TEN REAL

MW00527796

The Seventh Realm

Part 2

MICHAEL CHATFIELD

Cover Art by Jan Becerikli Garrido
Jacket Design by Caitlin Greer
Interior Design by Caitlin Greer

eBook ISBN: 978-1-989377-90-1
Paperback ISBN: 978-1-989377-89-5

Fallout

Vuzgal was gone.

Evernight shivered as she folded the letter containing her orders. She looked out at King's Hill and took a deep breath.

She walked down the corridor to Aditya's office. The guards opened the door. Pan Kun was sitting with Aditya. They were eating while studying the map on the main table. She waited for the doors to close before she pulled out the letter and put it on the table.

"Vuzgal has fallen. There is a change in policy. If anyone screws with Beast Mountain, we warn them once. If they do not understand it, we use force. Alva will continue to support us. Recruitment will be accelerated. Once the first line of defenses at our new borders are created, a second set will be created to increase our domain. The army will recruit and train its own members. Those that pass secondary selection will go to Alva."

Aditya read the letter as he listened to her.

"How?" he asked, glancing up at her.

"Like it says. A minor clan from the Seventh Realm sent a ship down and destroyed the city."

"A single ship?"

"A single ship." She took a breath, seeing the disbelief in their eyes.

"Things in the Seventh Realm are different than they are down here. What we know is that the Seventh Realm is the end of the line. The strongest clans and sects reside in the seventh, strong enough to make the associations take pause. Body Cultivation is common there and mana cultivation is high. They blasted through Vuzgal's depleted barriers with one attack and smashed through the walls of the city. Vuzgal is no more, and we have to deal with that."

"What about the lords, about the fighting force there?" Aditya drew himself up in his chair.

"They are hiding in backup dungeons before they can attempt to come back to the First Realm."

Evernight waited. The news had shocked her, and she had seen Vuzgal, knew of its impressive defense works and how totally they had been destroyed.

Aditya rubbed his face with a hand and stood. "Pan Kun, can we secure our territory?"

Pan Kun turned his eyes to the map, studying his army's positions. "It'll be tight. There's a lot of land to cover."

"You can use Adventurer's Guild members as mercenaries if you need to," Evernight said.

"Do they know about Alva? About all of this?" Aditya asked.

"We don't know. That's why everything will keep going as it has already, except more quickly. Make it look like we're consolidating our gains. Bring the kingdoms to the table and smack their heads together. Use Elise's and Emmanuel's support on the trade front to bend them over."

"Use the power of might over the seduction of words," Aditya said, folding the letter slowly and passing it back.

"Doesn't matter what we use as long as the Beast Mountain Range and Alva are secure from threats. Anything threatening either will meet the full fury of our forces," Evernight said.

"So, we keep working like everything is normal?" Elise asked.

"Since we got the news from Vuzgal, we've been running around trying to put out fires. Many have lost loved ones or simply don't know what happened to them." Delilah's level voice cut through the dungeon headquarters council room. "The plan that was created for such a situation is simple. Go to ground and continue activities on the surface without disruption. Prepare for an immediate attack on Alva, secure the Beast

Mountain Range, and increase the speed the drill works at. We need to let the dust settle and see where it lands."

The room calmed down as Elise sat.

"I'm sorry, I just..." Elise's sigh seemed to take her remaining energy. She rubbed her tired eyes.

"We're all worried about our loved ones." Delilah's voice softened.

Jia Feng reached out and held Elise's shoulder. Elise patted her hand and sat upright.

Momma Rodriguez stood up. "Let's go for a walk."

"What?" Delilah frowned. Momma Rodriguez had joined their meetings because of her ability to bring people together and because she was a mother to Rugrat and Erik.

"There are plenty of meetings and a lot of paperwork to get done. Do you think you can get it all done from here? Or do you think the Alvans would like to see their council leaders out *doing* things? Come on, Rugrat told me it is your tradition to have a meal during or after a meeting. None of you look like you've eaten much, so let Momma Rodriguez feed you."

"Bu—" Delilah's words died on her tongue as Momma tilted her head forward.

All Delilah heard was, *No one messes with Momma* in Rugrat's voice.

"Okay."

Captain Arenson, Jia Feng, Taran, Evernight, Melissa Bouchard, Elise, and Delilah bent their heads to Momma Rodrigeuz's power and shuffled out of the headquarters. They reached the street, where people were walking to and from work or tasks. There was a heaviness in the air. A shared worry.

"Come on, let's get something to eat. Captain Arenson." Momma Rodriguez put her arm on the police captain. "How is security?"

Arenson's tired features smoothed into a smile. "It isn't too bad. There are a few people that want to leave. We have some people working in the First Realm and other places. The fact that there are different rules for different people is making it harder."

Delilah massaged the back of her neck. "It's complicated."

"Why not uncomplicate it? Trade is allowed. Those with essential jobs in the realms can carry out their tasks. Others are advised to stay but not restrained," Momma said.

"But then we have more people moving around," Delilah replied.

"If you tell people they can't do something, they're sure to want to do it. Trust me, I had three children and a harassed cookie jar!"

Delilah smiled with the others.

"Though, people will run out of fear."

"Better to let the fear go away than build up. These contracts stop anyone from talking about Alva, no?"

"Yes, but—"

"You're overcomplicating it. Don't make something that works in every situation. Make something that works *for* the situation."

Delilah closed her mouth, thinking about it. "That should work."

"Good! And Jia Feng, I heard there're some discrepancies with the academy?"

"Attendance has dropped. They want to focus on training because it's cheaper," Jia Feng said.

Melissa stepped forward.

"Miss Bouchard?"

"We're seeing a lot of people coming in to do training as well. We have a lot of training facilities and supplies. But it might be a problem if we have the military training more people."

"Military always has priority for training rooms. People can make more if they want to if they adhere to our standards. Same with concoctions. If people are not studying, that is their prerogative. Make sure they know they will not be getting their money back," Delilah said.

"Is anyone feeling like soup? Mister Yi has a beast meat and noodle soup to die for," Momma said as she led the group.

They nodded to people who looked surprised to see them walking through the city.

"How are things with our supplies?" Delilah asked Elise.

"We have more than enough. The other floors supply all we could need. Rugrat and Erik got a lot of materials from the higher realms and sent them here first. We have a lot of people here from Vuzgal though: all the admin families, military, crafters."

"We have more teachers than students. Most of our people were in the Alvan reserves. It's a bit of a mess," Jia sighed.

"What about a job board like we had in the past? Have one in the crafter district. We can hold open the positions of the people that are serving in the military. We need to deal with the surge of people returning to Alva and plan for how to get them jobs," Delilah said.

"It's going to be crazier with everyone in Alva," Momma said as they passed through iron arches between buildings. The space opened up into a pond with benches, trees, and bushes positioned to create a weaving path through it all.

"Options?" Delilah asked.

"I hope the police force can get some more people. With the increase in population, we're not as big as we need to be," Arenson offered.

"Agreed. We need to make sure there is a service people can go to if they are ever in need," Delilah agreed.

"We can set up a tutor program. We will have more teachers going through the workshops, helping people refine their craft. That allows us to increase our production and put our teachers to work," Jia Feng said. "We can also increase the number of teachers in the Beast Mountain Range Consortium, slowly."

"Good idea."

"The factories still require a lot of people. We can build more to fulfill our military's needs. Now that we've gone through a siege, we know what kinds of items we use more of," Taran said. "We should push for the development of civilian factories too. They would provide more jobs for our people. Create ad hoc production facilities. Factories that exist to create other people's stuff. That way several companies can use one factory to produce their own items."

"I like it, and we have a lot of raw materials stored up. But what about material production on the other floors?" Delilah looked around but didn't find Egbert or hear his voice.

Elise cleared her throat. "Production has slowed on the other floors. With the merchants held here, or in the backup dungeons, there is nowhere to sell the resources. There is one thing I haven't touched on. The effect of our merchants not trading."

"Go on," Delilah prompted as they passed a burbling creek with water that ran down toward the pond.

"Our traders spread across five realms. In the higher realms, their impact isn't as large. But in the First, Second, and Third Realm, our traders have become a vital part of trade routes and economies. With them being recalled it's starting to show."

"How big of an impact would it be?" Melissa's brows pinched together.

"Kings and queens might rule the land in the First Realm, but traders own the people and the kingdoms," Evernight answered. "Entire economies could collapse."

"We can control the majority of the First Realm through the traders, or affect it one way or another," Elise agreed. "In the Second Realm, we can pick the powers that rise and fall. In the Third Realm, if our traders were under one banner, I think we could move as many materials as the top thirty trading conglomerates. In the Fourth Realm, we were trading as much as eight cities with our traders alone. If we were to use them as a weapon, it would be a potent one."

"If we keep the traders stuck here?" Delilah asked.

"I think that we would be revealing more than hiding." Elise spread her hands.

"Evernight?"

The woman frowned as they entered a copse of trees, passing a family out for a walk. Their two young children held their parent's hands.

"Such cute kiddos," Momma said.

"They'll grow up big and strong," Jia Feng agreed. The two women had become fast friends, reinforced by their love of food.

"Thank you, Miss Jia, Momma." The man smiled proudly as he bowed and his wife curtsied. The two boys gazed at the group of people with interest.

"Would they be allowed a treat?" Momma asked.

"What do you say, boys? Would you like a treat?"

"Mhmm!" The boy closest bit his lower lip, his eyes lighting up. The one holding onto his mother's hand pressed his forefinger against his mouth, watching and hiding behind his mother.

"What are their names?" asked Momma Rodriguez as she pulled out some freshly baked cookies.

"This one is Ryan." The man raised the hand of the smiling boy. "And the one behind my wife is Elbert."

E and R to start their names, a running theme in Alva. Delilah smiled as Momma gave the cookie to the first boy.

"Thank you!" He jumped up.

"Such good manners, young man." Momma laughed and patted him on the head. "Would you like a cookie too, Elbert?"

The boy looked from her, Ryan and his cookie, to his mother.

"She asked you a question, not me."

Elbert nodded his head and scrunched behind his mother.

"Here you go." Momma took out another cookie and passed it over.

"Here, something for dinner." Jia Feng pulled out a covered pot smelling of tomatoes, and held it out to the parents.

"Miss Jia," the woman said, looking to refuse.

"It'll only stay in my storage ring otherwise. Come on." Miss Jia winked. "They're my cabbage rolls. These boys must be big eaters. This should fill them up some. And save you both time in the kitchen."

The husband grinned and pushed his wife's elbow with a playful smile. She pressed her lips together and shot him a look.

Too cute. Delilah hid her smile behind her hand.

"Thank you, Miss Jia, you are too kind."

"Ah, it is a cook's hope that people might enjoy her food." Jia waved it off as the lady took the pot into her storage ring.

"Bye, Elbert and Ryan. Hope you have a great walk," Momma said.

The two groups separated and kept going.

"That's what we should have," Elise said.

"What?"

"A community meal. Bring everyone together. Just sit and eat with one another. In times like this, we need one another. We aren't like sects; we're a community."

"I agree, and I can have the students make food," Jia said.

"Pay all the vendors a fee so people can try out different things and boost the economy?" Delilah asked.

"Should relax people, but when to do it?"

"Two weeks. By then we'll have our people back. We'll know what happened and people will need one another more than ever," Momma answered.

"Momma, I'll leave that in your charge. Sorry, Evernight." Delilah put her hand on the other woman's arm.

"No worries, those kids are much cuter than me." Evernight smiled. "With the impacts of the traders remaining here, I agree with Elise. If we keep them hidden, the impact will be felt far and wide. If it were a gradual change, that would be fine. Traders change their routes all the time. But we just recalled them, tearing them out of the economies they were a part of."

"We have a lot of the Adventurer's Guild's members. See if they want a job."

"Okay, but we should keep their identities hidden. The Willful Institute badly wants to destroy the guild. If they trace them back to us, the Black Phoenix Clan could be right behind them."

"Talk to Jasper and make sure they understand."

"Yes, Council Leader." Evernight bowed her head.

Delilah stretched, taking in the park. They walked for some time in silence.

"We have an opportunity here," Momma said. "We must use this influx of people and resources to expand our abilities. If we just maintain what we have, everything could collapse. I've seen it happen on Earth. After wars, the cost can be too much. Countries fall apart because there are a lot of people returning, but there are no jobs for them."

"We can expand the number of traders, increase the number of factories, increase the staff in the Consortium and Kanesh Academy, and offer loans to people for expansion," Delilah contemplated.

"It will be a hard balance to strike," Momma said as they reached the end of the park. Through the arches leading out of the park, they headed to the seating that had been set up in the middle of the different restaurant stalls.

Why is it so empty? Delilah checked the time. It was the lunch hour, but there were only a few people in the chairs. Waiters sat in groups, talking to one another.

Seeing the group arriving, they stared at one another.

"There are so many good restaurants here. And it looks like we can get some prime seating," Momma said, raising her voice just enough for people walking by to hear her.

"Hiya, we might need two servers. I know Taran and Arenson have quite the appetites!" Momma said to a table of waiters.

They stared at one another before a man stood and tapped a waitress on the shoulder. She shook her head, and he pinched her ear.

She complained as she stood.

"We'll go with Mister Yi's soup to start, please! Could we get some of Miss Jo's boiled eggs as well? They're so runny in the middle," Momma said as the council sat on the low stools around the table. "We'll take some special fried rice from the Rice Emporium, please. And oh, hmm, come on, everyone. I need your help." Momma waved the waiter and waitress over, and they handed out menus.

When did I last eat? Delilah grimaced. *So many stamina potions and bars.*

"Oh, can we go for the black pepper frogs? Delicious," Jia Feng said.

"Soy ginger and honey ribs, please," Taran added.

The chefs at the stalls warmed up their grills as the council placed their orders.

"Need some vegetables. The cooked mixed greens and nuts, please," Momma said.

"The sushi rolls, could you tell me about them?" Melissa asked the waiter.

"Yes, Miss Bouchard. The fish is taken from the Water Floor each morning and we add seaweed from the Wood Floor, dried on the Fire Floor, and use rice from the Earth Floor, with mixed vegetables from both. The fish falls apart in your mouth and the seaweed has a clean crunch to it."

"I'll get a selection please," Melissa said.

"Certainly, one portion?"

"I'll go for a portion as well," Delilah said.

"Certainly, Council Leader."

"Could we start with the refreshing Mind Tranquility Tea?" Jia Feng asked the waitress.

"Certainly, I'll get that started for you."

"Thank you."

The waitress ran off to a stall. It was manned by a young man who eagerly accepted the order. He took out ingredients and prepared the tea in large clear tea ware so he and others could see everything he was doing.

Others, seeing the group there, took a seat at the tables.

There's much to do, Delilah thought. *Still, shouldn't forget the small things closer to home.*

"Shame." Marshal Edmond Dujardin traced his goatee. Behind him, a grand window showed sprawling gardens, hedges creating a maze, and roses that grew in carefully crafted and maintained beds.

"What do you want me to do, Uncle?" Esther asked.

"The Sha Clans are still under threat. And the Vuzgalians, if they survive this fight, the best thing for them to do is hide. The Black Phoenix Clan and the other dungeon lords will not sit by, nor will the Associations. Dungeon lords are a powerful force in the realms."

"The weapons they used?"

"Some are similar to my own; others are more advanced. They must be new arrivals from Earth."

"The Vuzgalians have reached high in the realms in a short time. There have only been rumors of new arrivals in the last couple of years."

"The leaders of the lower realms are sure to try to hold onto them. They can give rise to an empire. Lords West and Rodriguez might have been lords of the First Realm using new arrivals from Earth to build them better weapons. You do not hear much about the people who arrived around the same time I did."

"You think they are from Earth?"

"Other races were part of the Ten Realms in the past. But for the last several centuries, it has only been humans from Earth."

Esther nodded.

"We do not want to anger the Black Phoenix Clan. But we have to keep looking for people to ally ourselves with or we might share the Vuzgalians fate."

"Is it that dire, Uncle?"

"The Seventh Realm is much more stable than the lower realms, but power changes hands every day. We do not have the foundations or positions of other sects. We are a small tadpole in a vast ocean. We must stay at the edges. If we wade too deep, we'll be snatched up."

2

Recover, Repair, Rearm

ugrat."

"**R** A voice snapped him awake, and he grabbed his rifle. He reached out to the weight leaning against him and squeezed Erik.

Erik blinked and looked around. He breathed in through his nose deeply, checking his fire selector and patting the magazines on his rig.

"'Sup?" Rugrat asked Colonel Yui.

"Leadership huddle. Don't worry. We haven't been bumped."

Rugrat relaxed. Erik was still blinking, trying to wake up. Rugrat tapped him, shooting him a look.

Erik nodded and clipped his rifle to his sling and yawned. Rugrat did the same and stretched his neck, tilting his head from side to side and rolling his shoulders.

They'd fallen asleep against a pillar supporting the dungeon's ceiling. Troops were organized into squads. Few had cots; most simply collapsed into squad piles, clutching their weapons and wearing their gear they slept against brother and sister.

"Once we started dialing back the Conquerors armor, everyone started passing out. Those we could get off the line were dialed nearly all the way down. We put them on stamina and recovery buffs."

Erik hit Rugrat's arm, holding out a stamina potion. Rugrat nodded in thanks as Erik drank his and pulled out another.

"Yui, heads up." Yui turned and caught the potion.

"Thanks, boss." Yui tossed the potion back.

"How are we looking?" Erik asked.

"Glosil has the low-down."

"'Kay."

A group came in off watch. The sergeant woke another squad, rousing them for watch.

They left the sleeping troops and passed through halls, moving by armed and armored soldiers on watch.

Erik gave them stamina potions as he went. They raised the potions in thanks as the trio moved deeper into the dungeon.

They came out near the field hospital. Medics were moving between people, checking them. The craziness from earlier had subsided.

"Wounded?" Erik asked.

"All life-threatening injuries have been dealt with. They just need to recover from the armor's effects, so we can wean them off formation support. They might need another round of healing after that. But, with sufficient time, and their mana and body cultivation, they'll make a full recovery."

"Good," Erik said in relief.

They passed through another dirt tunnel.

"Earthy in here."

"We're under a hill. There are nearly six hundred meters of roots, dirt, and some stone above us. Lots of plants." Yui pointed at the vines on the tunnel walls. "Need them to change the air over."

They passed guards as they entered the command center. Field chairs sat in the left corner. Aides were piled up in the back right corner, sleeping. Tunnels ran out in every direction. Domonos and Glosil were talking to one another, leaning their forearms on the table.

Erik handed them stamina potions. They nodded in thanks and drank from them.

Glosil coughed and cleared his throat, storing the bottle. "Thanks."

Erik nodded.

Blaze walked into the room, glancing at the others in greeting.

"How are we?" Rugrat asked.

"Egbert?" Glosil shifted his feet and rubbed his face.

"Some wild animals passed overhead. Nothing on the teleportation formations or in the area above us. We are burning through mana stones to recover our people's strength through formations. The worst cases of mana fatigue we put into the mana cultivation pods. The stamina fatigue cases are hooked up to stamina IVs."

"Anything else?" Rugrat looked at the others.

"Our reg forces have two loads of railgun ammunition," Domonos said. "The reserves only have the regular Mark Seven rifles. Some of the newer reserve units have the bolt actions. We've cannibalized armor plates, passing them to the different groups and teams, which we've re-organized." Domonos looked at Yui.

"I've made a new squad list. The Adventurer's Guild didn't take any losses. Some of our reserves were hit. Our reg force is a mess. Did some reorganizing to bring different units up to strength. The air force ..." Yui shook his head. "They were one of the worst hit. Kanoa is commanding the other dungeon. We got a report from him, but nothing else. Two thirds of his birds are out; half of his people are dead or wounded."

Rugrat worked his jaw, looking at the map. "Fuck." He pressed the word out from his lips.

"What are the numbers?" Erik asked.

"We have one thousand five hundred and eighty-three still recovering and… eight hundred and fifty-seven dead."

Rugrat bit his lower lip, resting his hands on his hips as he studied a corner of the map. He felt hollow, as if someone had stabbed him in the stomach and there was nothing left there anymore.

Yui pulled out a handwritten list and put it on the table.

Erik opened the pages and spread them out with reverence.

Rugrat turned away and rubbed his face, his lower lip quivering. *Fuck. Tyrone and Jackie.*

He closed his eyes against the tears and sniffed, releasing a shaky breath as he kept reading the sheets. He leaned on the table, pushing back his hair.

Erik reached down, patting his back and squeezing his shoulder through the opening of his carrier.

Rugrat looked up at him.

Erik's face twisted in pain, his lips a white line against the tears.

"Fucking Tanya and Tan Xue!" Rugrat raised his hand as tears blurred his vision. He laughed, his lower lip trembling as he worked his jaw.

Erik pulled him back from the table. Tears broke from his eyes as Yui stood to the side. His jaw flexed as he looked at the ceiling. Domonos was rubbing his face. Glosil looked like he had taken a body blow as he leaned on the table, reading through the names. His cheek twitched as he wiped his face angrily, clearing the tears.

Erik hugged Rugrat as the two men shuddered with their soundless tears.

Rugrat got himself under control and patted Erik on the back. The two of them released.

"This is my fault. If Mistress Mercy didn't... then... they..." Domonos choked on the words.

"This fight was coming one way or another." Erik's voice was a whip crack, hard and rough. "*None* of us could predict what happened. We took on a sect from the Seventh Realm and we held them for weeks. Hell, we crushed their attacks."

"What do we do now?" Domonos smacked his leg.

Glosil stood up, but Erik held out his hand. "Sects would fall apart in this situation, but we have to remain strong. We need to pull ourselves together and carry out our duty."

Rugrat pointed at the names on the papers. "They paid the price to get our people out of Vuzgal. What we do next is in their honor. We need a lot more than what we've got to take on this Black Phoenix Clan."

"What are our orders?" Erik looked at Glosil.

"Recover, repair, rearm. We head to Alva. We get our people back to peak condition. We saw weaknesses in the battle, we address them. We repair our gear and gather or create the tools we would need to contend with the Black Phoenix Clan."

"Vuzgal was our foothold in the Fourth Realm, but Alva is our home. The First Realm has little in the way of natural resources, but it has one resource in plenty: people," Erik said.

"We need to talk to Elder Fred and his people," Erik said to Rugrat as they left the command center.

"Yeah."

The two walked in silence, passing soldiers at different posts.

Elder Fred and his family were in their own private room. They halted their conversation as Erik and Rugrat entered.

Fred stood to greet them.

"Thank you for your aid," Erik said.

"You freed us and were in need." Fred became quiet. "I wish we had arrived sooner. Gilly—"

"Was a great companion. She developed into a fine dragon."

"I remember when she was just a little thing, swimming in her pool every day." Fred grew quiet as William rubbed Elizabeth's arm. She turned her head into his arm, her hair covering her face.

Reaper studied his fingers and sat down.

Dromm shifted on his feet with a shaky sigh.

Racquel hugged Rugrat. He tensed before hugging her back. She gave him a small smile and backed away.

"She will be sorely missed." Erik pushed out the words.

Fred nodded and took a breath. "Is your offer to join Alva still open?"

"It is." Erik's head cleared as he frowned.

"Would you consider allowing us entry?"

"Sure, but why?"

"Why not? Traveling and adventuring for so long teaches you that without roots you cannot grow and blossom."

Erik nodded. "Welcome to Alva. There are contracts and other things that must be done." He looked up. "Egbert, did you hear that?"

"Yes, I will prepare the contracts!" The voice came through the dungeon.

"An odd one, that skeleton," Fred opined.

"We have a few strange ones." Erik smiled and looked over at Rugrat, who was talking with Elizabeth, William, Dromm, and Racquel.

"I will not keep you. I am sure there is much you have to do, Lord." Fred smiled.

"I have a lot of questions about the higher realms," Erik said.

"And I'll have your answers."

Erik turned to leave.

"Wait up," Rugrat called out.

Erik halted his steps. "I'm just going to check on the wounded and the troops."

Rugrat said some parting words to Racquel and jogged over to him. "I'll tag along."

"Sure you don't want to talk to Racquel some more?"

"We do it together man," Rugrat said.

Erik nodded as they headed into the tunnels again. They had just reached the hospital when Egbert waved them down and ran over. "What's up, Egbert?"

"Well, I have a dungeon core for you." Egbert opened his robe, showing the core floating in his ribcage.

Erik could feel the invisible pull of elements and mana into the dungeon core.

Dungeon Core
Grade: Lesser Sky
Range:
3250m
Controlled by:
Erik West
Jimmy Rodriguez

Erik noticed a list of other notifications but would deal with them later.

"I totally forgot," Erik said as Egbert closed his robe.

"Also, I looted what I could from Vuzgal. Took everything that was underground." Egbert waved his rune-covered finger bones. "Including core components of the totem as it was linked to the dungeon."

"Can we use it?" Erik asked.

"The power draw is massive. This dungeon, as it is, wouldn't be able to support it."

"Always good to have a backup just in case," Rugrat said. "We can use the resources in Alva. Instead of splitting our development between three cities, we'll focus on one realm and two cities."

"When we got Vuzgal, we put so much into it." Erik shook his head.

Egbert played with the hem of his robe. "I also have a request."

"Go on." Erik frowned, crossing his arms.

"While holding the dungeon core, I uhh, realized something." Egbert paused, opening and closing his jaw.

Erik and Rugrat waited on him.

"I can work independently of the dungeon if I have my own dungeon core," Egbert said in a rush.

"So, if you have a dungeon core in your body, you can leave a dungeon and not collapse? You can do that with enough mana stones, right?"

"Yes, but I have to consume the mana stones. I will always need to have more mana stones. If I was to have a small dungeon core and carve in a mana storing formation and gathering formations. I could cultivate mana. If I got a stronger dungeon core, I could gather more mana at a higher concentration."

"That's a lot of power if you're only restricted by the formations you carve into your bones," Rugrat said.

"Well, I would need to improve the, uhh, *materials*." Egbert waved at himself. "Though my skeleton gets stronger the more mana that runs through it. I can test out body tempering like the undead as well."

"What grade of dungeon core would you need?"

"A lesser mortal grade would be enough to keep me mobile and test with."

"Okay, hold onto Vuzgal's dungeon core for now and test it out. Do you have an idea of what to use the core for otherwise?"

"Yes, we should use it for the Alva defense grid and drill power bleed-off."

Erik and Rugrat turned their heads as Egbert stood there.

"And that would be?" Rugrat prompted.

"Oh, well, we have one main dungeon core that acts as the command center. We can break off a lot of smaller dungeon cores, create a network between them, add in those attack and defensive formations we talked about, and link them to the drill and mana gathering formations. That way we can control a massive area of land. When the drill cracks into the ley line, the power will divert through the floors of the dungeon and into their mana gathering formations, then spread out to the defensive network and the mana cornerstones. I recovered all of the mana cornerstones we had in Vuzgal as well."

"Dungeon, just add mana," Rugrat murmured.

3

Hunters and Hunted

Captain Stassov walked into *Eternus'* meeting room. Laid out at the head of the table were several boxes holding dungeon cores they'd retrieved from Vuzgal.

She'd been ordered to hold her position, burning mana stones in the low density Fourth Realm. Without the Vuzgalians, defeating the newly created dungeons and capturing the cores had been easy for Gregor.

"Most of the crafter dungeons were controlled by the Ten Realms. Only these cores were controlled by Vuzgal's lords," Goran reported, standing off to the side. Petros and Marco stood behind him, both looking at the floor.

Stassov's eyes swept the window. Vuzgal was a shell of what it was before, collapsed down on the underground city beneath. The sect camps laid empty and silent. A land of ghosts.

"The Ten Realms took the plan and started using it?"

"Yes, or they gave them blueprints and released control."

Stassov looked at Goran. "You think that they would do so?"

"They left several dungeon cores here in their city to create a regional dungeon," Goran offered.

A knock came from the room's door. With a flicker of power, Stassov opened it.

"Lord Commander Chmilenko's Talon, *Luminare*, has arrived

alongside and wishes to meet with you."

"I will meet him on the landing deck." Stassov took the dungeon cores into her storage ring.

"Wait here, Petros." She left the room. Guards ranged ahead as Ranko and Gregor trailed behind with Goran, who had taken Bela's sub commander role.

She stood on the formation under the dungeon core, surrounded by her party.

Formations appeared around them, and light flooded the area.

They reappeared in a corridor between stables. Beasts cried out in pain as their handlers tried to heal them. Blood covered the decks and the lifts that had raised and lowered the aerial forces.

Her group spread out and marched at her speed as her shoes rang out on the stone. They stepped onto a platform that rose to the surface of the *Eternus*.

Barriers are still messy. Stassov felt a breeze pull on her clothes as it passed over the deck.

The sun was shadowed as she looked at the *Luminare* dominating the sky. It was nearly three times the size of *Eternus* and had ten times the weapons and manpower.

The Lord Commander's group created red streaks in the sky. Their excess mana left a trail in the thin mana density of the Fourth Realm.

Their mounts cawed as they banked and glided over the *Eternus*. They rose up, flapping their wings and throwing up a wind before settling on their legs.

"Lord Commander Chmilenko." Stassov bowed. Gregor and Ranko cupped their hands as her guards dropped to one knee.

"Stand up. Quite the mess, commander. You track them down?"

"We have not found out where they are hiding yet. It appears they do control, or controlled, other dungeons." Stassov stood up.

"They hid under our radar for this long. I heard that your cannon was hit badly."

"Yes, my Talon is in need of repairs."

Chmilenko grunted, resting his fists on his hips. "Who are they?"

"Lord West is an Alchemist. His teacher is from the Alchemist Association. He's also a bit of a fighter. Lord Rodriguez, people call him Rugrat, is a smith. He is also a fighter. They ride a dragon and a red wolf with wings. Both of them and a number of people in their military were made elders of the Blue Lotus."

Chmilenko spat on the deck. "How were they able to stop you and inflict so many casualties?"

"They didn't have the levels, but they had the body cultivation and mana cultivation on level with some of our sub-commanders. They were used to the environment. We had only just arrived in this realm."

Chmilenko grunted and shifted the formation hooked to his belt, increasing the mana density around him.

"They used weapons and tactics we haven't seen before. Their army was disciplined, all different kinds of people working together with uniform weapons, clothing and armor."

"Were you able to recover anything from the city?"

"Everything was systematically destroyed, but we did recover this." Stassov pulled out a deformed bullet and held it out.

Chmilenko picked it up and studied it. "Earth grade ore, enhanced to increase the power of formations. Engraved with a formation, detailed work for the Fourth Realm. High journeyman. What is it?"

"It is the arrow heads, if you will, of the weapons they were using. This was pulled from one of my fighters."

"How many of these did they have?" Chmilenko raised the bullet.

"Hundreds, possibly thousands with weapons similar to what the Sha use."

Chmilenko rolled the bullet over in his fingers. "You think they are the Sha's dogs?"

"Yes."

"But they are not a clan. The Sha have other cities in this realm, do they not?"

"Yes, sir."

"Must've been trying to hide them. What a waste to have a sky grade dungeon core down here. *Which* they escaped with." Chmilenko's voice hardened as his hand balled into a fist around the bullet. "Find out where they are and get that dungeon core before you return. With your actions, you have left our flank undefended in the Earth Cloud valley. Now I will need to clean up your mess."

"Lord Chmilenko—"

"You went hunting for this dungeon core without asking me. Now you'd best find it. I hope you have stored up enough mana stones for this backwater."

Stassov gritted her teeth. "Yes, Lord Chmilenko."

He grunted and turned, leaving. "Have the ship ready to return to the Seventh Realm. Stassov, you had best have the mana stones it cost me to come down here returned to me soon!"

"Of course, commander."

She waited for him to leave before returning to her command center.

"Gregor," she said as she sat down in her chair.

"Commander?" He stepped forward as the sound canceling formation dropped around them.

"I have a mission for you in the lower realms. The United Sect Army is set on a path to find the Vuzgalians. They will not succeed with just their forces. They need support and I want those dungeon cores. Take your dungeon hunters and go to the Willful Institute. Make use of them. Create corvettes from dungeon cores under your command." She passed him a series of blueprints.

Gregor ground his jaw together.

"I don't know if it would be possible to create a corvette with the low-level dungeon cores in the lower realms."

"I don't care if you can make a corvette or a flying bucket. Build war machines to hunt down and destroy the Vuzgalians. All other resources are to be supplied by the other sects."

"Phoenix breath Cannons?"

"You think you will need it?" She sat back, framing her face with her hand.

"We don't know where they ran to. They kept the secrets of Vuzgal for years. They had a backup plan. Their people must have gone somewhere," Gregor said.

"If the situation warrants it, I will send one. Use their cannons and spell scrolls. There are plans for better mana barriers. You will need them to deal with the Vuzgalian weapons."

"The corvettes afterwards?"

"Once your task is complete, combine the dungeon cores and return to me. We need to wipe away this stain."

Gregor gritted his teeth and bowed.

"Yes, commander."

"Leave nothing of the Vuzgalians."

Elan Silaz, director of the Intelligence department, sat next to Qin, his heart twisting as he nudged her side with his elbow.

"Your food will go cold."

Qin stared blankly at the bowl of food in her hands, the heat dissipating rapidly.

She murmured something, grabbing her spoon and going through the motions of eating.

They were sitting in the cafeteria of dungeon one. It was filled with the last civilian members to leave Vuzgal. The stone walls were warm to the touch, keeping it comfortable. It was only a small dungeon, able to fit a few thousand in relative comfort.

People around them were playing cards, talking to one another, or getting drinks and food from the cooks that had taken over the large kitchen so they could do something.

Qin dropped her spoon, burying her face in her shaking hands.

"Qin." Elan hugged her. "Qin'er, it's okay, you're safe now."

She grabbed the front of his shirt as she cried.

"It's okay, Dad's here." Elan's voice broke as he shushed her, stroking her hair.

It took Qin some time to calm down, to get words out between big gulping breaths.

"I I-how… am I gon-na… tell Julilah?" She gripped his shirt tighter.

"All you can do is be there for her. Just… tell her and be there for her. That is what you must do as her friend, and for Tan Xue."

Qin shuddered. "She— the bunker. The attacks. There wasn't anything I could do."

"I know, my dear. I know. War does nothing to aid us. It only serves to tear us apart if we let it." Elan patted her head and rocked her.

4
Regroup

Elan checked his gear as Special Team Two checked their armor. Instead of carriers, they wore a motley collection of armor.

"How do we look?" Elan asked Erik, who was standing off to the side of the changing room.

"Like a trader and his guards. You ready for this?"

"It's kind of my job. The reports from the first group of agents that met with our contacts didn't find anything. Once I confirm that we don't have people searching for us in the surrounding area, we can move people to the lower realms."

"Okay." Erik looked to Storbon. "Keep him safe."

"Yes, sir."

Their sense of ease had disappeared. They'd become harder, more disciplined.

"Director." Storbon indicated for Elan to follow him.

"If we see trouble, we'll try to avoid it. If someone makes our position, we'll fight and flee. We cannot return to this location," Storbon briefed his people as they walked. "Do not use rifles unless it's on my command; then go straight to railguns."

"Sir," the others replied as they finished checking gear.

They walked past the medical tents, which had decreased in size over the last three days. Very few people were still in the buffing field.

They moved through the open gates that led to the teleportation formations and passed under the ever-watchful railguns.

"Bravo, you're up first." Yao Meng and half of his team, supported by CPD members that had been pulled for the mission, stepped onto the teleportation formation and faced outwards. They pulled out their weapons, preparing their mana.

"Launch in five!" a controller counted down. "Two, one!"

A flash of light and they were gone. Storbon grabbed Elan as the other half of the team rushed the pad, with Elan in the middle of them.

"Set!" Storbon yelled.

The pad flashed, and their surroundings changed.

They moved off the pad with weapons at the ready.

"All clear!" Yao Meng said.

Storbon relaxed his guard.

"Okay, now the second part. Let's get the mounts and carriage prepped."

Elan and his group crossed the rain-swept road to the inviting inn, away from the wet and dark.

Storbon opened the door, checking out the inn before signaling. Elan and the rest of the group entered. Water streamed from their waterproofed beast skins.

"Ah, Ackleod! I wish that you had better weather!" Elan chuckled as he moved to greet a tanned man who was sitting with a few guards off to the side.

The agent laughed. "It always rains when you're around. A round of drinks for my companions, Tyrrol!"

"Certainly."

"Oh, and a plate of your cheese, if you will."

"Right away, Mister Ackleod."

Storbon and Yao Meng took over two tables near the agent and Elan, watching the entrance and the rest of the inn's bar and seating area.

The inn keeper's people delivered beer and lay down a plate of cheese, bread, and dried fruits for Elan and Ackleod.

Elan paid the waiter, activating his sound transmission device, linking in Storbon and the special team members around the inn.

"We're connected now," Elan said.

Ackleod leaned in, dropping his smile. "Another Black Phoenix ship appeared over Vuzgal called the *Luminare*. Say it's a destroyer, one of the biggest warships seen in the Seventh Realm. They're using the Willful Institute to search for us while the Willful Institute is continuing to push their attacks, reclaiming their cities and attacking others."

"Go on."

"None of the sects have shown up here, or the Black Phoenix Clan. Alva has been relatively quiet. The decision to allow people the freedom of movement has been given. The council didn't want to reveal us due to a lack of movement."

"Wandering Inns, and the Sky Reaching Restaurants?"

"The Black Phoenix is investigating, but they've not pressed it. Since all this started, we've been trying to keep the Sky Reaching Restaurant separate. There could be issues in the Third Realm Alchemist Headquarters. But they would have to have much bigger balls to attack a restaurant in an Alchemist Association-controlled city."

"What of the guild's status?" Elan asked.

"The Willful Institute hit all of the known Adventurer's Guild locations. The Guild members are all located in the backup dungeons. Doesn't seem like they know about the trader's guild yet."

"We will have to create multiple guilds to break the Adventurers up and scatter them."

"Yes, sir." Ackleod pulled out a pad of paper and a pencil, jotting down notes as Elan broke off a piece of bread and took a slice of cheese, eating it.

"Have the Associations made any noises?"

"They're looking for us. We need eyes in the Seventh Realm badly." Ackleod rubbed his face and took a deep drink.

"What about the Black Phoenix Clan?"

"They've got every sect that was at Vuzgal looking for us. The sects' armies are attacking everyone they can. They need victories to remove the stain of loss.

Silence fell as Ackleod drank.

"What about transportation?" Elan said.

"We checked all the totems. We should be good to move our soldiers back to the first." Ackleod took out a packet and passed it to Elan. "Inside is the plan the council approved."

"Good." The packet disappeared into his storage ring.

Elan took out an envelope from his storage ring under the table carefully and handed it to Ackleod. "These are the names of the fallen. Take it home. Let their families know."

"Yes, sir. I'll have it sent out within the hour." Akcleod took the envelope, respectfully storing it.

"We'll start moving people tomorrow. Send a message to our people. Keep their ears to the ground. I want to know everything about the Seventh Realm and the Black Phoenix Clan."

"Yes, Director Silaz."

Delilah watched as the police officers took the lists and raised them to the board, nailing them in place. People huddled nearby, holding their husbands, wives, brothers, sisters, sons, and daughters close. They waited as the police officers finished putting up the lists and moved off, heading to the next noticeboard.

Delilah held onto her shirt.

"Come on," her mother said. They lined up with the others. She felt like a coward giving the task to Captain Arenson, but she couldn't bear to do it herself.

The Ryan family stood nearby. Zhiwei adjusted her and John's daughter on her hip. Greg looked drawn from his long days and nights working in the factories. Her mother was similarly tired looking. She had been working on the wounded transported from Vuzgal when the totem had been working. Her father held onto her and strode forward, guiding the family.

Suzy, Nolan, Kyle, and Rachel were with Delilah at the rear. Suzy and Rachel stood near Zhiwei. Suzy wagged her finger at the little one, entertaining her.

Nolan rested his hand on Delilah's back. He had grown large and strong in the fields. Delilah smiled at him.

"No, no. Not my little girl." The man at the front of the line touched the paper as if he could reach through and grab his daughter. His friends pulled him onward, supporting him. Some passed with relieved expressions while others collapsed under the loss; some demanded that the list be checked. Some yelled. Some were silent. Grief was not uniform.

The Ryan family was quiet as they walked down to the list, reaching the R section.

Her mother spotted it first; she simply started crying against her father's chest as his face shuddered and broke into tears.

Greg reached the words and turned back.

"Jamie and Joanna." He said the words as if he could take them back in the same moment. Delilah scrunched up her shirt in her hand, covering her mouth with the other as her stomach twisted. *No, no! He has to be wrong.*

Delilah pushed past him, stilling at the sight of her brother and sister's names. The hot and cold wave burned through her, dissolving the world around her. She didn't know when she started crying or who helped guide her back. Nolan hugged her, and she held onto him like a lifeboat as he clenched his jaw.

"What of John? Where's John?" Zhiwei pushed forward, studying the list. She gripped the blanket that wrapped up her daughter tight and let out a shuddering breath of relief.

"He's been wounded," Greg said, moving to help her as Nolan pulled over Rachel, who was crying. Suzy looked at the board, her finger tracing the air down the names before it fell limply by her side.

"Come on, let's go home." Joseph Ryan sniffed.

Delilah shook her head, wanting it to be not true, but the pain and the names burned into her deeper than any brand could go.

The Ryan family huddled together with pale faces, red eyes, and tears.

Delilah looked off at the memorial park and looked away. Today she couldn't face it. Today it tore at her within too much.

Taran stood before the house. He looked at the door, a weight on his heart and in his chest.

Tan Xue made me promise.

He gathered his courage and knocked on the door. There was no answer from inside. He waited, then knocked again.

Taran reached out and turned the door handle.

"Julilah?" he called out softly. "Julilah, where are you?"

He closed the door behind himself. He heard crying upstairs.

"It's Uncle Taran," he said as he climbed the stairs.

He followed the sound of choked sobs.

"Julilah," he said, pushing open the ajar door to Tan Xue's dark room. He flicked on the light, illuminating it.

It was sparse with a simple bed, a desk that looked out over Alva with different plans, protractors, pencils, angles, and rulers covering it. A closet stood to one side, and a picture mounted on a wall of Taran, Tan Xue, Qin, and Julilah at the crafting competition. The two girls looked horrified as they ate food. Tan Xue laughed at them, and Taran had his arms crossed and wore a wry grin.

Happier times.

Julilah was on the bed, wrapped around a pillow. She looked away from the door.

Taran didn't say anything. He just sat down and stroked her head. Julilah had accomplished so much. Sometimes he forgot how young she was.

"There, there Julilah."

She let go of the pillow and hugged his side.

Taran raised his arms in alarm before he wrapped them around her shaking shoulders.

After some time, she calmed down, falling asleep, exhausted.

As gently as possible, Taran picked her up and carried her to her own room, taking off her shoes and putting them to the side, tucking her into her sheets. He stepped away, making it to the doorway before his tears rolled down his cheeks.

I'll honor my promise, Tan Xue.

He turned to close the door, seeing the lines on Julilah's forehead as uneasy sleep claimed her.

He closed the door as quietly as possible. His shoulders slumped as he wiped away his tears. He looked through the house, remembering the times he and Tan Xue had worked on projects at the kitchen table, or when he had come to wake her to make sure she arrived at her classes on time. The laughter they shared, the smiles.

Now, it was just a house, quiet and dull. He let out a shaky sigh, looking for items, for things that drew his mind to Tan Xue, that brought with them memories. His feet-unbidden took him back to Tan Xue's room. Seeing the picture again, he smiled as fresh tears ran down his face. "One hell of a lady and a smith."

He chuckled, and raised his hand to the light, holding it above the formation, but couldn't bring himself to turn it off. He dropped his arm, taking a shaky breath. The room was just as Tan Xue had left it. Her boots lay where they had fallen when she'd kicked them off. The clothes she'd rummaged through to find something clean were still in a half-hazard pile.

These little reminders struck Taran harder than if the room had been spotless.

He turned, went downstairs, and sat on the couch. Memories floated through his mind of the people that had been lost as he stared out of the window.

The Alva totem flashed as traders walked through. They pulled off their gear as Egbert stepped out of the still moving carriage and floated mid-air with Davin flying right beside him. He clasped his hands behind his back and flew over to the council members standing off to the side of the main street. Alvans filled the streets. They were quiet as they stood on their tiptoes, looking for their loved ones. The traders took off their cloaks and armor, revealing fatigues. They walked down the street as the totem flashed again and again as more soldiers returned home.

Egbert hovered before the raised platform. "I have orders from the Lords to modify the dungeon to increase security and stability," Egbert said.

"It is good to see you again, Egbert. Davin," Delilah said.

"It is good to be *home*." Egbert sighed.

Davin bobbed his head and held his hands together in front of him.

"We will not keep you," Delilah said.

Egbert nodded, noticing the red eyes of the council leaders. *All of them lost someone they knew in Vuzgal. Not even rank can help you escape it.*

Egbert flew off toward the dungeon core. He landed before the headquarters.

"Davin, you can head off to the fire floor if you want to," Egbert said.

"No, I, uhh, think I'll stay up here." Davin looked like a shy child, unwilling to admit his thoughts.

"I can always use an assistant," Egbert said.

Davin's wings perked up.

Maybe I have been forgetting him. We are oddities, but the laughter is usually to hide the pain.

A guard checked his medallion. "It's good to see you again, Mister Egbert."

Egbert nodded and headed into the building. It was so quiet with no one here. "I've gotten used to having people around."

He walked through the building, passing different security formations, into the dungeon core room.

Do you wish to apply this blueprint?
Yes/No

Egbert checked the positioning. "That should work. Yes!"

The blueprint in his hand burned away as power diverted from the mana drill blasting into the ground.

"Onto part two." Egbert left the dungeon headquarters and flew over Alva with Davin.

"What are we doing now?"

"Now, we'll take the Vuzgal dungeon core, split it up and create a network of dungeons under the entire Beast Mountain Range. We've got a lot of work ahead of us!"

The rain disappeared with the Fourth Realm totem and warmth flooded in as Rugrat took in the familiar Alva Totem. *Home.*

He walked off the pad as it flashed again, bringing more people. He pulled off his wet cloak and gear, storing it as he checked Gong Jin and his people. They pulled on their headdresses and grouped up, heading out of the totem defenses together.

Leaving the gates, they saw soldiers walking down the road in groups. People along the street yelled and waved as they saw someone they knew. Soldiers ran to their families, hugging them. Some picked up young ones, others cried in the embrace of a parent.

Rugrat and the special team headed for the barracks.

"Jimmy!"

Rugrat turned to the familiar voice. Momma waved her handkerchief as tears ran down her face. He ran over to the side of the street and hugged her across the barricades.

"Oh, Jimmy! Jimmy, let me look at you."

Some things don't change.

As she had done every time he returned from deployment, she studied him. She turned his hands over, scanning him before she put her hands on his cheeks and brought him down, kissing him on the forehead, forcing him to bend over as she hugged his neck.

Rugrat hugged her back, careful to not use too much strength.

She let him go and patted his chest, pulling herself together. "Where is your brother?" She looked behind him.

"Erik is coming in a later batch. He's working on the wounded."

"That boy." Momma smiled and patted Rugrat's arm, her hand tightening on it. She sniffed and dabbed at her eyes, clearing them. "And who are they?"

Rugrat turned to see Elder Fred and his family.

"You know the people that were stuck in the dungeon I told you about?"

"Ahh, which one of them is Racquel?" Momma spoke out the side of her mouth in a low voice.

Rugrat winced as he saw the smile spread across Racquel's face. Her eyes flicked to him.

"She's the one on the right."

"Oh." Momma's eyes thinned as she nodded, weighing the woman. "Very pretty."

Rugrat introduced them. "Elder Fred, Reaper, Dromm, Elizabeth, William, and Racquel, this is my mother."

"It is very good to meet you all. Thank you for looking after my son. I hope that I can cook for you in the future."

They nodded and smiled as Momma Rodriguez cleaned some invisible thread from Rugrat's combats.

"Have to bring them around for dinner. Make them feel at ease here. I hope you can settle down a little more."

"Momma," Rugrat sighed.

"I know, I know." She patted his chest. "You've always been a free spirit. As much as it pains me, I understand. Come, come. I've made you a feast. Bring your friends as well. We'll do it like we did in the past."

"Okay." Rugrat nodded.

Taran looked around the food square, where people were gathered in groups. They served themselves, going to the stores that put food out for people to feed themselves.

Families and friends sat side by side with one another, sharing food.

Taran spotted Elan and Qin at a table. He guided Julilah, who was pale-faced. Her eyes were tired and red-rimmed. Qin looked the same.

"Elan, Qin," Taran said, making the two turn as Julilah looked up.

"Juli—" Qin let out a breath as Julilah wrapped her in a hug.

A dam broke as Qin cried with her and grabbed onto Julilah, holding her tight.

Elan and Taran nodded at one another and moved away from the two girls.

"Thank you, Taran," Elan said.

"Thank you, Elan, for suggesting this meetup. They both needed it."

"Yes." Elan nodded.

"What are you two doing without plates?" Momma Rodriguez asked from behind them.

They turned to find her wearing an apron and holding a spoon.

"Come on, let's get some food into you." Her voice was caring instead of demanding.

"Yes, Miss Rodriguez," Elan said.

"Get the girls something to eat, too. There's some soup and bread that should be filling and will warm them up."

"Okay," Taran said. "Where are Erik and Rugrat?"

"The boys are hiding in the corner. They take all of this on themselves. Could you talk with them?" She uncrossed her arms, a look of worry on her face as she glanced over to where they sat.

"We'll talk with them, Miss Rodriguez."

"Thank you both and make sure you get some food into you!"

She marched off as Taran and Elan smiled and headed to the food line.

Taran watched Qin and Julilah, who had ceased their crying and were now sitting on short stools. Qin talked to Julilah, looking at the ground. Julilah seemed alarmed and checked Qin for injuries before the other shook her off and kept talking.

She hung her head lower as she finished. Julilah grabbed the sides of her head, saying something to her before hugging her again. Qin hugged her back fiercely.

"Good," Taran said.

"It's a start. Alva has a lot of pain to work through," Elan said as he passed Taran a plate.

Taran sighed and took the plate. "Thanks. So, what now?"

"Now... now, we take over the First Realm."

5

A New Mission

Lord Aditya, newly promoted Lieutenant General Pan Kun, and Consortium Leader Quan rode to the Alvan Headquarters in a carriage.

Soldiers marched past him, grim faced and flint-eyed. They didn't flinch at the passing carriage. Their numbers had swelled since the attacks on Vuzgal. To compensate, Pan Kun's rank had grown.

A heavy air had fallen over the city, but new buildings were rising, and the city seemed busier than ever.

"Where is Miss Evernight?" Quan asked.

"She went ahead. Needed to report to the Lords," Aditya said.

They fell into silence.

What is the plan now?

They arrived at the headquarters and were ushered into the council chambers. Aditya knew of the people that sat at this table, but had only seen a few of them before. Each could control the First Realm by themselves if they so desired.

Aditya looked at the transparent formation-carved crystal which the dungeon core floated in, amongst other formations, watching the almost hypnotic beam of power spin together into threads. Elemental and mana energies bound together, drilling deep into the heart of the world. Its flickering colors illuminated the room.

The people at the table spoke with one another. Evernight walked over to the group.

"Pan Kun, sit behind Commander Glosil. Quan behind Jia Feng. Aditya behind Council Leader Delilah. I will be behind Director Silaz."

They nodded and headed to their seats. A few other people filed into the room, including an undead and a fire imp that sat behind Delilah's right side and to Erik's left. Near Aditya.

Chonglu sat next to him and nodded. Matt, who had helped to organize the building of King's Hill, sat behind Jia Feng. Elise looked tired as she sat next to Blaze. Their staff, like the military, was thin, called away to important tasks.

"Okay, I call this meeting for the future planning of Alva to order," Delilah said. "Director Elan, could you enlighten us on the current situation?"

Elan stood from his chair. "Several of the dungeon lord groups from the Seventh Realms have descended and are searching for us, as the Associations will be. The Willful Institute might be allied with the Black Phoenix Clan, or not; we do not know. None of them have made any progress in finding out who or where we are. It does not appear that anyone knows of our return to the First Realm. Evernight."

Elan sat as Evernight stood.

"The kingdoms that attacked us have recalled their fighters and brought more mercenaries onto their payroll. Other kingdoms are reaching out to us. Trade has started up again. The kingdoms are neither stopping nor allowing it. They are waiting to see if the Willful Institute will return."

Elan raised his hand. "There is no indication that they will come back. The United Sect Army is stuck in battle after battle to recover their position in the Mortal Realms." He nodded for her to continue.

"The kingdoms that attacked us are blaming one another. They are displeased about us increasing our border size, but have no plans to make their defiance clear in force. We've placed the blame on the other kingdoms and have been using that to spread word to others. Protecting our citizens, and after the attacks upon us all, the majority of people in the outposts now agree with a unified Beast Mountain Range. Our population has grown since we've proven our strength and that we care for our people."

Evernight sat down.

"Commander?" Delilah asked.

"We're continuing to train the reg force units and the reserve units. I hope that we can expand the Special Teams and the Close Protection

Details too. We need information from the higher realms. They are the strongest and highest leveled people we have, and they can support and be supported by the Intelligence Department."

"Understood. Training is in your realm. I will leave that up to you. Please update me if you need anything else."

"Certainly. It is also my hope to not only increase the ability of the Alvan army, but the Beast Mountain Army. We need more people to defend the newly expanded borders and the routes through the Range. The beasts have gotten stronger."

"Do it." Delilah nodded as Yui and Domonos turned to Pan Kun and talked to him.

"Miss Jia Feng?"

"We increased the number of classes we teach in practical and theoretical methodology, and extended overall education so we can teach the children, taking the time burden off their parents. I need to talk to Consortium Head Quan about spreading this to the Beast Mountain Range." She looked back at Quan.

"Basic education for people in the First Realm? Children will be more skilled than most adults."

"What about cultivation?" Delilah asked as Aditya focused.

"All Alvans will get free cultivation to open their mana gates, including forming their core. They will also be taught to temper their bodies to Body Like Iron while the military will train to Body Like Sky Iron." Jia Feng looked at Glosil, who nodded.

"Good. With the fall of Vuzgal and the withdrawal of the Adventurer's Guild, our population has ballooned. It will take some adjustment. Our traders are once again traveling through the realms. The dungeon's floors will be expanded in the coming weeks. We will develop the other floors of the dungeon completely. Now that all our efforts will be concentrated in one place, our plans will accelerate. We have planned for this." Delilah looked at Aditya.

"We plan to expand the Beast Mountain Range aggressively and increase our recruitment. Everything else will continue as normal. Every plan we have come up with to expand the Beast Mountain Range will now be put into action. We no longer care what the kingdoms think. If you can bring people over, whether they're peasants or lords, it doesn't matter," Delilah said.

"Yes, Council Leader," Aditya nodded.

"Lords?"

The room grew quiet. Erik and Rugrat looked at one another. Rugrat waved for Erik to speak and crossed his arms.

"In the rest of the realms, people think that the power of the individual is the greatest strength. How you get that power doesn't matter. It only matters who is stronger and weaker. We don't think the same in Alva." Erik stabbed his finger into the desk, scouring those around the table with a look. "We made them pay for every inch. We retreated in order. We did not flee. We were not routed. That shows discipline and coordination. What if we all had expert gear; if we had all increased our cultivations one or two stages, or we increased our levels to seventy?"

His words hung in the air.

"The Beast Mountain Range will be renamed Vermire Empire. King's Hill will be the capital. The outposts will undergo alterations to turn them into true defensive cities. Village cornerstones will be placed in each outpost. They will no longer be outposts, but strongholds and cities. Born from their lineage of carving out their living in the Beast Mountain Range, those that prove themselves will join the Kingdom. Noble houses and royalty will be abolished. The strongest members might join Alva to be trained and grow further. The Vermire Empire will be in the light, Alva in the dark. Alvans will continue to go to the higher realms for trade, for work, to expand. The Close Protection Details and Special Teams will spread through the realms, the sword to the Intelligence department's information. It might take months, years, or even decades, but we will gather our strength quietly until people come to the Vermire Empire instead of advancing higher in the realms."

Erik sat back. "We can live for centuries, why not use some of that time?"

Vermire Empire, take over the First Realm. Aditya's hands were trembling. *We could do it.*

He gripped his hand into a fist as he looked at Erik with heat in his eyes.

"Alva hears and obeys." Delilah bowed her head, relief flickering in her eyes. Her shoulders loosened slightly as she lowered one burden.

The others bowed their heads as well.

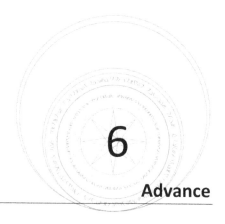

6

Advance

E rik put down the papers he was reading and rubbed his eyes.

"Have you slept since you got back?" Momma Rodriguez asked as she wiped down her sink.

"You know you could use a spell for that."

"I'm not afraid of the work. And you are avoiding the question."

Rugrat walked into the room. "I'm heading off to the workshop. Going to work on the new weapon plans."

"Good luck," Erik said.

"Thanks. Bye, Momma." Rugrat kissed her on the cheek.

"If you see Racquel, invite her for dinner, but tell me a day ahead!" Momma said as Rugrat paused with the door half-open.

"I don't know." Rugrat had his hand on the doorknob.

"Well, go and talk to her to figure it out! You've talked about her enough here and there."

Rugrat looked back into the kitchen. "What day is it today?"

"Tuesday?" Erik shrugged.

"Wednesday," Momma huffed.

"Huh," Rugrat said.

Erik shrugged again.

"I'll let her know if I see her. Bye." He closed the door as Erik picked up the papers.

"Go and sleep. Haven't your notifications driven you crazy by now?" She batted him with her drying towel lightly.

"Fine, fine I'll take a nap," Erik said.

"Good."

He cleared his papers up, went through the living room to the main stairs, and up to his room. *Damn notifications are blinking like mad.*

He let out a big breath. He was moaning about notifications when so many others...

He paused, his face falling.

"Fuck." He shook his head and accessed the notifications as he kept walking up the stairs.

Skill: Riding
Level: 72 (Journeyman)
Melee attacks while riding are 10% stronger Rider's strength increases by 5% when fighting atop their mount

Erik saw Gilly's broken body, heard her last breaths. It burned inside him, having felt her happiness. She had saved her master—saved him.

She—

He closed his eyes and grabbed the banister. He worked his jaw and let out a breath through his nose, pulling himself up the stairs.

Skill: Hand-to-Hand
Level: 72 (Journeyman)
Attacks cost 20% less Stamina. Agility is increased by 10%.

He saw the woman of lightning and man of mana and remembered the pain he felt, his lost limbs as they destroyed his body as if it were nothing more than rotten wood.

Skill: Marksman
Level: 89 (Expert)
Long-range weapons are familiar in your hands. When aiming, you can zoom in x2.0. 15% increased chance for a critical hit. When aiming, your agility increases by 20%

He recalled tracking his tracers through the sky, hitting aerial beasts and riders and watching them drop from the sky. The charge through the walls, the coming night as streams of tracers cut through the sky. Shooting through the hallway, not knowing if there would be a way out, or if this would be his last stand.

Skill: Healer
Level: 117 (Master)
You are a Master of the human body and the arts of repairing it. Healing spells now cost 20% less Mana and Stamina. Patient stamina is used an additional 30% less.
Upon advancing into the Master level of Healer, you will be rewarded with one randomly selected item related to this skill.

You have received the *Body as a system* theory book.
+10,000,000,000 EXP

He took the book and shoved it into a storage ring, something for Egbert to deal with. All he saw when he opened his bedroom door were memories, fresh and raw. Torn flesh and broken bodies. A myriad of wounds, fighting the reaper for his bounty. The faces belonged to those that had been claimed. The yells of pain as he worked. The sheer spirit breaking numbers.

You have reached Level 77
When you sleep next, you will be able to increase your attributes by: 65 points.

304,397,267/8,504,700,000 EXP till you reach Level 78

Erik shuddered at the sheer weight of power contained within his body. He closed his door and moved to his bed.

"Damn, feels like I'll pop." Erik laid down on his bed and quickly took out a sleeping aid.

He sniffed it, making his eyes swim, but it didn't work.

He took two big snorts, and then another before he slumped.

> You have 55 attribute points to use.

Agility and mana. When they were up against the Black Phoenix Clan they had to rely on their weapons and he needed the high agility to be faster. To heal people, he needed the extra mana. His thoughts traveled to the power the woman and man had displayed, even with thirty to forty percent of their strength stripped away.

With mana, he could cast larger spells like the one Egbert cast, and he could take on more of the power of mana through his body as a dungeon lord.

Erik looked at his points again.

Fifty-five. No small amount; Thirty to mana and twenty-five to agility.

He looked at the changes and confirmed.

Name: Erik West	
Level: 77	Race: Human-?
Titles:	
From the Grave II	
Blessed By Mana	
Dungeon Master V	
Reverse Alchemist	
Poison Body	
Fire Body	
Earth Soul	
Mana Reborn II	
Wandering Hero	
Metal Mind, Metal Body	
Earth Grade Bloodline	
Strength: (Base 90) +58	1554
Agility: (Base 83) +110	1109
Stamina: (Base 93) +35	2016
Mana: (Base 37) +134	1744
Mana Regeneration (Base 60) +61	76.02
Stamina Regeneration: (Base 162) +59	47.46

Blissful darkness took him.

Sparks of red-hot metal and mana sprayed around Rugrat's hammer. The simple-looking hammer had elemental lines of mana ran through its handle and up through its head.

Rugrat inspected the sword he was repairing. Mana infusion would help with the instability in the metal. He cast Scan. It spread out from his body, through the hammer, through the sword, the anvil, floor, ceiling, surrounding tables, raw materials, blueprints, and furnace.

Mana spread through the sword like veins. The heat dissipated and the layers of different materials bound together.

Rugrat turned the sword. Using a spell, the reddened iron spread down the blade, powered by his mana. He fell into the calming continuity of work. The labor didn't tire him anymore, not with his stats, but it kept him mentally engaged as he finished with the sword. Another spell appeared around the blade, drawing out the heat of the reddened area, his mana guiding the heat into the furnace.

"Good as new. Maybe even a bit better than it was before." The mana distribution should be better, easier to cast spells on or through the blade. He checked the blade one more time, turning it in his hands. He walked to the rack at one edge of his smithy and stored the blade.

He tapped his holstered hammer on his belt and stretched, the long hours wearing even on him.

He adjusted his short shorts and the wedgie crawling up his crack as he headed down through the smithys. "Shit, bit chilly on the cheeks without a hearth to keep you warm!"

He adjusted his shorts while walking through the smithy workshops. Some were closed off, but there were large instructional areas that were open to passersby as people toiled away.

Racks of weapons were lined out in the hall. Rugrat slowed to watch as an apprentice walked over to the racks filled with different weapons. She grabbed a spear, turning it over in her hands.

She went to a broken bin, grabbing some broken blades or cast-off metals and compared the metal of the spear against the metals in the bin. Finding the best match, she went back into the workshop, taking the materials to a Journeyman smith who checked the items before he threw them into the furnace and started to heat them, using different enhancers.

Expert and high Journeyman smiths walked around, offering help and assisting as needed. There were hundreds of smiths, turning the smithy into a small repair factory as broken weapons went into their forges and new weapons were put on the out rack to be sent back to soldiers or re-issued to new ones.

He detected a flare of mana in a furnace. A safety barrier snapped around the furnace, containing the flames as Rugrat grabbed the smith and his assistant, pulling them out of the way.

Formations in the ceiling drew the flames upward, draining the energy as the formation of the furnace was shut off.

Green flames blazed in the furnace like some demon.

George, who had been lazing on his shoulder, opened his eyes and jumped off his shoulder.

"George!" Rugrat admonished as the wolf dove through the mana barrier and into the furnace.

Rushing air filled the area as the green flames running up against the barrier were drawn backward.

What are you doing?

"Dude, that's just weird," Rugrat said.

"What is?" Taran asked, walking up beside him.

"George is… eating the flames? Sounds like a Dragon Force song. How you doing, man?"

"Second accident this morning. I suppose people are throwing themselves into work to dull their minds to the pain." Taran shrugged. "At least you were here to help them."

Rugrat grunted. "They just want to think that everything will go back to normal. Keep working on something, living their lives as they did in the past. You know."

"Yeah." Taran rubbed his head and paused, closing his eyes, and shuddered.

"Still going with the booty shorts, I see."

"Yes, I had to get a special run done by Zhou Heng." Rugrat adjusted his goggles and rubbed the lines they left under his eyes. "How's Julilah?"

"Back at work. She and Qin are inseparable again. They've thrown themselves into working on anything that will increase the power of their gear. They learned about the armor hangover and they're trying to do something to mitigate the effects. They're taking a look at their formations, in the stacks or the modular formations."

"I hear that they're working on the rail gun weaponry too?" Taran asked.

"Yeah, they've been tinkering with the formation sockets on the weapon. All the formation crafters have been working like crazy. It's impressive how they've broken down everything to rebuild it. They're coming up with some crazy formations and even updating the formations throughout the dungeon."

"Now that Egbert has his memories back, he has all the information on the formations. The missing gaps are being filled in. Are you working on anything?"

"Uh, a little something."

"Why does that make me hear screaming eagles and explosions?" Taran asked.

"Come with me." Rugrat waved for Taran to follow him and checked on George, who had sucked in the remaining flames. "Might want to ask them what that ingredient was. Makes one hell of a powerful flame."

George flew over to Rugrat and landed next to him, growing to the size of a dog. Among his reds and blues, there were faint green sparks now.

"Going to need something that hot?"

"I might." Rugrat shrugged and led the way back to his workshop. Taran closed the door and Rugrat pushed parts and half-formed metal off a blueprint.

"What is that?"

"That is fire superiority," Rugrat said. "It looks like a bastardized Russian PPSH or Tommy gun with a drum mag, mixed with a Gatling gun. I know. Basically, I made a man-portable Gatling gun. Each barrel uses railgun formations. Each round has a starter charge, enough to give it some acceleration from the drum into the barrel which accelerates it hard."

"Heat?"

"Smaller charge means less heat. But the sabot sheath will use new enhanced materials to gather heat. It will drain heat as it goes down the barrel. Then as it splits from the sabot, the sabot is good to go."

"How many formations do you have on this?"

"Well, you know the main thing is one formation, one piece of metal, right?"

"Too many formations and you'll just melt the sucker, if you're lucky." Taran nodded, studying the plans.

"So, we have a rotating drive formation that runs from the back plate through the drum and barrels to the front. It turns the whole thing. The barrels are the same as the ones we've been using in the railgun, but arranged in a group of eight with a band around them. They're covered in heat draining formations along with a rail under and above to hold scopes. Back plate will have a gelatin-like mix to take the impacts. I'll talk to the chefs and alchemists about that; springs will be under so much strain they won't be able to handle it."

"Mounted?"

"Yeah, primarily for mounted positions." Rugrat pulled out another plan. "On the left side, we've got a feed. Spent casings are spit out of the bottom. If you crank on the foregrip, then it works like a shotgun. Pulls the drum and assembly forward and forcefully rotates and ejects your rounds. Slam it forward and you're locked back in. Thought about having it just turn the drum, but you want to clear those stoppages as soon as possible."

"What's this?" Taran pointed to the ring sticking up from where the ammunition feeder connected.

"A storage device."

"We can't use storage devices unless we're touching them," Taran said.

"Uhh, well, kind of?" Rugrat moved to another work bench. George jumped up next to the furnace and laid down, basking in the heat.

On the workbench, there was a muddy brown line that had been carved into the wood creating a channel to a storage ring.

Rugrat put his finger on one side of the ring.

Taran studied the stained wood.

"What is this metal? Smells like iron."

"Blood."

"Euugh?" Taran's face pressed into a frown.

"Well, we can't use metal or inanimate objects to interact with the storage rings. I took a trick from Erik and used some of my blood to make this channel and bingo. I used some of Erik's blood, and it worked as well. Though I don't know if it will work for everyone. I will need to test or have them use their blood. This is what allows the weapon system to be man-portable."

"So, you fill the storage ring with ammunition and activate it through your blood channel and it just pours out ammo?"

"Pretty much. You run out of ammo, you hit the release here. It ejects the storage ring, and you smack in another one. I picked the storage ring sizing based on the number of rings we have in that size. We can't produce storage rings ourselves, yet. So, for now, we'll have to do with what we have."

Taran held his chin. "If we were to add something like this to the new mortars, you would only need a gunner and a team leader. Embed the ring in the side of the mortar and have the gunner activate it, dropping in whatever prepared round he wants. Just have to make sure they have the rounds prepped with different charges and shell types."

"You working on the new rail mortars?" Rugrat cocked an eyebrow.

"Yeah, same idea. Starting charge to get it going, then railgun formations up the barrel, separated by sleeves. They'll expand when the round is outgoing, speeding it up over a longer distance and draw back, hitting the heat release blocks when they come back. Should be able to increase the rate of fire by a factor of ten and increase the round's size, power, and range. Still, I'm not sure you don't have too many formations." Taran tapped the table, his eyes moving over plans unseen.

"I have the turning formation. It mechanically affects the other areas, but it doesn't apply mana to them. Then there's the storage ring for ammunition and spell plate so you can apply spells to the rounds. The sabot sheath has a formation. The sabot rounds can have their own formations, increased piercing, explosive, and so on. Then the barrels are the same as the railguns, independent ringed formations that don't overlap. There is one socket formation on the buttstock that affects the weapon overall, heat decreasing formation and silencing formation. That would be kind of fucking terrifying."

"A little. That all for formations?"

"Yes."

"How are you getting power to them all; you running them independently so you charge them all, or linked? And what about the heat core in the barrels? If that overheats, you're screwed."

"If you pump the gun, opening the chamber, you can rotate it to the left, unhooking the entire barrel assembly. Then you slap it to a heat-dissipating pack on your back. Drains the heat while you grab another barrel, rotate it to the right, lock it, and push the cocking handle forward." He tapped the foregrip. "Like a shotgun. Then it's all back together and you're ready to bring freedom through superior firepower."

"Power?"

"Ah, sorry, that is a bit of a tricky one. Need to run, basically, a superstructure, or spine of enhanced iron to charge all the formations through the weapon. This thing will be a power hog." Rugrat grinned.

"No shit." Taran shook his head. "Using enhanced iron to increase the power of formations?"

"Of course. I think I'll have to use sky iron to get the most out of this."

"Allow you to use stronger formations. We'll have to create the next series of railguns with sky iron. But we don't have machines in the factories to make them. And we still need experts to work with sky iron."

"Well, the body might need the sky iron and the superstructure. What I'm thinking is just hammering the sky iron into support rods and flat plates. Then we just need to cut them with a mana blade or use a fuse spell to put it together instead of building it all as a single piece."

"That could work. Yeah, make things faster."

"And the drum won't be sky iron either. We can replace that easily. And the barrels are just earth metal. Again, if we can get them mass-produced in sky iron, then we can weld them together and slap them into this. The buttstock is from the Mark Seven."

"So, the hardest thing would be making the sky iron sections. The rest is from earth iron which can be upgraded in the future."

"You got it."

"Smart." Taran studied the plans for a few more minutes. "What about your modified rifle, you giving that up?"

"Of course not. She's my baby." Rugrat looked Taran up and down as if he were crazy and took out the rifle. He pulled out the magazine and ejected the loaded round, catching it with mana.

He put it all down on the table.

"Though I think it needs some modifications." Rugrat leaned on the table.

"How so?"

"Change the recoil system to the same hydraulic systems to be used in the mobile-gat. Use the new heat dissipating sabots and increase the round size to twenty mil." Rugrat tapped the magwell.

"Won't that be a massive round?"

"It is large, yeah. But only needs a short stubby starter charge so cuts down the size a lot. More round, less powder. It'll be about as long as my middle finger and a bit thicker than my thumb."

"Going to need a whole new barrel."

"Just scale up the other barrels. The extra metal should increase the performance and the heat dissipation blocks will be bigger too."

"It'll be bigger than you are."

"Eh, I do plenty of curls." Rugrat couldn't hide the shine in his eyes. "I'm thinking that it gets used by the sharpshooters and those in the higher teams that want it. There's also a belt-fed version that can replace our belt-fed grenade launchers. Those things are good for a few hundred meters and not much else. A twenty-mil rail gun. That'll lay down some serious firepower over distance. Give them explosive formations and spell them up with explosive shot and someone's gonna have a shitty day."

"So, twenty mil portable cannons and a portable Gatling gun, too. If we have them, then we can take out the grenade launcher, modified Mark Seven, and the bolt action?" Taran asked.

"Yeah, the Mark Seven we just slapped on an attachment to take feeding through an open bolt and the bolt action wouldn't be able to break these fucker's barriers. All of them were nearly fifty percent their strength and our rail guns were having issues punching through. I like the grenade launcher, but it doesn't have the lethality we need. There is a limit to the number of weapons we can produce. The fewer the models, the better. When is the mark two rail mortar coming out?"

"It might be a few weeks. Going to close production on the mark one, start mark twos. We'll filter them through the service until we've replaced them all with mark twos."

"What about the artillery cannons? They're all getting changed to the rail cannons?" Rugrat asked.

"Yes, they're having heat issues as well. So wherever they're placed will have external heat radiators, circulate a cooling liquid around the barrels and pump that into a box with heat-dissipating blades. With the size of it, they'll have to run off formation sockets, so we can just replace the sockets. The portable versions are much smaller, requiring the formations to be built in. They'll have a shorter shelf life."

"Until we reach a point where formations are small as hell and we can replace them in small equipment as well," Rugrat said.

The two of them fell into silence.

"You think they're going to find us?" Taran asked.

Rugrat turned, leaning against the table, rubbing his face. He took off his cowboy hat and scratched his head before putting it back on.

"To be honest, man, I have no idea. It'll be difficult. But we are a large organization. There are sure to be some footprints. The Institute attacked the Beast Mountain Range through proxy." Rugrat opened his hands.

"Some people think we should just cut ourselves off from the other realms." Taran leaned against the worktable across from Rugrat.

Rugrat shrugged and pressed his lips together.

"I'm not the guy with the plan. I'm the guy that will be out there tearing the fuckers apart if they show themselves. If we cut ourselves off from the realms, we'll be weaker. We need materials. We need information. We're learning more every day, but it doesn't replace the fact that the information we get from people in the Ten Realms can open new doors and paths. We wouldn't be where we are now if we had isolated ourselves."

"We have the materials, and we have the knowledge. We just need to digest it and spend time on it," Taran said.

Rugrat opened his mouth and then closed it.

"When was the greatest period of advancement for Alva? Was it when we only had connections in the First Realm or a few months ago when we reached the Sixth Realm and brought back information books, new materials, and methods?"

"During the attacks, people were doing everything they could to create things to help out people on the front," Taran said.

"The closer the bullets are, the better the soldier is," Rugrat said. "People thrive under pressure. But, if we blindly follow our own path, we'll be idiots. Innovation and change are created through problems and information."

"Are you saying that fighting is good for us?"

"No, I'm saying that concentrated and focused effort is good for us. Pushing the boundaries is good for us. If we're cooped up in here, then does anything out there even matter anymore? Over time, will people lose their drive. Sure, there are weaknesses, but would we rather hide and lose our fire? That's the rub."

Taran was quiet.

"This is just my personal philosophy. Hiding from the world won't do anything. People need something to strive toward to have a fulfilled life. Shutting ourselves off, that is just admitting defeat. While we did lose, we were not defeated. The Alva military stands to defend the people of Alva so that they might live freely."

"Just… we've lost so much. And we could lose so much more," Taran said.

Rugrat nodded, agreeing with the man.

Erik and Rugrat inspected one another. They wore combat fatigues, pressed and cleaned. Their hair was freshly cut, and a fresh razor had cleaned away any scruff.

They checked their rank tabs, their special team and Alva patches.

Erik adjusted the blousing of his pants. "Good."

Rugrat nodded. They walked out of the special team office and into the command center. The staff was away. There were maps along the left wall of the First to the Sixth Realm with decreasing accuracy. There was a map table in the middle of the room. At the front of the room there were command desks, along with mounts where projection screens would be located.

They left the command center through a hatch, entering a hallway lined with doors marked one, two, three, and four. Behind each door were the locker rooms and armories of the special teams. Erik and Rugrat went through an unmarked door, a corridor between two and three.

They exited at the end of the corridor, leaving the building, and walked out onto a training square. Training equipment was stored around its perimeter.

The door opened from room two. Tully walked out and nodded to them.

"They nearly ready?" Erik asked.

"Yeah, just been a long time since we had to get all cleaned up," Tully responded quietly.

Rugrat went to doors three and four, knocking on them.

Erik went to door one and knocked on it, too. Erik and Rugrat met up as people started to come out of the team rooms.

We lost so many.

The teams stepped out in an extended line.

Team Three was only six people, nearly half their original team.

A lot of their wounded were still out of action. Their bodies were strong, so it took a lot to hurt them, but what did hurt them took a lot to heal.

"Get into formation, two abreast," Erik said.

Some of the special team had come off from medical and were stiff as they moved into it and got organized.

Erik and Rugrat moved to the front of the unit, checking on them as they passed.

"By the left, for—ward, march!"

They stepped off as one, marching forward. Rugrat's mana opened the gates as they exited the Special Team's training square.

The first training square had been cleaned. Families of the Special Teams, people that had served with them, or the fallen and the families of the fallen, waited there. Wounded team members forced themselves up to standing, ignoring their families' complaints as they helped one another and medics stood behind them as support.

"Teams, halt!"

Their boots smacked the rock with a crack.

Erik and Rugrat marched out and wheeled around to face the teams.

"Leftward face. Left turn."

They turned to face Erik and Rugrat, the families, and the wall between them.

Erik saw the movement of jaws and flares of nostrils.

Erik surveyed them and gave an imperceptible nod.

He looked at Rugrat.

They turned as one, facing the wall standing side by side.

"Sergeant Major Rodriguez, roll call!" Erik ordered.

"Yes sir, roll call! Master Gunnery Sergeant Xi," a muffled cry came from within the spectators. "Master Gunnery Sergeant Linda Xi!"

"Master Gunnery Sergeant Imani."

"Master Gunnery Sergeant Elle Imani!"

"Master Gunnery Sergeant Simms."

"Master Gunnery Sergeant David Simms!"

"Master Gunnery Sergeant Tyrone."

"Master Gunnery Sergeant Zedong Tyrone!"

"Master Gunnery Sergeant Qiu."

"Master Gunnery Sergeant Jacqueline Qiu!"

"Master Gunnery Sergeant Asaka."

"Master Gunnery Sergeant Asaka Tsuka!"

"Master Gunnery Sergeant Kachal."

"Master Gunnery Sergeant Yuli Kachal!"

"Master Gunnery Sergeant Ryan."

"Master Gunnery Sergeant Jamie Ryan!"

"Master Gunnery Sergeant Sang."

"Master Gunnery Sergeant Sang So-Hyon!"

The military members came to attention, focusing on the wall. Some of the families stared at the names of their loved ones.

Rugrat turned to face Erik.

Erik turned to face him.

"Roll call complete, sir!" Rugrat saluted, not blinking, holding back the pain as his jaw flexed.

"Thank you, Sergeant Major!" Erik returned the salute.

They turned to face the wall.

"To the fallen, salute!"

The special team members and the military members among those attending snapped up a salute, holding it before Erik slowly lowered his hand, the others following suit. Erik looked to Rugrat, and they turned as one.

"Teams, to your duties. Dis-missed!"

The teams turned as one and marched off to the side and then broke, moving toward the families and others.

Erik patted Rugrat on the back, working his lips as he took a deep breath, causing his nostrils to flare.

He saw Simms' kids and his wife as she touched his name, falling apart as her relations hugged and supported her. Her kids were too young to understand.

Setsuko Ket's father, Fehim, the leader of Alva's alchemists, supported her as she talked to Yuli's mother and father.

Delilah and the Ryan family were in tears as Yao Meng took off his headdress to talk to them.

Sang So-Hyon didn't have a family, but soldiers that had served with him, and some friends from the academy, supported one another; they had lost a brother.

Erik and Rugrat walked toward it, moving to the families.

The hardest part wasn't fighting. They were trained for that. The hardest part was putting to rest the ones that didn't make it back.

"Mister Imani, I can't understand what you're going through right now, but I wanted to tell you that Imani was one hell of a woman, one hell of a team member," Erik said.

The man's features broke as his eyes pinched together. Tears leaked out as another relation supported him.

"She… she was an amazing person, and it was incredible to have the honor to know her."

The man nodded, unable to say anything.

Erik glanced at the man supporting the other and nodded to him. Erik turned and nearly walked over two boys and a girl.

"Woah you three. What are you up to?"

"Mommy is crying over there and there are so many adults here," the oldest, one of the boys said. The younger boy was holding the youngest, his sister's, hand. Erik looked at the oldest. He couldn't be older than seven. *Simms will never see them go to school, never see them graduate, date people, go through heartbreak, marry, or have kids of their own.*

"Mommy just needs some time. She's sad. Where were you headed off to?"

"I heard there's a room of sweets!" the younger boy said.

"Always thinking with that belly." Erik smiled and poked his belly and tickled a bit.

The boy's shy laugh as he batted Erik's finger made others look over with smiles.

"I saw that there are three troublemakers over here," Momma Rodriguez said. She was wearing a black dress and an elegant black pin to keep her greying hair in check.

"They were looking for treats," Erik supplied.

"Treats was it, and maybe something to play with?" Momma asked, conspiratorially as she pulled out toasted sandwiches from her bag.

She made a head gesture to Erik.

"Come on, let's go and sit down. It's no good eating while standing!" She took them over to some chairs as Erik turned back to the grieving families.

He squared his jaw and stepped forward into it.

7

One Nation

Major Wazny walked into the hangar located in the sprawling Alva military training compound shared by the Army and the Air Force on the water floor.

"Attention!" one of the soldiers called out. The group loosely gaggled between the different displays of systems snapped to attention.

"Got some situational awareness," Wazny muttered to Captain Xia. Her left sleeve was empty, still regenerating with the scars on her face and patch over her eye.

"Maybe they can see better than me?" she asked wryly.

Wazny let out something between a grunt and a laugh as they stopped before the group. He saluted the man out front. "At ease. All right, so all of you want to be Sparrow pilots," Wazny muttered, finding them lacking.

"Reservists, raise your hands." Xia counted them. "Reg force?"

"Looks like a fifty-fifty split nearly." Wazny leaned on his cane and pulled out a folder and read it. "You lot are one fucking mess of training. Got riflemen, scouts, mortars, a few engineers, and some mages in there as well. You all tired of using your feet?"

"No, sir!"

"Hmm." Wazny checked the file again and put it away. "My name is Major Wazny. This is Captain Xia. Together we make a functioning human."

There were some moving lips, but no laughs.

Wazny raised an eyebrow. "I'll cut the shit. The air force got hammered. We lost." Wazny worked his jaw. "A lot." He sniffed. "And you lot are my new fliers. The Air Force struck the fear of sparrows and kestrels into the enemy and proved the concepts originally created by Colonel Kanoa. Sparrows are highly maneuverable and quick. They can hit the enemy before they know what's happening and fuck off before they know they're dead. Weapons include spell scrolls, spells, and repeaters, which will be upgraded to rail guns and bombs. Your defenses are your speed, your connection to your bird, and outsmarting the enemy."

A hand shot up.

"We have a question. Go on." Wazny rested both of his hands on his cane in front of him, pushing off his right leg.

"Don't the sparrows have mana barriers?"

"They do, but in the air there's all kinds of shit coming at you and going out. Best to rely on the things that work. You never know if a spell is gonna give you a light display or tear through your cabin, your bird, and you. You ever seen Lord West use his Finger Beats Fist move? Shit looks like nothing, but can blast a hole through a mana barrier and a block of buildings in a straight line and still kill you." Wazny surveyed them all.

"You might think that you're close to your battle buddy in the army, but the people in your wing, you have to be closer to and understand what the other will do as they do it. You have to anticipate one another.

"You might have noticed that things are a little thin around here. The fact that we're running training, half my body is fucked up and Captain Xia looks like she got into a fight with a fucking fire mage and lost, should tell you something." They were all focused on him now, hard faces. *They think they're ready, but it's my job to make sure they are.*

"I crashed into a building, sparrow dead, cabin cracked; we'd just evacuated the outer wall and were trying to break up the enemy, hitting the towers before the inner city. Captain Xia took on three aerial fighters that would have blasted me into an early retirement. She pulled paper. Her sparrow was dead.

"She lost an arm and wooden shrapnel from her cabin tore up her face." Wazny shifted his stance. "Still, she pulled me from that wreck, with one fucking arm and half a face, and carried me two kilometers to the nearest evacuation point. The reason we are thin is simple. Of our eight sparrow wings, *we* are the only survivors.

"Sparrows strike fear into the enemy's hearts. The sects cursed us as they died. Those that survive will remember us till the day they die. Sparrow pilots are some of the ballsiest, bravest, and stupidest motherfuckers you have seen. It is not expected that many of you will retire any other way than to add your name to that wall. Mark my words, we will not forget Vuzgal. We will demand payment from the sects and the Black Phoenix Clan—a debt of blood and bodies. I cannot guarantee your safety. What I can guarantee is that we will train you to strike fear into your enemy's hearts and destroy them. Nothing can stop a determined sparrow pilot. We own the skies so the army may own the ground."

Wazny watched their reactions as the cold wind from the water floor passed through the hangars, past the railgun models, whistling over the cabin cut outs, causing the spell scroll ribbons to flutter.

"You have all passed the physical standards and earned your place here. Many of you have been on the sharp end in Vuzgal. Take a day, think it through and talk to your families. Those of you that choose to stay, I will see you in two days, five a.m. here. Dismissed."

Wazny turned with Xia and he limped out of the hangar while the void of her combat sleeve flapped in the wind.

"We're disbanding the Adventurer's Guild?" Derrick smacked the table as he glared at Blaze. The other guild branch heads and administrators were looking to Blaze as he shook his head.

"We're not disbanding. We're separating into cells so we can continue to train, to live our lives, and gain strength."

"You saw the power of that sect. A ship made of stone and iron that floated in the air," Emilia said.

Stephen raised his hand.

"Go on." Blaze opened his hand toward the other man.

"I would like to apply for leave to go and teach in Alva."

"Teach?" Lin Lei asked from beside him.

"My teacher died and all of Alva is developing pure magic. I am fine with this administration thing. But with fighting, I am best used in large assaults. In handling a small guild, I will just want to get back to larger battles or train," Stephen said.

"You would leave us?" Joan slammed her hands on the table as her chair fell.

Kim Cheol placed his hand on her shoulders. "Stephen is not leaving *us*. We are Alva and Alva is us. Or do you forget who trained you, who made your weapons, who supported and taught our people to take cities?"

"People can do as they want; stay here in Alva, leave to pursue their own lives, or join one of the guilds. Our task is with the guild," Jasper said. "If we break into guilds, we can spread out and build up in different areas. When our groups interact, we can *build* alliances regathering our strength, but it changes our origins."

"What of the Willful Institute and this Black Phoenix?" Emilia asked.

"The Willful Institute has surged forth and retaken some of their cities. But they have bled for them. Now they are consolidating. If they get the support, I do not doubt that they will push to take more land. Elan reports that everything is not as it seems behind the scenes. The sect is pushed to their limit. They have gained some wealth, but they have fewer cities than they started with. If they do not want to fall apart, they need to consolidate what they have and reinforce it," Blaze said and then rubbed his face.

"The Black Phoenix Clan is a larger, less immediate, problem." He rested his head against his outstretched fingers. "They normally do not go into the lower realms. They have few contacts here, and other dungeon lords have arrived as well. They're squabbling with each other over hunting us down. Following a trail that has been muddied since the beginning."

"Are they coming for us or not?" Derrick asked.

"We don't know, but we should assume they are," Blaze said.

The room quieted. Joan picked up her chair as everyone sat with their thoughts.

"We have to rebuild pretty much everything. We have more connections in the lower realms. Most of the Alvan merchants have their own guards but as they have reappeared with more loans available. They need to grow," Jasper said.

"So we go from taking cities to protecting convoys again?" Joan clicked her tongue.

"That is what most of our people signed up to do. What most of them would have been doing before this war. It was what the Adventurer's guild party that was killed by those bastards at Meokar had been doing! Protecting convoys is honest and good work. We have the backing of Alva, with training, with resources, and information. If we attack the Willful Institute now, we'll get crushed by the people who want to use them to get closer to the Black Phoenix Clan. We cannot keep our people in these dungeons. Most of them don't even know they're in a dungeon. They think they're in hidden caves. A lot of them have families. They can't stay down here." Blaze pressed his forefinger and middle finger to the table.

Chonglu waited outside of Delilah's office in Alva. He had a forlorn look on his face as he scratched the patchy beard on his face numbly.

The door opened and Commander Glosil walked out.

"Sir." Glosil saluted Chonglu, not waiting for his response before he marched down the hall; his aides and officers fell in with him as he spoke to them, passing orders.

Chonglu rose to his feet with a long sigh. He pulled on his robe, breathing out, and stood straighter as he faced Delilah's office, bracing himself before he walked past the guard into the room.

She looked up from her notepad as he entered, her eyes piercing as she put her pen away. Her desk was organized precisely. While young, her face didn't show any childishness of her age. "Chonglu. Sorry. Just give me a moment to write up some notes." She bent her head and continued to write.

"Certainly, Council Leader," Chonglu said, standing in front of her desk.

"Please, take a seat." She waved at the chairs, not looking up as she continued to jot down notes. She circled and underlined a few key things, and then closed her notepad and placed it to the side, resting her pen atop it. "Chonglu, thank you for seeing me on such short notice."

Chonglu gave her a terse smile. "Look, Council Leader, I can save us both some time. Please thank Erik and Rugrat and the rest of the council for their faith in me for running Vuzgal. I lost the city and will retire quietly from the public eye for this shame." Chonglu bowed his head.

Delilah sat forward, resting her hands on the table. "Chonglu, that was hardly your fault. None of us could have predicted the Black Phoenix Clan. I sure as hell didn't." She sighed, looking tired as she sunk into her chair and waved her hand. "I don't want you to retire, Chonglu. I want you to run Alva."

"Run Alva?" Chonglu's eyes widened.

"When I started as Council Leader, Alva managed itself and had a few hundred people. We've just passed one and a half million Alvans. It might not be long before we reach two million with all the people from Vuzgal and the guild joining us. I cannot run this dungeon city and the nation growing around it by myself. So, would you be interested in being Alva's City Lord so I can be the nation's Council Leader?"

"You don't doubt my abilities?" Chonglu's brows knit together.

"Erik told me once: Don't watch what someone does day to day and forget to watch them when they are at their lowest. When one is under pressure, that is when to watch closer. Chonglu, it is because of your performance with Vuzgal that I am completely confident in asking you to run Alva Dungeon."

Chonglu was rendered mute as he cleared his throat. "Aren't you scared that the Black Phoenix Clan will find us again?"

Chonglu felt the mana in the room twist.

"Vuzgal and Vermire are just outposts., We can lose them if we must, but Alva. Alva is our home. They will need a dozen ships if they want to threaten us here."

Chonglu gritted his teeth, raising his head. "Council Leader, I would be honored to serve Alva." Chonglu stood, cupping his fists and bowing.

"Well, Mayor Chonglu, your first job—" She dropped books on her desk. "—is to get up to speed on Alva's developments."

Chonglu looked at the books. "More information books," he muttered.

"Oh, there's always more." Delilah smiled devilishly.

Chonglu gave her a nervous smile back. "What will people think of me sending my children to the Fighter's Association though?"

"You have your reasons. Sure, people will use that as a point of weakness, but Chonglu, you will not be the best mayor of Alva by being meek. You must promise me two things. One, that you will be dead, or right by me, as the last two people to leave Alva if we must flee. And, two, you will do everything in your power to support the people of Alva. We do not know how much time we have until we are found. We must use every second and squeeze every minute we have to be ready."

"I promise," Chonglu said solemnly.

"Then I picked right."

Rugrat reached the wood floor and stood on the porch of Fred's house. He raised his hand, pausing. *What the hell am I going to say?*

Noises approached from inside, and he expanded his domain just as the door opened.

"Why do I have to—" Racquel opened the door and looked at Rugrat. "Ah." She smiled, but something in her smile made his stomach twist.

"Tell him to stop wearing a hole in my steps!" Fred said from within the house.

"Do you have a minute?" Rugrat asked.

"What for?"

"I wanted to talk about… us. *This.*" Rugrat gestured between them.

"Okay." She turned her head back. "Going out for a bit, see you later."

She closed the door, and they stepped onto the road. They walked along rows of fruit trees and down the dirt packed road. Pickers filled the fields while the occasional cart moved down the road in the distance.

"I wanted to check in with you, see where we are. I feel like you've been avoiding me since we came back. You've been distant," Rugrat said, feeling his stomach twist in knots. He felt like he was walking to the edge of a cliff.

"It's just…" She sighed. "I feel like I'm in your way."

Rugrat frowned. "What do you mean?"

"You lead Alva with Erik. If we were to go out, then I'd be in that spotlight, and I don't want that. You're an adventurer, but you adventure with Erik. I adventure with my family. How much time would we spend together if we're in different places? Is that really a relationship?"

Rugrat sighed, but nodded. "Yeah, I get what you're saying."

"You and Erik have worked and lived together for so long. You're military people and I'm not. I don't understand what you're doing or why you're doing it. While that's okay for day to day, if we're in the fight, it could cause problems. You work well with the other teams and the trained groups. Look, I like you. I like you a lot."

He turned her head, seeing the hot tears in her eyes. The pit of his stomach readied to swallow him whole as her brows pinched together.

It twisted his heart.

"I really like you, Rugrat, but what if we did go out? There would be a limit. There would be an ending. Might not be next month or next year or even in a few decades, but at the end our lives are not compatible." She sniffed and turned her head away. "I want to go out with you so badly, but if there is no future—"

"Yeah, I get you, and it takes courage to say something like that. I like you too, but yeah." Rugrat shrugged, feeling like he had been plunged into the icy oceans and was grasping for a life jacket out of reach.

Racquel looked him in the eyes as Rugrat felt the fight draining from him.

"Our goals right now are different. You're looking to defend Alva and I just want to explore the realms. I was infatuated with you when we first met, and now you're larger than life to me. All of this is." She raised her arms to the dungeon with a short laugh. "This is your *home,* your people." She smiled. "You're one hell of a catch, but just not mine."

Rugrat laughed and rubbed the back of his head. "I feel the same way about you, but thank you for your honesty." He let out a heavy breath, releasing something that very nearly pulled him apart inside as he reached out his hand. "Friends, maybe fellow adventurers?"

"I'd like that." She smiled and shook his hand.

They released one another as a burning need to hug her overwhelmed him, but he held himself back, his brain and heart in conflict with one another.

"I'll see you around, Rugrat."

"See you around, Racquel."

Rugrat watched her walk away before he turned back and walked toward the Wood floor's main town. George leapt off his shoulder and grew to his full height, butting his head against Rugrat's shoulder.

"Thanks buddy." Rugrat scratched his neck. "Egbert, take us home please?"

He found Erik sitting out on the raised front porch, leaning back on his arms, his feet touching the ground.

"Beer?" Erik asked, and pulled out two bottles.

"Yeah." Rugrat took one, twisting the cap off and taking a few mouthfuls. He sat down on the porch and looked out at the city.

Erik tossed George a treat. He snatched it out of the air and laid down on the ground, devouring it in front of the duo.

"Not a bad sight," Rugrat said.

"Not a bad sight at all," Erik agreed.

8

The Beast Descends From the Mountain

The tent was a simple affair: four sticks with a piece of cloth draped over them and secured to the ground with ropes. Inside, the main table was covered in a map weighed down in rocks.

Several officers stood back from the table in their armor, sporting the new Vermire crest: a black mountain with a golden-colored wagon wheel impressed atop it.

"Are you sure?" Lieutenant General Pan Kun asked, looking to the previous Lord Aras. He wore a plain padded jacket for warmth and defense. He had a simple sword on his hip. His gaudy clothes and rings had been taken by the newly formed Vermire Empire.

"My Cousin, while he might be many things, is loyal to me before the Rodenheim Kingdom. He will comply," Aras said.

"Good. I do not want to spend more lives here. I will simply use spell scrolls upon the city." Pan Kun turned his head to the side. "How are the preparations, Colonel Quan?"

Quan braced himself. He shared similar features to his uncle, Consortium Leader Quan, who had once been the leader of the old mercenary group.

"Our forces are ready and waiting. We are set to move in twenty minutes."

"Good."

A messenger throwing the tent flap open, interrupting Pan Kun. "Message from Brigadier General Lukas!"

Pan Kun waved the woman over and received the letter.

"Ah, good. He's taken Zahir City without casualties. He is reinforcing it and creating interlinking towers." Pan Kun passed the message to Colonel Quan, who accepted it with both hands and read it.

"Lord Aras, I hope you're correct. You and your people will be at the front of our column. Let's get mounted up."

He left the tent with the other officers. Aras stuck to Pan Kun like glue. Outside the command tent, the army had formed into squares of melee fighters, mages, and ranged. Each wore different weapons and gear to denote their position while their gear was uniform in each unit.

Damn impressive sight.

His guards had his mount prepared for him. He swung up onto the mount as Aras waited.

"Head to the front of the line. You will do all in your power to turn the City of Shida."

"Yes, Lieutenant General." The man bowed his head and walked off toward the group of men and women at the front of the army. They wore simple clothes and walked on foot like the army. Pan Kun surveyed the army and looked behind him. The road had been expanded to nearly four times the size for them to pass.

Trees lay felled on the side of the road. Construction workers cut them up and put them on carts that headed to the rear, or tore out the stumps from the ground. After all the things they had done to cut through the Beast Mountain Range, they must have had the best crafters in the First Realm for road building.

Colonel Quan rode up on his beast.

"Sir, we're ready," Quan reported.

Pan Kun turned and looked out at the fields surrounding Shida. "They don't have much in the way of farms. Really, it's just a trading city. Pretty big, though."

The city's size was a third of the remodeled King's Hill City and sat directly on the road that led to the Beast Mountain Range. It was round in design, with one third of the city on the left side of the road, and two thirds on the right. The nobles' taller homes and places of business were on the right, far away from the road and the Beast Mountain Range. Sandstone walls made the city feel warm even as the wind threatened coming snow.

"Let's begin," Pan Kun said.

Colonel Quan turned to the signaler, who raised a horn to his lips and blew on it. The noise spread across the army and toward Shida.

The group of Shida residents, led by Aras, walked toward the gates of their home. Melee fighters, archers, and mages followed in their blocks. The sound of marching filled the air as their feet struck the cold, hard ground.

Pan Kun clicked his tongue, calling his mount into movement. "Barriers?" he asked.

"They have none and ours are active."

The army marched across the open ground under the watchful eyes of the city guards.

They moved in close to the gates, which remained closed.

"Bring the army to a halt," Quan said to the signaler.

The horn sounded again, and the Army snapped their feet together as one as the cold wind ran over their still, armored forms.

Aras and his group yelled up at the gate, talking to the people at the top.

Pan Kun used Eagle Sight to watch the exchange. A man yelled at Aras from the gate and Aras shouted back to him. Finally, the man on the wall gritted his teeth, turning and yelling to those around him. They disappeared from the wall and the gates of the city slowly opened.

The man that had been on the wall walked out of the gate with a group of twenty or so people.

A signaler waved his flag.

"Well, let's go and see what they have to say." Pan Kun canted forward with Colonel Quan and their guards.

They rode between the different units to the front, where the Shida groups were waiting.

"None of your attitude, cousin. They could easily take the city if they want to," Aras berated the other man. Even bound under contract, he hadn't lost his fire.

"I've got it. I've got it." The other man sighed.

People moved aside for the riders. Pan Kun's guards moved out, tense and ready to act at a moment's notice.

"Major General Pan Kun, if you allow my family to survive and do not take our belongings, then the city of Shida—" The man's jaw worked. "—surrenders to yourself and the Vermire Empire on the Ten Realms."

The formations on the walls of Shida faded. The city formation had failed now that they were no longer allied to their old kingdom.

"I accept your surrender."

You have taken control of the City Shida for the Vermire Empire.

"As of this moment, all Shida guards are dismissed. A recruitment station for the Vermire Army will be set up within the city. Aras, you will expand the farms to support the city. Trade will be opened to the rest of the Vermire Empire in two weeks. Everyone will have the right to basic education, three classes on novice crafts, and one class on an apprentice level craft. The First Army will move into the city to make sure that there is no counterattack." Pan Kun dropped a city cornerstone on the ground.

"Replace your old city cornerstone with this. It will link you to the Vermire Empire. And these." Pan Kun pulled out a bundle and tossed them to Aras. The ex-lord took a few heavy steps back from the weight. "Are to be posted throughout the city immediately."

Aras's cousin looked at Pan Kun and then to Aras.

"Yes, sir. We will see it done." Aras bowed his head and hit his cousin in the side with his elbow.

"Yes, sir," his cousin said, his voice faltering at the odd word.

"Good. Shida will be our second city of the day. Oh, and make sure you send letters to the lords and people that you know. Tell them we are looking for people. It does not matter if they are peasants or traders, we'll train them. After all, if I, a one-eyed cripple, can be the leader of Vermire's Army. There are plenty of opportunities for others to do the same."

"Brigadier Nasreen has taken her objective. We have now claimed all five cities without a drop of blood." Aditya pushed the marker on the map over the city.

He stood in his office with Consortium Leader Quan and Evernight.

"With the formal creation of the empire, we have unlocked the kingdom menus. We have made King's Hill the capital. The outposts are rated as villages and towns depending on their numbers, and the new cities should transfer over easily. It will allow us greater control in the future and increase our defensive ability. We gained access to two totems, one in Zahir and the other in Malakesh city." Aditya pointed to the cities.

"The armies cleared the ground ahead of the road construction teams to speed up the process. Other teams will be heading out with the Beast Mountain—Ah sorry. The Vermire Army will create and man the planned defensive network of towers." He waved his finger to the rough circle of markers that ran between each of the five cities. "At the same time, King's Hill will receive an upgrade." He rested his hands on the map and looked at the two others, smiling.

"A totem of our very own."

"Our construction crews are sure to be busy," Quan said. "Though I hear that the construction crews from Alva will be assisting?"

"Correct. They will assist with the towers. The totem is just materials which Alva will happily supply. As well as the teachers that we're sending out to each city," Evernight said.

"Teachers, or spies?" Aditya asked.

"Why can't someone have multiple jobs? We need people in the heart of these cities to know what people are thinking. Alvans are trained in many crafts. They can easily teach novice and apprentice level classes while gathering information on the people. Make sure first-hand that things are going well in the streets, not just based on the reports we get from the managers. Even if the city is producing, if people hate us, then we're sure to lose the city."

"I have been receiving letters recently from noble houses in the different nations," Quan said.

"They want to come back to the Consortium?"

"Yes, they claim they were not part of the actions against us, although we know most of them were." He gave a sidelong glance to Evernight.

"I made it clear that, at this time, we have too many students within the Vermire Empire and have no slots open for people outside the Empire."

"Their reactions?" Aditya asked.

Quan indicated to Evernight to answer.

"They're not pleased. They think it's a stupid idea to teach the people of the Empire; as if there are people that can learn and people who are too dumb. They think we will stop the practice and go back to them, begging them to join us because we will bankrupt ourselves trying to support so many people."

Aditya snorted and shook his head.

"I wonder what they will think in a few months' time?" Quan stroked his beard, the old man's eyes shining.

"Our priority is to hold the land we've claimed. Alva army will reinforce us, but we need numbers. What have the kingdoms' responses been to our letters?" Aditya asked.

"They ..." Evernight paused. "Well, they aren't pleased, but they'll accept them. Losing so much of their professional fighting force, they're watching all their borders. They're asking for the return of nobles before they give us compensation."

"They want to turn it into a barter?" Aditya asked.

"So, they attack us and want us to beg them for resources?" Quan echoed as he gritted his teeth.

"They are testing us. I think we should assert our position," Evernight said.

"How?" Aditya asked.

"We have nobles under contract. Let's send them back and liquidate their assets, turning them over to us. We claim their estates as our own. Most of them surround us, so it will expand our lands rapidly. People seek the protection of the strong. The citizens will seek our protection. We don't need this settlement. The kingdoms do."

"They attacked us once, and we put all the traders, camp followers and their armies under contract. Not sure our relationship can get worse. Just make sure that you get as much as possible out of their estates and cities before the kingdoms notice," Quan said.

"It might reveal some of our capabilities. I think it would be good to scare them a little. They'll be wary in the future then," Evernight said.

"Make sure we don't kill anyone unless we have to," Aditya said.

"Understood."

9

Guiding the Cultivation Path

A low-lying mist of mana filled the alchemy room, creating a suffocating pressure.

The cauldron in the middle of the room trembled and shuddered. The formations engraved on it flashed. The formation underneath the cauldron and a secondary under Erik glowed with power, supporting him and reinforcing his control over the cauldron.

"Norstron flower," Erik requested.

Department head Fehim raised a bowl of the prepared ingredient. A spark from Erik's hand turned into a tiger that snatched up the contents of the bowl and dashed toward the cauldron.

The top of the cauldron opened with a mana hand. A faint sheen of sweat appeared on Erik's forehead as his eyes closed. He was using Scan, focusing on everything that was happening within the cauldron as he moved his hands.

Heat rose from the top of the cauldron as beastly noises filled the room. The tiger roared, changing from red to blue as it dove into the cauldron. The cauldron closed with the *clunk* of metal on metal.

"Condense!" Erik directed, as he drew his hands together. The formations on the cauldron increased in brightness as Erik's alchemy robes and pendants glowed.

The cauldron rumbled as mana mist was drawn in through the walls of the cauldron.

"No, you ..."

The cauldron rocked before it exploded, striking the mana barrier that flashed into existence around it.

Erik sighed and waved his hand, gathering his flame beasts up once more.

"I hate this part." Erik waved a hand as a scoop of powder travelled through the air and into his open mouth.

Erik rolled it around on his tongue and swallowed, pulling out a canteen of tasteless potion.

Information filled his mind as he analyzed his results before he drank the potion.

"Well, that was better than some I've tested. Still not fun. I think we were trying to make it too strong and complicated. The pill reached peak Expert in Alchemy grade and it wasn't yet formed. We should go back to the weaker metal tempering pills. It might take more of them for people to temper their bodies, but we need to make sure the power isn't so volatile."

"You have already created several metal tempering pills of the low Expert grade Erik," Fehim reminded him.

"Yes, but all of them, while powerful, require people to be healed at the same time, meaning we have to make a secondary pill to complement the first. I want to make just one pill that can do it all. Call it a hobby." Erik shrugged.

"Some people call gardening, stitch work, or drawing a hobby; tempering one's body in one shot with a pill is no simple task." Fehim laughed as he stood.

"No." Erik smiled and rose as well. "Okay, next time we will work on the metal tempering potion. They are easier because they can be delivered intravenously. They're also easier to make than pills. The work you did with the formation department on the concoction concentration gear is smart. How did you think of it?"

"Oh, I was just walking through the integrated alchemy garden." Fehim hit a button on the wall. The mana mist in the room was drawn away as Erik opened the door for him.

They walked down the halls of the alchemy department workshops.

"It certainly makes sense. I think Delilah is working on a theory along those lines, but using elements directly to affect the ingredients."

Erik checked the time. "I have to get prepared for my next meeting.

I'll see you the same time next week?"

"Certainly." Fehim bowed his head.

"Thank you, Fehim!"

Erik broke into a jog and glided into the sky. His mana channels glowed as he manipulated the surrounding mana, casting discrete air and fire spells.

He smiled as he soared over Alva. He wouldn't be able to do all these spells at the same time or with the control he needed to stay up if he didn't have his domain. *Fricking mages and their cool mana cultivation.*

He stepped out. The mana solidified under his feet, responding to his command. He launched himself forward. It was like Rugrat said, a mix between skating and running.

A pair of mana wings appeared on Erik's back as he stepped into the sky, surging forward. He tilted and glided on his wings.

His smile faded as he slowly sank toward the ground. He would give it all up, his cultivation, being able to fly on his own, just to have Gilly back. It had been weeks, but it still hurt.

The faces and scenes played through his mind. He shook them away, focusing on his immediate actions to center himself, the rote repetition.

He landed on the ground near the hospital, pulled off his covering robe, and stored his buffing medallions and gear. He pulled out his medical band, putting it on his arm and took out his dog tags and healer's gloves as he walked out of the alleyway toward the hospital.

He checked their charge quickly.

Medic's Gloves
Weight: 0.3 kg
Health: 100/100
Charge: 100/100
Innate Effect:
Healing advantage—healing spell's effect increases by 15%
Enchantment:
Advanced Recovery—patient's Stamina recovery increases by 15%
Requirements:
Mana 40
Mana Regeneration 50

Dog tags
Weight: 0.01 kg Health: 100/100 Charge: 63/100
Innate Effect: Increase mana spell's effect by 5%
Enchantment: Linked-Connected to other linked items.
Requirements: Mana 12 Mana Regeneration 8
Engraved: 001 E West O+

Medic Band
Weight: 0.3 kg Health: 100/100 Charge: 85/100
Innate Effect: Calm mind, spells are 8% more effective
Enchantment: Assisted Recovery—patient's Stamina recovery increases by 12%
Requirements: Mana 57 Mana Regeneration 35

He walked up to the doors of the hospital. The waiting room was busy with people who had come with a friend to get treatment, or those heading to the training section of the hospital. Erik followed them, reaching the larger waiting room where people were filling out forms and passing them to the receptionists before taking a seat.

Erik walked past the waiting room and the police officer on guard, who held the brim of his hat in salute.

Erik nodded to him and entered the training area. The place got bigger every time he saw it. Training facilities were on every floor for body and mana tempering, but this was the heart of it all, hooked right into the dungeon itself.

He turned and headed past the stacked rooms filled with pods, medical staff, and people tempering their bodies and mana. He opened what looked like a storeroom and went to the back of the room to find a single mana pod ready and waiting.

"Okay, time to get prepped."

"You sure about this? It's only been three weeks since we got back," Erik asked, taping up the last IV in Rugrat's arm.

They were in one of the Alva cultivation rooms, pods filled with people tempering and cultivating.

"You're asking me when you were the one walking around like a stick of charcoal, leaking silver?" Rugrat snorted.

Erik grimaced. "The things I do for science."

"Using Vuzgal dungeon's mana, yes, I strained my mana channels, but they repaired, stronger than before. Waiting isn't going to do anything. When I cultivated my mana heart, it wasn't difficult. I had been able to do it for some time. I think I can advance further. I just need concentrated training time."

"You scared I'll catch up?" Erik grinned, pushing Rugrat backward.

"Scared? Hah! Can you even see me in the distance?" Rugrat looked behind himself as his back touched the mana cultivation pod.

Erik made sure that the lines were in the holes outside of the pod.

"Honestly, though, my mana pool is massive, my mana regeneration is high, and my body is strong. I just want to do some tests and I can't do that in Alva. The mana density isn't high enough. Once I had the mana density, I created my mana heart with just time. The fact you're catching up with me says something. Mostly, that I've been slacking, and you need to see someone about being a masochist."

"Thank you," Erik said dryly. He formed a mana hand, touching controls on the pad as he pressed on Rugrat's chest. The pod rotated backward. "I've got you on mana concentration and regeneration boosting lines. Anything starts going weird I'll drop the mana density and hit you with a healing potion." He locked the pod in the upright position and pulled a mask from the side of the pod, putting it on Rugrat's face.

"That sounds like a lot of fun." Rugrat was muffled by the mask.

"You wanted to do this." Erik hit another button with his mana hand and the top of the pod closed. Formations from the floor up activated as Erik stepped back, creating more mana hands that appeared around the pedestal, changing settings.

Rugrat closed his eyes as a thin sheen of mist covered his body within the pod; his mana gates glowed as power spread through his mana channels, circulating through his body, seeping through it, compressing and becoming brighter as he found his rhythm. The surrounding mist twisted under his control.

With a sound like rushing air, his mana gates pulled in the mana as if they had been starved for months.

"Show-off," Erik muttered, altering settings on the pedestal as the mana density inside the pod increased. "Mana density to elemental density is high. You have fire and earth elements with this Body Like Sky Iron. Time to introduce some metal elements. We'll start slow and low."

Erik breathed in, closing his eyes. The air shimmered around him as power from his mana core spread through his body, tracing out faint blue lines before they receded. His eyes glowed through his eyelids as he looked at Rugrat.

His face was slack and emotionless.

"Increase one percent metal to mana ratio." Erik's voice deepened, filling the room. The mana hands shed their form, turning into beasts, the same beasts that took on a flame form when he was working with his alchemy.

They adjusted the controls as Erik watched, observing.

"Hold metal element there. Increase mana density twenty percent."

The mist spread again, covering Rugrat, dimming his glowing channels. It reached the top of the pod and started to bead like steam against a mirror.

Mana drops fell, creating a thin surface of liquid mana.

"Body is holding. Mana channels are repairing. Dial back five percent on mana density."

Threads of mana appeared behind Erik. They formed into beasts, grabbing a chair and bringing it to Erik. He sat down, watching Rugrat.

Rugrat looked peaceful. His mana channels brightened and dimmed with each passing breath, drawing it into his body, circulating and compressing before it was drawn into his mana heart. His mana heart's crystalline structure grew as it processed the mana and sent it through the rest of his body.

Mana was a terrifying power. It could just as easily create as it could destroy. It continued to spread through Rugrat's body, creating new mana channels, threading more completely within his body.

10

Convergence

Jen found Melissa in the observation room watching Rugrat's cultivation pod. There was a flash of light as the book in Erik's hands dissolved, a stream of light channeling between his brows.

Melissa looked up from her notes and books.

"This your second office?" Jen asked.

"Only when these two are around. Too much information to be captured." Melissa sat back and rubbed her eyes.

Other scribes, alchemists, and medics in the room were writing down notes. There were some people in the room with Rugrat and Erik, using spells to observe Rugrat and write notes.

Erik opened his eyes and looked through the glass. He raised his hand in welcome.

"Hey, boss." Jen smiled.

"How goes the rounds?" He didn't open his mouth, but she heard him as if he were right next to her.

"Urggh!" Jen shivered and looked around. "What was that?"

"Sorry. I'm using a spell to talk over distance. My domain extends into the observation room. I can pick where I want to use it. It's like having a personal sound transmission device."

"Can you test that on the *new* medics?" She put her hand on her chest, a chill running through her spine.

"Sorry. I haven't explored the power of my domain yet. Been reading up on it while I was waiting for this guy." Erik pointed a thumb at the mana mist-covered pod.

"Is that liquid mana at the bottom?"

"Yeah, four inches of it and he's drinking it up like it's one-dollar beer night at the Roaring Boar," Melissa said.

"He's been slower cultivating his mana because of his cultivation accident a while back. Now... Well, we need to get stronger and he's got the capacity."

Jen saw the pain cross Erik's face, hiding as fast as it arrived.

"What's this?" one of the medics asked.

Erik's head tracked over. "Looks like the competitive bastard wasn't wrong." He stood up and moved to the pod as the mana's movements turned erratic.

Jen felt the throbbing power coming from the pod. Rugrat's body glowed as the mana around his heart started to shift and change. "What's happening?"

"I'm guessing he's taking on the Five-aperture Heart. He reached the peak of the Mana Heart a week ago. He must've been building up the power to break through into the next stage."

Melissa ran into the room to Jen's side.

"Can he?" Jen asked.

"He's regrown his mana channels into mana veins and channeled so much damn power through his body that it would've popped most people. I've been healing him." Erik looked at her. "I haven't seen stronger mana channels in anyone."

"So, he's really doing it—fifteen mana gates and body cultivation." Bouchard sounded equal parts excited and anxious.

Erik stood beside Jen and Melissa and used a Medical Scan to observe the changes in Rugrat's body.

In his right chest, his organs shifted, but there was no stress on his body, as if they were meant for their new location. His mana heart cracked, lines running through it as it expanded, transforming from its spherical shape. Mana travelled down the mana channels attached to the cracking and growing core. The mana channels strengthened. They spread through his body, connecting to each of his mana gates and extending the already advanced mana veins. Veins split off into capillaries, threading their way through his body. Three new, thick mana arteries grew from the mana heart as it continued to change. Two reached out to the left like tree roots. They curved up and down, splitting, before fusing into the lungs. They spread throughout, drawing in the mana and elements in the very air that Rugrat inhaled, pulling it into his mana heart while his mana heart sent pure mana into his oxygenated blood and through his system.

"His body isn't just creating a secondary system. It's linking with the circulatory system. Look! The mana veins are creating a secondary network with one another," Jen said.

"What about that descending last mana artery?" Melissa asked.

The last artery extended toward the bottom of the sternum.

No, could it be?

Erik touched his chest in the same place, feeling the thrum of power beneath. The true heart had become threaded with mana veins. A new channel traced from it, heading toward the same place under the sternum.

"Is it an element core?" Erik muttered as he looked for the elements in Rugrat's body. The Earth and Fire elements were as much a part of his body as blood.

"The elements are going through his blood and his mana channels. His blood vessels are altering as well."

The mana gates dragged mana through them and pumped into the cracking and transforming mana heart, which mimicked his original heart. His monster core siphoned off fire and earth elements. Rugrat's circulatory system directed metal elements with his pure mana. His lungs expelled water and wood elements.

"Fire and Earth element core," Erik said. "Same as his body cultivation. I thought you could only get that with the body cultivation."

"The heart powers the body. The mana core purifies the energies and contains it. The element core purifies the body and increases the power of the other systems. Three systems in harmony," Melissa said.

"His mana core is smaller," Jen said.

"It's like a mana stone core. The outer sphere has holes in it to draw in the mana. Then the core at the middle concentrates, separates and grows. Instead of storing mana in just his core, it's stored throughout his body," Erik said.

The changes slowed down as the liquid mana around Rugrat

decreased. He breathed in the mana with each breath, his mana gates responding to his breath.

Heart, mana heart, and element core worked in concert.

"Increase the mana density by two times," Erik said.

The medic did so as liquid mana bubbled under Rugrat. They held their tongues, watching and waiting. The medics and observers behind them made notes.

The mana consumption and supply leveled out as Rugrat remained asleep, his new body thrumming with energy.

"Jackass," Erik grinned.

"Monster core." Melissa tapped her chin. "Do you think he unlocked the bloodline cultivation?"

"Must have, right?" Erik said.

"You said the leaders from the Black Phoenix Clan had higher cultivation than you or Rugrat, right?"

"Yeah." Erik frowned. "And they had different colored tattoo lines on them. I wonder if that has something to do with the elements. Don't you have their bodies?"

"I do, but I haven't looked at them yet."

"Do you want to prep an autopsy?" Erik asked.

"I can, but do you want to join me?"

"Just give me a minute to get my head right. Jen, would you be able to watch over him?" Erik tilted his chin to Rugrat.

"Yeah, I can do that. It's really interesting how the elemental body cultivation interacts and works in tandem with the mana cultivation system." Jen coughed and blushed, calming herself.

"It is very exciting." Erik smiled.

Melissa went to organize things while Erik and Jen checked on Rugrat to make sure that there weren't any hidden issues.

"It's like he's tempering his body at the same time. The mana is not just in his mana channels anymore. It's spreading through his entire body. It should allow him to store a lot more power," Jen said.

"His mana core operates like a dungeon core instead of his cores' before. Instead of the elements being consumed by his core to get stronger, like with a dungeon core, they're separated. I'm not sure how he will increase his cultivation more than this, though." Erik bit his lip.

"What do you mean?" Jen asked.

"Well, his body and bloodline cultivation can be increased more easily now, but every evolution of his mana cultivation is a part of increasing your mana until it is a really high density and that transforms his mana system. Now his mana system is diffused."

"He can still hold more mana in his body, right?"

"Yeah…" Erik trailed off. "As you said, it's like he's tempering his body. Maybe the next stage of the mana cultivation is to temper the body with mana? What is the next stage called?"

"Uhh…" Jen turned to the researchers.

"Does someone know?"

A bookish-looking lady raised her hand. "The next stage is the seventy-two acupoints and then Mana Rebirth."

"Seventy-two?" Erik's eyes moved back and forth, recalling. "In a lot of the medical journals people mention the acupoints. There are supposed to be two hundred and ten minor points, seventy major points, and two divine points. A practice is to use acupoint needles in combination with your mana to heal the body or cover them in concoctions."

"So, it is related to the body. Maybe it is like the mana gates… We need to find the different points and open them up. Look through his circulatory system and see if there are any blockages."

They scanned his body closely, searching for an odd flow of power, something that wasn't quite right.

"I have one in his left hand around his mana gate. Where the mana veins and the veins intersect there are smaller gates."

They kept studying, creating a drawing of the different acupoints. There were places where the two circulatory systems interacted at key points. Instead of spreading out, they came to a dead end. They labelled those as minor acupoints. Where there were gates, they called them major acupoints.

"I wonder…" Erik muttered. "In most of the body cultivation it talks about tapping the acupoints, some of the techniques call for putting needles in acupoints to temper the body. Now that we have Rugrat's map, I can see if this works on me and put needles at these different points and see if it increases my cultivation."

There was a knock at the door as Niemm appeared. "Melissa has the bodies stripped and ready for you."

"We'll check the alignment again and watch over him," Jen said.

"Thanks, just a lot to learn today." Erik smiled.

"Always more to learn. Didn't you say that?"

Erik's mana opened the door.

Melissa was in the room with several medics who were going over the body, creating scans and drawing out everything they were seeing. Scribes along the wall recorded information.

The woman from the Black Phoenix Clan was laid out covered by a sheet.

"You sure she can't self-revive?" Erik asked.

"No, we tested it on animals, and we've seen it with people on different battlefields. They can revive over a longer period, but we shoved them into storage rings, and there is no way to survive after that."

"So, if we just left them on the ground?"

"They might have been able to recover." Bouchard looked at Erik. "You might."

Erik shivered and shook his head, clearing his thoughts as he approached, using medical scan.

"She has a monster core, and a five-aperture heart. Mana core is a variant Common Sky grade Wood and Metal." Erik frowned and looked at Bouchard. "Some traces of the fire element, but no others."

"Her body cultivation isn't high. She's tempered her foundation. Nothing past that." Melissa had the same frown as they shared a look.

"Does anyone have a background in formations?" Erik asked the room.

Someone raised a hand. "I do."

"These formations. Do you know what they do?"

The medic stepped forward, paling. "I-I'll need a closer look."

"What's your name?" Erik asked.

"Phil." The man bobbed his head, looking at Erik's chest.

"Don't worry, Phil. I won't bite. Please." Erik opened a hand to the body.

Phil stepped forward, hesitating. He steeled himself and checked the formations on her head, running down the sides of her neck. His movements became fluid. "Can someone help me turn her over?"

Erik grabbed her arm and rotated her into the recovery position.

"Thank you." Phil moved to the woman's back and tried to peer underneath.

Erik pulled out a mana dagger and cut the bindings.

Phil cleared his throat and bobbed his head in thanks again, removing the back plate to reveal a complex tattoo that was equal parts intricate, delicate, and beautiful. He traced out the different runes and circles without touching the body. "These are formations for metal and earth elements, I think, to control and gather them. They seem to have similar functions to the formations on the cultivation pods."

"They use formations to increase their cultivation?" Erik said.

"We do the same in the cultivation pods and with tempering needles. This is more of a permanent measure. They must be using these formations to jump past their limitations," Melissa said.

Erik used his medical scan again. "The formations run around to her elemental core, creating a third elementary circulatory system."

"Would allow them greater control with attuned elemental spells." Melissa cast several spells. "Strange."

"What?"

"Her mana channels and her body show heavy signs of wear and stress. When you use your elements, your body is attuned to them so there are no problems, and you can handle the stress, but remember what you told me about drawing in the wood element and how it hurt like hell?"

"So, she was in constant pain when casting?"

"Maybe? I think it's more likely she was careful to use those elements. The core contains them, but if the elements pass through her channels and her body, it could have wound her greatly."

Erik noticed the woman's left hand where she had held her sword of lightning. It showed burn marks and there was a blackening at her joints, as well.

"Wielding power that her body can't even handle." Erik clicked his tongue.

"Mages do not usually cast internal spells. They're all external. These formations gave a boost to her fighting power."

It is the ten realms, Erik added in for Melissa.

Erik looked at three tables on the side of the room that held their weapons and gear, from their storage rings to medallions.

Erik raised the formations, checking them. *Where are you?*

"Ah, there you are." He grabbed a box-like formation and drew out a Mortal mana stone from his storage ring.

He put the stone in the box-like formation.

"Like a reverse mana storing formation, it burns up the mana stone and fills the area with mana.

Mana mist appeared around the formation in a small cloud.

"What are you trying to do?" Bouchard asked.

"She has a five-aperture mana heart. I want to see how it operates with the isolated elemental core. Niemm, you mind covering me?"

The researchers moved to the wall as Niemm stepped forward, flicking his rifle off safe and aiming it at the dead woman.

"Is this necessary?"

"Miss Bouchard, I don't trust anything until I test it at least once." Erik pulled out his own rifle, checking it was loaded.

He used his medical scan again. Niemm and the other living beings were fuzzy, requiring more effort to look through if he wanted to. He focused on the dead woman.

He glanced at Niemm. "Ready?"

"Ready." Niemm's domain stretched out and contracted. Power flared through his body.

Erik used mana manipulation to pick up the formation he slotted in the mortal mana stone, the cheapest mana stone one could get, as it held the most elemental impurities. Erik wanted to see how the mana and the elements would react.

He placed the formation next to the woman's face.

The elements were drawn into the formations on her skin, creating an exterior elemental well. The semi-purified mana was drawn through her lungs, entering her mana veins, drawn by her five-aperture heart.

"She's not a body cultivator. Just a mana cultivator, using formations to increase her control over elements so she can wield elements with a greater proficiency without having tempered with them." Erik withdrew the mana density formation.

"The tattoo formation?" Melissa said.

"Bypasses the normal stages of elemental cultivation. Just need a formation, not the years or decades of body cultivation it would normally take. Still, I wonder what effects it has on them, and if we could do the same—get the elemental energy into the core and let it passively temper the body. Would that work, or would it overload a person and kill them? I wonder if it does anything to their bloodline." Erik rubbed his chin, turning off the mana density formation as Niemm lowered his rifle.

"I don't know enough about elemental cores to answer that," Melissa said.

"Beasts would know," Erik muttered and froze. Sadness spread across his face before it disappeared. "And we just happen to have several resident demi-humans. We should ask them."

"Good idea." Melissa nodded, half-distracted.

"Something on your mind, doc?" Erik asked.

"Using the elemental tattoos to draw in power from the surrounding world, we could temper the body at a constant rate. Even if they're walking around, and might not need a cultivation pod, a cultivation pod is better. But this would mean people aren't out of work for weeks or months at a time. Instead of getting blasted with elements or taking a pill, the tattoos would allow the body to get used to the element and get stronger passively over time."

"Thank fuck we were fighting them in our city," Niemm muttered. "If not for those debuffs…"

"I'm interested to find out anything more about them before I go bug Elder Fred," Erik said.

11

Hidden Above and Below

"**M**ira, go," Torf said, waving her off. "You got bigger things to worry about than our gear."

Mira Chonglu hesitated for a bare second and nodded. "Thanks, Torf."

"Go and see what the Branch Head knows."

She nodded and headed deeper into the Fighter Association's building. Grime covered her armor. They had just returned from their dungeon raid when she had heard about Vuzgal.

Now the Branch Head wanted to talk with her.

Her face was sweat and dirt-stained, her braided hair looped over her shoulder and ran down her front as she marched through the halls, holding onto her sword. Mira nodded to people and pushed on. She took the stairs three at a time, racing up them as she leaned on the banister.

She arrived in front of the Branch Head's office, breathing a few times to calm herself.

She raised her hand and knocked on the door.

"Come in."

She walked into the Branch Head's office. There was a map on the right wall that showed all the raids and dungeons in the area. A large window straight ahead looked out into the city. To the right, there was a large desk with a few chairs in front of it.

Branch Head Selkov sat behind the desk. Klaus, from Vuzgal, stood in front of his desk.

"Klaus," Mira said, walking toward him, grabbing his arms.

"Your children are safe and from what I know, so is your husband. Chonglu put your children in my care to protect and evacuate them and find you," Klaus said seriously.

Mira looked around.

"They are waiting outside. They're safe," Klaus clarified, squeezing her arms.

Mira shook with relief and staggered, breathing out.

"The Association is extremely interested in the capabilities of Vuzgal. Their defense revealed a variety of new weapons and systems that we have not seen in the past. The Association wishes to speak with the group, even, possibly, offering them sanctuary," Selkov said.

Mira shook her head, her brows knitting together. "What?"

"Your husband was the city lord. He must know about these weapons." Selkov shifted in his seat to face her head on. "We want to talk to him and see if we can purchase some of these weapons from him like we did with the repeater bows."

"You want me to pull my husband, and the group he's with, out of hiding to quite possibly die for some new weapon you're interested in? You want to leave your family naked and defenseless at the gates of your enemy because you're interested in seeing their new potion?" Mira's voice rose to a yell as she released Klaus' arms. "Are you an idiot?"

Klaus stepped back as Selkov's smile clouded over. "Watch what you say, party leader!" Selkov's voice rose.

Mira's power spread out, chilling the room. Her eyes turned icy as white frost appeared on her armor.

Selkov sputtered.

"Fucking idiot, then." Mira opened and closed her fist before letting out a yell filled with frustration as she turned and moved for the door.

Klaus held out his hand to Selkov as she punched the wall, taking out a chunk. She slammed the door shut and walked outside.

"Mom?"

Her anger fled like ice in the summer sun as Feng and Felicity stepped out of an adjacent office.

They ran to one another as she dropped to her knees, hugging them both. Tears rolled down their faces as they cried in one another's arms.

Mira kissed their heads, looking at them both for any cuts or bruises or anything.

"You grew," Mira said as she hugged them tight, breathing in their scent before letting out a shuddering breath.

They calmed down, and Mira pushed Felicity's hair out of her eyes. "You're okay now. Mom has you. What happened?"

"Dad told us to go with Mister Klaus and that he would take us to you. We wanted to stay with Dad, but he wouldn't let us. He said we'd be safer with you," Feng said.

"He gave us this." Felicity passed Mira a letter.

She took it lightly and sniffed. "Okay." She felt the weight of the letter before storing it away carefully. "I'm going to tan your father's hide after this."

She laughed, her face red as she cried again, hugging them to hide her tears.

She sniffed and scanned around, pausing as she held Feng's shoulder and Felicity's arm, looking at them both. "You advanced your mana and body cultivation?"

"Yeah, though we can't talk about it. We're much stronger now!" Feng flexed his arm with a boyish grin.

Felicity snorted and created fire in her hand.

She didn't need to say anything to cast the spell? Instantaneous casting?

She checked them closely. *All their mana gates are open! How?*

"Magic is better," Felicity said proudly.

"Don't start." Mira's voice lilted upwards.

They dipped their heads and stopped showing off.

"Come on, let's get you cleaned up." Mira stood and held their hands.

"Mommy, you smell more than us!" Felicity said. "Were you in a dungeon?"

"Yes, I was," Mira said, walking them toward her personal quarters.

"When do you think we can see Dad again?" Feng asked.

Mira opened her mouth to give him a half-hearted response to mollify him. She swallowed her words, seeing the light in his eyes.

He isn't a kid anymore.

"I don't know when we'll see your father again. Though... Sound Barrier."

The spell covered the three of them.

"Your father, Erik, and Rugrat, are not the kind of people to spend the rest of their lives hiding. They're determined, stubborn, and resourceful."

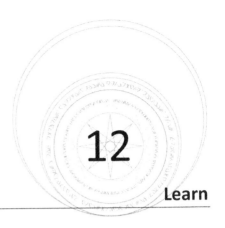

12

Learn

E lan walked along the path through the trees. Elder Fred's chair pushed him to standing and disappeared into the ground without a trace.

Elan stepped up beside the man, looking over a lake that ran through the wood floor, irrigating the trees that had rapidly grown.

"Mister Elan." Fred nodded.

"Elder Fred, I have heard much about you." Elan bowed his head.

"Don't believe everything Erik and Rugrat tell you. Shall we walk?" Fred held out a hand, indicating the side of the lake.

"Certainly. I don't get enough moving around from my assignments these days." Elan turned, and they started to walk along the lakeside.

"So, you want to learn about the higher realms in greater detail. I heard that Erik and Rugrat made it into the Sixth Realm with some of your special team members?"

"Yes, they ventured up to see what it was like and brought back a lot of materials and information. We debriefed them to find out about the realms. Though, we only know their experiences in several Sixth Realm cities and one dungeon. You have been from realm to realm and experienced much."

"The pursuit of knowledge takes time. There are many questions and few answers. Time seems to have sped up since we were freed from Bala dungeon." Fred smiled. He paused, looking up as he held his hands behind him.

"I have heard the saying that the differences between people or places can be heaven and earth. I didn't believe that until I reached the Seventh Realm. Sure, the Sixth Realm has many academies and dungeons, but they do not have the mana density of the Seventh Realm, or the competition. The Fifth and Sixth Realms could be explained as the studying realms, places where people are admitted to the great academies, and where they grow their knowledge. There is no lack of Journeyman and Expert crafters in the Seventh Realm. Fighters there have gained achievements in at least one cultivation system, if not both."

As they reached a creek, roots grew from the ground, creating a bridge for them to cross over it.

"The Seventh is where it all comes to a head. Knowledge grinds to a halt, secured and locked away after the mid expert level. No one makes it to that level without backing. If the Third Realm is the Alchemist Realm, the Fourth the Battlefield, the Fifth the Testing Realm and Sixth the academies, the Seventh is a political theatre."

"Political? There must be some stability for there to be politics involved." Elan raised an eyebrow.

Fred smiled.

"Few groups are willing to throw resources away, and people cost enough to support an entire Fourth Realm sect in the higher realms. In the Mortal and Earth Realms the Associations' power is absolute. In the Sky Realms, their power wanes. Other sects and groups, like the Black Phoenix Clan, are able to challenge and threaten them."

"How? The Associations have the strongest people, all the resources, and they work together."

"Yes, and they are the best way to reach peak expert level, but the gap from Expert to Master is massive. Not even the Associations can just cultivate people to that realm. They have the largest number of experts in one group, don't get me wrong. But they are outnumbered compared to all the other sects."

They reached the other side of the creek. The roots shortened and retracted to the opposite riverbank.

Such impressive control over elements and mana. From his profile, he was a tree.

Elan cleared his throat and his mind with it. "You keep talking about the Associations as a group."

"In the Seventh Realm, you learn the truth as the Mission Halls come into existence. The Associations are not just similar. They are different parts of the Tenth Imperium." Fred looked over to the side as trees moved apart. "Erik has arrived."

"Erik?" Elan looked over as they stopped walking. Erik and his team were approaching through the fruit trees. "You strong people and your domains."

"You'll get used to it. You are not far from reaching Body Like Iron," Fred said.

"That's what I mean, a big advantage over us mere mortals."

Fred just smiled as they waited for Erik to reach them.

"Elan, Fred." Erik nodded to them both.

"Director Elan is questioning me on the Seventh Realm and what I have seen there," Fred said.

"Oh." Erik's eyes widened. "Give me a sec. I just need to write down some questions to remember, but I'm interested as well. I know that Elan will give me a report, but ..." Erik shrugged and pulled out some paper.

Fred frowned and then nodded as Erik wrote down notes.

"Are you reading off the paper?" Elan asked.

"Yes." Fred chuckled "You will get used to it with your domain. It is strange when you start. You are used to just having control over one thing and affecting the world around you. With a domain it is like..." Fred looked away. "Like you are a part of the whole. The area that you control is a part of you. Like how you control your fingers without conscious thought. You barely think to raise your hand when you grab something on a shelf. You do the same with a domain. Just, when you raise your hands, you are manipulating the elements, the mana, and the world around you."

"Sounds like a learning curve."

"It is. You just have to let it happen and take your time. It's like adapting to anything new, like using a new spell. At first, it takes more to call upon it. As time goes by, you get faster at casting it. Eventually, you can make alterations to the spell without even conscious thought. It should be easier with your knowledge of this pure magic. Fascinating, really." Fred smiled and indicated for them to keep walking.

The Special Team fanned out as the trio kept walking along the side of the lake under the shade of the fruit trees.

"Your questions are rather interesting. I have some for you myself." Elan said. "You were talking about the political spheres in the Seventh

Realm.

"The Seventh Realm is the highest realm for the majority. Dungeons descend into the heart of the planet and cities reach the clouds. Associations are just another faction within the massive realm.

"Some clans hold position in only the Seventh Realm, never going lower and always pushing to go higher. No one that goes to the Seventh Realm wants to descend in case they lose part of their cultivation. They're reliant on the increased mana density of the Sky realm."

Fred cleared his throat.

"The highest realm, what about the eighth?"

"The eighth." Fred pursed his lips, finding his words. "It is better to call the eighth a trial, a test of the fighter. If you pass, you will enter the ninth. No need to reach level eighty, just level seventy. And you gain the right to attend Avegaaren Academy. Few pass the test. Those that do are powerhouses in the seventh."

"What is the trial?" Elan asked.

Fred raised his fore finger. "I do not know the answer to that, but I can tell you what the Associations really are. They, along with the Mission Hall, are pillars for the Tenth Imperium. They created Avegaaren, and it is rumored they created the Ten Realms as we know it."

"I've heard that before," Erik murmured, frowning.

"The Tenth Imperium created the Associations." Fred sighed. "Think of the Imperium like a group of the strongest people in the Ten Realms that do nothing but carry out the will of the Ten Realms."

"What?" Elan asked.

"Their mission in life is to carry out the quests that the Ten Realms gives them. In one way, they are the rulers of the Ten Realms due to their power. In another, they are a completely neutral force, only carrying out the missions that the Ten Realm sets forth. If there is no quest, then they will not act."

"Why would they do that?" Erik asked.

"I'm not sure, but the Tenth Imperium only exists in the Ninth Realm and has roots in the Seventh and Eighth. They are the quest givers of the Ten Realms. They created the Associations to supply them with gear and fresh numbers to make sure the Tenth continues to operate. In the Seventh, they created the Mission Halls. While the sects and clans might mess with the Associations, they would not *dare* to mess with the Mission Halls. The Mission Halls are directly under the Tenth Imperium; people can post missions there, even Ten Realm quests, and others will complete the quests for them. They will get some rewards, but the majority will go to the person who completes the quest. All groups, even individuals, are welcome to give quests. One can only get access to the missions if they have a One-Star Hero emblem." Fred took out an emblem.

Elan studied it.

"My family and I completed a One-Star qualifying mission. The medallion is issued by the Ten Realms, but you need to go to a quartermaster in a Mission Hall to get the physical version. With this, most groups would not want to attack us, and we can get access to One-Star level missions. We will need to take a Two Star qualifying mission to get the Two Star medallion and get more missions." Fred put the medallion away as they continued walking.

"Why is there a Mission Hall? Couldn't the Associations take on these tasks? I know they take on a lot of different missions," Erik said.

"Yes, and many of them are members of the Mission Halls as well. The Associations in the higher realms are different from the lower realms. Did you see the Associations in the Sixth Realm when you went?"

Fred waved his hand as the trees ahead grew taller so their branches were no longer at chest height, but above their heads.

"I saw some of them. They were smaller than I expected and most of them were just selling or buying resources. The Blue Lotus was the largest, with the Alchemy Associations and Fighter's Associations neck and neck for the second largest. The Crafting Association was small, almost hidden," Erik said.

"Yes, in the Fifth Realm, they recruit a massive amount of people. In the Sixth, instead of serving people as they do in the lower realms, they turn to teaching and nurturing their people. They have massive teaching campuses and control some of the strongest dungeons in cooperation with the other Associations."

"I thought that the cities must've been on a smaller scale so the Associations didn't want to have locations there."

"No, it is across the higher realms. They are more likely to control their own cities in the Sky Realms, focusing internally instead of externally."

"So, these Mission Halls, they're a central part of the Sky Realms?" Elan asked.

"Yes, they are a transaction point, you could say. All kinds of people take missions, and anyone can give them. Most people are so focused on training they don't care about quests and always need new things to be done. It is essential for the running of the realm and it maintains the stability."

"And you are protected with the One-Star Hero emblem?"

"Yes, it is essential for smaller groups, like my family. People who earn the emblem have done something of great merit. As such, the Ten Realms will issue a mission to the Tenth Imperium if a hero emblem holder is killed without due cause. There are legends of Celestials descending to render judgement on those that attacked a hero emblem holder."

They walked in silence for some time, each in their own thoughts.

"How strong are people from the Ninth Realm?"

"Strong enough to remove the existence of an Eighth Realm sect by themselves."

Elan raised an eyebrow. "They're only a level higher."

"Erik, how much experience do you need to level up?" Fred looked over.

Erik called up his stats. "Another Eight billion more or so."

"Well on your way to level Eighty. Impressive." Fred's eyes travelled up and down Erik's body. "Reach the expert level of a skill and you gain ten million experience. You would need to get twelve hundred skills to expert to level up. Killing those experts from the Talon provided a massive amount of experience. Without fighting in the higher realms, except in the dungeons, it can take centuries, or millennia for people to level up even once. Going from Expert to Master, one earns a billion experience. Then there are the five-star crafters. The first level starts at ten billion."

"Five-star crafters?" Elan asked.

"You didn't think that Master was the end of crafting, did you?" Fred raised an eyebrow as they continued their walk. They reached a new orchard of different fruits. Flying dungeon beasts were moving among the trees like fireflies, grabbing fruits and loading them onto larger dungeon beasts that looked like a hairy ox with six legs covered in baskets.

Workers in the fields waved and nodded as they continued along the waterfront past the ripening trees.

"How strong are the crafters?" Erik asked.

"I have heard about them. I do not know how strong they are."

"What else can you tell us about the realms?" Elan asked.

"People travel the skies in airships or the seas in massive ships.

Teleportation across the planet is normal. Dungeons create layered worlds underneath. There can be several cities stacked on top of one another, through multiple dungeons. Cities are rarely controlled by a single group. They are a political quagmire. Entire regions of the world are untamed. Beasts in those regions are correspondingly powerful and can cause great havoc. Limited access dungeons are all over the place. They only open every few decades or centuries, gathering their power, increasing the strength of their dungeon beasts and their rewards before releasing them.

"While the groups have to think twice about attacking a Two-Star emblem holder and would have to make very careful plans for Three-Star holders, they can and will engage One-Star emblem holders. Fighting is still constant in different ways and people challenge one another all the time for their belongings, their resources, even for power over one another."

Erik and Elan were silent as they absorbed the new information. Elan took out a note pad and wrote down more notes.

"Oh, and this might be useful for you, Erik, with your questions. Part of the reason that people do not leave the Sky Realms is because of the mana density loss. The other part is the elemental density loss. They are both higher in the upper realms. There are places that only someone with the right elemental cultivation can go to. Mana cultivation is used by most. With the high mana density and enough time and resources, one can reach the five-aperture heart level of mana cultivation. This allows them to form their monster or elemental core.

"Now, the elemental core is inert if you do not have body cultivation. If you have Body Like Iron, then the fire element can pass through your body and enter your mana core without issue, and so on with the other elements. If you haven't tempered your body with the elements, then your elemental core is largely useless. So, people came up with formations that would direct certain energies into their elemental core. It increases their control over the element."

"So, is that why they had elements not in the order that one would temper their body with?" Erik asked.

"Yes, if someone uses more water-based spells, then they would choose to add that element to their core first. It *only* affects their spells. They do not get the other enhancements one gets from tempering their entire body in the element." Fred came to a pause as the orchards fell away and they looked at open fields filled with different plants. Dungeon creatures walked through them, as did alchemists, checking on the rows upon rows of ingredients.

"So, they're jumping over the tempering system."

"Yes, it is the fastest way to gain strength. With time, they might attempt to temper their body to gain experience. Otherwise, they get the benefits they want for their casting. They don't care about being stronger or having more stamina. Their mana pools are massive, and the mana is so dense that they don't have to increase their mana regeneration much to refill their mana pool in a short period. They are creatures of their environment." Fred looked over the fields. "Shall we continue? The path along the water is covered with powerful ingredients with restrictive formations." Fred indicated to a road down through the fields.

"Sure," Erik said, and looked at Elan.

"Yes, sorry writing notes." Elan smiled.

"These formations in the skin, they look like tattoos. How are they made?"

"Tattooists are a mix between alchemists and formation masters," Fred said as they kept walking.

"That makes sense. Seems stupid to jump over body cultivation, though."

"Erik, it might only take you a few weeks, but it takes them years. Yes, they scan people and look at their bodies, but alchemists rule in the higher realms. They care about making pills and concoctions. They don't care about the individual using them. Unless they are paid to care. With a mix of crafting practices, alchemists will learn formations to become tattooists. They also use acupuncture to open the seventy-two acupoints. They disdain healing, for the most part, because they compete over whether healers or alchemists are the strongest."

"So, pride stops the alchemists from doing healer things?" Erik grimaced.

"Pretty much, and it works well enough. As long as it works, people will use it. Everything is so expensive that you get what you pay for. What you have *here*, the sheer amount of research, even in clans and sects, that information is more likely to be passed down from master to disciple only and *never* spread. If it did, then they would lose their edge and money-making ability. Add in your crafters working together, being multiple disciplines when they start, and that information is open, and you are not like the groups in the higher realms at all."

Elan groaned. "So, it's like the lower realms. People hoarding information, only releasing it if you're part of their group?"

"Yes."

They walked in silence again with only the noise of the wind passing over the ingredients they passed.

Elan wrote down notes furiously. He looked over to movement, soldiers raised walls from the ground, reinforcing and building them in seconds.

Dirt created the first. The ground was pinched together and drawn upwards.

Roots shot up and twisted into a second wall. Dirt and wood twisted together to form a third wall, bushes growing out of it.

Damn. Elan paused, seeing the casual display of power. The squads walked around the walls, with their sergeants pointing to different areas.

"Us beasts-turned-demi-humans and body cultivators have an advantage. We have tempered our bodies with the elements. That is why creatures in the higher realms are deadly. They have a massive number of elements to draw from and cultivate their core with. Once they temper their own element to the sky grade, they undergo a change which develops their mana system and allows them to absorb even more elements. The more elements they absorb, the stronger they get. Many keep increasing the power of one or two elements until they reach celestial. Everyone plays to their strengths only.

"Beasts cultivate the body and get some benefits from the mana system. The humans cultivate the mana system and get some benefits from the body cultivation system. Doing them together, there are more people that do so in the higher realms, yes. But most of them are the older generation that have reached the limits of what they have done in one area and start working on another area. It will take them a long time to cultivate that element to a point they would find useful since they are advancing their strength in that element from the starting stages."

"Like how people don't open all their mana gates and just race to condense enough mana to create their mana core. Shortcuts to power," Erik said.

"Yes, but that is not to say they are weak," Elan said.

"Not at all. The strong are everywhere," Fred said.

They came to a halt on the dirt packed road. Their special team escort stopped as well. The group of soldiers that had been building the walls started to attack the walls with different spells.

"What about the Black Phoenix Clan?" Elan asked.

"Dungeon clans are a strange group. They keep to themselves. It is rare for them to expand to be too large. They are aggressive toward one another. Their people cultivate the same as everyone else, but they have the bonus of tailored dungeons that have the sole purpose of making them stronger. They can level faster. However, they have smaller numbers, which evens out most things. I heard that there is a conflict between them and the Associations. I guess that is part of why they are hunting you and why they aren't allowed to just take over dungeons in the higher realms." Fred shrugged. "I have some answers, but not all of them."

The woods that framed the main road to the Vermire Empire opened up. Lumberjack steel met wood as carts carried logs clear and beasts toiled to pull out stumps, their hot breath coming out like furnace bellows in the chill of late fall.

The forest had been cut back to clear the way for expanding farm fields.

Aureus pulled at his hood and folded scarf that covered him from the eyes down against the cold. He swayed with the carriage's movements smoothed out by the new road works, rubbing his neck, which had been tense from the jerkiness of the unfinished mud and stone filled ones.

The caravan rumbled on, the line of carriages filled with trader's supplies and travelers waving in greeting to the working farmers as they passed the convoy.

They look happy enough. Must be true that the Beast Mountain Range is open for trade.

Aureus' blue eyes tracked the flag on the city's walls, a black mountain with a golden wagon wheel on it, showing the different outposts. The flag snapped out in the wind, revealing a red, white, and blue star-spangled banner in the top right.

"Aren't people scared of Vermire?" Aureus asked, pulling his cloak tighter.

"Bah. More like excited. Vermire don't want nothing from us but to pay the rent and do whatever we want, as long as we don't screw with their rules. They even offer basic training on the crafts. You could become an apprentice in a craft without paying anything. I heard that the trader groups are clamoring to join Vermire."

"Aren't they scared that the kingdoms will attack again?"

The driver's smile spread into a toothy grin. "I bet people would be excited to do so just to lose." He laughed and slapped his leg as the cart rumbled forward. "You know what happened to their armies?"

"They were defeated and captured," Aureus said.

"And contracted, hundreds of thousands of able-bodied men and women, and all their traders, and the camp followers too!" He let out a low whistle. "Though they weren't done. The kingdoms were reeling. Vermire gave them terms—agree to their land claim, send them resources, and decrease the taxation on their goods. Kingdoms tried to reduce the terms, you see. So, the Vermire Empire sent the nobles back to their estates."

"The grand migration?" Aureus asked.

The driver snickered. "The grand migration! All those nobles, big and small, returned home. No one knows how, still. Then in secret, they gathered their families and possessions, and then fled to Vermire. Noble families with centuries of history packed up everything they had and brought it to Vermire."

Aureus frowned.

"Seems wrong that they stole all of that from others."

"Who said they stole it? When they reached Vermire, those under contract returned to serve the Empire. But their families, their trading groups, were all welcomed. Nobles don't get any say in running the Empire. But they had all that wealth and weren't bound to their old city, or kingdom anymore. Yeah, sure. Some of them went to other kingdoms, but most of them settled in the outposts. See, they wanted to come to Vermire. War is coming, you hear? Those other kingdoms are weak now and others are watching them. Vermire is the safest place in the First Realm. Hah! Who'd have thought a mountain range famous for its strong beasts would be a safe haven!"

The driver chuckled as the convoy started to slow.

"Ah, looks like we're almost there! Are you and your son staying here or moving deeper into the Empire?" the man asked.

"We'll be heading deeper."

"Make sure you go with a trade caravan with guards. While the Empire is strong, so are their beasts, and they've gotten stronger in the past years."

"I'll keep that in mind." Aureus nodded his head.

"I'm looking forward to seeing my wife and daughters. I brought them here not two months back—a month after they took the city. Haven't looked back."

Aureus looked at the soldiers patrolling the walls and standing to the sides of the gates. They seemed disciplined and wore the same armor. *Their production speed with their smithies might not be as exaggerated as I thought.*

There were two gates beside one another, one for foot traffic and the other for convoys.

The convoy leader talked to a woman on a raised platform from his carriage. Guards walked along the convoy and looked inside, checking the goods and people before they spoke to the lady on the platform again. The convoy leader paid the lady, and the convoy moved forward through the city's gates.

The wall was a good five meters thick before they came out into the city. On the right there were warehouses and slums, on the left were crafter shops, market squares, and noble houses. The main streets were thick with trader carts. The entire city had been designed for the movement of goods.

"Warm food and bath with your room. Only forty coppers at the Black Ram!" Criers called out to the traders and travellers coming into the city.

The noise of a city, animals, carts, and people's voices filled the air.

Men and women in black and white armored uniforms and hats patrolled the area, talking to people here and there, more personable than the helmeted and heavily armored soldiers that marched through the city.

"Ah, the police," the driver said. "They're another group that Vermire introduced. They deal with issues among the people, while the army deals with the fighting between kingdoms, protecting the trade routes."

"Yeah," Aureus said. *Police, the American flag... There* have *to be other earthers here.*

"I'd suggest getting a room at the Green Tulip. Got good food. Not as boisterous for the kids. Linda is the mistress there. She'll know about traders heading into the Empire if you're interested."

"Thank you, I'll pay her a visit."

"Let me formally welcome you to the Empire. It's a hell of a place."

The convoy rolled on for a while before coming to rest on a large street.

"Green Tulip is up this street, third road on the right. You'll see it, has a great big green sign and yellow glass windows." The driver pointed down the road. The sidewalk was busy, as stores lined the street with sellers trying to entice people inside. Carts tried to get through tiny spaces, weaving down the road.

"Thank you." Aureus paid the man and stepped down from the carriage. His blue eyes tracked the area, taking in the people. They were brisk. The veterans avoided eye contact with the storefront sellers.

He moved to the rear of the carriage. The tarp had been thrown off as people got out.

Aureus offered to help Jian, but the young boy jumped down from the carriage, landing on the cobblestone road. He looked around with wide eyes.

"Come on, there's an inn up ahead," Aureus said. He made sure Jian was following as he walked into the stream of foot traffic. Jian followed him closely, looking at the people's clothes and the stores.

"Young man, you look famished from your ride! Don't you want some honey roasted pork?"

Jian headed over to the seller.

"Jian." Aureus' tone deepened as the boy frowned and lowered his head, trudging back to Aureus.

Aureus sighed and guided the boy with a hand on his shoulder.

"Look at that," Aureus said, pointing to some police officers that blocked off the road.

Jian looked, but he was too short to see over others.

Aureus picked him up easily.

The mages used spells to raise stone pillars from the ground that connected and spread out, creating tall walkways that would allow foot traffic across the busy road without stopping the moving carts.

They raised other walkways around the intersection in a matter of minutes before the carriages were released to continue on their way. The mages checked their walkways and used them to cross the street with the police officers. People used the walkways after them, testing them out and looking down over the flowing carriages.

"Those mages are so strong. They pulled those pillars out of the ground, then *berscheerp*! They created paths in the air. So cool!" Jian used his hands to gesture as Aureus lowered him.

"See how they all worked together to make the walkway? Now people can cross overhead and not get hurt by the carriages."

He followed the driver's instructions and turned down the third street. It was quieter without the same stream of traffic.

"Sir!" Jian said, pulling on the hem of Aureus' shirt.

Aureus looked at where he was pointing. A group of men and women walked down the street. Those in front used spells to open the ground several meters deep and a few wide. People next to a cart threw down large pipes. A group of mages fused the pipes and covered them up again before adding storm drains.

"They're putting in sewers so water and snow don't fill the streets but can flow away. Come on now," Aureus said.

They kept walking.

People with shifty eyes wearing cloaks hurried past them, moving to a bar where young men and women in similar attire gathered in groups. Their eyes widened as they looked around. Aureus saw a flash of metal under their cloaks. *Armor, they must be hiding weapons under their cloaks.*

"There it is!" Jian said, pointing at the Green Tulip.

It was up the street from the bar where people were gathering.

Aureus nodded, increasing his pace, keeping a hand on Jian's shoulder. Aureus circulated his mana.

Aureus opened the door to the Green Tulip. There was a reception in front of the door. A set of stairs and corridor to rooms lay on the right while a small eating area with a few people sitting down was on the left.

A young woman came from the left where she had been standing next to the green windows, looking at the bar they had just passed. "Hello, come for shelter, food, or a room?"

"You know about...?" Aureus tilted his head in the direction of the bar.

The woman's face darkened as she sighed and shook her head. "Nobles being nobles. Think that because the Empire has been nice to us that they are weak. They'll find out soon enough."

"The police have showed up!" said the young man by the window.

"What are the police?" Jian asked.

"They're peacekeepers." Aureus pulled the boy along. They joined the other patrons, looking through the windows.

The groups of young men and women had spread out to the street, not hiding their presence as they created a line at least thirty strong facing the ten police officers.

"Lady Zou, please present yourself. There is an arrest warrant for you for disturbing the peace. If you do not comply, we will be forced to enter the premise and use force."

The door of the bar opened, and armored guards marched out. The people in the street tore off their cloaks to reveal armored gear underneath. Most were wearing a mixture of gambesons and hides with some metal pieces. The knights had metal breastplates and two or three other pieces of polished armor.

The police held batons and wore a belt of tools on their hips, baseball caps, and uniform black pants and black vests. They seemed unaffected as nearly five times their number appeared, armed and armored, making a skirmish line.

A middle-aged woman with flawless makeup walked out, the guards staying close to her. She wore a silk robe with stitched designs and drooping sleeves.

"Officers, you are misinformed. This city has been wrongfully taken. And I vow to take it back from the Vermire Empire. They have lied to you. Promised education and resources. They only seek to enslave and conquer. Join me and find your own position. We will take this city together and rally the armies to attack Vermire and remove their cancer!"

"Look, Lady, you're the fifth noble I've had to deal with that uses some noble sounding crap to back up why you want to take over the city for yourself." The leader of the police sighed and placed his hands on his belt. "Now listen up, you lot! Vermire hasn't lied to you. Education is available to all. Mercenary groups, traders, all need young people who can fight. Walk away and go get a job. Don't get used by this lady for her cause. It'll lead to you dying for her greed."

The fighters looked between one another.

"Lies! I do this for the people!" She waved her hand as watchers shed their cloaks, freeing their weapons to stand with Lady Zou's fighters.

"That's over a hundred fighters to ten police officers," one of the men in the Green Tulip said.

"Can they hold out?" a woman asked, holding her boy close.

"I heard the Vermire Police are worth twenty of any normal fighter," the woman who had helped Aureus said. "That said, if something does happen, there are exits down the corridor and through the kitchen to slip out the back."

Some families heard her words and gathered their young ones to scurry out.

Aureus felt the power waiting for him to use it, form into spell to enhance himself with.

"Lady Zou, I am sorry I'm late." A man knelt in the street to Lady Zou. She dismissed his words with a perfunctory flick of her robes.

The police officers moved around, limbering up and talking to one another; they didn't seem afraid.

Strategizing.

"These dogs of the Vermire Empire refuse to open their eyes! We cannot let them continue to spread their lies."

"Lies, huh?" The leader of the police's dry laugh echoed through the street as his aura surged. "Let me test my non-existent education against your beliefs."

"Attack! Now!"

The fighters yelled and surged forward.

There was silence in the Green Tulip as mana was drawn from the surrounding area toward the ten police officers. Their easy-going smiles disappeared as eight officers pulled canisters from their belts and stepped forward, leaving the leader and another officer behind their protective line.

"Ed, you ready?"

"Yes, sir!" the officer at his side said.

"Spray it!"

The fighters were just three meters from the officers when they raised their canisters. A jet of liquid shot out as the lead police officer and Ed cast wind spells, spreading the liquid across the charging fighters.

Streams of liquid hit the fighters' eyes. They hadn't brought helmets, leaving them unprotected as they screamed in agony, dropping their weapons to clutch at their eyes and fall to the ground.

Like a wave, the liquid, aided with the magical spells, spread through the fighters. They screamed, rubbing at their eyes as they puffed up and tears ran down their faces.

The atmosphere in the Green Tulip was somber.

"Poison that eats the eyes, horrible," someone hissed.

"It doesn't eat their eyes. It just makes them itchy," the Green Tulip lady said.

Even Lady Zou was yelling out among her guards, her makeup a ruined mess as the police officers put away their canisters.

A series of carriages with metal bars turned down the street and toward the police officers. Two groups of three walked through the flailing fighters, gathering weapons, and securing them.

The police officers driving the carts joined in cleaning up the fighters.

"What will happen to them now?" someone asked the Green Tulip lady.

"They'll have a public trial, under contract, to see if they were fighting for their beliefs or if they were doing it for their own means. Those that were doing it to cause chaos will be executed; the others, well, the Vermire Empire is grand and there are a lot of people that need to eat. They'll be contracted as farm hands for a while. They should've taken the police officers' advice." She sighed and headed back to the reception desk.

"Did you see their spells? That wind magic. They used air with that spray!" Jian said, getting excited.

"Yes," Aureus said.

"Will I learn how to use magic like that?"

"If you study hard, yes." Aureus guided the boy toward the desk.

The woman smiled. "Sorry about all the excitement,"

"No problem. Can we have a room for two and a meal? Do you know of any caravans that are heading deeper into the Empire?"

"Yes, there is one in three days. Are you and your son thinking of joining the Empire?"

Jian quieted.

"We're going to hunt beasts in the Range and hopefully get some education."

"Dangerous line of work."

"Yes, but one must confront their fears or else be ruled by them." Aureus squeezed Jian's shoulder as the young boy's head tilted down, biting his lower lip.

The touch seemed to draw him out of his darker memories and reassure him as he nodded, blinking his wet eyes, and looking up with a sniff.

13

Leading Steps

E rik sat back from the meal. Fred had joined them at the insistence of Momma Rodriguez, equal parts interested and amazed in this man-tree.

"So, I heard that you were raised in a dungeon," Momma asked.

"Momma," Rugrat said, nearly spitting out his coffee.

"It is true after all." Fred smiled and drank from his cup. "I was. I didn't have consciousness for several decades."

Momma Rodriguez pulled stories from him of the others growing up, being rescued from the dungeon, and going on adventures in the Seventh Realm.

"So," Rugrat said, "people in the higher realms are using formation tattoos to bypass the body cultivation system or make it work faster by introducing more elements to their bodies or elemental core. Smart. I was thinking of buffing only, but that makes sense over a longer period."

"Dungeons that are high in one element, like the different floors in Alva, are highly sought after. Sects will go to war over them. Some are called elemental springs. The greater concentration of elements within their elemental core, the stronger their spells will be. Of course, there is also consuming monster cores, monster meat, and concoctions."

Where is Momma?

At some point, she had cleared the table but hadn't returned.

Erik stood up, indicating for them to keep talking as he headed to the kitchen.

"Wouldn't the cores be the fastest way?"

"Yes, the fastest and purest way. But do you really want to fight a Sky Realm beast? Some of them have achieved sentience already, and most know several powerful spells. They're not like the creatures in the lower realms that fight with their bodies and only have a few spells at their disposal. Sky Realm beasts have raised their body cultivation to such a height that, once they gain sentience and cultivate mana, they'll quickly increase their overall power. In the Seventh Realm, the human sects are powerful because of their numbers. But the beast sects are incredibly powerful on their own."

"There are sects of demi-Humans?"

"Of course! My father and I were asked to join many of their groups!"

Erik found the dishes cleaned and put in the drying rack. Looking to the side, he saw Momma cleaning up her tear-stained face with her towel.

"I'm just cleaning up the plates. I'll be in, in a minute," she said, trying to hide her tears.

"Momma." Erik knelt and hugged her gently.

She couldn't hold them back, crying softly into his shoulder.

"What's wrong?" he said, patting her back.

"I-its—" She moved her head back and forth, tears rolling down her face. "I know you're going to the Seventh Realm. I know the dangers you'll face, and it tears me up something fierce. It is who you two are. You seek adventure; you seek to see what you haven't seen before. You are honorable men. I know that I cannot hold you back. I know that you'll leave, that in your minds, even if you do not know it, you will go to the Seventh Realm. You will seek to become stronger."

She looked at him. Erik couldn't say anything.

I want to go, I want to be stronger, to… go.

"I understand that's who you are, but it scares me. Fear tears me up inside. Not knowing if you're in danger. If you're fleeing for your lives, or not. I've only just found you again."

"Momma," Erik said.

She put a hand on his chest. "Erik, I may not be your mother by birth, but I know you as well as I know my son. Don't try to give me empty promises. Just…" She shook as she let out her breath. "Look after one another, and while danger might find you, please do not seek it out."

Erik didn't know what to say.

"You remain here out of your sense of duty. You don't want to leave Alva when they need you most. But, Erik, you created Alva, and while you might not know it, they won't let you give up your titles because they want you to rule them. They want to honor you and Rugrat. You were the spark, and they were the tinder to become everything that Alva is now. Go to the Seventh Realm, the Eighth, the Ninth, the Tenth. Don't let Alva hold you back. Instead, realize that they have and always will support you and Rugrat." She held his face with a soft smile before she moved his hair into order.

Erik let out a breath and lowered his head. "Thank you, Momma."

She didn't say anything, only taking in a heavy breath before kissing his forehead.

Laying in the cultivation pod, Erik inhaled fire, earth, and metal elements. They seeped through his pores into his muscles and bones before being drawn through his body to his elemental core.

He grunted as the elemental density increased in his mana channels, making it feel like his whole body was stretching. Some elements were okay, but pure elements were more likely to rip his mana channels apart. *I'm looking forward to getting a five-aperture heart.*

He was tempted, highly tempted, to draw in the water element and start work on his body cultivation, but held back. He couldn't risk weakening like he had with the metal body cultivation. *We could be attacked at any time.*

He promised to start cultivating his body when Alva was stronger. When he wasn't needed at the helm to pull and guide it.

Erik drew in more mana and elemental power, relaxing his mind with the repetitive and focused actions. He studied his elemental core, three swirling nebulae: red, yellow, and white. The clouds of light were mist-like on the outer edges and thicker with sparkling radiance as they condensed in their centers.

He already had a greater earth grade element core. He just needed to get through grand and break through the sky grade. He snorted, disturbing the eddies of elements surrounding his body. *Makes it sound easy.*

Erik focused his mind again.

Unlike mana that could be only drawn through his mana gates, the elements could be drawn in from across his body. He commanded the elements completely, drawing them through and into his core, cultivating and circulating it. While his control was much better than when he had first reached the Ten Realms, compared to the elements, it was night and day.

He opened his eyes, looking at Fred and Bouchard.

"With the increase in my core size, it is easier to draw in more elements, though it needs a hell of a lot more to increase in level. I'm not sure what it'll take to reach sky grade, but it has to be a huge amount. Looks like they just went for the quest completion instead of the title. That would help, but gotta wonder if they're not slower at cultivating their elemental cores in the later stages," Erik rubbed his scruff.

"You and the Alvans have taken completion to a whole other level. Most of the people in the higher realms haven't opened all their mana gates still, and you have done it as a basic requirement. Skipping steps does make them stronger faster, but not as complete, as you say. I think it's how beasts who have only increased their body cultivation through a single element and opened up their bloodline to be purified are able to compete with the humans who have both mana and body cultivation at their disposal."

"So, you think that through the beast's dedication to cultivation, slow and methodical, it gives them an advantage?" Erik nodded in his pod.

"Yes, when I achieved body tempering, power from my elemental core spread through my body. My bloodline was unlocked, and I was able to cultivate mana. My monster or elemental core was a sky grade earth element variant. Since I last saw you, I went from having little mana within my body to opening all my mana gates and forming my core. I went through mist, vapor and I'm only a half-step away from forming my Solid Mana Core. My body cultivation surged as well. I can suppress other elements with the earth element. I rapidly made up for the shortcomings in my body cultivation." Fred fell quiet.

"Even with little mana, I was fairly strong because I had control over nature and understood it. Many thought I was a mage by trade. With spells, mana is the fuel. The elements are the guidance. The greater attuned you are with the spell's elements, the less the spell will cost and the greater the control."

"That much is what we've seen already," Melissa said.

"We know the Ten Realms have these systems, but Earth doesn't.

What is different about the two? Why are these systems so essential?" Fred asked.

Erik's thoughts skipped. "What do you mean?"

"I mean that it must take a lot of power to bring you to the Ten Realms and takes more power to change your bodies in a way that has never been seen before on your planet. Why?"

Erik couldn't help but pull up one of the very first notifications he had got in the Ten Realms.

Welcome to the Ten Realms!

You have been randomly selected to join the Ten Realms. One may choose to ascend the Ten Realms, thereupon making a request to the Gods of the Realms.

Only those who are Level 10, 20, 30, 40, 50, 60, 70, 80, and 90 may ascend to the next realm.

Fortune favors the strong!

"Fortune favors the strong."

And who are these gods? I've never heard of them, even after reaching the Sixth Realm. "Everything in the Ten Realms is about ascending and getting stronger. Even the Ten Realms system pushes it, but why?" Erik muttered.

"What do you mean, isn't the system the system?" Melissa asked.

"You think the system is like a computer program that you need to put in the right answers, and it'll give you a solution?" Erik smirked.

"Well, yeah, like those game systems that offer quests and things."

"Building the dungeons, while it was pretty straightforward, showed that the Ten Realms was malleable. We gained experience with projects made of multiple projects instead of a single part. Again, it showed some changes from the norm. But the biggest deviations are the fact that dungeon cores exist, are so protected, and how the Ten Realms will give quests that support and help out people and innocents."

Erik opened his eyes and watched the drifting elements within the pod pouring into his body.

"It is a system, but that doesn't mean that it is *just* a system. A system must have a purpose and this system needs us to fix mistakes and problems in the realms and it wants us to get stronger."

"Then why not just give us experience and cultivation?" Melissa asked.

"The gifts you are given are never as appreciated as the ones that you earn," Fred said.

Mistress Mercy sat at the head of the table. Niklaus sat to her right side and the other leaders of her army arrayed around the table. They looked suitably pleased with themselves.

In the last couple of months since Vuzgal, they had re-established their dominance and secured newly gained cities. Critical alliances with the Stone Fist Sect and the Black Phoenix Clan were looking favorably on them with their combined victories, and their positions within the sect were stronger than ever.

Niklaus finished talking about army placements and rotations. The leaders jotted down orders that applied to them.

Maybe unification was a good thing. Many of the clans she would never have been seen with had shown value.

Her eyes hid a cold gleam as she made a note of those who had shown promise. They might be allies now, but who knew what the future would bring? Sects were rarely peaceful in times of peace.

The leaders rose as the meeting came to an end and bowed to Mistress Mercy and Niklaus before leaving the two cousins.

"It seems that Uncle's and my trust was not misplaced in you, Cousin," Mercy said.

"Thank you, Cousin. I would not have done as well as I have without your support."

Mercy nodded. "What do you think will happen now?"

Niklaus pinched the beard he had grown during the campaign. "We have held our positions, but we haven't secured them. Dungeon clans and sects of all kinds have descended to Vuzgal searching for clues. Information is power. If we could capture the powers the Vuzgal leaders held, we would be beset on all sides by the dungeon lords until we couldn't exist anymore. If we were to offer information that leads them to the survivors of Vuzgal, we can draw them to our side. If I were the sect leader, then I would be doing everything possible to get information and get the dungeon sects to patron us."

"You don't think that we can stand on our own two feet?" Mercy arched her eyebrow.

Niklaus paused, picking his words carefully. "We lost much and gained more, but it takes time to digest what we have truly gained."

"So, what is our next move?" Mercy asked.

"Gather our army's strength and follow the leads you have. Search out this Silaz family and gather information on where Vuzgal, the Adventurer's Guild, and the Vuzgal lords might have gone."

Mercy deflated and rolled her eyes. "Find the Silaz family. That could take years of combing the Second Realm. What about the Lord Chonglu? He's married to that Fighter's Association member?"

"She's a Fighter's Association member, a strong one too. The Associations are never going to let us."

What if we don't ask?

"And don't even think that." Niklaus said.

"Think what?" Mercy's eyes thinned as she sat up.

"Something that will get us killed at the very least, and could implicate our sect at the most."

Mercy grumbled outwardly, assessing Niklaus. He had gotten them this far. It would be good to keep him close.

"Very well, Cousin. I will leave it in your hands. Let me know how things go. Until then, I have to cultivate. Oh…" She pulled out a scroll and put it in front of Niklaus with a pill bottle. "These are mana vein tapping pills. I'm told that they can help open one to two mana gates even if they have created their Vapor core. Make sure you read the instructions." She stood as Niklaus looked at the pill and scroll as if it was his newborn child.

"Thank you, Cousin!" He bowed as she waved her hand in dismissal.

One must make sure to reward as well as punish. He has been a good one. She headed for the door as it opened inwards.

"High Elder Cai Bo!" she said in surprise, cupping her hands and bowing.

Cai Bo and her guards strode in, her shoes like thunder upon the stone floor. Low Elder Kostic trailed behind. She studied the two bowing Kostic members.

Mercy straightened up with Niklaus, stiffening at her Uncle's warning glare.

"What can we do for you, High Elder?"

"I am in need of information. *Discreetly.* Information on Lords Rodriguez and West. I want to know where they went to hide. How have you been in tracing them back?"

"We have found traces of the people around them in the lower realms, but they move around. It will be hard to find them."

The room became stifling as Cai Bo's expression tightened. "Mercy, oh Mercy, this is not a request. You and your army will do everything in its power to track down these two lords."

"Yes, High Elder." Mercy bowed.

"And not a word to anyone other than myself or your uncle. I do not want the Black Phoenix Clan to hear anything about this."

Mercy looked up with a frown before bobbing her head. "Yes, High Elder."

"Good, Mercy. Niklaus, you have done well in the lower realm. I look forward to results. Do not come looking for me until you have something. We must track them down and their dungeon core. Elder Kostic."

Cai Bo turned in a whirl of her dress. Mercy and Niklaus bowed deeply while Elder Kostic bowed his head as her guards opened the doors and moved around her.

The doors closed behind her.

"You have done well for the clan," Low Elder Kostic said. "This is an opportunity that will allow our clan to become a premier clan and push the sect into the higher realms. We must not fail. Come, take a seat. There is much to discuss. I want to know everything that you have learned so far."

14

Create

Erik sat back in his chair. The plans for Alva's Gatling gun were spread across his desk in different sections. He also had a railgun barrel on his desk.

He massaged his traps and rolled his head, his neck tight from spending hours looking over the design for faults. He'd found a few and added additional notes.

"Damn body." Erik used a vibration spell on the muscles in his neck, loosening them as he stretched and rolled his shoulders.

He summoned metal and fire elements with his right hand. His arm darkened with threads of silver and veins of magma ran down his shoulder, elbow, and through his hand.

Erik's left hand emitted heat as he reached out. It should have hurt like hell, or had some reaction, but all he sensed was a slow reduction in his mana.

He created a flame in both hands.

The one in his unchanged hand was a warm yellow, while the one in his right hand was red with blue flickers.

Using his body cultivation and igniting his bloodline, taking on the characteristics of the elements he'd tempered with, increased his mana draw, but also increased his control over the elements. When he used it to fight the Black Phoenix people, they were shocked. None of them showed the ability to alter their bodies in such a way, possibly because they hadn't tempered their bodies all the way.

Erik added in the earth element. Threads of yellow ran down his arm as his body's strength and vitality increased. It acted as a buff and all he had to do was add mana. The mana cost decreased as he increased the rating of his elemental core, although it would be more accurate to call the cultivation systems the mana cultivation and elemental cultivation system.

People called it the body cultivation system, probably because the effect was that the body's abilities were increased.

Erik drew the elements into his arm once again.

"I guess they don't advance enough to learn that it's not about increasing the body's ability, but rather the body taking on the characteristics of the elements that increase one's overall strength."

And the bloodline, it has an effect on the entire body.

Erik shrugged and pulled out a new recipe he had created, putting it on the table and moving the barrel.

"Should take the edge off the conqueror's armor. With the boost from that thing, the body is running so damn hot that coming off too fast could kill the user."

Step-down
Grade: Expert
Form: Pill
Places body in recovery, decreases stats by 25% Increases recovery by 215%

Skill: Alchemy
Level: 98 (Expert)
Able to identify 1 effect of the ingredient. Ingredients are 5% more potent. When creating concoctions, mana regeneration increases by 20%

Rugrat squeezed the trigger. The rifle bucked in his shoulder, and he heard the second metallic reply as he hit the target seven hundred meters away.

"Well, it works. Thankfully, we were able to add that silencing formation or else we wouldn't be able to hear," Taran said.

"A reciprocating barrel dulls that jump and recoil, spreads the energy. Going to be hell for someone with a lower body cultivation to use this thing in anything but mounted. The arrowhead muzzle brake helps." Rugrat reached forward and patted it at the end of the barrel.

"The formations are running a little warmer than I would like," Julilah said.

"What if we were to add a formation to the magazine to remove heat as well?" Qin asked.

"That would work, but what about when it's belt fed and mounted?"

"Add it to the mount. It will be more metal and spread out more, allowing for heat to dissipate quickly," Rugrat said.

"That would work," Qin said.

The two women made notes as Rugrat looked at the rifle. "Not bad for a twenty-mil rifle. In World War Two, people would use these to take out tanks."

Rugrat shook his head. "Okay. I'll put a few more rounds down range and get this thing zeroed in."

He took out the magazine and replaced it, hitting the bolt catch. The heavy assembly slammed forward. He fired again and again, leaving a grouping on the iron target. These rounds didn't have formations, and paper targets would have been torn up.

Rugrat checked his grouping and adjusted his sight.

He flung a metal spell that repaired the target and fired again, pulling the weapon closer and closer to zero.

It took him all afternoon. Taran, Qin, Julilah, and the others watched him and studied the weapon.

Rugrat finished shooting and stood up.

"Just need to test this out as well." Rugrat grinned a little as he braced the rifle as he stood.

He flipped off safe and fired. The recoil pushed him backward. Mana solidified behind him, supporting him.

"Okay," Rugrat said thoughtfully as he lowered the rifle. "So, while I can shoot it fine, the recoiling force is so damn high and I'm so light that it forces me backward. Without support, I'll fall over shooting it upright. I guess magic needs workarounds where physics is concerned."

"Mounted?" Taran asked, pointing to the tripod. Its feet were buried in the ground which had been hardened around it.

"Read my mind."

Rugrat put the rifle into the mount with a few pins.

"We based it off of the old mount for the Mark Seven semi-auto," Taran said.

"The one that looked similar to the FAL?" Rugrat asked.

"Yeah."

"Range is live!"

Rugrat took the larger belt feeder and slotted it into the magazine well. It had catches that went over the well to secure it firmly.

He turned the formation on the belt. The rollers fed rounds up to the beast and he hit the release, sending the bolt forward, housing a new round in the chamber.

Rugrat checked either side and sat down, bracing the mount with his legs, and putting his hand on the trigger assembly. He pulled on the trigger, feeling the weapon buck slightly.

Rugrat watched the tracer, seeing it strike near the target.

He unlocked the mount, shifted his aim, locked, and fired again, tearing holes through the mortal iron plate.

Rugrat unlocked and shifted, finding another target on the range. He locked in and fired.

He repeated the process several times, shooting in long and short bursts before draining the remaining rounds that were tossed out the side of the weapon.

"She's accurate as hell. Barrel is tight with the new techniques. The power flow is awesome. As the round fires, the formations catch it almost immediately and hurl it right the hell out. With the smaller powder charge, the felt recoil in the gun is less. Still reactive force. You throw anything, a tree or a stick, you'll have some kickback. Though that heat management..." Rugrat pressed his lips together with his finger and opened them with a kissing noise. "Oh, my days, that is sweet. Stroke of genius there, ladies, putting a heat draining formation connected to the hydraulic compensation system in the rear. Just strips that extra heat out. This thing hits like, what? Five times harder than my modified railgun, probably more? The recoil is only slightly higher and cools faster."

"Just give us time and we'll make it better," Julilah said.

Rugrat nodded. "Always room for improvement."

He unhooked the Beast and inspected the weapon.

The Beast
Damage: Unknown Weight: 14. 57 kg Charge: 9,568/10,000 Durability: 124/124
Innate Effect: Increase durability by 24%
Socket One: Empty
Socket Two: Empty
Integrated Enchantment: Silence- Silence weapon and attack Heat Exchange- Remove heat from area. Dissipate-expel fire element
Range: Long range Requires: 20mm rounds
Requirements: Agility 60 Strength 50

He opened the notifications, seeing the significant increase to his blacksmithing skill.

"Nice! I love good old-fashioned cooperation."

15

Honorary Lords

The command center's conference room beneath the barracks was stark. Everything in the room was there out of utility.

Commander Glosil accepted the paper from Yui on his right next to Kanoa. Domonos sat to his left.

Rugrat spoke to Niemm. Roska and Storbon. Elan finished speaking to Evernight before nodding to Glosil.

"All right." Glosil cleared his throat, making sure he had everyone's attention. "I think we're about ready to begin." He intertwined his fingers and put them on his notepad.

"Since the fall of Vuzgal, we've recovered our fighting forces from across the realms. Reserve units have continued training, and we have been recruiting aggressively. The Reserves have been rushed through refresher courses and we've taken steps to ensure they can complete their jobs proficiently. Close Protection and Special Teams were the worst hit. They also take more time to train. The goals of the military in the coming months are as follows." Glosil moved his hands to read the notes on his pad.

"One, to continue training our military forces, Alva, regular, and reserve, as well as the Vermire Empire's military, which is the only thing standing against the kingdoms right now." Glosil looked around the room and back to his notes. "Two, establish a defensive grid over Alva. Egbert has taken Vuzgal's dungeon core and created an expanded defensive network that covers the entirety of the Vermire Empire. We have offensive capabilities and can expand the dungeon rapidly to gather a massive amount of power." Glosil shifted in his seat. "On the topic of defenses, our back up dungeons will be expanded, stocked, and prepared for fallback. I know it isn't glorious, but we need to make sure that, no matter what, the people we protect survive."

Those around the table nodded their heads.

"The third goal deals with the Special Teams and the Close Protection Details. We got blindsided on this one, and we still don't know much about the Black Phoenix Clan. All units will be geared toward raising Close Protection members. It has traditionally been the role of the Special Teams to go into the higher realms to gather information. While the Special Teams will be the tip of the spear, we need military units in the different realms. Just training here will do nothing for them. We need people that have experienced the realms. Following orders is good. Knowing their enemy, knowing the terrain is better. We don't need yes men. We need thinking soldiers. The action against the Willful Institute and in Vuzgal showed us how even a small force can overwhelm a stronger opponent. While we're being low profile in our actions, training all the time in the city will blunt our edge."

He surveyed the room. "Now, we all know our goals. Erik and Rugrat will head to the Seventh Realm to gather information about the Black Phoenix Clan and possibly make contact with the Sha. Gentlemen?"

Erik sat forward, leaning on the table. "Thank you, Commander. Our mission is twofold. First, to find out more on the Black Phoenix Clan, then the Sha Clan, and second, to get our hero emblems, as it will act as a protection against most people. Killing a One-Star Hero can come with a nasty backlash. We'll be inserting with Elder Fred and some of his family and going in a small group without Special Team guards to reduce suspicion. Plus, they know the area. They will have to go up on a separate mission to claim their emblems."

Erik nodded and sat back.

"Very good. That details most of our upcoming missions. Half of the Special Teams will rotate in operational roles. One team will act as a quick reaction force. The other will be on missions across the realms under the Intelligence Department. The last two will be training and testing people that wish to join the Special Teams," Glosil said, and jotted down some

"What about the elemental drill? It takes a lot of power and we don't know what will happen if it hits that ley line we're hoping to find," Colonel Yui asked.

"Egbert is doing everything he can to make sure that whatever happens, the dungeon can deal with it. We have multiple peak earth grade dungeon cores, one on each floor to bleed off and purify energy. Also, a grand sky grade dungeon core at the peak, with *hundreds* of lower-level dungeon cores spread out across kilometers to bleed off power and collect it. Each of the defensive towers the Vermire Empire created will act as mana gathering formations."

"What if it gives away our position?" Yui asked.

"It could, but the power that we tap into is more than some airship can gather," Rugrat said.

"Even if we don't tap a ley line, and just get really damn deep, the heat coming off from that, the elemental energy, would be massive. Our dungeon cores are too strong for this realm. Even with the contained Alva system, the ingredients, the crafting, the powerful people... There is not enough mana or impurities here to even strain the dungeon cores. If we tap the earth with the drill, the elemental and mana energy transformed into pure mana will be strong. If we can increase our mana density, we can increase the cultivation of our people faster, grow stronger ingredients, improve nearly everything that we make. Right now, we've got so many dungeon cores and systems in place, we would be dealing with more mana density than the Sky Realms to breach our containment and alert others."

"It is a valid concern, and a risk, but this is something that can secure Alva from future attacks." Erik was looking at Yui, but scanned the others in the room to see more questions.

Glosil checked. No one was making notes or writing messages.

"Director Elan, could you update us on the situation in the higher realms?"

"Yes, Commander. Right now, the Black Phoenix Clan is pressuring the Willful Institute and every other sect to give them information on us. They have taken the dungeon cores in Vuzgal and looted it. They are slowly moving through the Fourth Realm between mana dense pockets. Their ship can't remain in one place for too long as the mana is too thin. They'll absorb it all and have to move using their mana stones instead. Frankly, they're power hogs that can only exist in a place with a massive mana density.

"The Willful Institute has made alliances across the realms and consolidated their gains. They recovered several cities and have used some for bartering. They are consolidating; they and the Stone Fist Sect have never been closer and are going from strength to strength." Elan intertwined his fingers together on the desk.

"That is not our immediate problem. We have information that some of their people are getting close. We traced back to where these spies were coming from. The Kostic family seems to be searching for us. It looks like they are doing it without the knowledge of the Black Phoenix Clan."

"They're going independent?" Storbon asked.

"No. I think they know the Black Phoenix wants something from us, and that it must be valuable, so they're waiting them out. The Black Phoenix Clan can't remain there forever. They could get beached in the Fourth Realm without the necessary mana stones to realm transit."

"They're still searching for our dungeon core," Colonel Yui said.

"That is our conclusion as well," Elan said.

"It doesn't matter if they do or do not find us. We must prepare as if they will arrive at any minute. We can never truly plan for the when, but we *can* plan for what happens," Glosil said.

Erik, Rugrat, Glosil, Chonglu, Delilah, and Momma Rodriguez sat around the table in the council chamber.

Rugrat looked at his mother who had called the meeting, eating the cookies she had put in the middle of the table. "Oh." The cookie crumbled partially. Rugrat looked around quickly before he cleaned it up with his storage ring.

"Can't take you anywhere," Erik whispered.

Rugrat swore him to secrecy with his eyes.

"Use the plate, Jimmy," Momma said.

"Mo-om," Rugrat said with some cookie in his mouth.

"Did I teach you to speak with your mouth full?" She cocked her head.

Rugrat shrank his neck and closed his mouth.

She sighed and looked to the rest of the table. "So, I wanted to clear something up. These two boneheads are constantly leaving to go on their scouting missions and see the rest of the realms. They feel guilty leaving the dungeon because they're lords and feel like they should always be an active part of it. You all run the dungeon and the evolving Alva nation. For everyone's sake, I think it's best to clarify the roles of these two." She looked at Erik and Rugrat.

Delilah cleared her throat. "We understand that they go to the higher realms and are gone for long periods. That doesn't matter to us. They did so in the beginning, and it was the materials, knowledge, and information they brought back that allowed us to evolve and grow so quickly. They created the council to look after the dungeon, and now the growing nation and interests of Alva." Delilah turned her powerful gaze on Erik and Rugrat. "While we do not believe in chaining them down, Alva will *not* accept them abdicating! They are our lords, our leaders, and the ground stone of Alva. Alvans support them, and while the council might change, while there are new roles, they will never accept someone else taking on the role of Alva's lords."

"I agree with the Council Leader," Glosil said.

"I know the people agree and so do I," Chonglu said.

Rugrat leaned his elbow on the table, rubbing his face before holding his chin.

"I thought as much, and I have a compromise. Do you need Erik or Jimmy for the running of this city?" Momma looked at Chonglu.

He paused for a moment and shrugged. "No, not really."

"The army?"

Glosil shook his head. "No Ma'am. They passed complete control over to me. And I only hope that I am worthy of the trust they placed in me to defend our people."

Rugrat and Erik looked at Glosil, reinforcing their continued belief with their eyes.

"Alva and its national interest?" Momma looked at Delilah.

"No."

"So, the council and the groups they've put in charge, or have been put in charge of Alva, are capable of operating without Erik and Rugrat's input all the time." Momma stated to a general nodding of heads.

"So, I propose a change, a small one. But one I think will put Alva at ease that Erik and Jimmy will not run away someday and never come back. And Erik and Jimmy won't feel guilty every time they leave Alva because they feel they aren't doing their duty."

Rugrat used the arm of his chair to shift in his seat as Erik cleared his throat.

"Delilah?"

Delilah nodded and opened the journal in front of her. "We wish for Erik and Rugrat to remain in control. They would have the right to veto, overturning any decision that the council makes. They can order the council and Alva to carry out tasks as they desire. This is not a responsibility. When they return to Alva, information on all high-level decisions will be given to them. In this way, they will be able to guide Alva without having to be here all the time. It will keep Alva operating and ensure the council never oversteps their boundaries. While the council makes plans for the next several years, they will be making plans for the decades to come." Delilah looked at Glosil.

"The military will be loyal to our Lords first and foremost and the council second. They will be the overseers of the Special Teams, their trainers, and in times of battle, the Special Teams' leadership. We will support their missions to the higher realms, assist as we can, and pass on missions of importance to them."

They looked at Erik and Rugrat.

"Erik? Jimmy?" Momma Rodriguez asked.

"So, we would be able to call the shots and leave, but otherwise you would be managing Alva?"

"Yes, you would be like the royalty in the UK, but you have much more power to shift the nation," Momma clarified.

Erik and Rugrat looked at one another.

Rugrat pressed his lips together and shrugged with his hands open.

Erik nodded and tilted his head.

"It sounds good to us. We do keep feeling like we're failing Alva whenever we leave. Are you sure you want us to remain as leaders?" Erik said.

Rugrat looked over the table at the frowns on different faces.

Glosil leaned forward, his face softening. "Without you two, the first Alvans would have died in some backwater village and never have had a chance. You created this place. You shaped it against what was the norm. You could have been tyrants with your dungeon core. Instead you welcomed us, taught us." Glosil let out a breath. "You defended us; you gave us an opportunity that we never had in the past. If we do not honor that, then what does that say about us?"

Silence spread through the room.

"I was wandering through some of the schools for the children as part of an inspection a few months back. I snuck into a classroom teaching history. In the realms, history is usually relegated to one's clan or sect. This lesson was about the founding of Alva. I sat in the back of that classroom and listened. That teacher was from the First Realm. She talked about the founding of Alva in the beginning, the defense of the town, the trials that the dungeon went through when there was just one floor. She spoke with such passion. In her eyes, in the eyes of the children, you are their heroes." Delilah looked at Erik and Rugrat.

"All of my staff were in the room with me. I could see how much it affected them. Many of them had lived through parts of that history themselves. You are our history and our core. If we stopped you from adventuring, then we would tarnish that history and you would no longer be the people you are. Alva is your home as much as it is ours."

Erik and Rugrat looked at one another.

"We accept," Rugrat announced.

The room relaxed.

"Damn, had me scared for a moment." Delilah sighed into her chair.

"I think I need a drink," Glosil said.

Rugrat laughed. He hadn't realized their fear of losing their leaders had weighed on them as well.

Rugrat looked at Erik. "Guess we did some good."

Erik laughed and smiled. "Some."

Cai Bo passed an eye over the other elders and Head Asadi. The council chambers had been cleaned and redressed, the broken desk replaced. All the elders wore their most expensive and powerful robes. Even Head Asadi wore his best robes and jewelry.

The glares and snide comments had been hidden away, showing a united whole as they waited.

The high elders snatched glances at the main door to the council chambers. Cai Bo forced herself to not do the same.

The doors flew open, bringing them all out of their seats.

Cai Bo cupped her fists and bowed to the red armored man who strode into the room as if he owned it. She could feel the heat prickling against her skin like she was standing too close to a furnace.

Gregor paused, grunted, and walked to the empty chair, guided by Marco Tolentino.

Two of Gregor's fellow dungeon hunters stood behind his chair, ominous statues wearing black armor with yellow highlights, their hands resting on their belts, away from their swords.

"Please sit." Gregor's voice rumbled through the room.

The doors to the council chamber closed as the high elders and the Head sat under his command. It was natural, given his level of power and backing. He was someone from the higher echelons of a Seventh Realm power, his power a step above even Head Asadi's.

"I have been sent here with a single mission, one that unites our cause—to hunt down the Vuzgalians and destroy them."

It was exactly as Cai Bo had thought. They couldn't let it go. They needed a victory, one to regain their honor. *And they don't know the lower realms, but we do.*

Cai Bo had wondered if they would continue the fight. The Sects were badly damaged from the fighting at Vuzgal. They had lost thousands of fighters and resources in the attempt.

If the Vuzgalians kept hidden, we would look for them to make sure they would not attack us from behind, but we could leave them alone, regaining our strength and fighting easier opponents.

"We will provide you with all the support you need to take them. Warships and mana barriers to defeat their weapons, to close with them, and attack them directly from above."

The high elders sat taller in their seats.

"I have the plans, but I have not been given any ships so we will have to make our own."

"What will you need?" Head Asadi asked.

"Earth grade dungeon cores. I know you do not have dungeon hunters, but as long as you can find the locations, my hunters and I will take the dungeon core. We need a shipyard to build them, as well as cannons and crew."

"In return?" Asadi asked.

"We will make no claim on the loot. We only desire the Vuzgalian dungeon core."

"None of their weapons?"

"We know the clan that manufactures them. We know how they operate already."

So, someone else made these weapons?

"There is someone supporting them?"

"We believe they are part of the Sha Clans or have a connection. They also use these types of firearms."

Cai Bo hid her grimace as a few of the high elders' faces paled.

Asadi was quiet for some time before he responded. "We will assist you in building these warships and welcome your support against the Vuzgalians."

The Elders nodded their agreement as if it were the only thing to do.

Idiot, you think that we have the resources to do so? Cai Bo held her tongue as her calm returned and her eyes fell on Gregor.

Asadi was a thorn in her side, treating her as a lapdog, and unaware that she had maneuvered her way to control some of the strongest clans and groups inside the Willful Institute. *The Willful Institute stands on a knife edge, future unknown. the Black Phoenix Clan has a bright future.*

A plan started to form in her mind. Even if they won, the resources needed to support such an army to lead an attack would be immense. They were reclaiming territory and putting the loot to use in filling their treasury. They could earn much from defeating the Vuzgalians, but the cost would barely equal the gains.

If she were to give Vuzgal to the Black Phoenix Clan, she could leverage that to join their clan, or at the very least shift the balance of power and take Asadi's position.

She hid the glimmer in her eyes and joined in the congratulatory speech.

"I need to know where the strongest dungeons are with powerful dungeon cores so we can start to build warships," said Gregor. "I have plans for your crafters to speed up the ships' completion. I hope that we will know where the Vuzgalians hide by the time the ships are complete." He pulled out blueprints and put them on the table before standing.

"I look forward to our partnership," Asadi said.

Gregor grunted. "If you find a man with a fire wolf or a man with a dragon from Vuzgal, they're mine."

The room rose several degrees as whispers were silenced.

"Of course." Asadi bowed his head in agreement.

16

Recruiting the Best

ureus peered through the thick Beast Mountain Range forest with an arrow on his bow. He had pulled his hood down, revealing his short cropped blonde hair and blue eyes.

"Watlings," Jian said, checking the paw prints on the ground once more before he looked at Aureus.

"Are you sure?" Aureus stopped scanning the area to look at the boy.

"Uhh." Jian looked at the prints again, biting his lip. "I think so?"

"Okay, so what do we know about watlings?"

"They're small creatures. They don't move fast, but they're good at hiding. They dig warrens and like rocks or forests to hide in. A lot of other animals hunt them."

"Good," Aureus said. "And they make good food but have tough hides. All right, let's go and find them."

Jian bobbed his head and stood up. He had a small crossbow that fit his frame as he followed the game trail.

They kept going through the forest. Aureus clicked his tongue and pointed with his bow at some plants resting between two rocks off to the side. "Red berry bittersweets."

Jian looked from the red berries to Aureus.

"They're poisonous unless you burn them. Then the dust can be used in health potions. Grab them," Aureus said.

Jian moved to the berries and took out a small pouch. He quickly pulled the berries from the small plant.

"Make sure you don't touch your face after picking them or else you might die," Aureus said lightly.

Jian paused, shaking. "Uhh, Mister Aureus?" Jian gulped, his eyes going wide.

"So, what do you do to clean your hands?" Aureus raised an eyebrow, glancing at Jian before he kept watching the area.

Jian screwed up his face, trying to pull out the knowledge from deeper in his head. "Soap and water?"

"Right, soap and water will save your life more often than any bow or sword. Now, where is there water?"

"Uhh…" Jian stood up and looked around. "I don't know."

"What did we get before we came out here?" Aureus asked.

"The map!" Jian dropped his pouch and made to grab his map.

"Stop," Aureus ordered.

Jian looked around with wide eyes.

"You'll get the poison on the map. Get all the berries," Aureus said.

Jian looked at the pouch. A few of the berries had fallen out.

"Make sure you know what you're dealing with before you touch it. Get the berries in your pouch. We'll use my soap and I'll pour water on your hands to clean them," Aureus said.

"Why didn't you say so?" Jian pouted and stomped his foot.

Aureus glared at the boy. "I am not your father or your family member, boy. Just because you are young, it does not mean that you get everything you ask for. Do you want to hunt monsters or be a complaining child that throws a hissy fit whenever things don't go right?"

Jian bowed his head, trembling.

"Hurry up, the trail is old already, and it gets older with your pouting." Aureus kept his vigil over the forest.

Jian bit his lip and grabbed the pouch. He gathered the berries and secured the pouch.

Aureus sighed inwardly but didn't show any outward kindness.

Jian finished with the berries. Aureus passed him a bar of soap and wet his hands with a water skin. Jian washed his hands and passed Aureus his soap back.

Aureus rinsed his hands, and the boy wiped them on his sides.

"Very well. Now, let's find where those watlings went."

Jian led the way. They would stop occasionally, Jian checking the trail as it widened.

"Wait." Aureus put his hand on the boy's shoulder and tilted his head. "There is water up ahead."

Aureus led the way forward, his bow ready.

They crept through the brush. There was a stream less than a meter wide going through the forest. Trees and vines linked overhead.

Aureus slowed as he saw three large loken. They bore a resemblance to deer, but instead of antlers, they had twin horns like a ram. Two of the beasts were drinking, another was eating shoots near the water's edge as the fourth chewed on something, standing tall, his ears flipping in the direction of noise.

One of those drinking raised its head, water falling from its chin with the first before growing bored and drinking once again. Jian released a slow breath, pitching his voice low to Aureus.

"With loken, you need to aim for their neck. Make sure you use the paralysis concoction on your arrowhead."

Jian made sure his crossbow was on safe. He took out a small pouch and put his arrowhead in the greenish-pink gunk in the pouch, then wiped off the excess, making sure to close the pouch properly and store it.

The water erupted as a beast similar to an Earth alligator tore out of the water and latched onto a loken's neck. The other three took off at a halting run that turned into a quick escape as they fled. The loken that had been caught fought the alligator, pulling back and trying to get away as the alligator hauled it deeper into the water.

"Shoot one of the loken in the side," Aureus said as Jian watched the two groups with wide eyes.

"Do it, boy!" Aureus drew back his bow and aimed at the alligator.

Jian stood and aimed at the loken.

Aureus released his arrow. It hit the alligator in the side, making it shake from side to side.

Jian fired, hitting a loken. The others bounded out of range.

Aureus drew another arrow and fired on the loken in the alligator's mouth. It collapsed with the paralysis arrow.

The alligator floated on the water. Its movements slowly stilled.

"Quickly now." Aureus and Jian moved toward their kills.

Aureus had a fresh arrow on his bow as he grabbed the hoof of the loken in the water. The alligator's jaws were snapped tightly around it and it came out of the water with the loken.

Aureus pulled out a blade and stabbed it into the alligator, a tombstone appearing. The first loken showed a tombstone as well.

Aureus looked at Jian who stood in front of the loken with his knife.

"Quickly. We'll get into the trees and clean them up. I don't want to stay next to this water in case another alligator comes," Aureus said as he put his gear away and grabbed his kills, his superhuman strength allowing him to drag them with ease.

He put them to the side and moved to Jian.

"Okay, right here. Nice and clean." Aureus pressed between the loken's ribs.

Jian put his blade where Aureus had put his fingers. With a yell, he drove it through the tough hide and into the beast's heart.

The beast twitched, but a tombstone quickly appeared.

"Okay, good. Now let's get these three cleaned up and we can head back to the city."

Aureus left the lightest loken and carried the heaviest along with the alligator, dragging them back into the forest. He dropped them off and helped Jian, then got him working on field dressing the beasts. He needed some help with the alligator, as that was new to him.

Aureus showed Jian the two monster cores, storing them in a bag on his hip.

"Okay, let's get these back to the city." They picked up their kills and headed back the way they had come. Aureus looked around as Jian struggled with his beast.

No boy back on Earth could walk with such a beast over their shoulders, but this ain't Earth and his stats are plenty high enough.

They reached their cart, dumped their kills into it, and covered them.

"Okay, well, that should get us some good coin. Let's get going."

Aureus picked up the handles of the cart and they headed through the little bit of forest that remained before they reached the road.

"You did good work, Jian. That alligator came out of nowhere. Not much that we can do in those situations. Also why watering holes might look nice and calm, but they can have all kinds of hidden dangers."

Jian nodded.

"Don't worry. I won't take you to face the strongest beasts until you're good and ready," Aureus said.

Jian nodded again. Aureus grinned and rubbed his head. Jian scowled and moved his hair back into place.

Aureus heard horse hooves and pulled up his hood. They passed traders heading to the outposts.

"Good day!" the leader of the caravan said. Aureus nodded, and Jian waved a hand. The road was nice and big, large enough for four carts to go side by side.

The trade caravan carried on at a rapid speed. He spotted several new carriages along the road, fresh from the Vermire's workshops.

"Those carriages are so fast," Jian said.

"The Consortium has a lot of smart people to work on them."

"Is the Consortium the school you talked about?" Jian asked.

"No, school is the place I'm sending you to for three days a week to read, write, and learn some basic crafts. The Consortium takes the brightest and strongest people from the school and makes them stronger."

Jian's eyes lit up. "Like a sect."

"Sects are in the Second Realm, and the Consortium is in the First Realm. They're a group of strong people. Sects want you to pledge your life to them. The Consortium just wants your coin, and they help Vermire Empire's people first. If you can learn all the things the school has to offer and become a strong hunter, then you can get into the Consortium."

"What about the guards? Couldn't I be one of them?" Jian asked.

"Sure," Aureus answered.

"Couldn't you join the guards? Miss Inez from the tavern said that the Empire's army is the strongest in the First Realm; there ain't no one that can stop them. I'm sure you could join, Mister Aureus!"

"I'm fine with my hunting for now," Aureus said.

"I'd be a good fighter. They say that the army only takes the strongest and that they make you even stronger. Strong as people in the Second Realm!" Jian exclaimed. Aureus let the boy ramble as they made their way toward King's Hill.

He could see it in the distance, the spires over the land. It stood on its hill, now spreading down the hill and to the flat ground around it. Ground had been cleared around the city. An outer wall protected the farms that were necessary to support the massive city and keep out the beasts of the range.

Massive works were underway near the edge of the city.

"What are they doing by the river, Mister Aureus?" Jian asked, looking at where he was.

"They're widening it to fit barges and put in a lock system," Aureus said. "It will allow them to have ships that reach the Eastern Seas without having to take everything by land."

"Why would they do that?"

"You can take a lot more cargo by water compared to overland in carriages."

Jian turned quiet.

Aureus looked at the jewel of the Beast Mountain Range and the capital of the Vermire Empire. King's Hill city spread out expansively. The new city had been well planned, broken into a grid structure to ease the movement of people and supplies. A secondary city lay over a large bridge on the other side of the growing river.

The Consortium, which many had thought would die after the kingdoms removed their noble sons and daughters, had ballooned in size. Farmers, merchants, mercenaries, tavern owners, and blacksmiths were all in attendance. Everyone that became a Vermire citizen had the right to attend the consortium with pay for their needs for two years. Many had rushed to take advantage. Nobles were in the minority. Those parts of the beast mountain range had previously pledged their loyalties and filled up every available seat in just days. It had led to thousands joining Vermire.

The city and campus were orderly and planned, unlike the other cities that had grown organically, turning into a mess.

The gates were a flurry of activity as people entered and left the city. There were beast hunters, adventurers, mercenary groups, miners, loggers, farmers, and traders.

"Clear the way!" a woman's voice cried out as the sound of metal striking metal filled the quieting air. Aureus joined the end of the line to enter the city.

Those in the path of the exit quickly moved to the side.

Vermire's soldiers marched out. Their armor wasn't polished to a fine sheen, but was dull, and their oddly colored jerkins weren't like those of the proud armies of the surrounding kingdoms. It made them look like a patch of forest, which was exactly what they were meant to do. The camouflaged group marched out of the city as sergeants moved on either side of the group, forcing the men and women up to standard.

Other than the soldiers in the lead, or the ones that were swarming around the group, watching every deficiency and correcting them, none of them had a rank tab on their shoulders yet.

"Wow," Jian remarked, seeing the soldiers as they passed.

That was another thing; back on Earth, soldiers might exist in the same city or next door, but most of the time you never saw them.

"And the other kingdoms thought to attack our empire," a man wearing a basket on his back commented to his friend.

"The kingdoms had no idea what they were running into. Hah, bet they never had a real fight in their lives. Even us herb pickers know how to use a blade in these forests." The man patted his blade.

Aureus stopped listening to the duo, who showed a pass so they didn't have to pay to enter the city.

It didn't take Aureus long to reach Tobi, the butcher. They went around the back, and Jian knocked on the door. It opened after a few minutes, revealing a large man with a grand moustache.

Tobi grinned. "Jian, Aureus! Got some spoils for me?"

"Two loken and an alligator!" Jian said proudly.

"An alligator, huh?" Tobi said, as he inspected the meat.

"Should have some good value meat on it," Aureus said.

"I'll say. Those beasts are hard to catch, hiding in the rivers and streams all the time. They're old as bones and strong hunters." Tobi used a spell on the meat.

"You're in luck. This one is old. The meat will provide people with a buff!" Tobi grinned.

Jian looked at the alligator and then to Tobi in shock.

"How much for them?" Aureus asked.

"I'll give you three silver for each of the Loken. I'll give you seven for the alligator."

"Seven, and I keep the hide. I know some people that could turn that into armor."

"What about six and I leave you the pelts?" Tobi said.

"All right," Aureus said.

"Good, I'll have them cleaned up and ready for you tomorrow."

"Thanks. Jian, give me a hand in getting these inside," Aureus said.

Jian moved to help, taking one of the loken into the butcher. Aureus looked between the stores, spotting a tanned lady taking the time to tie her shoes.

I've seen her before. Is she following me?

He grabbed the alligator and headed into the butcher shop.

Tobi paid them out and Aureus put the coin in his pouch, taking

Jian and his cart off to the house they had rented.

"Jian, clean up the cart. Make sure there isn't any blood left. We'll get dinner at the Noble Ram tonight."

"Okay!" Jian went to the well and filled up a bucket to clean the cart.

Aureus cleaned off the monster cores and stored them away before heading to the marketplace.

He heard it before he smelled it—the sound of people calling out their offerings, talking to one another, picking up and putting down wares as coin changed hands.

There were stalls along the streets, but Aureus went to a grand looking building with glass panels and the words Silaz Trading House on the wall. Guards stood at the door, the kind that looked like they had put their weapons to recent use.

"Hood off," the guard directed.

Aureus took his hood down. The guard looked him over and grunted.

Aureus went inside. The glass window had monster cores of all kinds on display and a mana stone sat in formation covered glass.

He passed the monster cores that were arranged around the room and moved to a curtained-off area.

The curtain opened and an armored woman walked out. She stared at Aureus and then around the room before she left quickly.

"Next," the older man behind the curtain called. He stood at a desk with a monocle hanging from his vest pocket.

Aureus walked up, and the man used a spell to close the curtain. Aureus took out the monster cores and put them on the tray.

"A lesser and a common mortal grade." The man took some time inspecting the alligator core.

"A variant, earth and water." The man sounded impressed. "Albeit a weak one."

He put the core down.

"Two mortal mana stones and six gold, all in gold."

Two thousand and six gold. "Done," Aureus agreed.

The man nodded as he picked up the tray and wrote out a note.

He put it through an opening in the wall beside him.

A few seconds later, a man with a pouch came out.

"I can sell you a mana stone for thirteen hundred gold," the appraiser offered, as he accepted the coin from the other man.

Aureus reached out and paused.

"Do you have something that would keep it from leaking mana?" Aureus asked.

"Of course." The appraiser smiled and passed the pouch back.

The other man reappeared after a few moments with a smaller pouch. The appraiser accepted it and put it on the table.

Aureus looked inside, seeing the shining gold coins and the simple mortal mana stone.

He closed the pouch and weighed it in his hand. He couldn't sense any mana from it.

"Pleasure doing business with you," the appraiser said.

Aureus grunted and hid the pouch. The curtain opened and Aureus left as another mercenary walked forward to make their sale.

They must have had a lot of mana stones to allow him to buy one for only three hundred above the asking price. *Jian can use this with his cultivation techniques.*

Aureus rubbed his forearm as if it were tight.

He left the trading house and headed back to his rented home, passing several police officers walking through the streets. He had been here for weeks now, and other than people mentioning that some disappear, and the outward displays, like the flag, he couldn't sense anyone from Earth.

Aureus continued on his journey through the city. He stopped at one of the vendors, checking their wares, glancing out the corner of his eye past the people meandering through the packed market.

There you are. Aureus saw the woman again. He turned back to the stall, checking the wares for a few more seconds and leaving as the trader turned to him after finishing with her latest customer.

Aureus walked down the street, mentally mapping out where he was. He continued in the general direction of the Ram, going down a side street, passing a man pulling a cart stacked with goods. Aureus looked around the quiet road. Supplies were stacked and netted. Carts were tied to the back of different stores. A group of bored looking guards glanced up at Aureus as he quickly moved down the street and walked through an alleyway.

He made it out onto a busy street, mingling with the crowd. The woman burst out of the alleyway. Looking around for a bit, she locked onto him and started moving after him. Aureus turned his head, making it clear he was aware there were people following him without staring at the woman who was tying her shoes again.

Aureus turned and headed into the alleyway. He circulated his mana and gritted his teeth as he drew it into the formations carved into his very bones. He could see the runes through his skin and the power that flared from within. He moved to a jog and using the walls of the alleyway he jumped upward from side to side, until he reached the top of the adjacent building, then pulled himself onto the roof.

Aureus crouched and watched the alleyway. The woman appeared and sped up toward the end, coming to a square with several alleys leading off from it.

"Shit," she hissed, pivoting and turning around to take in the square.

Aureus dropped from the roof. She turned at the sound of his flapping clothing he rose from his crouch, drawing his dagger pushing his hood back, clearing his peripheral vision, studying her. "Why are you following me?"

She was lightly tanned, which had only grown darker from long hours spent working under the sun. She was middle-aged and had that energy of someone who had fought life to get there.

She was shorter than Aureus, but looked stronger and well fed.

"Was wondering if you put the stars and stripes on the flag. You're the only person I've seen from Earth," she answered.

"You?"

"The great state of Nevada. Moved to Arizona. You?"

"American." Aureus lowered his blade.

"What state?"

"I was saying you are. Why were you following me? Why did you think I was from Earth?"

"Your teeth. Not many pearly whites around here." She shrugged.

"When did you arrive here?" Aureus asked.

"Few months back. You?"

"Some time ago. You run into other people from Earth?"

"No. I heard that there was a group of people from Earth that supposedly disappeared here and then I saw the flag."

Aureus nodded.

"Not really the talkative type, are you?"

Aureus grunted. He looked at his blade and put it away.

"Come on. I'll buy you a drink," she offered.

Aureus raised an eyebrow before nodding and indicating for her to lead. She took him to a nearby tavern.

"Two beers, please," she said at the counter. The bartender nodded, filling two mugs and putting them on the side.

"That'll be eleven coppers." The bartender put some nuts in a dish on the side as well.

"Thanks." The woman put her coin on the side and grabbed a beer and nuts. Aureus grabbed the other beer, and they moved to a corner of the room. "So, what's your name? I'm Delfina." She wiped her hand on her clothes and held it out.

"Aureus." He shook her hand.

"So, what do you make of all this?" She waved at the tavern.

"It's a nice place to drink," Aureus said and picked up his mug and drank.

Delfina let out an exasperated sigh. "Not the tavern—the empire—this city. Has to have been made by someone from Earth or who knows about Earth. You hear about people getting invited to the Consortium? How they can disappear at times?"

"Tales of an imaginative mind. There are totems that can take you planets away. It's not odd for people to go missing for a few days or weeks. Crafts are not easy and can take long hours of study and practice to master." Aureus shook his head. "It's not like we have cellphones that allow us to check up on them, or the internet."

"But the soldiers, their training... There are assembly lines controlled by some traders," Delfina said.

"Yes, there are Earth elements. But if the people are from Earth or from here and they are using them...." Aureus shrugged.

"Real optimist, aren't you?"

"A realist."

A man walked up to the table and sat down, drinking his beer. Delfina and Aureus watched the man gulp down half his beer, then sigh. He wiped his beard with the back of his arm. "Thirsty work, all this recruiting. At least you two are together. Makes my job a bit easier." The man smiled.

Aureus' hand dropped to his dagger. Delfina's hand moved for her own unseen weapons.

"Oh, I'm by myself. Don't worry. I'm just here to give you these." Two letters appeared in his hand and he put them on the table.

"Storage ring?" Delfina said.

"I'm not from Earth. Know a bunch of people who are though, those letters are invitations."

Aureus let go of his mug and grabbed the letter. He opened it with his dagger and started reading.

"You want to recruit us to the Consortium and give us citizenship." He glanced at Delfina. "These are contracts, agreed to by the leader of the Vermire Empire, Lord Aditya himself."

"Yeah, it guarantees your safety," the man clarified, and took another sip of his beer.

Delfina opened her letter. "It also seals our lips so that we may never say what we see."

"A precaution. The First Realm isn't as calm as it appears on the surface. There are spies and people wishing us ill out there." The man opened his hands as his smile returned. "If you sign on the line, your questions about our flag and the empire will be answered."

The man sat back and drank his beer.

Aureus and Delfina looked at one another.

"Shit, I've signed some bad contracts before. What's one more?" Delfina nicked the side of her hand and dropped the blood on the contract. Runes flared out from the point of contact as a glow fell over Delfina.

Some people looked over and then went back about their business, something to break up the monotony of the day. People were signing or making contracts all over the realm.

Aureus turned the letter over and looked for any smaller script on the contract. Not finding any, he cut his hand and dripped some blood on the paper.

"Very good. Well, no time like the present. Come with me." The man finished off his beer.

"Might as well store those. Don't want them to go to waste.

Delfina and Aureus ran an eye over the man.

"You're new arrivals. Don't tell me you sold your storage rings already?" The man shook his head. "Waste. Come on, then."

The man walked to the tavern entrance. Delfina shared a look with Aureus. He nodded back to her and put his blade away.

They followed the man into the street. They walked for some time before they arrived at a large smithy. He went in through a side door. Smiths were covered in soot as they worked in front of the raging flames.

The man passed through. A young boy opened a door for them to a storage room filled with iron and enhancing materials. He closed it behind them.

"This one is always a bit tricky."

A formation glowed through the dirt floor, and a flash of light covered all three.

Aureus pulled out his dagger as the light faded. His eyes widened in shock, feeling the man's power flare.

"Watch your stabby device there," the man said. "Not here to harm you, but to offer you an option. Blade," the man admonished, looking at Aureus.

Aureus studied the man and slowly sheathed it.

"Good."

Light flashed, and they were in a large room with teleportation formations. Other people were arriving and being guided to the only door out of the room. Guards wearing carriers and rifles watched the room. Twin bunkers stood on either side. Aureus saw barrels in the bunker's slit as they passed them.

Aureus and Delfina followed the man through the door.

There were people everywhere, all kinds of clothes, rich, poor, hale and hearty, or missing limbs, families, or just solo travelers.

The man guided them into a large auditorium. "Please, take a seat. The presentation should start soon." The man left, meeting up with other guides who'd left others in the auditorium.

Aureus and Delfina found a couple of free seats. The auditorium was clearer than nearly any room he had seen in the First Realm. There were magical lights, the seats were padded, and everything was uniform. No dozen of one chair, a handful of another.

What the hell did we just get ourselves into?

A man walked out onto the stage.

"Charles, is that all of them?"

"Just a few more," Charles said from where he stood next to the door.

"Okay." The man on stage grabbed a glass of water and took a drink.

More people walked in.

"That should be it!" Charles projected his voice over the rumbling of chatter that died away as Charles closed the door.

"All right!" The presenter clapped his hands together.

"My name is David. Thank you for coming here today. This is not the Consortium. No, you are in Alva. Now, a little bit of history about Alva."

Silence permeated the auditorium. David had spent nearly an hour and a half talking about how Alva was formed, offering them conditional citizenship, and telling them the benefits of Alva.

"Now that is my part over, please go through the door." David opened his hand to where the guards stood. They opened the doors. "There are recruiters on the other side. They will review you on a case-by-case basis before giving you conditional citizenship for Alva. Remember, we do not care who you are; we care about your loyalty and your willingness to perform."

Aureus and Delfina turned to one another.

"Two soldiers turned dungeon lords." Delfina shook her head.

"We are on another planet filled with magic, powerful creatures, and people swinging swords around," Aureus said.

Delfina shrugged.

They followed the people out past the guards. The recruiting offices looked like passport control, but there were doors that opened, letting in families or individuals.

Some people were sent out to where guards were waiting to escort them out of a side door.

"What do you fucking mean? This place was built by people from Earth, dickhead! You think that you can throw me out! Wot, you want the fucking peasants! Are you thick?" yelled a young British man as he leaned over the desk.

"Sir, Alva needs the best people," said the woman interviewing him.

"What you trying to fucking say?" The man reared up, his face turning red as he held his hand back and open.

"That you are rejected." With the last word a wind picked up the man and tossed him out of the office. "Next!"

"You fucking thick bitch. Your lords'll hear about this. You'll be begging me to come back. I'm from fucking Earth!" A guard grabbed the man by the back of his neck and held him up as easily as if he was a coat. The man swore and struggled, his hits striking a carrier around the guard's body.

"Next!" The door ahead of Aureus opened. He walked into the office, finding a woman behind a desk and some chairs in front of it.

"Please take a seat," she said. "My name is Melinda, what is yours?"

"Aureus."

She made a note on her papers before she steepled her hands and looked at Aureus. "Do you have any pressing questions about Alva?"

"Is what you said about education true, and the cultivation?"

"Yes, we offer free education to the Apprentice level for all citizens. Beyond that, you will need to pay to join classes. With cultivation, reaching Body Like Iron and forming your mana core is a right by being a citizen, as is medical care and aid." She smiled.

Aureus moved his jaw. "There's a boy with me."

"Your son?" She raised an eyebrow.

'No, his parents were killed in a beast attack. I brought him here to instill some confidence in him by having him fight beasts," Aureus said.

"And you are wondering if he can join as well?"

"Yes."

"I don't see that there will be a problem. He will have to get a contract as well. We don't want to break up families or dependents," she said.

Aureus relaxed slightly.

"Are there any jobs that you are interested in?"

"Hunting?"

"We are affiliated with the adventurer… ah sorry, *several* guilds in the lower realms. A number of them work out of the empire and other places and have hunting contracts. Otherwise, there is the military."

"Not the military. Not my style," Aureus said.

"Okay, so then the guilds?"

"That would be interesting," Aureus said.

"Good, then you will have an interview with them tomorrow. You are free to apply to any job that is available in Alva." She took out some pamphlets and passed them to Aureus. "There is information on Alva, on your living quarters, and food as well as job opportunities. Are there any issues?"

"Uhh, no. Will I be able to go and see the boy? I promised to get him dinner and I've been gone for some time."

"Once you get settled into your quarters, contact the transition staff in your building and they will go with you. I'm sorry, but it is a security precaution." She smiled.

"Okay, I understand. Thanks."

The opposite door opened.

"Welcome to Alva, Mister Aureus, and watch out. The mana density can be a bit of a shock the first time."

"Thank you."

Aureus came out on the other side of the booths. There was a final hall that they went through with more guards, and a formation.

"Be careful," a guard called out. "You are moving into a high mana density area. Take your time. Please call for assistance if you need it. Go through the gradual mana tunnels if you have children!" He pointed to formation covered tunnels.

Aureus passed the guard line. He staggered under the mana that crashed into his body but got his feet under him.

"Kind of crazy, isn't it? Mana is so dense here that I think it's increasing my cultivation without me doing anything," Delfina observed.

Aureus got upright. opening his mouth to talk, but stilled looking at the city.

"Looks pretty modern, huh? Got all those towers, the parks… There's even a tram line that runs through the streets. Guns and carrier vests, too."

"Wha—" he said as he looked at it all.

"Yeah, impressive shit. I wonder if the higher realms have shit like this?" Delfina said, putting her hands on her hips.

A big grin spread across her face. "You know, if there's a tram line, then it means that they have propulsion on wheels which means…" She looked at Aureus with a smile that threatened to split her face and with madness in her eyes.

Aureus unconsciously took a step backward.

"Means that I can make the Ten Realms' first ever car."

Aureus paused his retreat as she laughed taking in the city.

"Alva Dungeon." Aureus watched a family moving past. The wife held onto a boy who was trying to charge ahead. The husband carried their young daughter who was unhappy and bucking around. He also held the hand of his other daughter, her eyes darting around to try to take in *all* the city in as short a period as possible.

Their clothes were simple, dirty, repaired and worn, like they had just come in from the fields.

"You seem confused." The man that had brought them through the teleportation formation wandered over.

"There was someone from Earth that was kicked out," Aureus started before he paused, feeling embarrassed.

"Alva wants people that will strengthen Alva. Just because you know more doesn't mean that you're the best fit. Alva is well past the point where it needs people from Earth. Sure, it's nice to have Earthers to strengthen our knowledge, but don't be surprised if you learn more from Alvans than you teach them."

"What do you mean?" Delfina asked.

"We recruit people from across the realms. We've taken knowledge from Earth, the realms and adapted them to one another and built upon them. We only pick people who are ready to learn and apply themselves. We don't care where you're from or what your background is."

"You no longer need people from Earth for their advanced knowledge? Then the biggest thing is you want more citizens to teach more people and increase your strength. You're not recruiting to get talent. You're recruiting to train talent," Aureus observed.

"Smart one you are. You should join the Intelligence Department. They're always looking for sneaky smart types like you. Come on, jump on the tram and it'll take you to your temporary quarters. I'm coming with. Then, Aureus, we can go and pick up your boy. Melinda told me."

Aureus nodded to the man.

"Intelligence Department, what is that?"

17
Moves

Julilah and Qin finished talking to the group of crafters.

"All good?" Qin asked Taran and Rugrat, who dropped the covering tarp over the mounted weapon system.

"I think we're ready," Rugrat said, looking at Taran.

"You just want to tear that target apart." Taran grinned and nodded to Qin and Julilah.

They walked over to where the officers of the Alva Military were assembled.

They've rapidly grown in number, Qin thought, picking out her brothers who were near Commander Glosil. Behind them were their own officers.

The group quieted as they arrived, standing next to a table of gear.

"Listen up." Glosil raised his voice, silencing any remaining chatter.

"Thank you, everyone, for coming out. First, we will go over the upgrades." Qin indicated to Julilah.

"The size of the stack formations is the same, but the new formations increase energy efficiency and the heat dissipation technology. The barriers will be stronger and less prone to overheating."

"We're phasing out formation plate technology. The stacks are easier to handle and can be prepared in various configurations. One for a mana barrier, another to increase the power of your casters," Qin said and grabbed the stack formation from the display table, moving it to a formation plate on the ground.

"The only formation plates are these baseplates. Their purpose is to increase the range of the stack and increase the power supplied and heat regulation." She put the stack into the middle of the formation and twisted it into the stack. The formation lit up with power. She turned it back and pulled it out.

"As easy as that." She indicated to Julilah again as she walked back to the table.

"With the first version of conqueror's armor, we saw considerable cooldown time. Once people use it, they need time to recover before they can do anything else. Erik and the alchemists have been working on concoctions to help with this. New formations will increase the percentage buffs and we have secondary recovery formations." Julilah picked up a formation fit for the formation socket.

"This specialized formation can be switched out in the armor, increasing the regeneration. They're linked to one another still so everyone's recovery will speed up. With trial and error, for every one minute of using the one hundred percent buff, you'll need twenty-four minutes of recovery. After sixty minutes, you'll need to rest for an entire day. If you increase that to two hundred percent, then for one hour of power, you get four days of rest. Three hundred percent, sixteen days of rest, though I'm not sure that the body would be able to handle that much."

She had the officers' rapt attention, some writing down notes.

"When Julilah says using the armor, she means that you're not just wearing the armor. You have it activated with its complete buffing abilities. You're hurling out spells enhanced by the armor and using all your newfound strength. If you just stand there in your armor, you'll recover. Slower than if you were using the recovery formations, but you will recover."

"What if we use both formations? One cooldown in a stack and the buffs with the armor?" Glosil asked.

Qin looked at Julilah.

"Once you're over the one hour mark, you'll start to have issues. Recovery time is longer than use time, so you'd need four minutes to cool down. Now, while you are in the armor, you are buffed and fine. Taking the armor off is the issue, or if your armor is damaged. If you're injured, then the problems will quickly compound. Which is why the first course of action is to hit someone with a revival needle right away, then go about your first aid. And make sure that their dog tags are still functioning and keeping them buffed."

Glosil nodded in understanding.

Julilah looked at Taran.

"The weapon formations?" he asked.

Julilah nodded and looked at Qin, who tilted her chin back at her.

"The formation masters have been working hard to improve the socket formations for your weapons. They're stronger than before. Replacements are being manufactured for all weapon types."

An officer raised a hand.

Julilah indicated for him to go on.

"With the weapon systems, which ones will we be working with now?"

Rugrat cleared his throat. "May I?" he asked Julilah.

"You know more than I do. We don't have anything else to add."

Qin nodded.

"Thank you." Rugrat stepped forward with Taran to Julilah's side. Julilah put the formation back and moved to Qin's side.

"The primary weapon will be the mark eight rifle with automatic capabilities. That will be phased out in favor of the mark three railgun which will be the primary weapon of the Alva Military. The other will be the mark five. Gather round." Rugrat moved to the mounted rifle. The officers grouped around it.

"Semi and full auto, firing the new twenty-mil round. Can be used by people who have Body Like Iron from the prone. Standing, this puppy kicks like a mule and is likely to knock you on your ass unless you're buffed up or have higher body cultivation."

Rugrat pulled off the feeding belt and pulled back on the heavy action, clearing the weapon. "It can be mounted and belt fed." Rugrat aimed and pulled the trigger, releasing the action.

He pulled out a round and turned to Taran. "Do you want to go over the rounds?"

"Sure." Taran took the round and passed it to the nearest officer, then pulled out a few more for them to pass around before he stepped back. "Formation enhanced rounds. With the help of the formation masters—" Taran glanced at Julilah and Qin. "—we were finally able to mass produce formation carved rounds. Using a new formula of gunpowder, we don't need such a large cartridge. The new carved rounds are going to be produced not only for the mark five, but for the mark three railguns, as well as mortar rounds."

The officers passed the rounds on, each inspecting them.

"The weapon is filled with formations. In the mounted role, it has a place for a formation stack." Rugrat tapped the ground. The tripod rested on a baseplate with a socket in the middle for a stack formation.

"The mark five is meant to replace the grenade launcher, mana cannons, and our marksman rifles. She will provide heavy supporting firepower with devastating results. Think of it as hitting an enemy at mortar ranges, but with the power of a mana cannon spell." Rugrat patted the weapon system.

He moved to the tarp covering the next mounted item and pulled it off.

"This is the mark thirteen." The officers stared wide-eyed at the Gatling gun. "We've been modifying things to be machine guns since we started. This baby, from the ground up, is designed to spit out destruction at a high rate of fire. We actually decreased the overall speed of the weapon to improve accuracy and decrease the number of rounds used. Still, at one thousand enchanted rounds per minute, it seriously puts a kink in anyone's plans. There is a quick barrel change system, and you might notice that there's no ammunition pack. An integrated storage device feeds the weapon and keeps it portable."

The officers were looking hungrily at the two new weapon systems,

"So, who wants to shoot them?" Rugrat grinned.

The entire group leaned closer.

"That's what I thought."

Erik released his charging handle, loading his M8 before storing it away in his storage ring. He checked on the rest of the group, who were preparing their gear before the defenses around Alva's totem. They wore sunglasses, ball caps, and long sleeve shirts that had been covered in formations with standard issue pants and boots.

He caught Rugrat's eye. "Good to go?"

"Ah, you know it, West," Rugrat said. He patted his gear.

George made a noise on his shoulder, displeased with the movement.

Erik looked around before he felt the emptiness in his gut.

She's not here anymore.

Fred approached and cleared his throat.

"You're sure there's no one from the Black Phoenix Clan or others that might recognize us in this place?"

"I'm sure," Fred said. "There are no Sha or Black Phoenix Clan in that area. Cronen City is a major port city with air, sea, dungeon, and land routes that connect to the rest of the Seventh Realm. There's plenty of information, resources and missions to be found there." Fred wore eastern styled robes. His hands were hidden in opposite sleeves. Fine embroidery showed the formations that had been sewn into the fabric. Erik rested his hand on his hip where he used to holster his pistol. Dromm, Racquel, and Reaper moved away from Elizabeth and William, who would be staying in the dungeon.

They had become fast friends with the beaver family from the Metal floor, who had largely taken over the Water floor, akin to how Davin managed the fire floor. They'd had a great feast with Xern and were sleeping off a food coma.

Dromm looked like a mercenary with his mix of beast leather and metal plates. Reaper wore casting robes, and Racquel wore gear similar to Dromm, but with more leather than metal to allow for greater movement.

"Ready?" Fred asked.

The others nodded.

Fred looked at Erik and Rugrat.

"Lead on." Erik held out a hand toward the totem.

Fred nodded, and the group passed through the gates around the totem. So early in the morning, there was little traffic. The soldiers saluted as they passed and stood on the pad around the totem. Fred held out mana stones. The totem drew in the power and light wrapped around the group.

The bright blues of early morning sun and the sound of a bustling city replaced the yellowing darkness of Alva. It was like jumping from a hot summer day into a pool. All his pores seemed to open at once, drinking in the mana and elements around him.

He staggered under the weight of mana. It was so thick and felt dense enough to be vapor.

Erik adjusted to the influx of mana density.

You are in the Seventh Realm.

Mana regeneration increases by 100

The only thing comparable was the mana density in the cultivation pods.

Rugrat raised his eyebrows around his sunglasses.

"Clear the totem pad! Move it people! Plenty of people coming and going!"

"Make sure you have payment ready! Traders on the left, individual travelers on the right!" guards yelled out, organizing the chaos.

People wore High Journeyman level gear as regular clothes and Expert pieces were the norm. Tattoos glowed with power, drawing in mana and elements.

They're much brighter up here with the increased mana.

Fred led them to the guards, quickly flashing his badge and paying a reduced fee.

Once outside, the city revealed itself; ancient Chinese towers dotted the landscape. People moved in groups, showing off their colorful and elegant emblems. While many had weapons and armor, few rested their hands on their weapons, relaxed as they proudly displayed their affiliations.

The roads were made of stone that had been rubbed smooth with the passage of time and feet.

The city was hazy with the smell of incense that seemed to drift through the streets.

People wore clothes with fine needlework that created scenes that played in the light and drew one's eyes. Tropical ocean blues, flowering reds, and powerful golds were woven with vibrant greens, dashing purples, and bright yellows. The clothes were alive with color. While the streets were busy, there were no stalls for traders. Buildings were walled off in their own compounds, the walls adorned with the emblem of the controlling clan or sect.

"There are few traders here, but there are many crafters. Most are of the Expert level, with some who have reached Master. There are quite a few that have reached Expert in a few areas. Trading is different than in the lower realms. In the lower realms, people just buy the product. Here, people meet with one another in their compounds. Their trades can be massive, and they will usually be for a term," Racquel said, walking nearby.

"A term?" Erik asked.

"Of several years or several dozen. Expert and Master crafters take a lot of time and resources to raise, and the resources aren't easy to get. So, traders and crafters wine and dine one another. A trade here is akin to an alliance between two groups."

"So, they have a meeting every time they buy something?" Rugrat asked.

"Yes, other than the mission halls. You need to have connections in the Seventh Realm to succeed. The mission hall is where most of the *trade* happens. Otherwise, there are a lot of auction houses." Racquel pointed to a grand building with its doors open as people in magnificent carriages arrived.

Rugrat let out a low whistle.

"What's up?" Erik asked.

"Those carriages, they're covered in powerful formations, sky metal, enhancers, formation activation ingredients. Damn, that is one expensive buggy."

"How is your crafting now?"

"Uhh, well, with working on the guns and being part of the team, I'm a Master in blacksmithing and I reached Expert in formations. How about you?"

"I've reached Master in healing; mid Expert in alchemy. They've both slowed down. I'm not making complicated pills or concoctions and there aren't many injured people that need help anymore, so no way to increase healing. Not that I want to deal with wounded."

Rugrat grunted.

They reached the base of a tall tower where aerial beasts landed and took off.

"I thought this was the city that had the Mission Hall," Rugrat said.

"It is." Fred led them into the tower, paying another fee, and led them to a platform.

"So why are we here?" Rugrat asked.

Fred smiled mysteriously as Dromm and Racquel grinned. "You'll see."

The platform came to a stop. People boarded different birds and aerial creatures with scaled up passenger cabins on their backs.

Fred led them up a set of stairs into a large carriage that could fit fifty people. Chairs were arranged in rows with windows that looked out onto the aerial beast hangar.

The passenger cabin quickly filled.

The walkway was removed, and the exterior door closed.

"For takeoff, please remain seated," a woman at the front said, and bowed to the people inside the compartment.

The passengers were as varied as the people Erik had seen on the street.

The cabin shifted from side to side as the beast moved to the edge of the tower.

"Well, nothing like beasty air," Rugrat said.

Erik snorted and looked out the window. "Damn." The city stretched for kilometers in every direction, filled with compounds and towers. Erik clenched as he saw an airship.

"Don't worry. There are many airships here," Dromm said from behind, through the space in the seats.

"Lots of dungeon lords use their dungeon cores to transport materials from one place to another. Can even raise some in transit. They move materials, growers, and traders."

Erik studied the large airships and their glowing formations threading through the city.

They reached the edge of the platform and the bird jumped. His wings extended, catching the air as they glided downwards and gained speed. Then the beast flapped its wings several times, increasing their altitude.

"What the hell?" Erik said, seeing the edge of the city beyond. Below it were more buildings.

"This city has three levels above ground and twenty below. Shaped like a pyramid." Dromm chuckled.

The bird moved with the eddies in the air as they glided through an open section in the floor. They passed through into the larger city below. Massive pillars and towers reached up, supporting the floor above. All the buildings were closer together. Formations on the bottom of the upper level made it appear as if the sky was right above them.

Aerial creatures of all kinds flew through the towers. Their mount joined a line of aerial beasts that flowed between towers. Birds broke off occasionally before they once again glided down and through a hole in the second level.

"Welcome to the under city," Reaper said.

It wasn't as bright on the ground. Everything here looked functional and rough.

"Looks like an industrial area," Rugrat said.

Pits led into the dungeons underground, where light shone out. The compounds didn't have the elegance of the cities above. Smoke filled the area, creating a dark fog.

Towers extended downward into the ground. A network of formation enhanced pillars rose to support the second city. They were covered in buildings that had been built along their surface.

Erik looked over the ravaged ground. There wasn't one space for trees or other greenery.

"Everything down here is for the dungeons. Any supplies from the dungeons are sent to the airships or the higher cities. Supplies the dungeons need are brought in from the higher cities or the airships. This entire city is dedicated to the transportation of goods," Dromm said.

"Most of the groups here are people who have banded together, working to move goods or to adventure in the dungeons. This is where they go to relax. It's not lawless, but things are a lot more relaxed here and there are dueling arenas everywhere," Racquel said.

They continued flying, heading away from the stacked cities.

Light spilled down, the cities above creating a line ahead of their bird.

Airships of different kinds cast shadows as they came to land in pits that were ringed with towers.

"They'll land in the pits so they don't burn through their mana stones. The airships have to keep moving to draw in fresh mana to stay in the air. The towers on either side have ramps that attach to the ships so they can load and unload goods," Dromm said.

Erik studied the snaking roads filled with carriages that wove through the lowest city and looked at the pits. "So, the dungeons, can anyone access them, or do you need to pay?"

"You pay to get entry to the different dungeon cities and forts. It's complicated down there. Some places will accept you; others don't want anyone but their clan members around. There are open dungeons that anyone can use as long as they pay a fee. There are also free dungeons. But they are pretty much wild dungeon areas with beasts that are too strong or don't have enough resources to interest groups strong enough to set up an outpost in the dungeon. Then there are resource nodes, places where dungeons create mana stones, or ingredients, or materials. People vie for those locations daily and farm them, collecting resources repeatedly," Reaper said.

Erik nodded. The world got suddenly brighter as they left the stacked cities. They followed other aerial beasts, passing the airship pits that lined the ground.

In the distance, there was the sea and a massive harbor that could be rightfully called its own city. The stacked city stood proudly on a high point and expanded in every direction, taking over the valleys and reaching into mountains, with dark openings across the hills and mountains.

"How far does the dungeon go?" Erik asked.

"Don't know. They think that the whole of the Seventh Realm is covered in layers of dungeons. There are even dungeons under the seabed. But no one has a complete map because the dungeons change constantly," Racquel said. "Look, that's where we're going." She pointed at a black and silver building.

"Everything is bigger in the Seventh Realm," Erik said.

"I thought that was Texas," Rugrat quipped.

Erik rolled his eyes.

The mission hall was a black and silver spire shaped like a drill that reached into the sky. It was a hundred stories tall, and all roads seemed to lead to the spire. Airship pits lay around the base, ringing it. Aerial beasts landed in the spire.

Their own bird banked, bringing them on a slow glide before he reared up, flapping his wings as he came to land inside the spire. He moved forward and settled down with a few flicks of his wings.

The stewardess opened the door as a walkway connected and the cabin started to empty.

They walked off the bird and down another set of stairs.

Erik took his sunglasses off and put them on the top of his hat. He could see through one side of the spire to the other. Flashes of light were happening everywhere as people appeared and disappeared.

"This way." Fred guided them toward a teleportation pad with a sign above it. *Tenth Imperium Quartermaster.*

In a flash of light, they appeared in a hallway that reminded Erik of the grand cathedrals he had seen in Europe with their massive arched ceilings.

"This is all the quartermaster of the Tenth Imperium. If you are a member, you can purchase anything you might need, get your gear repaired, and sell off any gear or loot you don't want." Fred raised his voice to be heard over the noise of people talking in the hall and moving between the open arches that led to counters where staff assisted heroes.

"Thought that more people would be wearing armor and carrying weapons," Rugrat said.

"Most people become heroes by completing missions for the mission hall instead of doing heroic acts," Racquel said. "Many became heroes earlier in life when they were fighters, but that was decades or centuries ago. Now, they've taken up different skills and work on those instead," Fred said as he led them past the busy stores to the quieter regions. People appeared in teleportation formations between the stores, a place of constant activity.

"I keep forgetting how long people live for in the Ten Realms," Rugrat said.

"All of us could live for several hundred years," Fred said.

Erik peered through the archways. People stood at quiet counters. Some passed over storage items. Those at the counter checked the contents and passed back a new storage device. One man pulled out several beast heads and put them on the table.

The person at the counter sighed and started checking the heads.

Erik looked at the sign, which read: Missions drop off.

"If you're a One-Star Hero, you can purchase high Expert grade materials and gear, Two-Star, low Master grade, Three-Star high Master, and with Four-Stars you can get *star rated* stuff," Dromm said. "Can only use mission points, though. A One-Star will give you ten mission points, Two-Star mission a hundred points and so on."

"Or you can trade with trainers for private training, or libraries for access into their archives," Racquel said.

"Smart, they're probably raking in mana stones while we just believe that these points are worth as much as a sky grade mana cornerstone," Rugrat said.

"Kind of like paper money back on Earth," Erik said.

"Yeah, or credit cards. We believe they hold enough value for us to purchase things, but that value is only supported by belief, not resources." Rugrat shrugged.

"Here we are." Fred walked through an archway.

People walked up solemnly to the counter and handed in pieces of paper. Those at the counter read the paper before pulling out medallions.

Those receiving the medallions showed joy as they accepted the contract that bound them to the Mission Hall.

"Come with me." Fred led them through a line to a bored looking woman who glanced up at them as they approached.

"Medallion papers." She opened her hand.

"Hello. Sorry, we don't have papers. The Ten Realms told us to see you."

The woman perked up. The group backed away, giving Erik and Rugrat space.

She focused on something that only she could see. "Naturals, huh? Been some time since I saw a natural."

She grunted and pulled out two books from under the counter and two medallions, dropping them on the counter as she tapped the book and searched under the counter with her other arm.

"This outlines the rules of the mission hall. These are your one-star hero medallions and this is your contract." She pulled out contracts and put them on top of the books. "The contract is simple. You promise to uphold the rules of the Mission Hall, meaning no killing Mission Hall or Association members. Assist them if you can, and if you cannot complete a mission or don't want to do a mission, then you will resubmit the mission so that others might attempt it."

Erik skimmed the contract. "What if we're affiliated with a sect or association?"

"That's fine. As long as your sect or association doesn't intend the Mission Hall or its people harm there shouldn't be a problem."

Erik read the contract over.

"What about this? Answering the call?" Rugrat asked.

"In times of need, a mission hall might call upon you for support. Say if there is a dungeon eruption creating a beast wave. There is a pay table in the book for how much you will get paid depending on the situation."

"What if we don't have combat abilities?"

She looked at them both with a raised eyebrow before she cleared her throat. "*If* you weren't fighters, and a fight broke out, then it would be your duty to tell someone that could deal with the situation or assist as you can. If there's a beast tide, you could be asked to create defenses, maintain weapons, repair gear and the like."

Erik cut his finger and dripped blood on the contract. They had already read the rule book, thanks to Fred and his people having a copy.

Rugrat followed suit.

"Welcome to the Mission Hall. If you are under threat, the Mission Hall will protect you. You have access to the mission board, all our services including training facilities, a place to stay and materials. Have a good day."

"Is there a way we can get information?" Erik asked.

"Yeah, go to the Library Department. They have maps you can purchase, information on the different areas you might travel in, and books to learn crafts, spells and techniques."

"Thanks." Erik and Rugrat grabbed their medallions, putting them on their shirts and storing the rest of the materials.

Erik took the time to check his medallion.

One-Star Hero medallion
One-time emergency contact for the nearest Mission Hall. Creates a powerful barrier to protect medallion wearer.

"Just need to clear ten One-Star missions and we can attempt a Two-Star mission and become a Two-Star Hero," Erik said.

"Welcome to the mission grind club." Dromm laughed.

"Now, let's go and see the scroll keepers. They should have the information you're looking for," Fred said.

Through some more teleportation pads, they arrived in the mission halls library.

"Does this place have anything other than massive spaces?" Rugrat asked as they walked up to the counter.

Erik looked up at the several floors filled with books, people, and librarians with hero medallions flying through the air silently.

The floor was quiet as people read books and made notes.

On the bottom floor, there were different counters covered in formations. Servers moved between the racks of books behind the counter and different storage chests, pulling out books for those at the counter who tapped their medallions to a formation before leaving and passing over a sound canceling field.

"You can purchase spell books, information books of all kinds, cultivation manuals, and regional information from the different counters," Fred whispered. "One can only get access to the library with the One-Star emblem. Some books are restricted by the star level. The higher your star level, the more books you can get and the greater your discount. We can wait for you here."

"Thanks," Erik whispered back.

They had to tap their medallions at turnstiles to get into the library.

Erik and Rugrat walked up to a counter by themselves, passing through the ear-popping sound cancellation field.

Erik worked his jaw as they reached the counter.

"How can I help you today?" a man behind the counter asked.

"Do you have information on groups or clans?" Erik asked.

"We do on a number of them. Do you have a name?"

"Black Phoenix Clan," Erik said.

"Sounds familiar. Medallion?" The man pointed to a formation.

Erik put his medallion into the formation.

"I'll see what I have." The man wandered back into the racks, quickly disappearing into the books.

"Doesn't know them off the bat?" Rugrat looked at Erik.

"Well, everything seems to be bigger in this realm. You saw how many airships were out there," Erik said.

"You've got a point."

The man walked out of the racks with a skinny book. "This book contains One-Star information on the Black Phoenix Clan. They are an airship clan to the northwest, in the elemental plains. It costs ten sky mana stones."

"No points?" Erik asked.

"The information isn't that complete. When you're a One-Star, you can get basic information. For more in-depth information, you'll need to find an information broker or increase your overall star rank. It doesn't warrant the fee of a mission point, which is used primarily for training, new items, and gear."

"What information would we get if we were Two-Star?" Erik asked.

"Two-Star you can learn about events going on within the groups. Tensions, how strong the ties are between people."

"Thank you," Erik said, and checked his storage ring before checking another, then another.

"How much do you got?" Erik muttered to Rugrat.

Rugrat frowned and looked through his storage rings as well.

"I have nearly three sky grade mana stones worth. You?"

"I've got four, got a ton of supplies, pills, and ammo." Erik scratched his head.

"I'll ask," Rugrat said and jogged off.

Erik smiled awkwardly. "Sorry, just going to see if we can borrow a friend's stones."

"Mhmm." The man slid the book to his side of the counter.

Racquel returned with Rugrat.

"I'll buy it." She put some mana stones on the counter.

The man checked the formation underneath.

"Thank you." He passed the book to Racquel, who passed it to Erik with a teasing grin. "Didn't think I'd be the one lending you two money." She shifted her lips, holding back a laugh as she gave Rugrat a side-long look.

"We can pay you what we have now." Erik started pulling out the stones.

"Don't worry about it. Pay me back after the mission is done."

"Thanks, Racquel," Erik said as they moved away from the counter.

Racquel waved him off as they reached the rest of the group. Fred led them to a private room, Dromm closing the door behind.

Information Book: Black Phoenix Clan

Do you wish to activate this information book? Doing so will destroy this information book.

YES/NO

"Yes." Light poured in between his brows and knitted together before the light dissipated.

"Anything good?" Rugrat asked.

"Just the basics, where they operate, what they trade in, some background." Erik organized his thoughts. "They were a mining clan. They worked in one of the cities and gathered dungeon cores, then spread out into different areas. Attacked several small mana mining clans that had airships through competitions, and took their ships, dungeon cores and their regions. They have a reputation as pirates and mana stone miners. They mainly operate in the elemental plains, a region where tears are common and elemental energies run rampant, creating many anomalies. They ride in their airships through mana storms to create mana stones that they sell on."

"So, they're a group of miners?" Fred asked.

"With big ships." Erik shrugged. "While they do have a number of allies, as enemies, their number one is the Sha. Says that their competition is linked to the Violet Cloud Realm tokens."

"What's that?" Rugrat asked.

"Hell if I know. It's just listed. Bet we would have to buy more information books to find out," Erik said. "Basically, the two groups attack one another's regions and their ships to get an advantage."

"Sounds like it might be a sub-realm or tear realm," Reaper said and looked at Fred.

"Wait, a tear?" Rugrat asked.

"Oh, in the higher realms there are things such as tears—openings that connect the realms to somewhere else. Sometimes tears can lead to places with resources or information. Most are filled with powerful creatures. The wider the tear gets, the stronger the creatures. Some people farm these locations. The beasts that come through are strong, but they can have multiple beast cores."

"Where do they come from?" Rugrat asked.

"We don't know. If you go through a tear, then you don't come back. The Mission Halls take on these tear missions all the time. If there are tears in areas not under anyone's control, the Mission Hall will issue a mission themselves," Fred said.

"It might be there are many competitions among people over who can enter which realms. There are the Ten Realms that we reside in, but in the Sky Realms and higher there can be portals that connect the realm to other places. Sects and groups can hold competitions for people to enter these places under their control. There can be many resources and information on the other side." Reaper added.

" Wait, are they competing or fighting one another?" Rugrat asked.

"Oh, they're straight up fighting massive airship battles. They're just fighting it out in the elemental plains," Erik said.

"Most rivalries within cities are dealt with in the arenas. But outside the cities and in the chaotic areas, death is still common." Racquel said.

"So, how did they find Vuzgal?" Rugrat asked.

"It has to be through the Sha. I don't know how, but that's the only thing that is common," Erik said.

"Fuckers." Rugrat leaned forward on the table.

"We don't know the full story," Erik said.

"We might not, but something the Sha did made the Black Phoenix Clan get interested in Vuzgal, and us." Rugrat looked at Erik.

"Yes, but we might need them if we want to defeat the Black Phoenix Clan. Otherwise, we'll have to make our own fleet of airships powered with Sky grade dungeon cores."

Rugrat clicked his tongue.

"The enemy of my enemy is my friend. The Sha wanted to talk to us before," Erik said.

"So we make a deal with them?"

"Doing so right now might not be in your best interests," Fred said. "You're just One-Star Heroes right now. If we deal with the Sha, you'll be at a disadvantage. If you're Two-Star Heroes, have some more levels, then it will give you a position of power to deal with them."

"One thing at a time," Rugrat said.

"One thing at a time." Erik agreed.

"So, it sounds like we need a mission," Dromm grinned.

"Let's head to the mission hall."

18

Missing Adventurers

"**W**elcome to the club!" Dromm said. "Ready for your first mission?"

"Sure, let's go check it out." Erik glanced at Rugrat.

"We can swing round the library after?"

"Sounds good to me."

"Okay, now all missions are posted on the mission board, which is…" Fred looked at the signs on the walls between arches. "That way." He pointed and followed his finger.

"I thought it would be brighter up the spire," Erik said as they walked.

"Oh, we're not in the spire. We're in the Cronin City headquarters in the middle of the dungeon."

"Wait, so we got teleported into the dungeon?" Erik asked.

"We wanted to show you a bit more of Cronen, in case we get a mission that takes us across the planet. The Mission Hall spires are all over the place. They're teleportation hubs that send you to their city headquarters." Racquel held out her hands to the halls.

"The power use?" Rugrat said.

"Mana here is dense enough that the power requirement is minimal," Fred said as they reached a teleportation pad with Mission Board above it.

In a flash of light, they appeared in a new hall. They followed others leaving the pads through an open archway and entered a massive room as large as four football fields. Help desks created a ring in the middle of the room. Between the help desks and the boards, teleportation formations flashed with people leaving.

The walls were covered in pieces of paper and scrolls with different missions, looking like a chaotic noticeboard.

Glowing terminals dotted the walls in small alcoves. Lines gathered behind them as a person or group flickered between images.

Some pulled paper from the wall, going to counters between the mission walls.

"The walls are broken up into mission types. There are missions to collect certain resources, others to create items, clear out a dangerous dungeon, or protect a ship crossing the skies or seas. There are also missions hunting down people that have committed grave crimes or beasts that have attacked the local people." Fred indicated to someone that pulled off a scroll.

"You take the mission from the board and pass it to the people at the desk. They make sure you have the right qualifications and give you the mission and any associated information. Some missions have a requirement for a party to complete. The terminals show missions that one can apply to from other mission halls."

Erik saw a woman toss out papers. Mana pulled on the nails embedded in the wall. The papers and scrolls rested in place before the nails drove home.

People cast sight enhancement and moved closer, checking on the new missions.

A few people snatched missions and headed to the desk, grinning at their good fortune and quick eyes.

"The clans and bigger groups of the Seventh Realm rely on trade agreements and alliances. But sometimes they don't have the right alliances and need a few things, or they don't want to admit they're weak and hire on the Mission Hall to take care of issues. There are also plenty of people that make it to the Seventh Realm but have little in the way of backing. The Mission Hall is a protection and where one can find employment," Racquel said.

"Okay, so, mission then?" Erik asked.

Rugrat glanced at the board. "Why don't we each get a mission and check which one we want to do?"

"This is the starless floor. Most people without a star rating are called nulls. We need to go upstairs to get One-Star missions," Fred said.

"What's the difference?" Erik asked.

"Missions down here can be accepted by anyone as long as they've placed a deposit. If they complete enough missions, they'll become a null star and can take missions that allows them to increase their level and become a One-Star Hero." Fred led them across the busy hall to a group of teleportation pads of copper, silver, gold, and crystal.

He took them toward the copper. Their medallions glowed once they stepped on the teleportation pad. The light settled down as they found themselves in a room nearly identical to the first, but a third of the size and with only a few dozen people instead of hundreds.

"Well, this is a bit easier," Rugrat said.

"Take a look around and see the different mission types. Those are for healing and for crafting weapons and concoctions." Fred indicated to the boards.

The group broke apart. Erik went by himself toward the healing board and mused over the different issues. Some people were trying to open more of their mana gates. They had progressed quickly through their cultivation and were trying to reinforce their cultivation. It would be much harder, even if they opened their mana gates. The mana channels hadn't had the kind of mana flowing through them as the rest of the body. It would be so easy for the mana channels to take in too much mana and burst.

He moved through the board looking at the requests.

"Anything Interesting?" Reaper startled Erik.

"Ah, yes, most of them are related to cultivation. There are some that have physical issues. While they might have started or manifested in the body, I think most of them are related to cultivation."

Erik looked around, seeing only a few healers. At the alchemy board there were nearly three times as many alchemists and they were pulling missions off quickly.

"Alchemy is much easier to deal with," Reaper said.

"Did Fred find us some missions?" Erik asked.

"Yes, he sent me over here to get you."

"All right, let's go see what choices we have."

They chose a table out of the way of the mission boards to go through their options.

"Okay, I picked out four missions. One is the retrieval of a book in a haunted caster's keep. The client wants the book. Anything else we find is ours. There is a tear near a city, and the city has issued a mission to close the tear."

"How do you close a tear?" Erik asked.

"You have to break through the creatures and put down a formation near the tear and defend against attacks as the formation closes the tear. There is a group requirement of ten. We would need to match up with four other One-Stars. Some missions have a minimum party size." Racquel shrugged.

"Okay, so something else to start?"

"Probably best," Fred said. "A party from the Mission Hall has gone missing in Kralea dungeon. They were null's, but they were looking into possible dungeon raiders along a resource trade route. Anyone else?"

"A new part of a combat dungeon that has opened. They want us to map it out and they'll pay us for the map. Probably be combat and dungeon creatures," Dromm said.

"Getting a book from a tower sounds kind of easy," Rugrat said.

"Kind of. There are supposed to be all kinds of creatures of the dark in the area. We would have to sneak or kill them all to get to the tower, and there's no telling what kind of traps are along the way before we can get to this book."

"Well, we know dungeons and those people that went missing could use our help," Dromm said.

"I agree. We joined the Mission Hall for their protection. Shouldn't we help out others when we can?" Reaper said.

Erik and Rugrat looked at one another.

"We're in."

Fred looked at Racquel, who nodded.

"Very well." Fred tossed the other missions in the air, and they flew back to the wall.

They walked up to the counter. Fred took off his medallion and presented it to the lady there. She put the medallion into one formation and the mission into another that showed lines of information.

"This is a time sensitive mission; you must set out within the next twenty-four hours." She looked up at Fred.

"We understand."

She nodded and looked past him. "Medallions visible, please."

They held out their medallions. She activated the formation again, casting a spell that streamed out to their medallions.

"You are all registered with the mission now." She pulled out Fred's medallion and handed it back to him.

Quest: The Missing Adventurers
Searching for possible raiders in the Kraela dungeon, a party of adventurers have gone missing.
Requirements:
Report to the Mission Hall once you know their condition unless they are in danger. In that case, you are to do everything in your power to recover them and bring them back to the Mission Hall.
Rewards:
+100,000,000 EXP +1 star mission Rewards may be increased based on performance

A teleportation formation on the counter flashed, revealing two scrolls that she pushed across the table.

"Thank you." Fred took them both and gestured at some rooms away from the mission hall.

Racquel led the way as Fred stored one scroll, pulling out his map and touching it to the second scroll. His map populated with information, lines sprawling across it to create roads, towns, and cities.

They entered an empty room, and he put the map down. Reaper moved to it with his map, copying the information.

Fred pulled out the second scroll and started reading as Erik and the others updated their maps. He scanned through the pertinent information and shifted the scroll to the side for the others.

Erik read through the information as Fred talked.

"It looks like the leader of the adventurer group was a guard. He went to the area to hunt down bandits. His sister and young son were killed. He gathered a group of others who were angry with the bandits, and they tracked down and killed different groups in the Azraadale area. They had just taken down a hidden bandit stronghold and were aiming to head to the Mission Hall to get their One-Star emblem when something made them head out hunting again. They activated an emergency token inside the Kralea dungeon. Their friends and the Mission Hall have been unable to contact them since. So, now a mission has been raised," Fred said.

"We head to Kralea dungeon, find out where the adventurers are, and bring them back home. Time since the alert?" Erik asked.

"A day," Fred said.

"Damn." Rugrat clicked his tongue and frowned.

A day since they sent out an alert. Not good.

"I suggest that we leave as soon as possible and see if we can save them from whatever is happening. Has anyone not copied the map?"

Fred's hand hovered over it before he picked it up and stored it. "First, we'll head to the city Azraadale and then onto this dungeon." They followed Fred out of the library and through a teleportation pad.

Sounds rushed in as they found themselves within an underground city. There were taverns and random stores dotted around the area. In the middle was a large totem with defensive walls around it. People streamed in and out of the gates, walking into the city from their adventures, or leaving on their next, disappearing and appearing across tens of teleportation formations around the totem.

Fred led them toward the totem. Racquel grinned; Erik and Rugrat's eyes were wide as they looked around.

"These are the training facilities, homes, inns and taverns of the Cronen City Mission Hall. If you go down one level or through the teleportation pads, you can get to the other halls that we saw earlier," Racquel said.

"What about the stores?" Rugrat asked.

"How do they keep going? With the Mission Hall's own stores?" Racquel said.

"Yeah."

"The Mission Hall supplies standard equipment. If you want something custom or special, you need to come to these stores. Also, the Mission Hall doesn't sell food or drink, or sleeping quarters. All of this makes up for the things the Mission Hall lacks."

Fred walked them over to a stall near the totem with realm guides on a signboard above.

"Hello, we need a guide to Kralea Dungeon or Azraadale," Fred said to the man behind the counter. The man nodded and used a formation and a sound transmission device.

"Guide should be here in a minute. Will be ten Sky mana stones," the man said.

Fred passed the mana stones.

"Good doing business with you."

A man ran over from a nearby café moments later and talked to the man at the counter.

"You need to go to Azraadale?" the new arrival asked.

"Nothing closer to Kralea?" Fred asked.

"No. Traders still use carts in the area. It's still rural."

"Okay," Fred said.

The guide nodded and led them through the defenses around the totem.

Erik studied the guards. Men and women walked around, runic and line tattoos stretched across their bodies. Around the totem stood metal statues covered in runes.

"Those statues?" Erik elbowed Rugrat, feeling the power coming off of them.

"Golems, strong ones. They're made from enhanced Sky metal. I can't see all that deeply into them," Rugrat said.

They passed through and reached the totem, where a flood of people came and went.

"Stones?" the guide asked.

Fred passed him the sky mana stones.

The guide used the totem. The stones collapsed, the pure mana draining into the totem before light wrapped around the group.

Erik felt the breeze, the smell of fresh rain. Wet wood and mud mixed with the chill of night and stone.

It was early morning in Azraadale, the world washed clean with rain.

Grey stone inscribed with runes formed the totem.

"Welcome to Azraadale. You can get a carriage to the dungeon from the western gate. It should get you there in a few minutes," the guide said. He disappeared in another flash.

Fred led the way to the lines of people that were leaving the totem. They passed through with a flash of their emblems into the lit city. Mage lights illuminated the roads as people moved through the streets, going about their jobs.

There was a lack of towers, but there were several large buildings that reminded Erik of warehouses.

"So, like, how strong are kids that grow up here?" Rugrat asked as they walked along the sidewalk to the west, following the procession of people traveling in the same direction.

"They have more open mana gates than those in the lower realms and have Body Like Stone upon birth," Fred said.

"At birth?" Erik asked.

"Yes. Mana, while it is powerful, is also destructive. With so much mana around, it tempers the body. As children are formed in the womb, they're tempered from the base up. Open more mana gates, higher body cultivation and mana cultivation."

Erik sunk into thought as they kept walking.

Azraadale wasn't on the same scale as Cronen City. It acted as a resource hub and a city of trade; caravans of carts and carriages moved through the streets.

Erik saw an airship rise in the north. Its formations glowed with power, creating eddies in the surrounding mana, distorting the air. Sails ran out across the ship, catching the early morning wind, setting off toward their next city.

"There are a lot of people around for it being so early," Erik said.

"Everyone in this realm is at least level sixty. How high do you think their stamina regeneration is? The Seventh Realm doesn't sleep," Reaper said.

It didn't take them much longer before they reached the Western gate.

A large square lay just inside the wall. Caravan owners offered safe travel to dungeons, other villages, and cities to all manner of people without the funds for aerial travel or heading to a place that didn't have it.

"I've got it." Dromm waded into the groups.

"Okay, so what's the plan?" Erik asked.

"They were last located in Vativa outpost. We go there, wander around, and see if we can find any clues as to why they were there and what they were doing there." Fred shrugged.

"What do we know about the mission they were on?" Erik asked.

"They were tracking down raiders that have been plaguing these trade routes. Kraela produces Striped Redweed, a powerful stimulant that can increase one's reaction speed and mental faculties. It is highly addictive because of the enhanced speed. The raiders have been targeting these shipments primarily," Fred said.

"So they came in and went to the places where it was being

produced?"

"No. They hid in the caravans and waited. Then they would spring their own attacks and hunt down the raiders. At first, they simply killed them. With time, the caravans they were on were no longer attacked. They had to switch tactics. People knew them, and the raiders were learning of it."

"Spies among the traders or the population?" Erik said.

"Yes, they thought that this wasn't a small issue, but a much larger one. Instead of killing all the raiders, they pulled information from them. It led them to a stronghold. They killed everyone inside. There haven't been any raids since."

Dromm returned to the group.

"Okay, I got us a ride to Vativa. Ready?"

The group nodded and followed Dromm.

They headed out of the city. The ground had been cleared, a large ten-cart wide road leading off into the distance. There were caravans waiting outside the city in large squares. They were transferring their cargo to smaller city-going wagons.

Dromm led them to a group of carriages and held up a slip of paper to a guard around the square.

"Cart four," the man grunted as he scanned them with his eyes and looked toward the city with boredom.

They reached the carriage, where people were clambering up.

Erik smelt a medicinal air around them. He frowned as he climbed up into the carriage. Each person inside had a distinct smell that marked them as an alchemist. Their concoction fumes had infused their clothes. They were wiry and pale, having spent weeks, months or even years preparing ingredients and creating concoctions.

"Huh, just like back in the day. Guess transport trucks never really change much between carriages and troop transports," Rugrat said.

"I just hope this one has better suspension. Damn, I thought the thing was going to flip every time we were in it." Erik sat down next to one of the passengers. "What takes you to Vativa?" he asked.

The man looked him over. "Striped Redweed." The man frowned as Erik heard the silent *of course*.

"You going to turn it into pills, powders?"

"No." The man shook his head, knitting his eyebrows. "I'm a Journeyman alchemist, so I'm just harvesting the plant. Only Expert alchemists are trusted with using the Striped Redweed as an ingredient."

"Oh." Erik nodded. Journeyman alchemists as laborers; the jump from the Mortal Realms to the Earth Realms wasn't anything compared to the jump from Earth to Sky Realms.

"Next stop, Vativa Outpost," the driver said as he put up the rear gate, securing them in the back of the carriage.

A few minutes later, they headed away from Azraadale and onto the road.

The carriage jolted as it got onto the road.

"Just like with the sidewalks, the roads are enchanted. With so much ambient mana, they don't need to be refilled with mana stones," Reaper said.

Erik was glad they were using their sound transmission devices to talk or else he'd feel really stupid not knowing the basics of the Seventh Realm. He looked through a slit in the carriage covering as they sped down the road. The beasts stomped along, used to the speed.

"Shit." Erik shook his head and waved Rugrat to look out through the slit. Rugrat leaned over.

"Crap, must be moving well over a hundred kilometers an hour."

"Beast power beats horsepower," Erik said as he shifted in his armor, putting his hands over one another in the top of his armor, letting his arms hang.

Erik turned his head, pushing it against the materials so he could see out of the carriage. A road branched off from their own. He could see a fort of stone at the end of it.

Rugrat, Dromm, and Reaper discussed something as Racquel sat back to sleep. Fred pulled out a book and started reading.

They passed several other roads before they turned on one. The caravan slowed on the side road as they reached the gates of a stone keep.

The guards talked to the traders, accepted a token, and allowed them past.

Through the walls lay a small town. There were warehouses, stables, and carriages in many places. Taverns, inns, and crafters that supported the traders dotted the side of the road.

The caravan moved down the wide main road to a second, thicker wall. Another check and they passed through the second set of walls. The road sloped down and into the ground, mage lights illuminating the path ahead as other caravans and carriages came out from the depths.

They headed into the ground. The smell of earth and stone dust made Erik sneeze.

"Thicker elements," Erik said.

"Earth, water, and some wood, hints of metal." Fred moved his mouth around as if tasting the air.

"Well, it is a dungeon," Rugrat said.

Their speed picked up as they descended. The tunnel opened into a massive cavern. The ceiling glowed with green, blues, and pinks. On either side of the road were glowing dots to illuminate the road like a runway.

Plants growing like grapevines stretched out along the road, covering kilometers. The ground was perfectly smooth, leading toward a town in the distance. It lay in the middle of the vineyard that extended in every direction.

"Looks like we're almost there." Erik looked across the vineyards and cast Eagle Sight. He spotted smaller stone defenses at the limits of the cavern, blocking off the entrances to the rest of the dungeon.

Alchemists used their tools confidently, trimming the plants, harvesting their wood. Erik only saw a few in the nearby fields, but they stretched out into the distance without end.

Formations activated in the ceiling, releasing rain.

Erik used his sight to look at the posts holding up the vines, reaching out with his domain to sense the changes in elements. Even the supporting posts were carved with formations to help the plants grow. *This is ingredient growing on a massive scale.*

They reached the town in a matter of minutes, coming to park in another square.

The driver came around and opened the rear of the carriage.

"Welcome to Vativa." He moved out of the way. "Watch your step when getting out of the carriage."

They dismounted and headed toward the gates.

Another check by the guards, and a small fee, and they were inside Vativa Outpost. There were taverns, a few with inns attached. Apartments built from stone housed alchemists that worked in the outpost. Warehouses stored and finished preparing the Striped Redweed before it was sold to the traders.

"Reminds me of those gold rush towns. Everything here is built around growing and harvesting Redweed," Rugrat said.

"Dungeons are the main area of industry for the Seventh Realm.

These ingredients will be shipped to Expert alchemists and turned into the final concoction before being sold to clans and sects," Fred said.

"Do they not care about the fact it's a drug?" Erik asked.

"Drug?" Reaper asked.

"You know, something you take that changes the body."

"Like concoctions?" Reaper frowned.

"Well, there are good ones and bad ones. Drugs that you take and then want them all the time to get that feeling again," Erik said.

"Those seem useless. There might be some that use those," Reaper said.

"Isn't this Redweed kind of like that? It gives you a momentary boost, hooks you, and then you want it all the time?"

"Yes, but you can take another concoction to clear it out of your system. If you could increase how fast you could react and move, wouldn't you? You level up. Isn't part of leveling up to get stronger?"

Erik was stumped and shook his head. "So, this Redweed is good?"

"Sure, if someone is thinking over a problem, a commander overseeing a battle, this can be a key ingredient in increasing the speed of their thoughts. Even people in a fight, just like any buff," Reaper said.

"Though, like your conqueror's armor, if you buff people well beyond what their bodies can take, it can have a negative effect that you have to work to counteract," Fred interjected.

"Makes sense," Erik said.

"Where should we go to find out more about this group?" Rugrat asked.

"Who would you talk to if you heard there was an attack in the area?" Racquel asked.

"Guards," the group said as one and turned toward the nearest guard tower.

"Well, best get started," Fred said.

"If we can get them talking, I can watch them, ask them a few yes or no questions for me to get a baseline. Then I can see if their heartbeat increases, or if they start to sweat or release different hormones," Erik said.

"You can do that?" Rugrat said.

"Yeah."

"We can do the same," Raquel said.

"Wait, what?"

"Well, we are beasts first. Our senses of smell, hearing, and sight are better than you humans and we're all a bit stronger." Dromm grinned.

"Great, so I am working with a group of walking lie detectors," Rugrat said.

Using their emblems, they quickly got to the guard captain on duty.

"Hello! The name is Verrick. How can I help you today?" he asked as they walked into his office.

"You are the captain of the guards here?" Fred asked, leading the questioning. The others remained behind him, using their senses and spells to analyze the captain.

"Uhh, yes. Why?"

"Just wanted to confirm. Have you been here long?"

"Yes, two decades now," Verrick said.

"Many beast waves here?"

"No, the dungeon is calm. Prefers to create plants instead of beasts. The Redweed fields keep the elemental mana low, so the dungeon doesn't use it to spawn beasts."

"We heard there were some raids happening in the area. We're going out tomorrow to hunt down the raiders. We were wondering if you'd heard anything about them?"

"There are always desperate people who want to steal from hard workers." Verrick sighed and shook his head.

"Do you have a record of any raids in the area?"

"No. If something happens within our borders, between the entrance walls into the dungeon and out to Azraadale, then we keep records. Beyond there, it's the Ubren clan's domain."

"Do you know who might know more?"

"You should check with Miss Mercia. She is Vativa's biggest seller of Redweed. She knows nearly all the trading companies. Supplies most of them, too. She has holdings in other outposts, too. She'll know more."

"Where might we find her?"

"Got a map?"

Verrick put down a marker on Fred's map, and a notification appeared.

Quest: The Missing Adventurers

> Searching for possible raiders in the Kraela dungeon, a party of adventurers have gone missing.

Requirements:

> Report to the Mission Hall once you know their condition unless they are in danger. In that case, you are to do everything in your power to recover them and bring them back to the Mission Hall.
>
> Talk to Mercia. She should have more information on the missing adventurers.

Rewards:

> +100,000,000 EXP
>
> +1 star mission
>
> Rewards may be increased based on performance.

"Thank you," Fred said.

"No problem. Have a good day."

They left the tower and headed toward the marker the captain had placed.

Erik broke the silence once they reached the street. "Either he is an incredible liar or has some help. But I don't think he knows anything about this."

"I agree," Dromm said.

"Well, on to Mercia then."

Mercia's estate was fenced off, with a garden setting the house back from the roads and giving the residents privacy.

Ten minutes later, they stood outside Mercia's office. A door opened and a short pale woman and a taller man with tanned features and a thick beard and turban walked out.

"Well, I wish you good luck on your travels, Fernandes. You're lucky we got a bumper harvest last month," the woman, Mercia, said.

"Your alchemists are the best in Kralea. The others can't seem to grow more than their stated quota. Really, it is only a matter of time until you take over all of Kralea."

"I just own one small plot of many."

"I will not keep you. I wish you a good day and will see you soon." Fernandes shook her hand and passed Erik's group.

"How may I help you?" Mercia asked.

"We heard that there were some raids in the area and came to check it out. We heard that you have a lot of farms and may know more about the situation on the roads," stated Fred.

"I only know a little. I'll do what I can to help heroes of the Mission Hall." She smiled, but the vein along her neck pulsated faster. Beads of sweat appeared on her hands, and her pupils dilated.

Oh, that's interesting.

They headed into the office. Once inside, Mercia moved to a pot of tea and opened the covering.

Erik smelled the tea.

Calming properties. This could hide her signs.

"Thank you for the offer. We cannot stay long," Erik interrupted.

Fred looked at Erik, then back to Mercia. "I am sorry for his outburst. We can, of course, stay a short time," Fred said.

Mercia laughed and lowered the lid on the teapot. "It's not a problem."

Erik watched her closely.

"Do you know where these raiders might be?" Fred asked before she had time to pause.

"I'm not sure. Otherwise, I would head over there with my own caravan guards and teach them a thing or two."

That's a lie.

"Have you been trading in Redweed for a long time?"

She poured herself a cup of tea. "I hope you do not mind," she said. "Yes, my grandparents started the first farm; my parents expanded it and I took over with my brother."

Anger?

"Though he died some time ago."

Some truth, some not.

"Do you know where a good place to start looking might be?"

She faced away. "I heard that a group of raiders were slaughtered a few weeks ago. I think that was the last of them."

I can't get a reading on her.

"Do you think that is the end of raiders and bandits in the area?" Fred asked as she turned and drank from her cup.

"No. Where there are high-priced goods, there will always be people that want to take them for their own use. It is the Seventh Realm. As you, from the Mission Hall, know. Power is everything. If you do not have it, then you'll be crushed under it."

She looked right into Fred's eyes, then looked away and shrugged.

She's hiding something. Erik kept his expression neutral.

"Thank you for your time. While *some* —" Fred looked at Erik. "— want to rush off, we must make sure that we know everything about these bandits before we try to find them."

"No problem. Whatever I can do to help."

"Thank you." Fred bowed his head and turned to the group, heading out of the room. A stout man stood outside the door with several others. They were all wearing clothing that made them look like laborers.

Erik felt their eyes on him, studying and assessing them.

These guys have killed before.

"I could do with another beer," Dromm said.

"Or four," Rugrat said.

"One tavern to another with you," Racquel said as they walked down the corridor. Using his domain, Erik could see the group turning and watching them as they left.

"Ding Rong, get in here," Mercia said from her office.

The group of fighters walked into Mercia's room. Formations activated, stopping Erik from learning what they were talking about.

"That lady is holding onto secrets," Erik said, as they left the building.

"Yeah, she was using the tea to calm herself and smooth out her response. Once she drank it, I couldn't read her anymore," Racquel said.

Quest: The Missing Adventurers
Searching for possible raiders in the Kraela dungeon, a party of adventurers have gone missing.
Requirements:
Report to the Mission Hall once you know their condition unless they are in danger. In that case, you are to do everything in your power to recover them and bring them back to the Mission Hall. You sense that Mercia has not told you the entire truth, investigate more.
Rewards:
+100,000,000 EXP +1 star mission Rewards may be increased based on performance.

"We should follow her or get into her study and see if we can find any information," Reaper said.

"People like that don't keep records in their office. No, if I were her, I'd be getting my guard dog to carry out any tasks I didn't want to be linked to. She can cut him away and say he was acting on his own if it goes sideways," Rugrat said.

"And that group that was waiting outside. I'd wager they were there in case something went wrong."

"All right, we'll see what we can find out in the taverns and with the people working here. Erik, Rugrat, do you want to find out who those guys are and see if you can figure out how Mercia is connected to all this?" Fred asked.

"Oorah," Rugrat said.

"I was hoping that tendency stopped when we crossed over into the realms. You know, gaining the ability to read came with it?" Erik said.

Rugrat rolled his eyes and sighed. "I word good!"

Erik grinned. "Okay, meet up at the gate we came in through tonight if we don't find anything, but use the sound transmission devices if you find out anything of value."

They nodded and broke apart.

"So, how do we find out how this lady is connected?" Rugrat asked as they walked away from Mercia's office.

"We follow the minions. You spot any good vantage points?"

"Oh yeah. That building over there just has workers in it and a view of the entire house. Anything comes out, we'll see it." Rugrat nodded toward a worker apartment. It was a simple building made of stone and replicated to create blocks of housing.

They looped around the building and walked up to the front, waiting for someone to come out before they slipped inside. They jogged up the stairs, which were empty because everyone used the formation elevators.

Rugrat cut a hole in the roof and Erik jumped through it and landed in a squat.

"Clear," he whispered, forgetting his sound transmission device would cut out his voice, anyway.

Rugrat jumped the three meters vertically. With their strength, jumping wasn't much of a challenge anymore.

They got down on their bellies, moved to the edge of the building, and looked down on Mercia's building.

"I'll take left and front, you take back and right?" Erik said.

"Oorah, brother."

"Is this a phase I need to know about?" asked Erik as he cast Eagle Sight, looking along the sides and front of the house. They faced the left side of the mansion, with the gardens to Erik's right and the dirt patch area, where carts and carriages brought in food stuffs and supplies out back.

"Nah, just been some time. It's nice to go back to it. Been holding myself back from saying it for a bit now. Didn't want to say it in front of the troops and get them all confused like."

"You are a marine, man. They won't care," Erik said. "Makes you, you."

Rugrat was quiet for some time before he grunted. "Once a marine, always a marine, oorah?"

"Army Strong."

"Urgh, didn't momma teach you to not swear like that in public?"

"You giving me a lesson about not swearing in public? Wait," Erik saw a door open on the side of the house with people moving out. He focused his sight on the group.

"Well, hello, Ding-something."

"Rong."

"That's it." Erik scanned the group as Ding Rong gave them instructions. They headed off in different directions.

"Shit, they're splitting up."

"Don't worry, we'll wait and see. You watch big Dong and I'll scan and check up on his minions."

"Really?"

Silence greeted Erik.

Ding Rong did a loop around the house, scanned the street, talked to the gate guards, then looped back around to the rear and into some stables.

"Shit, he's in the stables. Can't see him. Got scrying formations blocking me."

"Just keep watching; he's gotta come out at some point. Make sure you're looking for height and body language. Keep your eyes fresh. All the guys he sent out went into the city or are patrolling the walls. I'm going to watch the building again."

"Got it."

Erik scanned right to left and picked out different points around the stable to look at.

"I have a beaten-up cart hooked up to an old beast. Male, unknown, leading it toward the house. He's wearing a cloak and a doupeng," Rugrat said.

Erik kept scanning the stable and looked closer at the man leading the animal.

"Dude, I don't see anyone else wearing straw hats or cloaks in here. Only place it rains is out in the fields. Why would there be an alchemist hanging out in their stable?" Rugrat said.

"Keeping an eye on him and the stable."

Erik split between watching the stable and the cart that stopped near the house. A woman wearing servant's clothes walked out to the cart and got on the riding bench.

"You see that?" Erik asked.

"Yeah, wait one." Rugrat pulled out a tube with formations and looked through it. "Yeah, that's Mercia. Skin's pale as anything, same height."

"If she goes, how do we track them? It's morning here. Lights coming up," Erik glanced at the moss that glowed brighter, creating a daytime. The formations over the fields had lit up with artificial sunlight.

"Semper Fi, my dude." Rugrat raised his hand, mana flowing between his fingers.

"What trick you got up your sleeve?"

"Tracking spell, baby," Rugrat said. "You watch the area. I'll hit them with it."

"They aren't going to notice?"

"Not if I target their cart and they're outside the mansion with its formation enhanced walls."

They waited as the cart left the mansion. Rugrat readied his spell and cast it. Erik saw a splash of green in a spell formation on the rear of the cart as the woman looked behind giving Erik a full view.

"Oh yeah, that's her all right. Though she looked back for the spell."

"Well either they sense it, or they don't." Rugrat shrugged.

"Where was the confidence from before where you said they wouldn't sense it?"

"That was ten seconds ago, man. Can't be holding onto the past like that. Come on, we've got some tracking to do." Rugrat got up and crouch walked back to the hole in the ceiling.

"Shit, much easier than tracking deer through brush."

They fixed up the ceiling and followed the tracking mark on their map.

"Hey, guys and gals, Miss Mercia left her mansion. Rugrat and I are tracking her and her right-hand guy. Gonna see what they're up to."

"Track 'em down and get them to reveal everything?" Reaper said.

"Something like that. I'm thinking more like we restrain them, hit them with a contract so they have to tell the truth," Erik said.

"Why not do that in her office?" Racquel asked.

"Got all her people around. Don't want to get into a fight in the middle of an outpost we don't know." Erik looked at Rugrat who glanced down at the map on the inside of his wrist. "*Just* yet."

"Give us a marker and we'll head toward you," Fred said.

Erik put down a map marker and shared it. "Make sure you aren't followed. They sent out more people and I don't know where they went or what they're doing."

"We'll be safe," Dromm said.

Erik and Rugrat left the building, heading in the direction their map showed the tracking symbol.

Erik scanned the roads between warehouses as a cart disappeared from sight. He waved his hand to Rugrat who ran and jumped, launching himself onto the stone warehouse wall with an irate fire-wolf-scarf. Mana materialized around him, sticking into the wall, hauling Rugrat and George up the side.

"I'm up." Rugrat's voice came through Erik's ear as he glanced up. Rugrat had disappeared.

Erik moved from where he had been standing, walking through the warehouse district. He had ditched the glasses and cap to blend in. He reached the street where there were people working on loading a cart. They all looked over. Erik stumbled for the wall making heaving noises and dropping food out of his storage ring.

The loaders looked over to him.

"Ughh, damn dungeon dwellers. Bunch of drunks," one of the loaders said.

"Hey!" another growled.

"Shut up, the two of you," a foreman snapped, coming out of the warehouse with a clipboard. "Get out of here before I have my boys throw you out!"

Erik waved his hand at them. He staggered and dry heaved again.

"You're a terrible actor, but I'm on the other roof," Rugrat said.

Jackass.

Erik staggered away from the street, wiping his mouth. He made it around the corner. Seeing no one, he straightened and continued on his path.

"Okay," Rugrat said. "I've got a good position over where they stopped. Looks like a regular warehouse, bit more reinforced." Rugrat paused. "Make that a lot more reinforced. It blends in well, but this place is built like a bomb shelter; sound canceling formations, reinforcing formations."

"Weaknesses?"

"The roof, reinforced, but no alarms like there are on the ground."

"You got a sight line into the place?"

"I can see heat signatures; that's about it. Can't hear anything."

A cart trundled up the road ahead to Erik's left, heading to his right.

"Might have incoming," Erik said.

"I've got a few moving carts. Looks like this just got complicated."

"We've reached the latest map marker," Fred said.

"One sec. I'll find a secure location and we can meet there," Erik said.

"Check this warehouse out." Rugrat put down a marker. "It looks like it's in use, but it has barely anything in it. I'm guessing Miss Mercia didn't want many people in the area."

Erik turned up the street and headed for the warehouse a row away from the one Mercia and Ding Rong were in.

"I've got two carts coming toward the warehouse from different directions. They look like fighters."

Great.

Erik checked the warehouse Rugrat had talked about. He scanned the walls and ground, seeing the alarm formations. He checked around, backed up, took a starting run, and jumped toward the wall. Reaching out with his domain, he pushed it into the wall and to the side, creating an opening. He solidified the ambient mana, creating solid squares of mana under his feet. He stumbled, catching himself on the solid mana and closed the wall, returning it back to its original condition. Erik looked around for traps.

Where are you? He walked several feet above the ground, his domain spread out. There was one power convergence, which might be where the formations' power was coming from. *But I'd have a backup.*

Erik wandered through the warehouse taking note of every location where mana gathered and concentrated.

"Okay, the carts are nearing the location. They circled around. Three more coming in. Looks like a party," Rugrat said.

"Okay," Erik said, distracted by an odd flow of mana. "Hey, Rugrat, these formations, they use the ambient mana, right?"

"Yeah, easier and cheaper."

"Thought so, thanks."

Erik looked at the points where the mana was being pulled.

Okay, so one main backup power source, three separate power draws, and two points of power convergence.

He closed his eyes. Spears of mana appeared around him. His domain spread out across the warehouse.

"Put a silence spell on the building first," Rugrat said.

"Good idea." Erik raised his hand. A white and black spell appeared in his hand before he released it against the warehouse wall. It faded into the building as Erik sensed it spreading through the brickwork.

He waited for it to cover the entire building. It took a serious amount of mana for one cast.

Erik breathed out. The spears shot out, cutting through a small office in the corner of the warehouse and several points across the warehouse. The mana in the area became erratic, the normal flow changing. Erik drew in all the mana from his domain. Mana vapor and mist were drawn from the ground and spilled out from the formations as Erik, with his powerful cultivation, sucked up all the surrounding mana.

The flaring formations dimmed, powerless.

"Might set off an alarm, might not. Wait one." Erik released the mana under his feet, dropping to the ground below.

He looked around, his eyes glowing as he looked through the dead formations, through the warehouse, checking to see if there was a flare of any anomalous mana.

"Okay, looks like we're all good. I'm at Rugrat's map marker."

"We will be there in a few minutes," Fred said.

Rugrat perched on a flat warehouse roof that gave him a vantage of the target warehouse's southeast corner.

Old mugs, blocks of stone used for chairs, and the litter of a long-forgotten break area spread across the roof. A square protrusion that was sealed up and locked led down to the warehouse below. George remained near the stairs.

Rugrat had raised some stone from the roof, using it as a perch for the beast, giving him a vantage over the knee-high warehouse wall.

"Carts are lined up along the southern side of the warehouse." Rugrat checked out each of the five carts. The riders headed into the building as soon as they arrived. They made sure to secure their beasts before they moved to the eastern side where the other drivers had gathered.

"We're all in the warehouse now," Erik said.

Rugrat watched the drivers. One pulled out a pipe and lit it. Others pulled out stools.

Rugrat glanced at the warehouse Erik and the others were in. They were one row of warehouses over to the south, but to the west of the warehouse where Mercia and her fighters were gathering.

"Got it. The riders are going into the warehouse and the drivers are hanging around. I'll listen in on them."

Rugrat pulled out a Focused Hearing spell scroll and activated it. The spell disappeared into his body. As his ears opened, he heard people moving around and breathing in Erik's warehouse.

He turned his focus to the drivers.

"All this waiting around is getting annoying." One of the drivers spat on the ground.

"What does it matter if we're getting paid?" another asked, sitting on a chair and clearing out his pipe.

"You might be okay with it. You got that juicy trader before those adventurers started attacking us."

The other drivers grumbled and muttered.

"Fucking righteous pricks."

"I heard that they were going to get their star. Then they got a tip off," a woman carving a piece of wood with her knife said.

"A tip off? Wait, they're still here?" the first driver asked.

"You think the boss will let this go? After what they did? They killed her brother." A man with red tattoos down the right side of his face sat back in his stool.

The man who had cleaned out his pipe lit it, creating a halo of smoke. "If they got their stars, no saying they wouldn't be back." He released the flame from between his fingers and grabbed the bowl of the pipe as he puffed. "We can't do anything against One-Star Heroes, not with the protection the Mission Hall gives them. Adventurers, bah, easy targets."

"You think?" the first driver asked.

The woman paused her carving. "The boss didn't get to where she is by being merciful."

"Shit, they're adventurers." The man started pacing.

"Calm yourself, Serix," the red tattooed man said. "Not like adventurers haven't disappeared before."

"Yeah, but there's a group of One-Stars here now," Serix snapped.

The others paused.

"What are they here for?" the last person of their group, a young woman asked.

Serix grimaced as the others pulled back from her. "Heard from the guards that they were asking about raiders in the area."

The group went quiet.

They all shifted and looked east. Rugrat changed his point of aim, seeing the riders coming out.

"Get over here, stop lazing about!" a man growled.

The drivers broke up and quickly moved to their carts.

"All right," Rugrat said. "Looks like Mercia is linked to the bandits. I think she might be the leader. The adventurers were hunting them down. She might have put out information to bring them back here and into her outpost. The bandits are leaving. Should only be Mercia and Ding Rong." Rugrat used the modified heat spell. His eyes glowed with a cold blue as he looked through the walls of the building. Two people were inside the building facing one another.

Rugrat scanned again.

"Okay, the carts are away. Get ready to jump on Mercia and Ding."

Quest: The Missing Adventurers
Searching for possible raiders in the Kraela dungeon, a party of adventurers have gone missing.
Requirements:
Report to the Mission Hall once you know their condition unless they are in danger. In that case, you are to do everything in your power to recover them and bring them back to the Mission Hall.

> Mercia and Ding Rong are connected to the Bandits in the area. Find out what they know about the missing Adventurers.
>
> **Rewards:**
> +100,000,000 EXP
> +1 star mission
> Rewards may be increased based on performance.

Rugrat dismissed the quest update and watched the carts hurry away from the warehouse district.

"We need Mercia and Ding alive," Erik said.

"Agreed."

He was just under two hundred meters away.

Rugrat put the beast away and pulled out his M8. He checked that the silencing formation carved muzzle break was attached, made sure that it was loaded, and the magazine had NL he'd written on its side. *Non-lethals.*

He aimed through the scope and adjusted his positioning. He scanned the warehouse Mercia and Ding, finding their heat signatures as they were walking out of the warehouse.

"They're coming out and going for the cart. What do you want me to do?" Rugrat asked.

"You got non-lethals?" Erik said.

"Loaded."

"Okay, tell us when they're moving the cart around. That should trap them in. You signal when you're firing. We'll go after a three count and make sure the rounds worked. Everyone good?"

"Good to go," Dromm said.

"Yup," Rugrat agreed.

"We're ready here, Rugrat. On your call," Erik said.

Rugrat was working on his breathing now, clearing as he felt the wind against his skin.

Dead in here. Higher humidity. Neither should play a factor at this distance.

Rugrat watched the two of them walk out to their cart. They looked around before climbing up.

Ding took the reins, clicking his tongue as he pulled back on the animal's reins. The beast started to back up.

Rugrat shifted from left to right, between both.

He aimed at their backs, casting silence on the rounds.

Ding stopped the animal from moving backward.

"Go." Rugrat fired as he breathed the word. He changed his point of aim to Mercia and fired again.

He let out the rest of his breath, scanning.

The impact of the round had thrown Ding forward, leaving him folded over his own legs.

Mercia was lethargic. A faint purple smoke hung around them as she looked at Ding and tried to get off the cart.

Rugrat fired again. She flopped to the side. He saw the flash of the stun spell. The poison coating turned into a puff of purple smoke as the silence spell canceled the noise from the duo. She went boneless, hanging off the cart.

Erik and the rest of the team ran across the street while Rugrat scanned both sides of the road, looking for movement.

He saw a cart pass far down the street.

Rugrat aimed at them. The driver looked over but kept going. Rugrat didn't see a change in his bored expression as the older man sighed and flicked his reins. Out for something to do, continuing on with the day's tasks.

Rugrat lowered his rifle and scanned.

"They're both out cold. I've given them something to keep them that way. We'll move back to the other warehouse," Erik said.

"Okay, be quick about it."

Erik and Dromm grabbed the duo. Racquel and Reaper watched. Fred got up on the cart, turned it around, and took it down the street.

Erik opened the wall to the abandoned warehouse, running through the gap with Dromm. Fred and the cart moved through after them. Racquel and Reaper went last. The wall closed back over without any signs of change.

"All clear out here," Rugrat said.

General Ubren appeared to be a middle-aged woman. Her hair was cut to shoulder length with shades of silver and grey, giving her a refined look against her purple and black armor with silver adornments. Green and blue tattoos added elegance to her appearance; they glowed with power, emanating light.

The corvette, *Anatov,* was silent as it shot through the skies. *Aemis* hung to her right flank.

She sat on the topmost level of the command deck at the rear of the ship overlooking all. The wind howled, but none of it reached Ubren and her staff. Wrap around windows showed the casting deck of the ship. Mages, wearing outdoor air gear, held onto the deck's railings.

The cannon ports were all closed as the formations surged with power, propelling the airship forward.

Those damn heroes, meddling in other people's affairs. First the adventurers had come around, trying to take her fame from her, killing her bandits. She had bowed and scraped with a smile, praised and showered them with coin, all while getting reprimanded for not clearing out the bandits herself.

She snarled and balled her fist, increasing the power flow to the corvette's engines as it increased in speed.

Just as I was about rid of them, they planned to investigate me and my people!

"We just got a report from Azraadale. They confirm that a group of One-Star Heroes headed for Vativa Outpost," Pena said from his seat to the right of her command chair.

She slammed her fist into her chair. "Did I not say that I wanted to know when there were heroes or adventurers coming in through the cities?"

"Yes, General. I will make sure that those who were tardy in passing the message are punished."

Ubren turned away from Pena, looking ahead of the warship. She combed her half back away from her face with forced controlled actions. *That stuck up Mercia best keep her mouth shut. The way she looks at me as if she's superior. I should have killed Ethan long ago just to see that look on her face. She will learn her place.*

Ubren imagined Mercia with a dead expression, a puppet to her will, an uppity rich kid that she had turned into her tool. She opened and closed her hand as she relaxed. She had broken and beaten them. There was nothing she could not overcome. She had brought order and created her own empire. Family members who had looked down on her for having low cultivation were under her boot since she now surpassed them in wealth, position, and cultivation.

She took out a small vial, placing it under her nose. Taking a sniff of the redweed, her mind awakened, calming her. She felt her control of the ship through the dungeon core—power that extended across the land below and sat straighter.

"We are coming up on the landing zone."

"Very well. Prepare to land," Ubren said.

The cannons under the warship tilted until they were parallel with the warship's underside.

Ubren focused on the landing zone as she decreased speed and altitude. She brought the airship over the landing area in a hover, before lowering to the ground.

She brought them in as close to the wall as she dared.

"See to the shutdown, Pena," Ubren said, standing from her command chair.

"Yes, General."

Ubren felt a thrill through her body from the word. She left the command deck, Pena following her. They moved to the rear of the command deck, taking the platform down. They reached the main deck. Large twin doors opened, showing the casters and their formations. Ubren's personal guard were mounted. Their beasts ran forward and stretched out their wings, catching the launch formations at the front of the ship, sending them skyward.

The stable master had Ubren and Pena's beasts ready, the finest Krakol had to offer. They were deep grey beasts with intelligent purple eyes and black wings.

Ubren pulled out her riding helmet and put it on, getting on the back of her beast. The beast ran forward out of the rear decks and across the main casting deck. He spread his wings as they met the lifting formation.

They shot into the air. Her guards moved around her as she looked down on the dungeon entrance to Vativa. "Let's go!"

They banked, cutting through the sky, and dove through the tunnel. They sped up with the tunnel formations, shooting out over the redweed farms.

Ubren snorted, her lip raising in distaste at the tiny outpost.

Still such a backwater.

She and her guards flew straight for Mercia's mansion and landed in the street outside. People moved out of the way as her guards dismounted and rushed ahead.

She followed with Pena, walking into the mansion.

Mercia's butler was waiting in her office.

"Where is the little bitch?" Ubren snarled as she moved around the desk and sat down in Mercia's seat.

"She was coordinating the clean-up of the adventurers, General."

"The heroes?"

"They came around and talked to her. They are wandering the city now."

A formation shook on Ubren's necklace. She picked up the buzzing black bead and stood up slowly. "What was the rank of the heroes?"

"One-Star, General."

"General?" Pena asked, stepping forward.

"Something happened to Mercia. If our secret is in danger, she'll cast a spell that will activate this formation. We need to find her! Where did she go?"

"She went to the warehouse district."

Ubren strode around the desk, Pena opening the doors for her. She rushed down the stairs and out of the manor.

Those damn heroes. I'll need to silence them to make sure the Mission Hall doesn't learn anything. Why do a few adventurers matter?

"Mount up!" she yelled at the guards standing in a huddle near their mounts.

"Are you sure about this?" Pena asked Ubren.

"Heroes go missing all the time." Ubren shot him a look as her mount was prepared and brought forth.

Fred pulled the cart to a stop inside the warehouse, positioning it between the tall aisles filled with dust, forgotten containers, and random materials.

The draft animal snorted at the collected dust.

Fred got down and patted the beast. "There, there. All is okay." Fred pulled out some treats. The beast looked at him with a lazy eye before nibbling at the food in Fred's hand. He patted the beast again and put some more food on the floor. The beast bent his head for the treats.

There were grunts from the other aisle and the clink of chains and metal snapping closed. He walked over. Erik and Dromm had secured the unconscious man and woman to iron chairs with weakening handcuffs on their wrists and legs.

"Racquel, can you frisk her? Check her hair down to her feet, false teeth, bunch up her clothing like this." Erik grabbed Ding Rong's pants, bunching them up in his hand.

"Okay." Racquel moved to Mercia and started checking.

Erik opened Ding Rong's mouth, searching around before mana pulled out a tooth. Erik's mana put it on a shelf as he took off storage rings, several daggers and hidden storage items.

He took off Ding Rong's shirt and the armor underneath.

Racquel finished with her check. They'd created a collection of gear on the shelf.

"Reaper, can you sort through all that?" Erik asked.

"Sure." Reaper waved a hand, plucking it all from the air.

"Go into the next aisle if you can. Don't want them to see it."

"Okay." Reaper left.

"So we need to question them. Should we record it?" Erik asked.

"That would be the best," Fred said.

Erik nodded and pulled out a recording orb. He put it behind and to the side of the duo so it would see them, but they wouldn't be able to find it easily.

"Rugrat, what did you learn from the drivers?" Erik moved farther down the aisle to where Fred was. "Racquel, Dromm, can you watch them for a minute?"

"Yeah," Dromm said and Racquel nodded.

Erik gave them a thumbs up as Rugrat replied on their party wide chat.

"They're linked to the bandits. I think Mercia is the leader. They were raiding traders. Her brother was killed by the adventurers. They were going to return and complete their One-Star mission, but she might have sent out information to lure them here. The bandits didn't know what happened to them."

"When we were close to the warehouse, I could taste metal. It could have been blood," Racquel said.

"Okay then." Erik walked back to the duo. The chairs sunk into the ground a bit; stone climbed up the chair legs, creating new bindings around Mercia and Ding and securing them to the ground.

"Okay let's start." Erik pulled out a vial and put it under their noses. They twitched against the smell.

"What? You!" Mercia was the first to awaken. She glared at the group and then relaxed.

"Miss Mercia, welcome to the land of the living. What did you do to the adventurers?"

She sighed. "I lured them here, and I killed them."

Erik looked at the others and back to her. "Why?"

"I had to," Mercia said.

"Because they learned of your connection to the bandits?"

Ding Rong groaned and blinked, glancing around.

"Because I had to." Mercia's eyes were tearing up. "Ding Rong."

"Thank the gods," Ding Rong said, leaning back into his chair. "You came. We hoped you would when we let the adventurers send out the message. Mercia is under contract, don't release her. The contract will compel her to kill you."

Erik felt the hairs on the back of his neck rise. "Check the area. Rugrat, how are we looking?"

The group dispersed. Fred remained near Erik. The others used holes and windows to look outside.

"She's on her way, but we should have some time. She was alerted once you entered the outpost. You need to get out of here," Ding Rong said, bringing Erik's attention back.

"Who is *she* and what are you talking about?"

"Mercia and her brother are contracted to General Ubren. She used to be the ruler of this outpost. She tricked them when they were younger and got them to uphold her—"

"Don't say another word." Mercia hissed, but her expression was sad. Like a puppet with its lips controlled by another, the two at odds with one another.

"She cannot reveal any information. But I am only bound to Mercia through contract. I can do what is in her best interest."

"I'll kill you!" Mercia yelled, throwing her body against her bonds as tears ran down her face.

"Can you gag her and block her eyes and ears?" Ding Rong pleaded.

Erik took out a sound canceling formation, activating it and putting it near Mercia. He quickly took out a sack and put it over her head.

"Sorry. She is so sworn to General Ubren and has to do everything to defend her and keep her unassociated with the situation. She'll attack and murder because of the contract." Ding Rong shook his head with wet eyes.

"What the hell is going on?"

"General Ubren used Mercia to learn everything about the redweed trade, and she used Mercia's brother, Markholm, to create bandits. She used them to steal from other traders and be her foil to increase her rank within the guards. She controls Azraadale's forces and the surrounding areas. She controls all the redweed trade and has been slowly taking it over through Mercia."

Quest Completed: The Missing Adventurers
The Adventurer group has been killed by Mercia.   You have found out that she is the puppet of the general who controls this area. Inform the Mission Hall.
Rewards: +100,000,000 EXP   +10 Mission Points   Rewards may be increased based on performance.

Hero Star Emblem
1/10 1 star missions until you can take the Star Level 2 test

Quest: Puppetress
General Ubren is implicated in banditry, forcing two orphans to work as bandits and to break the law for her to increase her position.   Kill General Ubren
Rewards: 100 Mission points   2-Star Hero medallion   Rewards may be increased based on performance.

"You must tell the Mission Hall. Kill the general! She is the one that made us kill the adventurers!" Ding Rong strained against his chair, looking at Erik and Fred.

"I don't see anything out there," Racquel said.

"Me either," Dromm said.

"Rugrat?" Erik asked.

"I have no movement out here."

"She's already on the way with her corvette airships. Now that Mercia has been discovered, she's bound to know. She put a formation tattoo on Mercia. If she is knocked out or incapacitated, it sends Ubren a message. You need to tell the Mission Hall and get the hell out of here. There are tens of tunnels that lead out of the outpost into the dungeon. There's a map in the blue storage ring that shows them all."

His heart rate, while elevated, wasn't in a pattern that made Erik think he was lying. Same with his breathing, eyes, and sweating.

"Fred?" Erik looked to the other man.

"I don't think he is lying. The fact that a quest has been created shows that they aren't lying. I'll contact the Mission Hall now."

Erik nodded and Fred walked around some shelving to send his messages.

"Where are their bodies?" Erik asked.

"With the bandit leaders. They're taking them out of the outpost to plant in a rival's location, to put the blame on them." Ding Rong said.

"For what purpose?"

"So the general can find the despicable traders working with the bandits and kill them. Raising her position. Mercia will take her rivals' property when they are executed. The bandits will work as traders. Then, with time, we will take more of the redweed trade." Ding Rong seemed sapped of energy and sat back against his chair. "I knew that they had a way to contact the Mission Hall. I let them use it. We wanted you to come here."

"What for?"

"To end all this." Ding Rong shrugged.

Fred returned around the shelves.

"What did they say?" Erik asked.

"Escape. They'll put up the mission."

"They say how long it will be before a Two-Star picks it up?"

"No, but if the General knows that we've told the Mission Hall, she'll run and hide."

"Will the Mission Hall give up?"

"With time they might. They were adventurers, not heroes and this is a backwater region."

"Don't mean to burst your bubble," Rugrat said. "You know how I said things were clear a few minutes ago? Well, they aren't anymore. We have flying beasts coming in!"

19

Hard Decisions

here!" one of Ubren's guards said, pointing at a nearby warehouse. "T The mages and guards in the air circulated their power, ready for battle.

A mage shattered the warehouse door with a blast of air. Guards jumped off their mounts, freeing their weapons and rushing in.

A guard ran back out of the dust that had been thrown up. "It's clear. We've secured them! There's only Mercia and her guard!"

Ubren dove toward the ground on her mount.

"General," Pena said, but held his words at her frosty gaze.

She strolled into the warehouse, taking it in with a glance.

Mercia and Ding Rong had been drugged and were secured to chairs.

"Wake them up," Ubren said.

A guard stepped forward and used a healing spell to wake them up. They looked around groggily.

"What the hell happened? Why were you unconscious?"

"I was stunned by the heroes." Mercia said.

"You what?" Ubren said.

"They know everything, and they've told the Mission Hall!"

Ubren slapped her, sending Mercia and the chair to the ground.

Mercia looked back, but she was held in place by the contract. Tears and fresh blood marred her features. Ubren could see it now, the burning light in Mercia's eyes. Ubren yelled, and smacked her again.

"Think that you're the one running the show, little bitch?" Ubren snarled. "After all, I did give you the adventurers to avenge your brother."

Mercia's lips trembled as she winced at the pain in her cut cheeks.

Ubren stretched her hand, feeling a slight sting on her palm.

She punched Mercia in the stomach, throwing her in her chair, backward into a shelving unit.

Mercia coughed against her bonds.

"Where are they?" Ubren demanded, turning on Ding Rong.

"I don't know."

"Useless." She smacked him with the back of her hand.

She saw Mercia recovering and kicked her in the stomach. She yelled as she kicked her again and again.

"Stop it! Stop!" Ding Rong shouted.

She was breathing heavily and flipped her hair out of the way. "You think I care what a dog's dog would say? Now that they know, what use do I have for either of you?" Ubren snarled. She drew a sword from her storage ring, stabbing through Mercia and the chair.

Mercia coughed and choked in surprise.

Ubren leaned forward. "Say hello to that useless brother of yours."

Ding Rong yelled as the power in the room fluctuated. He bent his head and grabbed his top button between his teeth. His eyes turned red with anger as he stared through Ubren and pulled the button, tearing the spell scroll inside his shirt. She kicked Mercia free of her sword, turned, and ran, battering Pena out of the way. Pena stumbled behind her as the guards all started to run.

She could just make out Ding Rong's last words.

"I love you, Mercia," Ding Rong said.

Ubren was nearly out of the warehouse when the spell ignited, tossing her forward.

Erik looked back as a spell tore through the warehouse district. They rumbled along on the cart that Ding Rong and Mercia had used. "What the hell was that?" he asked, but deep down he knew what it meant.

He studied the destructive spell as the mana dissipated before forcing himself to look away. "Shit."

They continued in silence for some time.

Guards rushed past them in droves, heading toward the warehouse district.

George shifted on Rugrat's shoulders, growling.

They stared in the direction he was looking.

"Those are the same aerial beasts I saw heading for the warehouse district. There are less of them now. Did the quest complete?" Rugrat asked.

Quest: Puppetress
General Ubren is implicated in banditry, forcing two orphans to work as bandits and to break the law for her to increase her position. Kill General Ubren
Rewards:
+100,000,000,000 EXP 100 Mission points 2-Star Hero medallion Rewards may be increased based on performance.

"No, she must still be alive," Erik said.

Rugrat studied the group of fliers as they cut overhead. "That one." He pointed at the flier wearing better gear than the others and with the strongest mount. "That has to be her."

Rugrat looked at Erik.

"We have to go after her after the shit she pulled." Dromm spat, trying to clear the bad taste in his mouth.

"We're One-Stars. That's a Two-Star mission," Erik said.

"Look, guards are all distracted. Can't watch all the wall, right? Dunno which ones are corrupt and not. We get out of here, figure out what direction Ubren's heading. Give the Two-Stars a head start," Rugrat said.

"We can't just let her go," Reaper growled.

"Wouldn't feel right," Racquel offered.

Dromm grunted in agreement.

"Fred?" Erik asked.

"Your choice."

Erik looked at them all. "Shit, it pisses me off, too. If we get caught…"

"They'll have one hell of a fight on their hands. You think some little outpost guard will want to fight a One-Star Hero? He might take bribes, but he won't put himself and his family in danger for someone else's problems," Dromm said.

"All right. Rugrat, find us a place to get over the wall. We'll go on foot. I have some agility buffs that should help us out."

General Ubren blinked against the light as she and her remaining guards shot out of the tunnel leading down to Vativa. They angled away from the entrance toward the twin corvette airships waiting outside the Western gate.

She stifled a cough, resisting the urge to press her hand to her throbbing side. If she hadn't thrown Pena in the way of the blast, using his barriers and protections, she would now be dead. *Shame, really. He was a useful second-in-command.* She pulled out a healing potion, drinking it in a few gulps and tossing it away as her body's repairs sped up.

She used her sound transmission device as her beast slowed, coming in to land on her *Anatov*. "Major Vedat, take your forces and head into Vativa. I was ambushed in the warehouse district. Pena died in the attack. Leave a skeleton crew behind. I will give you the majority of my people to assist you. My guards have informed me that I need to head out of the area for my safety."

Her mount landed on the deck. She slid off and her guards formed around her.

"Yes, General! I will see to it, at once!"

Good. That way, I keep those that are loyal on my ship and thin out the people on his corvette. If he's ordered to come after me, he'll need time to get his people together.

"Make sure we're ready to fly as soon as we're free of the stragglers," Ubren said to the closest guard.

"Yes, General."

20

The Hunt

T he cart cleared the entrance to the dungeon. People yelled, trying to get out of the way of the guards who were shooting through the entrance on the back of their flying beasts.

Guards from the outposts jogged, or mounted ground beasts, and headed into the depths of the outpost.

"There's a lot of guards on aerial beasts," Rugrat said.

"You thinking something?" Erik asked.

"They have to be coming from somewhere. Their gear is better than the guards here. Wait, dungeon cores power the ships, right?" Rugrat closed his eyes.

Erik couldn't feel any difference as they snapped open not a second later, looking to the west.

"I can sense two powerful dungeon cores close to the wall over there."

Right where all the aerial beasts are coming from.

"What are you thinking?"

"Why don't we go west, see what's over there? I have a feeling."

"Fred?"

"To the west we go, a band of righteous heroes in a cart that's made of more wood worms than wood. Doubt anyone would think a group of heroes would travel in such, style."

Erik caught a hint of a grin from the corner of Fred's hood as he guided the tired beast toward the western gates.

They trundled down the road. People looked out of their houses and shops, taking a break from their lives and work to watch the guards streaming away from the walls and into the dungeon.

"Get your fool cart out of the way. Guards coming through!"

"Sorry, sorry!" Fred said as they pulled as far over to the side as possible.

The sound of rushing air followed a large group of aerial beasts.

Erik peered into the sky. Slowly, a small airship rose over the city's walls, framed by the midday sun shining off its cold, lethal angles and weaponry, its formations glowing with power.

"Damn, those are some sweet rides," Dromm said from his seat beside Fred.

It was ten meters tall and ran fifty meters long, a mean beast of war.

The sleek airship didn't have the sails of the merchant or trader ships. It looked like an old sea-going ship that had had its upper sails removed and its masts cut off at the waterline.

A set of skids at the front of the bottom of the ship kept it raised from the ground, protecting the formation-carved cannons on the underbelly of the ship. Gun ports ran down the ship's sides, closed but ready to fight off any that would dare to stand in its way.

Large pivoting cannons jutted out of the ship's forecastle.

Erik looked in the sky, using his Eagle Sight. The warship's formations increased in power as it turned, blowing up dust and debris before it applied power, heading to the north east.

"She could get away," Racquel said.

"Will the Mission Hall penalize us if we requisition a corvette?" Rugrat said, gathering silence.

Erik looked at him. "Are you serious?"

Rugrat shrugged.

"There's a gate guard up ahead. Why don't we ask him?"

Fred angled the cart toward the gate and kept rolling forward. Erik could only see one young guard on duty.

He scanned the wall but couldn't see any signs of guards patrolling.

Did they really send all their people into the dungeon?

"Halt there!" the guard said as they rolled toward the gate that had been closed.

"Woah, woah," Fred cooed to the beast, slowing her.

"No one is allowed out of the outpost right now. I'll need to see some identification before you head back into the outpost.

"Sure, sure. No problem. Get out your medallions, everyone!" Fred grabbed his as the guard moved in closer. "What's with all the commotion? There are a lot of guards heading down to the lower levels. Then that airship took off. I haven't seen a warship like that up close in a long time." Fred chuckled, and the guard relaxed a bit.

"Something happened in the lower dungeon. Apparently, someone tried to kill General Ubren. She rushed back here, and all the guards rushed down there, even her aerial fighters," the younger guard offered, eager to share his inside knowledge.

"Aerial fighters as well! Well, it speaks highly of your training to trust you here with the gate."

"Ah, it's nothing. Just have to turn people away. Don't want to piss off a general." The young man laughed. "Could I see your affiliation?"

"Sure." Erik watched Fred open his hand around his emblem.

"Wow, One-Star Hero?" The man looked at the rest of the group's Mission Hall badges as they opened their hands. He rested the butt of his spear on the ground. "My ma will never believe this."

"We're on an important mission and we have to head out to complete it. Can we exit here?"

"No can do. The corvettes don't want anyone near them. I'm sorry, but you can try the northern exit."

"Must be hard with so few of you here," Fred said, making to turn the cart around.

"Yeah, it's a bit difficult, but we'll manage. Who would attack the Ubren outposts?" The lad laughed as the cart turned slowly.

There wouldn't be many people on the other warship. At the very least, there weren't many people on the wall. They could check it out and run if they needed to—or take their chances.

Erik looked at Rugrat and nodded, leaning to the side.

Rugrat raised his M8 from under his cloak.

Erik heard a noise from the boy behind him before Rugrat fired and the boy slumped.

"Don't worry, non-lethals. Gonna feel like he got kicked by a mule, though."

Erik and the others jumped out of the sides of the cart. George leaped from Rugrat's shoulders and swelled to the size of a large dog. There was no one else around the gate. Erik's domain scanned the young guard before he grabbed him and put him in the back of the cart. Fred pulled the cart to the side.

Dromm found an entrance to a stairwell, opening it for Reaper and Racquel, who ran up the stairs.

Rugrat, then Erik followed with the last two following afterwards.

Erik came out on the twenty-meter-tall wall with his rifle ready.

"Next guard is a few hundred meters out," Reaper stated.

"Here, let me use this."

Racquel pulled out a spell scroll, aimed, and activated it; the spell fell over everyone.

Distracted Eye spell scroll
Others will unconsciously look away from those affected by this scroll, drawn off to other interesting sights.
Low Expert Grade

"Sweet."

Rugrat prowled toward the wall. Erik followed him as they peeked between the stone crenellations.

"Nice parking job, right between the lines," Rugrat said.

The corvette was about a hundred meters away from the edge of the wall. Sunlight burned through the shadows that would have covered it in the morning. Formations were set out across the deck, waiting for mages to stand on them. Erik's eyes tracked to the open doors at the rear of the flat deck and at the base of the bridge at the rear, catching sight of a crew member.

"I have one at the large door on the main deck," Erik said.

"I have one moving on the bridge," Rugrat said.

"It might be a skeleton crew."

Fred and Dromm moved up to spots on either side of them.

"Every second she is getting farther away. If we don't go after her, she could be in the wind forever," Rugrat said.

Erik turned from the wall, putting his back against the crenellation. "What the hell? Let's steal a corvette! No killing anyone; just knock them out. We don't know who're Ubren's people and who's just doing their jobs. It could be that she left the people who aren't on her side."

Erik waited until he saw the acknowledgement in everyone's eyes.

"Rugrat and I will work on locating and capturing the dungeon core to control the ship. Dromm, and Fred, you're Team Alpha. You secure the weapon decks. Racquel, Reaper, you're Bravo. Secure the mana stone stores. Rugrat and I are Charlie. Once we secure our individual objectives, we'll move through the ship to clear out any remaining forces. Good?"

"Good," the group replied together.

"Okay, from now on, switch to talking on the sound transmission devices." Erik glanced at the corvette again. The deck was running toward them and the bridge was the furthest thing from them.

"Rugrat and I will go first with George; we need to clear out that bridge and take control as soon as possible. If we can take the bridge, you'll be free to jump onto the deck without anyone spotting you as long as you take out the guard watching the door at the base of the bridge."

He wished he had more time to go over the plan, but they didn't have the luxury of time.

"Let's get to it."

Erik tapped Rugrat's back and raised his rifle as he rolled forward, heel to toe down the wall. He watched the guard that was a few hundred meters away. The guard looked into the outpost instead of out at the corvette.

"You want me to take him?"

"Do it," Erik said.

Rugrat paused for a half step, steadying, and pulled the trigger. The guard dropped to the ground without a noise.

"Gotta love these formation-silenced rounds," Rugrat said as Erik sped up, glancing between crenellations at the corvette to their side.

"How do you want to do this?" Erik asked.

"Jump down to the top of the bridge. Go down the side. Use mana blades to cut through the walls and make entry."

"Works." Erik looked over the wall. They were in-line with the bridge of the ship.

"Not on this jump, little fella," Rugrat said to George, who padded alongside them.

Rugrat moved up next to Erik. "Up for it?"

"Being able to fly in this thick mana is doing wonders for my fear of heights," Erik said as he took off his cloak, storing it away and walking to the opposite side of the wall. He strapped on his helmet and secured his rifle. Rugrat did the same.

Erik tightened his helmet more and glanced at Rugrat on his left.

"Oorah!" Rugrat grinned and started running.

Erik grunted and ran after him. They leapt over the crenellations, sending them hurtling forward toward the corvette. George followed them. His wings flapped open as Erik shifted his arms around and he fell toward the roof of the corvette.

Erik's domain stretched out, gathering the mana together, slowing his descent. He reached the top of the bridge and rolled, taking out the impact of his landing. He rose to a knee, scanning the area, mana swelling through his body, ready at a moment's notice.

He checked Rugrat, who had landed back from him. "Good?"

"Good to go."

George landed at a sedate glide.

Erik and Rugrat ran toward the rear of the bridge. Rugrat jumped off the edge and turned, facing Erik as he dropped. Erik jumped after him. They drew on the ambient mana to fly.

They dropped next to the bridge, just above the main windows, releasing their rifles and aiming at the breach point.

"Set!" Rugrat said, as mana blades formed around him.

"Breach!" Erik yelled.

Rugrat's blade stabbed into the wall and turned counterclockwise. With a grunt, he mule-kicked the cut panel, hurling it inwards.

Erik squared off with the breach, taking out a guard to the right as he pushed inside. He snapped to the left, shooting another standing up from the workstation. Erik's feet carried him inside as he checked the room. Rugrat entered right behind him and stood abreast on his right side.

Erik breathed out, clearing his vision and focusing his mind. "Clear left. Chair in front. Three low barriers. Workstations to front. Stairwell left leading down! No read on domain."

"Clear right. Obstacles to front. Stairwell leading down! Domain, clear!"

"Push to the left. You clear the stations. I'll watch the stairwell," Erik said.

"Got it."

Rugrat moved over to Erik, the two going shoulder to shoulder.

"Push!"

They moved forward. Erik covered the stairwell and Rugrat on his side.

"Hold!" Rugrat said.

Erik took a knee, watching the stairs. Rugrat pushed up to the stations, staying low, his weapon up and ready. He stepped out, seeing in front of the stations. "Clear!"

"Good. Drop alert formation," Erik said.

"Understood."

Rugrat took out a formation, turned it, activated it, and tossed it down the stairwell. It clattered on the metal stairs before it stopped.

"Other stairwell." Erik turned. Rugrat had his rifle up and watched the area.

"Alpha, Bravo, this is Charlie. Bridge is secure," Erik said.

"Understood," Fred acknowledged.

Erik and Rugrat made it to the other stairwell and repeated the process from the first.

"All clear," Erik stated. He lowered his rifle, pulled out a life detect scroll and tore it. He saw movement outside, a silent flash of green light that landed somewhere below before four shadows dropped onto the deck and split up, heading for stairs that led into the corvette.

"Formations are thick in here. Hard for my domain to get through it all," Rugrat said as he walked to the rear of the bridge and the two downed bridge members.

"At least these detect life scrolls are strong enough to let us see a bit more."

"Can you cover me?" Rugrat asked.

"Sure." Rugrat had reached the first person Erik had taken down.

Rugrat secured his rifle as Erik moved to the side so he had a clear line of sight and could keep the second member of the bridge crew in sight.

Rugrat checked the man, pulling off storage rings and tossing them to the side before he slapped on mana dispersing cuffs and put the man in a nearby workstation chair; he manipulated the metal, bending it around the man's body.

Rugrat shifted to the second member and repeated the process quickly and efficiently.

"This is Bravo. We have secured one mana stone storage area. We're storing the mana stones and moving to secure other locations," Racquel said.

"Understood, Bravo," Erik acknowledged.

Rugrat sat at the command chair in the middle of the bridge. The dungeon core was stuck in the floor in front of it with complicated formations all around it.

"You got any idea how to fly this thing?" Erik said.

"Just takes some redneck ingenuity." Rugrat's eyes glowed with spells as he examined the seat. Rugrat's mana blade appeared and stabbed into something at the side of the chair, while another grabbed a necklace from the nearest prisoner and put the emblem into the armrest.

Formation lines ran from the emblem through the rest of the chair and around the dungeon core.

"I guess that's the ignition," Rugrat said as George padded around the chair, having come in through the new floor to ceiling window Rugrat had created.

Rugrat moved to the chair and sat down. "Take control. That's interesting. Hey, Erik, it's asking if I want to take over control from a Major Vedat. We don't know what will happen. It could alert him."

"You think you can get us airborne in the amount of time it will take them to get back here?"

Rugrat grinned. "Shit, we've got a general to chase down. I'll have her up and running in no time."

"Okay, take control. You going to be okay here?"

"Yeah, George will cover me, and I think I'm going to need you on those guns."

"All right." Erik looked through the decks.

"This is Alpha team. We have secured the main decks. I'm not sure if they were able to get off a message or not," Fred said.

"Okay, I'm heading down. We need to make sure there are no stragglers on board."

Erik looked at Rugrat and nodded.

"Yes." Rugrat waved around screens. "I have control over the ship."

The formations around the dungeon core glowed as Rugrat tested them out.

"Get going," he said without looking up.

"Okay."

Erik turned and moved to the left stairwell. He activated another detect life spell scroll. It rolled outwards, showing glowing ghosts of people and aerial beasts. He headed down the stairs, passing a large living area that must have been the commander's. He went down another floor as an officer looked out his door.

Erik dropped the man and moved for the doorway. He couldn't see anyone else on that floor with detect life, so he checked inside. Erik grabbed the man and hauled him into the room. He secured him with cuffs to the metal desk that had been fused into the floor. "Sleep tight."

He left the room, closing the door behind him.

He quickly cleared the eight officer rooms and headed lower. There were training rooms and then two decks of stables. Most of the pens were empty, but there were about ten wounded aerial beasts.

"There we are, my lovelies. Don't worry. You'll get to go on the next time," a lady said as she stepped out of a blind spot and moved to the beasts with a food pail.

Erik stepped out from the edge of the pens and fired. She collapsed with the stun enchantment, dropping the food pail and spilling it.

He moved up and looked at where she had come from. He found a break in the pens; beyond was a storage room.

"Hah! Gimme those mana stones!" one man said as others groaned.

Card game?

Erik moved toward the noise. He peeked through the door to see a bunk room with three beast handlers playing cards. One man leaned over the table to rake in the mana stones.

Erik opened the door fully with a flare of mana, firing a burst into each of the handlers. One fell out of his chair with the force. The man grabbing the stones splayed over the table and the last rolled back in his chair.

Erik fired as he moved, going from right to left.

The stones and cards fell after the players.

He cleared the rest of the floor and headed down to the next. The floor held empty pens and the unconscious guard at the door that led out to the main deck.

"Bridge tower secured. Heading below the deck. Rugrat, how is that dungeon core?"

"This thing doesn't come with a manual, but I'm figuring it out."

"Alpha, Bravo?"

"There are four floors under the deck. We have taken the third and fourth floor," Fred said.

"We just cleared the lowest two decks. Should be all clear then," Reaper said.

"Okay." Erik checked his watch.

That was quicker than I thought it would be.

"Okay, let's get these people off the ship, and we can get moving. The general is getting away and we might have a major coming after us any minute." Erik grabbed the guard at the door by the belt, picking him up as he ran to the side of the bridge tower, away from the wall.

He opened a window and tossed the man out, solidifying mana around him as he dropped several floors safely.

Erik headed back up, grabbing the handlers and repeating the same process. He reached the officer he'd secured in his quarters when Rugrat spoke up.

"I don't mean to be the bearer of bad news, but I'm seeing a bunch of aerial beasts rushing this way on our sensing formations," Rugrat said.

"Shit." Erik grabbed the officer and ran to the tower side, and threw him out of a window.

He ran back down toward the beast pens.

"Get us in the air as fast as possible!"

"Can do!"

"Damn complicated machines," Rugrat muttered as he asserted his control through the ship and felt his domain shift. "Huh, that's cool."

The dungeon core altered the different formations of the ship to control it. Usually, multiple people controlled all the different formations together.

Rugrat expanded his domain, covering all the formations in the bridge.

"All right, little bit more complicated. Who said a Marine can't navigate a ship?"

"Everyone, remember the do not touch buttons lectures?" Erik muttered.

"These are heat and those are wind formations. That should give us some lift." Rugrat ignored Erik's negativity and completed a formation. Power moved through the ship and into the formations below. The ship shook and shuddered when the flow of power suddenly decreased. "Racquel, I need you to put back those mana stones!"

Rugrat looked at the aerial beasts charging across the outpost.

"Where the hell are the defenses on this thing? Weapons? Okay, there are mana barriers, I think? What about guns? There you are, but I can't elevate them high enough. Racquel!"

"There!"

Rugrat routed the power into the warship which pushed it through the completed formations.

The corvette lifted at the rear, suddenly, dragging its forward skids toward the wall.

"Looks like you scared the guards!" Erik yelled.

"More power to the front!" Fred yelled.

"Back seat warshippers!"

Rugrat turned on other formations.

"Shit this is more like completing water pipes to get it to go in the right direction than flying."

"Brace!" Erik yelled.

The right side shifted, turning them to hit the wall side-on and *scraping* metal and stone against one another.

"There goes the paint!" Erik glared. Rugrat couldn't *see* it, but he could feel it.

"The *front* Rugrat, *not* the *front right*." Fred yelled.

"Everyone's a critic." They got free from the wall, turning in a circle as it sped up.

"Rugrat!" Erik's voice rose in something like panic.

"One sec!" Power was rerouted as they crashed into the wall again.

"Fly the damn thing! Stop trying to use it as a sledgehammer to knock down their wall!" Fred growled.

Reaper snorted and laughed, clapping while Dromm was whooping up a storm.

At least someone is enjoying this. Rugrat adjusted the formations. He swung out from the wall and powered others, slamming right back into it. "Sorry!"

"Are you doing this on purpose?" Racquel yelled.

"No backseat corvette airship formation friggin ship driving! Piloting?"

Rugrat powered several formations under the ship, and they rose rapidly, causing the aerial beasts that had come close to rear back.

Rugrat altered the flow of mana, turning the airship. "This thing is like a brick with thrusters."

Rugrat turned as he rapidly gained altitude, forcing him into his seat.

"Dungeon Sense."

Like a pulse, he felt it stretch out, reaching far and fast.

Dungeon cores in the ground. Don't need those. Where are you? Come on, come on. "There you are." Rugrat slowed the ship's turn to a halt.

"What the hell are you doing? This is an Ubren Clan Warship!" The two stunned crew members tied to chairs looked over aghast.

I totally forgot the two dudes up here.

Rugrat looked at George, who returned a displeased look.

With a grimace, Rugrat poured power into the engines at the rear of the bridge.

They *shot* forward with eye-peeling acceleration that had Rugrat grinning like a redneck strapped to a rocket.

The frankly *alarmed* look on George's face as he was forced back into his seat made Rugrat reduce the power output to more manageable racecar speeds.

Nice, that's another mana storage locker filled with stones.

"I found her; we're moving to pursue. She's hauling ass and near the edge of my range," Rugrat told the others.

He closed the channel at the mixture of groans and expletives, good and bad. He had other things to worry about.

"Who the hell are you? You're the ones that attacked the general!" The man who had woken up kept talking. They sounded shaky from their trip. Rugrat swore they had been horizontal at one point, holding on by their cuffs.

Dammit I should have kicked them off the ship.

In a lapse of concentration, the airship ducked and weaved, taking Rugrat a second to maintain control over the beast.

"Will you shut up? I am trying to pilot a frigging airship!" Rugrat glared at the pale-faced man, changing back to his sound transmission device.

"Hey everyone. Thank you for flying redneck air! We are currently cruising at a speed of fast, looking to go really fast, though it will burn through a damn ton of mana stones. Huh..."

Rugrat activated a series of wind formations; wings of wind appeared on either side of the craft, jostling the ship.

"Will you please concentrate on flying this thing?"

"It's pretty cool, right!?" Rugrat said as they wobbled again. "Right, going back to this whole flying gig."

Rugrat canceled the sound transmission device. "Hey, you, bridge boy. How the hell do I fly this thing?"

"Why would I tell you?"

"Because if I go down in a big fiery ball, then *you* go down in a big fiery ball as well."

The man swallowed, looking at Rugrat as if he was a madman.

Rugrat gave him a winning grin, as the man started to tremble and sweat.

"Okay, but I am *only* doing this so that my people might not die."

"Cool, now, how do I get more power out of the formations?"

Ubren lounged on her favorite chair in her room under the command deck. She drew in the liquid mana, purified by the dungeon core above, through her eight mana gates. She stretched. Popping and cracking noises rang through her body as her weariness fell away.

The best training scrolls she had been able to find filled the walls. She rubbed her temples, feeling the raised lines of her tattoos. Her damaged armor lay strewn about the room, as did several healing and recovery potion bottles.

She yelled and pulled out a dagger, hurling it across the room. It sunk into the wall up to the hilt, breaking the weapon. Several other broken items and discarded armor lie around the wall.

"That little bitch!"

She smashed her hand into the armrest of the chair, breaking it. She kept hitting it again and again until it separated from the chair and fell on the floor. She turned and kicked the chair sending it flying into a wall of scrolls, spilling the priceless training manuals across the deck.

She breathed through her nose, her fists balled at her side.

Mercia had always looked at Ubren as if she were something less than her, like she was some kind of dog. *She didn't see it when I pulled her into that contract, sealing her and her brother's fates, becoming my playthings. Oh, how sweet that was!*

A twisted smile rose on her face as she let out a controlled breath before she ran to where the chair lay and stomped on it.

"That. Fucking. Useless. Butler. Prick!"

He must have been planning it for days, weeks even, using the adventurers, then sowing a spell scroll into his clothes.

She drove her foot through the chair.

A knock came from the door, interrupting her thoughts.

"What is it?" she snarled.

"General, Major Vedat wishes to talk to you. The *Aemis* is heading toward us at her best speed," a guard called through the door.

"One minute!" Ubren kicked away the remains of the chair, talking as she pulled on a spare set of armor. "Have all the weapon batteries checked and ready to engage."

She slowed as she waited for the response.

"Yes, General. Right away."

Once this was over, she would have to replace her guards. Their weaknesses were showing.

She quickly dressed, checking the sword on her hip and the hidden daggers and weapons on her body.

She left her room and headed up to the command deck. She swept in and sat in her command chair.

"Continue to block the major's transmissions. Prepare our weapons."

It should have taken him a lot longer to gather his people and come after them.

"The Mission Hall must have gotten word to the clan. We must rely on one another. Once we get rid of the *Aemis*, we can escape to our stash and disappear. If we can't lose them, the rest of the clan and the Mission Hall will hunt us down."

She saw the stiffening of backs, the lost looks turn hard.

"Be ready on the guns. Prepare for combat."

"We don't have enough people aboard to man all the guns," her new head guard said to her quietly.

"Well, then send some of our guards down. You and three others stay here," she snapped.

"Yes, General."

"They're powering weapons!" a watcher observed.

The forward cannons on the *Aemis* fired, covering its forward bow in a cloud of released energies.

"Barrier!"

The barriers snapped up around the warship. The cannon blasts struck the rear of the ship, creating twin ripples that flared across the bubble of a shield barrier.

"Increase the power to the rear barriers. Decrease the power of the forward." She glared at the guards rushing down the stairs to the lower decks.

Erik adjusted his aim as the mana cannon refilled with power rapidly.

"Nice hit. They'll feel that one," Rugrat complimented.

"How long to close with them?"

"Fifteen minutes!" Rugrat said.

Erik's mana cannon recharged. He checked his aim quickly. The ship shook as the other forward cannon battery fired, controlled by Reaper.

Erik fired his cannon. It shot backward as the chaotic mana travelled the distance and crashed into the other ship's mana barrier.

"Okay, keep it up!"

They raced across the skies. Rugrat drove the ship like a madman. He had improved rapidly since their take off.

"Ship is turning to bring its port batteries to bear! Brace yourselves!" Rugrat said.

The forward corvette turned to the left, revealing left-side guns that rolled out through its two decks of gun ports.

Reaper fired his cannon.

Erik checked his as it locked back into firing position, the power nearing full.

He fired as soon as it was full. The *Anatov* bucked in a display of light and destruction. The cannons' attacks struck the forward barrier as the warship shifted under Erik's feet, turning toward the *Anatov's* new course.

"Hold on!"

Erik grabbed onto handles around the mana cannon as it pushed back up into its firing position.

Maneuvering formations on the front side of *Aemis* activated, swinging them around faster and tighter. The force pressed Erik against the side of the ship before the engines thrust increased, pushing him to the rear.

"They're banking! They're trying to bring their cannons to bear," Rugrat yelled.

"Gives me a bigger target," Erik said, his cannon charged. He checked his aim and worked the formations, shifting the cannon onto target, firing again as soon as he was lined up.

Reaper fired afterward.

The *Anatov* shifted to bring the port side batteries onto target releasing a barrage.

"Erik, Reaper, now is a good time to head back!" Rugrat said.

"Got it."

Erik fired the cannon once more and left his armored room. Reaper followed him a second later. They ran through the cannon deck; it was open, with cannons on both sides charged and ready for action.

They took the stairs up two at a time, entering the crew's living quarters. Then another run to a set of stairs to the deck.

Reaper and Erik ducked as the *Anatov* replied to their volley, striking the barrier behind them. The noise rolled over the deck as they raced for the door at the bottom of the bridge through the aerial beast stables.

They ran across the deck, illuminated with cannon spells impacting against their mana barrier.

The other corvette loomed ahead. Its cannons fired as fast as they could, decorating their mana barrier with attacks.

Erik could see what Rugrat was aiming for with a glance.

They ran up the stairs, reaching the bridge where Rugrat and the rest of the group were waiting with their two prisoners.

"Brace for impact!"

"It's a corvette, not a damn landing craft!" Erik yelled as he grabbed onto a workstation and a nearby chair that held a terrified looking prisoner.

Yeah, there's a reason marines shouldn't drive the ships.

The rest of the group waited near the rear of the bridge that was open to the sky. Dromm stood next to the other prisoner strapped to his chair.

"No, you don't!" Rugrat shouted as he banked, raising the air blades along the side of the ship and forcing power through the thrust formations on the right side of the *Aemis*. The air blade formations along the left side of the ship failed as the ship tilted to the right, starting to roll.

He activated the left side cannons, firing all ten up and into the underside of the Antaov.

Rugrat sent one last command through the dungeon core. Everyone jumped out the rear of the Aemis as Erik and Fred sliced the prisoner's free and ran out. Erik's mana wrapped around them and dragged them along, screaming as Erik and Fred jumped out of the warship.

Rugrat checked the formations were in alignment and tore the dungeon core from the floor, running after the others as the ship tilted. He ran on the wall and jumped.

Claws grabbed onto his armor and there was a rushing wind of wing beats.

The group raced away from the corvette, jumping across the clouds as they formed mana around their bodies.

They descended toward the ground as Rugrat looked back.

Two, one, zero! Did I time it wrong?

Rugrat's doubts faded when the sky and ground were blotted out in noise and light. The *Aemis* erupted in a rippling explosion that tore it and the nearby *Anatov* apart, sending both warships toward the ground.

The shattered ships had their spines broken, coming apart as they dropped, landing among mountain ranges filled with sparse woodland. Trees were flattened with the impact; explosions tore the ships apart.

Erik dropped to the ground with the still screaming prisoners. They were sobbing as they held onto rocks and dirt.

"Thanks for the flying lessons, lads," Rugrat joked as he dropped off their storage rings and gear on the ground away from them.

He stored the dungeon core and freed his rifle, unloading and clearing it and inserting live rounds.

"Everyone okay?" Fred asked.

"Good!" Reaper said.

"Damn, that was some piloting. I liked the part where you knocked down their wall," Dromm said.

Rugrat scratched the back of his head. "Took some getting used to."

Racquel rolled her eyes and shook her head, resting her hands on her twin blades.

"Looks like we're all good. Our goal is to clear the ship as fast as possible and catch Ubren. Potions."

They took out the green and lightning blue potions Erik had given them before and drank them.

Rugrat felt the thrill through his body.

You have taken an acceleration potion.
Increased agility by 23% For: 00:09:59s

"Tastes like I ate a taser." Rugrat smacked his lips together.

"You do *not* want to know what the failures tasted like." Erik's haunted expression gave Rugrat the chills.

The group left their dazed prisoners behind and moved off in the direction of the two crashed ships in the middle of the mountain range.

General Ubren winced as she moved. She spat blood to the side as she shifted in her chair; people around her were groaning and complaining. *The ship blew up. We saw them jumping towards the ground.*

She reached out to the dungeon core. Her senses spread through the ship. It was broken halfway down its spine. It had smashed through trees, landing on its left side.

"They'll be coming soon. Get potions into you and check your gear!"

She grabbed the dungeon core, going through different options.

Destroy Dungeon: Anatov
You will receive:
2154x Sky realm Iron
6547x Earth Iron
1x Lesser Sky-Grade Dungeon Core
32x Humans
4x Damaged thrust formations
232x Sky grade mana stones
4x Sky grade cornerstones
1x Shield Spell Formation
56x Krakol
8x Heavy Mana Cannons
Do you wish to destroy this Dungeon?
YES/NO

"Yes."

Items shot toward the dungeon core and into her storage devices before the dungeon core entered her storage ring.

Everyone that was inside of the ship, including the beasts, were teleported outside.

Ubren fell a few feet to the ground, grunting. Her people were scattered around but the Krakol were nearby.

Her recently appointed head guard helped her to her feet.

"They're only five fucking people. They don't have a ship to hide behind anymore. Go and kill them!" she yelled, her mana spilling out.

She spread her hand, pushing her disorderly hair from her face, composing herself. "Whoever brings me their heads will get an extra two percent of the cache!" Ubren raised her voice so her remaining crew could hear her.

The ramshackle crew drew weapons and charged in the direction they had come from.

"Get us mounts," she hissed to her head guard through her sound transmission device. She wanted to be gone from this place as fast as possible.

The guard moved away, cuffing a younger man. "Go secure us Krakol before they run off. You two watch the area. We don't know if we disturbed any of the beasts nearby. There could be some strong ones in a place this remote!"

Maybe this one isn't a complete idiot.

The guards quickly grabbed Krakol, pulling the irate and confused birds to where Ubren and her remaining guards stood. The rest of her crew were still rushing through the enemy corvette.

One man jumped from one airship section to the other; he never made it. A spray of blood shot out of his back and he slumped between the two sections.

Those on the top of the corvettes dropped silently in sprays of blood.

What?

"They're attacking. They're in the tree line! They have an ar—" The guard's last word ended in a gargle as he cradled his neck, looked at Ubren, and collapsed.

Ubren turned and ran toward the Krakol, keeping the ship between her and the forest.

Crunching metal and explosions came from the direction of her people charging the tree-line, casting spells into the trees blindly.

Accurate pinpoint spells and ranged weapons cut down the charging rabble.

Ubren jumped onto a Krakol, kicking it forward.

"Come on. you damn bird! Faster, damn you!" She hissed, kicking harder and wiping the blood from her forehead.

The guards yelled and kicked their beasts after her.

An explosion on Ubren's back buffeted her forward. An unlucky guard coughed blood, gravely wounded. His mount had been killed in the blast and dropped away from the group. Other attacks hit around the group as he faded away.

"Keep up!" Ubren yelled.

She risked a glance toward the ground. Three people ran out from the forest, blurs of speed. Two men and a woman. Behind them two mages walked out; their spells crashed into the attack spells that her remaining crew hurled at the blurs.

Her crew continued to be killed by a sixth hidden person. Leaping from the ground to the debris, the blurs reached the edge of the warship's graveyard. They leapt from one piece of broken ship to another, a woman with twin blades leaving sprays of blood in her wake, staining the ground as she weaved between Ubren's crew.

Another conjured spears of wood from the ground, grabbing and throwing them or raising them to meet those charging him.

The last waded forward with a two-handed hammer, denting his opponents' armor and sending them careening backward.

Roots and greenery shot from the ground between the ships, grabbing people from the sky, snapping at their feet, giving the trio openings.

The crew's forward momentum was arrested as they turned and ran away.

Ubren felt a chill as she looked back at the tree line. The sixth member appeared with an odd-looking weapon in his hands. She could swear he was looking at her.

She gritted her teeth and pulled out an old, tattered spell scroll. The mana around her seemed to still. The beast underneath her shook.

Cold sweat ran down her back as rage burned in her heart. "Bastards."

She ripped the spell scroll open. The pages bloomed with imbued mana as the clouds shifted. A spell formation appeared above the crash site. Swirling storm clouds gathered as the spell scroll burned with purple and blue flames.

There was a tension in the air, a hidden fight as the elemental mana poured into the spell and mana circulated throughout the formation. Elemental mana was torn from the skies and the ground. Black threads from the clouds turned white. Flames of red gathered, sucking away the heat of the land.

Trees and plants withered and died as green, yellow, and silver energies tore from the ground. The ships started to fall apart, dissolving.

Her crew ran for the remaining Krakol that were trying to escape, their instincts overriding their training.

The group ran toward the ships.

Fools!

"Why the hell are we heading *toward* this thing, Rugrat?" Erik yelled even as he ran into the middle of the ships.

"We can't outrun it and there are no aerial beasts. We're going to have to improvise. Pull out your stack formations," Rugrat yelled as he threw down the old corvette's dungeon core.

It struck the ground and started to rebuild itself.

Rugrat took control of the dungeon. The blueprint for the Aemis was still input into the dungeon core. *Just need some modifications.*

"You sure?"

"We got any other choice?" Rugrat asked as he threw down a stack formation base plate and an attack stack formation. The shifting metal moved it around and under the dungeon core, creating a console.

Metal moved like water, creating what looked like a metal cart with raised sides. Wings grew from the sides and runners formed underneath.

He turned, grabbing the stack formations in Erik's hands. He threw away some formations in the stacks and added in new formations. The metal twisted around the stacks and pulled them into different locations.

His domain and mana arms worked on three stack formations at the same time as the metal created a roof and started to rise, cocooning them.

"Racquel, do you have that sky mana cornerstone?"

Formation runic lines were pulled from the ship underneath, connecting the various formations.

"Here!" She threw it out. His mana hands grabbed it and pulled it to the deck of the ship. Formations spread out from it and connected to the rest of the ship. The stack formations drew in power that shot into the dungeon core at the front of the metal cart, then directed into the sky grade cornerstone. Mana stones grew like ice across a windshield, spreading through the craft at a rapid rate.

"Rugrat, if you're going to do something *now* would be the time to do it." Reaper sounded panicked. The surrounding ground lifted, the elemental energies dragged toward the swirling formation above. Colors twisted together as they bled from the outer rings to the inner rings and runes.

"That should do it! Hold on!"

The cart accelerated forward as the part of the ship they had been standing on started to rise into the sky. The cart they were in began to lift too, the metal creaking and groaning as they broke away from the corvette, speeding up as they got farther from the eye of the spell scroll. Trees, dirt, rock, parts of the other ships lifted as they hit the ground again.

"Rugrat!" Racquel yelled, pointing at a section of a ship rolling over to block their path.

Rugrat poured power into another stack formation, pushing them to the side and increasing the power.

He created solidified mana for the runners, creating a half-pipe, bringing them up and over the section of the ship before they turned and dropped back down again, gaining speed. The edges of the left wing hit the side of the moving section of ship as they rose into the air then dropped to the ground with a bump. Rugrat checked the power available as more mana stones grew in the middle of the cart.

"Add in your mana stones!"

They threw down their mana stones as Rugrat gathered his power.

"Okay, so I'm going to need your help! George, grab the front! Everyone else, spells to lift us!"

Everyone drew on their mana as George grew to his full height and stretched out his wings, grabbing onto the front of the cart with his rear paws.

Spells appeared under the cart; mana solidified as fire spells bloomed behind the cart.

Rugrat poured in the power to his formation stacks, diverting it all.

They hurtled into the sky. Rugrat altered their course to avoid the trees torn free from the ground into the spell formation above.

They swung through the heavens as the spell finalized. It was as if a god had taken a sip of the planet's atmosphere. Time, sound, breath were stolen from them all in that one second.

The elemental energies swirled together into a chaotic pillar that reaped vengeance upon the ground. The surrounding mana purified, their elements ripped from them as it descended.

Sound and light sparked into existence. The different elements violently interacted with matter and one another, mana fueling their combined destruction. Rugrat felt the world shifting around him. The light took his vision as he closed off his ears with mana against the roar of nature's vengeance. He bent his will to his craft.

A wave of force crashed into the ship. He fought to keep them level, to not send them tumbling, running on the tide of destruction to escape the wall of annihilation that chased behind it.

Hard fingers wrapped around him, rooting him in place and protecting him from smashing against the sides.

Another wave hit them, tossing them forward.

Ubren and her guards were thrown forward with the blast of the spell scroll.

Her beast tried to right himself, but the winds were too powerful, sending her cartwheeling forward. A singular wave cut through the forests, ripping them up. She saw it come and pass as she was thrown free of her mount. She screamed, but it was lost in the noise.

Her replacement protection medallions and formations activated before she hit the ground. Pain flared through her legs and back as she tumbled, striking her head on the ground.

She hissed in pain as she lay still.

She didn't know for how long she laid there. Her hearing came back with a painful pop as she grunted to pull out a healing potion. She knocked off the stopper with a rock and poured it down her throat and on her head.

She breathed heavily, the pain throughout her body. She pulled out other healing potions and drank them. She needed to go. If she stayed here, the clan or the Mission Hall would find her. *Those Heroes couldn't have survived that.*

Erik breathed in suddenly, grabbing his rifle and freeing it as he looked around. He started coughing from all the dust in the air. *Broken left*

shoulder, bruising, nothing too bad.

He looked around. Trees had been blown over and scattered as if they were matchsticks, leaving them in piles all over and revealing the dirt and stone of the mountain underneath.

"Call out your name if you can hear me!" Erik said as he pushed himself to his feet, spreading out his domain to find the others.

"Racquel!" She grunted as she stood up and dusted the dirt off herself.

Tree roots sprouted from a pile of rubble, parting it, revealing Fred.

"Fred!"

"Reaper!" His voice was high and through his teeth. Erik moved toward where his voice was coming from.

"Rugrat!" George let out a howl as he dug through trees that covered Rugrat.

"Dromm, where are you?" Erik said as he reached Reaper. Parts of a tree had exploded and peppered his back.

"Ah, nothing but a scratch for you," Erik said as he pulled out the medical kit from the rear of his vest.

"I've found him," Fred said.

"How is he?" Erik yelled as he pulled out a revival needle and stabbed it into Reaper's back, closest to his wounds.

"He's out. Breathing, I think!" Fred said, his voice rising in panic.

"Rugrat!"

"I'm coming!" Rugrat's voice was deadly serious as he clambered over the fallen trees and broken forest.

"Bit of an odd day," Erik said to Reaper.

"Ye-*ARGH*" Reaper screamed as Erik used that moment to pull the shards of wood out of his back.

"Don't worry. The potion is already at work. You'll be good to go in no time."

"Damn, that hurt," Reaper grumbled.

"Next time, try to avoid flying tree shards. Usually, you're the one throwing them about."

"Rugrat, talk to me!" Erik said standing.

"He's okay. Broken arm, but no internal. Brain is as good as it's going to get." It was more Rugrat's calm tone than his words that let Erik breathe freely.

"Okay, Reaper just needs to get bandaged and we can get moving."

Erik bandaged Reaper and got him to his feet.

"Ah hell, why do I have to wake up to your face? I was dreaming of the most gorgeous women in Coren," Dromm complained.

"Welcome back to reality." Rugrat laughed.

Erik looked around the area and at the group and then checked his quests.

Quest: Puppetress
General Ubren is implicated in banditry, forcing two orphans to work as bandits and to break the law for her to increase her position.   Kill General Ubren

Rewards:
     +100,000,000,000 EXP
     100 Mission points
     2-Star Hero medallion
     Rewards may be increased based on performance.

"Looks like she's still alive," Erik said he applied Fuse Bone to his shoulder, pulling it back into form. His body started to heal naturally.

Rugrat closed his eyes.

"I sense a dungeon core, other than ours, not that far away, moving slowly. I think she got downed too."

"Okay, let's move forward slowly."

Erik heard a yell from the left. He looked over to see Fred's spell break the incoming spell.

Erik turned and fired on the guards with his rifle, running for some cover he had scanned moments before. A mana barrier snapped up, covering the group.

Rugrat fired, causing the barrier to flare angrily.

"Stoppage!" Rugrat yelled as he dropped to a crouch.

Racquel ran forward and threw out a slash. A bolt of lightning struck her and smashed her through several logs as her attack went wide.

Erik fired over the top of the log and ran toward where she landed.

"We're no good to her dead. Keep going!" Erik yelled, feeling the lull in the fighting as he quickly reloaded.

Dromm charged forward. An arrow narrowly missed him, turning the stone and fallen trees he had been standing on into a crater.

Fred raised his hands; trees flew into the air, coming apart in spears back in the direction the arrow had come from. They broke the mana barrier and staked the mage maintaining it.

Dromm slipped as the lightning attacker came under his guard, slashing his side. He lost his footing completely and rolled, crashing into trees.

Erik fired on the lightning swordsman who had turned to finish off Dromm, hitting his personal barrier and sending him tumbling.

Ubren's other guard ran for it.

Erik's gun jammed. He reached out, conjuring a stone spear out of the ground, impaling the lightning man.

A hand made from weaved trees reached out of the earth, grabbed the last man, and squeezed with a cracking noise as Dromm righted himself and Erik cleared his rifle.

"Where the hell is she?"

Ubren panted as she leaned on the boulder.

How can people spend all their lives walking in the dirt?

She groaned and moved forward from the boulder.

There was movement across the forest—a group of three people walking north.

She squinted, using a spell on her eyes.

Her guards. But she was weak right now. If she waved them over and they chose to attack her, there would be nothing she could do other than threaten them with spell scrolls. *No, they don't know where I hid my treasures.* She made sure that she was the only one piloting the ship when they dropped off items and that the sensors were off so they couldn't update their maps. If she killed them here, she wouldn't need to share the cache with them or waste any time killing them later.

She crouched between the logs, out of view of her old guards when she heard a yell. She looked over and a vicious expression crossed her face as she pulled out a spell scroll.

I'll kill you, you damn bastards.

She readied her scroll. She nearly cheered as the swordswoman was sent flying through a pile of wood, and then the warhammer user was cut down.

She took out her scroll, but was tossed to the side before she could rip it. She looked around, stunned. Her barriers had disappeared, and she was a few feet from where she had been.

She felt the same chill she had experienced when looking at the crash site when the same group had torn through her people.

The sixth one.

She saw him kneeling with that odd weapon and then the flash of pain in her stomach.

She tilted over to the side and dropped on the rocks. An inglorious ending for the once General Ubren.

Erik heard Rugrat's rifle bellow and saw an explosion behind a boulder to the right.

The wooden hands collapsed as two tombstones appeared between them.

Rugrat fired again as notifications rang out. Erik ignored it and cleared his weapon before reloading it and scanning the area.

A pulse covered the land, detecting all life.

Erik didn't see anything in any direction that looked humanoid other than their own group.

Fred released the attackers as he ran forward. The forest created a path under his feet as he ran for Dromm.

Erik ran for Racquel, calling on the branches to make a smooth path for him.

"Reaper, you're with me. Check on the guards. There's another one behind that boulder over there," Rugrat said.

Erik reached Racquel who'd gone through a pile of trees.

"Hey Racquel, can you hear me?" Erik asked as he pulled a revival needle out and unslung his gun, putting it behind his knees. He stabbed her neck with the needle. Her eyes were swimming, looking up at the sky above.

"Hurts," Racquel offered.

"Yup, I bet it does," Erik said as he pulled out other potions.

Internal fractures, internal bleeding, Nasty concussion as well. She's seeing stars.

"I need to go and help." She started to stand up, looking around. "Where are my swords? I remember having my swords. I just had them sharpened."

"Don't worry, everyone's safe. They took care of the guards," Erik said calmly as he used healing spells on her to relieve the pressure on her brain and the internal bleeding.

"Hey, Fred. How is Dromm?"

"He's fine. The sword just about made it through his armor. It was the lightning's stun effect that made him slow down and fall. How is Racquel?"

"She's fine, just a little fuzzy. She hit her head," Erik stated as he worked with calm, easy movements.

"Okay."

"Rugrat, how are we looking on your side?"

"We have the guards here. We've looted them and the one behind the rock, you'll never guess who it is." Rugrat paused for a half-breath before Erik could think it all the way through. "Ubren."

"No shit? I guess I know what that notification was about then."

He changed off the sound transmission device.

"Don't worry. I'll have you good to go in no time, but you have to stop moving around," Erik said.

Racquel nodded and sank to the ground again.

"Sorry, I'm working on Racquel right now. Give me a few minutes, will you? Can you clear the perimeter," Erik asked.

"Can do," Rugrat said.

Erik focused on his work and not on the transmission channel. He quickly sealed up the internal bleeding, moving from the skull down. Then he reduced the swelling in her brain as Racquel blinked, coming back to the world of the conscious.

She groaned and turned away from the light.

"Don't worry. You'll be good in no time. Stop moving around or you'll undo my work."

Racquel nodded and closed her eyes, biting her lip as she suffered through the brightness.

Her features relaxed as Erik got the swelling under control. He checked on her internal injuries.

"All right. Sweet. It looks like your body is doing all the heavy lifting.

It's working on your internal injuries, sealing them up completely and clearing out the clots. How do you feel?"

"Like I smashed through that!" Racquel pointed at the wood pile in front of her.

Erik laughed and gave her a potion.

"Take this; , it will help. It's specially made to deal with internal bleeding and swelling."

"Not just a regular healing potion?" She took the dark green and yellowish mixture with chunks of both.

"No." Erik sat back on his rifle. "Someone figured out that many injuries we have in the higher realms are not puncture or stab wounds, they're internal. They were a healer, so they looked at spells in this area, but they didn't find any that were effective. Went to the alchemists and came up with this."

"You Alvans are a resourceful bunch."

"You're talking about yourself now," Rugrat said.

Erik laughed at Racquel's perplexed look. Grabbing his rifle from behind his knee crease, he stood, checking the notification he had ignored.

Quest Completed: Puppetress
You have killed General Ubren. Head to the Mission Hall Quartermaster to receive your rewards.
Rewards:
+100,000,000,000 EXP
100 Mission points
2-Star Hero medallion
Rewards may be increased based on performance.

Racquel sat up and drank some of the potion in a small sip, waiting a few more seconds before taking another sip.

Erik heard footsteps coming in their direction. Through his domain he picked up Dromm and Fred.

Fred was creating a path through the trees, and he visibly relaxed seeing Racquel.

"Shit, I think you made more of a mess than I did," Dromm said, walking over.

Erik cast a cleanse spell on him, removing the blood from his clothes and armor. There was still a silver line through his armor where the blade had cut through.

The better the armor, the better the weapons.

"I have one question. Where the hell are we?" Dromm asked.

"Good question," Rugrat said as he walked up with Reaper. Racquel stood up to prove that she was okay.

"Let me use my Dungeon Sense. That should at least tell us where there are a lot of dungeon cores," Erik said.

"Where there are dungeon cores, there are people." Fred sighed as he raked his long hair back and sat down on a rock.

"Do your quests usually go like this?" Reaper asked.

"There are usually some fights, cool places to see, though the airships are a new twist."

"And you creating a bathtub with wings?" Racquel asked.

"Bit more of a surprise."

"Okay, I've picked up some large-sized dungeons in that direction." Erik pointed.

"Let's head out."

"Well, this might make things a bit easier," Fred said as the wood grew up and into a cart.

"Seems like it is a day for carts and carriages," Dromm observed.

"Let's get out of here before it gets dark." Reaper said.

They got onto the cart and Fred sat up at the front. The fallen trees and other plants reached up to move the cart forward under Fred's direction, quickly carrying them across the area where Ubren's spell scroll had reaped its destruction.

21

To Come Together and Fall Apart

omma Rodriguez looked over the factory floor from the lobby window. Hundreds of machines worked in tandem with people to create the supplies needed by the military. Everyone worked furiously, but the long nights and little breaks in between showed in their expressions and movements.

She sighed as the manager, Adam, walked out of the swing doors and into the lobby.

Adam smiled, holding out his hand. "Miss Rodriguez."

"Adam Wainfleet. And Momma Rodriguez is just fine. Everyone else around here calls me that," she said with a disarming smile. She took his hand and patted it, somehow getting her hand in the crook of his elbow as she turned him toward the doors into his factory line.

He looked confused, but let himself be led.

"What can I do for you, Momma Rodrigeuz?" Adam had a slight rise to his voice as they pushed through the swing doors onto the loud factory lines.

"It is incredible what you have achieved here, Adam. I bet your wife and children are proud."

"Well, I think my wife might say I spend too many hours at work, even when I'm at home." Adam chuckled.

She patted his hand. "It's hard to be with someone that is so dedicated to their job. I understand, but it also means that you put them above work which is your love and joy."

Adam nodded with a small, tired smile.

She gave him a knowing smile as they moved through the factory. "You were working on enhancement formations before?"

"Yes, for carriages and carts specifically. We sold formations to the traders to upgrade their carts, then they sold it to their friends. We had one of the top three transportation formations out there. Increased reliability for your cart and decreased strain on your beast of burden, allowing you to carry more and travel faster."

"Then when the military asked factories to take on contracts to fulfill material requirements, you took that on as well, producing stack formation base plates."

Adam stood straighter. "Yes, ma'am. We weren't that good with the detail work, so we wouldn't be as fast producing the individual plates that go into a stack formation as other factories, but we can produce high quality larger plates, a perfect size and skill match with the base plates. Wanted to do our part, you see."

"And you're producing more base plates than any other factory in Alva. What would you put that down to?"

"I put it down to the staff, their dedication and ability." He smiled and glanced around.

Momma patted his hand. He was a good man, doing the best he could. She paused and watched the lines. Metal came in through one side, machines pressing and cleaning them as people checked their work and added in details. The metal was carved, and the lines filled in before they were tested at the end of the line and added to others that had been completed that day.

"Adam, how do your people look?"

Adam was confused by the question and looked at the people working on the line.

Momma followed his gaze. They were drooping. Some tried to stretch in between what they were doing. Others rubbed their eyes.

"Do they look tired to you, Adam?" Her voice was soft.

"I guess that they do," Adam said, still studying people up and down the line.

"Adam, your people work the longest hours out of any factory. They might have large stamina pools to draw from, but many of them are technicians and you have them on the line instead of working on their machines. Many of them have few hours at home to see their family and then they're back at it. Adam, when was the last time you saw your family?"

"Uhh, it had to be yesterday, o-or the day before." Adam grew quiet, trying to recall.

"It was a week ago, Adam," Momma said.

Adam's face fell "Oh, no."

"Alva was not built in a day, and it was not made by one person; it was made by many. If you keep working your people as you are, they'll fall apart and there will be none of them left at the end," Momma assured him.

"But the war..." He sounded as drawn out as he looked.

"We do not know if the war will happen next week or in several years. We are preparing, but if our people are reduced to nothing but husks while preparing, does it matter?"

They walked in silence for some time.

"Your workers, how many of them attend the school?"

"Around eighty percent, maybe ninety percent. Many go to the new drop-in courses so they can continue to work and support their families."

"Eventually, many of those people will become crafters of the Journeyman, even the Expert grade. Will they want to sell their designs to you for mass production if you did nothing but work them to death?"

Adam opened his mouth and sighed. "No, they won't."

"I understand. You're working hard to build the supplies the military needs. I know you want to work as fast as possible to produce as much as possible. But what would Alva become if we were to sacrifice everything we have to become a military machine. We can't let this war define us. We must defeat the enemy in combat, but we must not allow them to defeat our minds and break the culture that has supported us for so long."

Adam rubbed his face. "Then what do I do?"

"Go back to your normal hours and listen to your people. Yes, work on increasing production, but not at the cost of your people's lives. So many of them have been working for two or three days straight, afraid that they'll get fired if they dare to come in any less."

Adam groaned as his face pinched together. "I wouldn't fire them for doing the work they were contracted for."

"I can see that you care for them. You don't need to tell me; you have to tell them."

Adam nodded, and Momma moved with him, continuing their walk.

Adam fell into silence, thinking.

He stood straighter, a new light in his eyes. He looked at the different stations as if to verify it, a kernel of an idea unravelling in his mind.

"Momma Rodriguez, I think I might have a way for us to increase our working hours and production speed without increasing the number of people working on the line."

"How so?"

"Contracting! We use a lot of machines and crafters to make components to a standard that are sent down the line and fitted to other parts to make a complete whole, right?"

"Yes." Momma nodded.

"Making the smaller components takes the most amount of time. Combining them is faster. Instead of us making the components in-house, what if we were to contract them out?"

"The Academy is already working on projects for the military and the city. You won't be able to use them." Momma sighed.

"Well, that's where the next bit might need your help. What if we were to contract out to other crafters in the Ten Realms, external to Alva?"

"External." It was her turn to pause. "I, well I don't see—"

"You might be wondering if we would be letting go of our secrets? If they make specific small components, it would be hard for them to figure out what they are a part of. Sure, we'll lose out on some experience, but if we're looking at production speed, that should make things faster," Adam said.

"What do we have in Alva that is not produced by Alvans?"

"Uhh," Adam looked up at the ceiling. "I don't think there is much. A lot of the things that we create are used internally, either because we can produce it faster, or at a higher quality for cheaper."

"So, what would happen if we get other people to make these parts?"

"I could take on workers that aren't crafters and just have them assembling things. Most of the equipment I've built is around assembling so it would be automated."

"What would you need to turn that into a reality?"

"I guess the only thing would be for the government to okay it."

"All right, I'll have a talk with them and see. In the meantime, what will you do?"

"Return to normal working hours, listen to my people, and keep the production at stable levels," Adam said.

"And?"

"And?" Adam frowned.

She rapped her knuckles on his shoulder. "Go see your family and sleep! I know the signs of someone that is kept standing by nothing more than continuous stamina potions!"

Adam rubbed the back of his neck, looking like he knew he had done wrong. She withdrew her hand from Adam's elbow as they reached the swing doors back into the lobby.

"Thank you, Momma Rodriguez." Adam bowed to her.

"Don't worry Adam. We all slip up from time to time." She smiled and patted him on the shoulder, leaving the factory floor.

Delilah finished reviewing her latest documents, signing the note she had affixed to them. She held her temples, rubbing them as she leaned back in her chair and flipped a formation that would notify her staff that she was available.

"Miss Delilah, Momma Rodriguez is here to see you with Elise." Her assistant's voice came through a sound transmission device on her desk.

"Let them in." Delilah forced herself forward and stood from her desk, moving around it. Not a few moments later, the door opened as the duo walked in. "Elise, Momma, what can I do for you?" She indicated to the couches and table to the side of the room.

"We want to see if we can trade with other groups on items that the factories need to complete their military orders," Elise said as she sat on the couch opposite.

Momma pulled out a plate of cookies and held them out to Delilah. "Chocolate Chip, your favorite" Momma smiled. "Take two!"

Delilah smiled, grabbing one of the still-warm cookies that seemed to melt in her hand. Elise took one as well.

The sugar rush served to clear Delilah's mind as she mulled it over. "What kind of items?"

"Parts. We could get crafters in the Ten Realms to make, say, a section of inscribed runes. Over seven different factories they create several sections. They're brought back to Alva and fused together to create an entire formation," Momma said.

"I fail to see why we can't do that here?" Delilah frowned as she started eating her second cookie.

"I was talking to one of the factory owners. He is working his people to the bone to fill the military orders. His people are making all the parts, but if he were to have them delivered, already complete, it would allow him to increase production," Momma said.

Delilah looked to Elise. "Can we do it?"

"Yes, it wouldn't be that hard. If we split it up across regions and realms, they won't have any clue what it's for."

"The time will come that Alva is revealed to the world. Our people's level of skill varies across the board. But eventually, they will increase in skill. As they do, fewer and fewer will be interested in making simple parts that pay little. Making pipes that heat and move water might not be glamorous, but they will forever be something that we need." Momma said.

"As Momma says, you and I both know that relationships between nations are built upon one thing above all others— trade." Delilah crossed her arms as she finished off her second cookie.

"Since Alva started production, we've been bringing in raw materials and pushing out finished products for people to sell. Bringing in components to build advanced technology would allow us to change the dynamic," Elise said.

"I want to make sure that our military projects are kept within Alva, but I don't see why we couldn't purchase parts externally for other projects." Delilah pointed out.

"Okay, I'll talk to the traders, crafters, and factory owners, and have the plan on your desk in three days," Elise said, standing.

"How are things with the Adventurer's Guild?" Delilah asked.

"Good. They gave their members references to guilds in different realms, so it looks like the guild has fallen apart. A lot of them are joining Alva directly. Training has increased. They started some training halls in the higher realms. Again, separate from the other guilds. They're set up in cells so if one is compromised, they'll only learn of a few connections, instead of the entire network. Though it has proliferated through the guilds that while they are free to do as they want, they have a backer and if it is needed. They will support their backer as the backer supports them."

"How are they adjusting to the changes?"

"There are rough patches with any kind of big change. There are still many interested in the dungeons and places they were hiding. Most of them are angry at the Willful Institute. When we make our attack, they'll lead the charge."

Delilah felt the familiar darkness around her, the weight that rested on her body.

"Yes," she murmured, distracted as she looked at the wall without seeing it. She shook herself internally and smiled at Elise. "Thank you. I'll let you get back to what you were doing. I look forward to reading your plan."

"Thank you, Delilah. See you later." Elise glanced at Momma Rodriguez, but she waved Elise on.

Elise shrugged, smiling and waving good-bye as she walked out of the room.

Delilah looked at Momma Rodriguez. "Is there something else you wanted to talk about?"

"You," Momma said.

"Me?"

"You carry the weight of Alva on your shoulders. It's not an easy burden. What troubles you?"

Delilah smiled. "There's not much that doesn't trouble me. Hoping that we have the supplies we'll need for the coming war. That we'll win this war."

Momma Rodriguez pushed the plate of cookies to Delilah, who took one. "Do you trust Commander Glosil?"

"Yes, of course."

"Then trust him. It's his job to worry about the war. Your job is to worry about the people. I know the two are linked, but don't get so focused on the war that you forget the other things. Alva needs not only warriors, but builders. If we become so focused on war, we forget that. Then we will lose Alva."

Delilah nibbled on her cookie in thought, feeling the knot in her stomach, the tension in her face. "What if we lose?"

"Then we lose. We lost at Vuzgal and we have only increased our abilities. The realms are vast; we should not look at them as if we are against the entire realms. We will never win with that mindset. To create change, we must first change ourselves."

Delilah sunk into silence and looked out the window of her office. "Since returning from the Fourth Realm, Egbert has been working tirelessly to increase the size of the dungeon and install the defensive and offensive formations across the entire Beast Mountain Range. What we have here is so precious, if we were to lose it—"

"What is broken can be repaired, and what is destroyed can be rebuilt. We must stop looking at the now, this day, tomorrow, this week, and the next. We must look at next month, this year, next year, this decade and the next. Time is power. Just think of what change we can effect with a bit each day piled up?"

Delilah looked at Momma Rodriguez. It felt as if something had unlocked in her head. In the silence, her imagination bloomed, seeing the dungeon expand as buildings rose, fields grew and were harvested. The academy continued to sprawl with its workshops increasing in ability, the factories increasing in production.

Her mind turned to the Beast Mountain Range, seeing King's Hill expanding, the outposts turning into cities and reaching outward as they tamed the wild land between the outposts and the border cities and turned to fields. Smaller villages and towns appeared.

"This, too, shall come to pass. As Alva continues to grow, so will our crafters. So will our population. So will our fighters and traders. Alva will reach out further than ever before. We are but one small group in a vast network of ten connected worlds. While our problems with the Willful Institute and their allies are large to us, they are barely worth talking about with some groups. There are people that don't even know of the Willful Institute, or the Stone Fist Sect, and we never knew about the Black Phoenix Clan until they showed up in their warship." Momma Rodriguez took a cookie and sat back on the couch, giving Delilah time to digest what she said.

"It is Glosil's job to deal with the threats while I deal with the people and the future of Alva. I should stop worrying about a job that's not mine, and do the job I need to, preparing for Alva's future—whatever that might be."

Delilah felt the weight on her release slightly as her eyes flickered. Where there had been dread, now she felt energized.

"There you go."

Momma Rodriguez walked through the street toward her home. She smiled at people as they passed, causing some to return the gesture, while others bowed in a panic.

"Taran, why would you be loitering near my door? Would you like to come inside for some tea?" Momma Rodriguez said as she approached the front of her house.

The burly smith looked up from the stair he sat on. "Sorry, I was lost in my own thoughts."

"Take a seat in the chairs, please." She gestured at two rocking chairs on the porch.

She walked past him to the seats. He looked torn before standing up and sat in the opposite chair as she pulled out glasses and a pitcher of chilled tea.

"So, what can I help you with?" she asked as she filled the glasses and passed the first one to Taran.

"Thank you, Miss Rodriguez. I'm worried about Julilah."

"Oh?" Momma put the pitcher on a table between them then took a sip from her iced tea, relieving her itchy throat.

"Since Tan Xue passed away, she's been wrapped up in her work. Throws herself in without care. Passes out only when she can no longer stay awake; she is skilled and highly sought after for projects. Qin works with her and has been doing the same thing. I-I just want to make sure that she's okay."

Taran's voice turned gruff as he looked straight ahead, drinking his iced tea.

Momma sipped her tea.

"I'm not good with this talking thing. Not sure what to say to her that will make this all right, you know? Dunno if there is anything I can say that will. Shit, I miss Tan Xue as well. Just ..." Taran grunted as he leaned on the left armrest of the chair, away from Momma, and pinched the bridge of his nose.

"You're a good man, Taran Choi. You knew how much Tan Xue cared for Julilah and have looked out for her admirably. Have you tried talking to her?"

"I mean to, but every time I open my mouth something else comes out. Just trying to avoid it, you know?" Taran sniffed, turning to Momma. "I don't know what to say. I don't want to say something wrong and hurt her or make a rift between us."

"I can talk with her, though I can't do that work for you. You still need to talk to her. You care for her deeply and she has to know that." Momma reached over and grabbed his forearm, holding it. He looked back at her, nodding, his eyes still wet.

"Thank you," he choked out, the tension bleeding off from within his body.

She patted his arm and rocked in her chair as she drank her iced tea.

Marshal Edmond Dujardin was feeling melancholy, looking at the fresh faces around the conference table. There were only a few that remained from the old days, the days when the Sha Clans were in their infancy. Back then, the Sha Clans were a group of people working and fighting together, using their weapons to make up for their weaknesses and forge a path ahead. As they rose, they gained access to resources, increasing their cultivation, adding more people to their ranks, reaching the staggering height of the Seventh Realm.

That was then. This is now.

Most were dead or had vacated their positions of power for the younger generations.

He looked at the four eldest members of the table. Robert Larionvich was a pale man with golden hair and a trimmed beard. His dull grey eyes seemed to look past the world, bored with the day to day. His hair showed fringes of grey and shifting to white.

Kameela wore a face covering, revealing only her deep dark eyes, the fringes of a silver tattoo at the corners. She shifted her covering, resting her head against her hand, sliding her gaze to meet Marshal's.

He saw the pull at the corner of her eyes, the amusement dancing there.

Marshal fought to control the corner of his mouth that threatened to rise in a smirk, turning away to look at Harrod. The man wore a mishmash of armor, out of touch with the surrounding finery. He disregarded the meeting, scribbling notes in his journal, raising his hands and pen, visualizing his latest creation. Those on either side had learned to sit back from the table, lost in thought as he was. His head was shaved, and he had a squashed nose and rock-like teeth in a too big mouth.

I still remember when he would chase Esther and Milo around the garden, acting like an ogre. One of the few times he put down his notes.

His stomach clenched as he looked at the last remaining member, Lady LeBlanc, Esther's mother. She sat there, prim and proper, her eyes half-lowered and vacant, her mind somewhere else.

22

Two Stars

"Yₒᵤ sure this is all necessary?" Dromm asked. He wore low quality clothes and simple armor.

"Cassmir's Totem is in clan Ubren's territory. I don't know how they'll treat us, so best to be cautious," Erik said as he drew his finger along his upper lip, growing a moustache. He wore a trader's garb of gaudy reds and purples with a gold fringe.

Reaper had taken down his hood, revealing his white and electric green hair and eyes. He shook his head as his hair grew, turning brown. When he opened his eyes, they were a light brown. He stored his cloak and removed his armor, revealing dusty and worn clothes underneath.

Racquel and Rugrat wore simple clothes, while Fred's were flashier, making them appear like a mentor and his apprentices.

Rugrat had grown out his hair some, spoiling his high and tight haircut.

Erik finished with his moustache and grew out his hair with a grow hair spell. He used a tie to pull it back out of his face. "Well, I think that about does it. We'll go through the gate in groups. Once inside, we'll head for the totem and teleport to Cronen."

Erik finished with his hair tie. "Let's get the hell out of here."

Erik's group left the forest first, joining the road, and starting their trek toward the city.

"So, why did we loop all the way around the city?" Reaper asked.

"Old tactic. If they know that we were in the south, then they'll be watching the southern gates. But, if we loop around to the east and come in through the easterly gates, guards might not be on high alert," Erik said as they walked.

"And the appearances?"

"Breaking up the group and changing our appearance should throw them off. Instead of five guys and a woman, we're three guys, or two guys and a woman."

It took a few hours before they saw the city gates. The gates were huge, as wide as the road, and could fit six normal carriages side by side.

They passed a large wood-topped berm that acted as defenses. Houses lay back from the road a bit, farmers and those who didn't have the money to live inside the city chose to call these home.

Erik blinked as he looked closer at the people. "Are they..." Erik was confused as he saw ears in different positions, some with tails and other beast features.

Dromm followed his eyes. "Those are the beast-kin. Some call us demi-humans."

"Like, I know that you are, but I didn't think there were so many."

"Much more common in the higher realms. In the Sixth there are a rare few, but in the Seventh some really powerful beasts attained a humanoid form. Most of the creatures in the Seventh Realm, even if they still retain their beast form, have the intelligence of a young human child. Never underestimate them."

"Becoming a demi-human, do you just need to increase your body cultivation?"

"You need to improve your body cultivation and unlock your bloodline. Once you do that, you undergo an evolution; humans get their elemental core. Us beasts already have it. Instead, we develop our mana systems out. The mana system seems to be linked to the humanoid body. Our body shifts and changes, becoming more humanoid, and our brains develop. Our intelligence shoots up. We can then access mana, along with our developed elemental core. And we scare a whole ton of people with our very existence." Dromm smiled evilly.

"You make it sound so easy, but it changes you completely," Erik said.

"Yeah, we have a few more changes, and while it makes the first generation much stronger, the second generation will have to work for it.

Just like humans," Reaper said.

"If the first generation are powerful cultivators, then their kids will have a leg up, but only so much. To get to the stage their parents are at, or higher, they'll have to work hard," Erik said thoughtfully.

"Yeah, most of them are probably a few generations removed from the beasts that unlocked their bloodline," Dromm said.

"You said beast-kin and demi-human. What's that about?"

"Most people call us demi-human. There are not many of us that like the term. It makes it seem as if we are less than human. We prefer the name beast-kin. It shows that we are part beast, that we have not forgotten where we come from, but while we're related. We're not like them," Reaper said.

"There is a long history of beast-kin being used by humans and others. We're something different. Not everyone likes differences," Dromm said.

Erik grunted and nodded. They reached the gate, and he looked at the guards. They were all wearing the Ubren Clan armor, but there were a lot among them that were beast-kin.

Groups were pulled to the side of the road and checked; the guards seemed extra vigilant.

They're looking for us. Each of the groups had five men and one woman.

Guards patrolled the lines, looking at people, their hands resting on their weapons.

Erik pressed his lips into a smile as they rolled over him with a bored expression.

The group ahead were called up to a cubicle. They split up the road, looking like toll stations that one might find on a land border.

"Next!"

Dromm and Erik stepped forward. Erik pulled on Reaper's sleeve, pulling the startled man into movement.

"Ah, sorry, just—yeah." Reaper laughed awkwardly as they reached the station.

"Purpose of your visit?" The guard asked, glancing at all three of them as they stepped onto a formation between stations.

"To head to Kraseem City," Dromm said.

The guard checked something out of sight. Erik rubbed his thumb, watching the positioning of the nearby guards through his peripherals.

"Three Sky Stones each."

Dromm paid the fee as Erik winced. He really needed to get some more stones, and soon, to pay them back.

The guard took the stones and looked past them. "Next!"

Casmir's wall blocked out the sun as they walked through the entrance tunnel. The noise of beasts, carts, and people bounced off the stone walls.

The noise shifted as they reached the other side and found themselves in a bustling city filled with people.

"All right, this way," Dromm said, leading them through the streets.

Erik scanned as they walked, noting where the guards were, watching for any sudden movements, or if they had picked up a tail.

"Looking for a place to stay, or for some work? I know just the people to talk to!" a man said, coming up to the group.

"Passing through," Erik said.

The man's smile slipped into a sneer as he clicked his tongue and turned back to the city's entrance.

Erik observed the different ingredient shops, inns, and taverns. There was an airship lifting off in the distance. "There are a lot of alchemists around here." He kept his head on a swivel. Trying to break up the nervous silence.

"Well, we do have a greater sense of smell, taste, touch, and hearing than most humans. Gives us a step up in some areas," Reaper said as they turned a corner, coming face-to-face with a group of guards.

Reaper ducked his head.

"Ah, sorry about that," Dromm said as they weaved around the guards and hurried down the street.

"Hey!" A voice rose from behind.

Erik looked back. The guards stared at him and started to walk toward them. People on the sidewalk moved out of the way and hurried on with their day or watched in curiosity about what was about to unfold. A large man wearing leather armor, some kind of beast pelt, and a feather that curled from his helmet down his back spoke first. "You three stop right there!"

The rest of the group trailed after their leader, eyeing Erik and his people.

Dromm glanced at Erik, who opened his hand without raising his arm.

"Is there anything we can do for you?" Erik asked, turning around with a smile.

"Move it, animal fucker." The man with the feather shoved Erik and grunted as Erik failed to move.

Erik looked down at his chest as the man recoiled and cradled his arm.

"What the…" one of the guards said.

"Lookie here. Seems that we have a tough guy. These bunch of animal rejects cut us off on our nice stroll and now they're acting suspicious." The leader opened and closed his hand, getting up close to Erik.

Erik backed up so he wouldn't have to tilt his head up to look at the man.

The man kept advancing.

"Think you're all big and tough? Think that you're bigger than the guard, huh? Hanging around with some wee beasties now? You saw it boys, didn't you? He was going for my sword!"

"That's enough, Tolos," another man said, and clipped the side of his head. The guard covered his head with a grimace, making way for a man with a darker, more perfect feather who pulled out a scroll and looked at the group.

He squinted before he shook his head. "Never mind. It's not them. Let's keep going." The man turned and started walking away.

"But, Captain," the guard whined.

"Tolos, you might be good with a blade, but that doesn't mean you have anything between your ears. You keep pissing off the beast-kin you'll wind up in a pool of your own blood and no one to blame for it but yourself."

"I'd like to see them try," Tolos growled as he looked at Erik, his hand gripping his sword.

The guard captain hit Tolos so hard in the helmet he staggered into the street. "You going to make my job hard for me, Tolos! I don't like the demi-humans, and I don't care if you do. Just don't make my job harder than it needs to be. You got me?"

Erik, Dromm, and Reaper backed away.

"Get out of here," the guard captain snarled.

They turned and left quickly.

"What was that all about?" Reaper asked.

"Some people are just assholes. Once they get a bit of power, it goes to their head and they think they can do anything they want. Think that their way is right and there is no way they could be wrong." Erik observed sourly.

"Come on. We're nearly there."

They got to the totem without further incident. The guards there were stricter than the ones at the gate. They checked everyone over before they reached the stations that would let them reach the totem.

They stepped up to the stations as a sound canceling field locked around them.

"Were you in the outpost, Vativa, two weeks ago?"

"I think we were in Vativa around two weeks ago. We were there for work. Why?"

"Why were you purchasing Redweed?"

"I am an alchemist." Erik pulled out his Journeyman level alchemist emblem. "I need to get my emblem updated. I was doing a job in Azraadale and now we're heading to Kraseem city with the guidance of my friends."

"Were you part of the attacks on the Ubren Clan?"

"Attacks on the Ubren Clan? I don't know of any attacks on the Ubren Clan." Erik smiled.

The woman looked at something only she could see and sighed. "Go on."

Erik smiled, and the group walked forward. They reached the totem and Dromm pulled out the stones. They disappeared in a flash of light. Barely had the world started to form around them when Dromm used more mana stones and they disappeared from Kraseem City and appeared in Cronen's Mission Hall.

"Damn, how the hell were you able to get away with that. She must have been watching for us lying, right?" Reaper asked as Erik slumped.

"When she asked about Vativa, I said I was working near it. Which is technically correct. We were there for work. The mission was work. We didn't aim to attack any of the Clan. We weren't acting out against the group. We were attacking one person for the Mission Hall. Everything I said was technically the truth. You make yourself bubbly and happy enough, give them long answers and they'll want nothing more than to push you off and get to the next person."

They walked away from the totem and showed their emblems to the guards. They used the teleportation pads, appearing in the gear hall.

They found some benches near the Quartermaster Hall.

Erik took the time to check on his skills and any notifications he might've missed.

Skill: Marksman
Level: 96 (Expert)
Long-range weapons are familiar in your hands. When aiming, you can zoom in x2.0. 15% increased chance for a critical hit. When aiming your agility increases by 20%

You have reached Level 85
When you sleep next, you will be able to increase your attributes by: 50 points.

2,932,100,000/128,249,000,000 EXP till you reach Level 86

You have 50 attribute points to use.

"About time you lot showed up. We were going to send out a search party," Dromm cracked.

Erik waved the screens away, looking at the rest of the group.

"How was your trip?" Rugrat asked.

"Just some asshole along the way. All smooth otherwise. You?"

"No problems," Rugrat said.

"Shall we turn in this quest, finally?" Fred said.

Erik and Reaper stood as the group headed into the Quartermaster office and right up to the mission desk.

"Medallion." The bored lady indicated to the groove in the desk.

Erik put his medallion into the groove. The formation in the table flashed with colors a few times. A screen appeared in front of the lady. She quickly read through it. Frowning, she looked at the group before she flicked through a few more of the screens. She tapped a sound transmission device, talking to someone before she pulled out the medallion and pushed it back toward Erik.

+100,000,000 EXP

> +100,000,000,000 EXP

> **113,042,097,548/128,249,000,000 EXP till you reach Level 86**

"Your mission points are stored on your medallion."

Erik took the medallion. Feeling it heat up, he turned it over. The other side was transforming, and a second star appeared on the medallion.

"Please come up one by one."

Erik appraised the medallion.

> **Two-Star Hero medallion**
>
> One time ability to contact the nearest Mission Hall in an emergency.
>
> Creates a powerful barrier to protect medallion wearer.
>
> 110 Mission points.
>
> Access to Low Master Grade level materials and gear

One by one they went up, getting their mission points and upgrading their medallions.

Fred took them off to a training room, paying the mana stones to enter.

"What's this for?" Erik asked.

"Add in our new attribute points and test out your abilities safely before heading back out into the world," Fred said.

"You go first. I'll watch." Erik bumped Rugrat's shoulder.

"All right, sounds good to me."

They took sleeping aids and Erik watched the experience energy in their body enter their mana system, their muscles, their bones, their brains, altering them according to the changes they'd made in attributes.

There was always a background amount of mana to the ten realms and a signature of a person's mana, changed by their attributes, their cultivations, their techniques, and styles.

It was like they were becoming a part of the ten realms, or the ten realms were altering to become like them.

Rugrat shuddered awake and looked around, giving another shudder as he looked at Erik.

"God, you're ugly."

"You look like shit." Erik smirked and helped him to his feet.

"Ready for naptime?"

"Bite me, Louisiana."

Erik laid down and used a sleeping potion.

You have 45 attribute points to use.

Erik looked at his stats, reviewing the numbers. His stamina pool had the lowest in terms of attribute points, but it was still larger than his mana pool and his stamina regeneration was much lower.

Regeneration gets it back faster.

He put ten points into mana regeneration and forty into his stamina regeneration before he could over-think it.

Name: Erik West	
Level: 85	Race: Human-?
Titles:	
From the Grave II	
Blessed By Mana	
Dungeon Master V	
Reverse Alchemist	
Poison Body	
Fire Body	
Earth Soul	
Mana Reborn II	
Wandering Hero	
Metal Mind, Metal Body	
Earth Grade Bloodline	
Strength: (Base 90) +58	1554
Agility: (Base 83) +110	1109
Stamina: (Base 93) +35	2016
Mana: (Base 37) +134	1744
Mana Regeneration (Base 60) +71	82.22
Stamina Regeneration: (Base 162) +99	55.86

The teleportation light disappeared as Erik and the rest of the group looked out on the living quarters of Cronen Mission Hall. It took them a day to adjust to their new stats. With their overall stats high already, it was a minor modification.

"Shall we head to the Rusted Spoon?"

"Sounds appealing," Erik said.

"Their stew is great, their roasted meats are incredible, and I have the fierce need for something strong to drink!" Dromm said.

He led them through another teleportation formation into the depths of the sprawling madness of inns, taverns and more.

The city had a warm glow to it. The lighting made the underground city seem as if it were in perpetual dusk; candles and mage lights flickered around taverns and inns, inviting people in.

Many of the buildings were made from different brown and red woods.

The enticing aroma of food was present on every corner, accompanying people as they settled in for a late dinner. Tavern doors opened, leaking out the sounds of live bands, people dancing and singing along with the noise of rowdier groups. Erik took his time looking around.

"So, is this city just for Mission Hall members to find somewhere to eat and drink?"

"And sleep occasionally." Dromm laughed.

"People from the Mission Hall are usually wanderers going from one place to the next, wherever the job takes them. Few have houses, and while some belong to clans, most of them are low-powered clans. Staying here, you can meet other heroes, party up, find out about new missions that are posted up, and get information on places that aren't mentioned in the information the scroll keepers have," Fred stated.

"It can be a neutral refuge for some. Say they pissed off the wrong person at home. They can run their ass here, get a job, and have a roof over their heads. No one cares who you are or where you came from as long as you follow the rules," Reaper said and then grimaced. "Even if some of them are stupid."

Reaper shook his head, returning his hair to its original white and green.

Erik shed his hair, as did Rugrat.

They reached a tavern of wood and glass windows. The oddly shaped glass pieces distorted what was happening on the other side of the glass.

Above the door hung a rusty spoon.

Fred opened the door.

"Ah, Fred! What brings you around here? Looking for a table?"

"Hey, Tim. Please, for six?"

"Certainly. We have some room for you in the back."

Erik entered the room. It smelled of aged wood and food.

People ate and drank around the room; there was no music, just people talking and eating.

The lighting was dimmed to make it feel like twilight. A bar with several taps was set against the left side wall. On the right were tables.

Tim, an older man with black hair and a wide smile, led them to a table in the back right.

"We'll go for your house bread, your soup special, and spicy fish please," Fred said as they reached the table. He pulled out a chair, and the others arranged themselves around the table.

Tim laughed. "I couldn't pick better myself. Anything else?"

"Beer, Timothy. A beer for everyone," Dromm said.

"I can do that!" Tim headed back toward the bar.

"Sorry for ordering for you both, but the Rusted Spoon is supposed to mean that you would spend so much time eating their famous soups that your spoon would rust," Fred said.

"No worries. Makes the decisions easier," Erik said as he leaned back in his chair, watching the door to the bar and relaxing.

They talked a bit, winding down. Their beers arrived quickly and were doled out.

"Well, here's to becoming Two Stars." Dromm held up his mug.

"To the adventurers trying to do the right thing." Racquel held up her beer.

The table grew quiet as they held their beers, thinking.

"To the adventurers," Dromm agreed, crashing his mug against Racquel's. Erik and Rugrat tapped their mugs on the table before they took a deep drink.

Rugrat cleared his throat after a few minutes, using the sound transmission device so only they could hear him. "We still haven't talked about the loot we got from General Ubren and her people."

"We can split it evenly six ways," Fred said.

"I agree, but, well, there are the supplies from two corvette warships, all of their training aids, some storage rings, a pendant, and a little map I found in General Ubren's storage ring."

Everyone looked at Rugrat. "I'm willing to take more materials over straight mana stones and gear," Rugrat said.

"Same here, and Alva will give you a fair price for any other materials you have," Erik said.

"This map though, where does it lead?" Dromm asked,

"I think it was to Ubren's lair, or at least to where she was stashing her gear and the things she's gotten over the years," Rugrat said.

"We need to get that information and return to Alva," Erik said.

"I'll take you up on the offers to trade, but I have another group of friends I promised to work with," Fred said. "I'll keep an eye out for any information on the Black Phoenix Clan and pass it on."

"I'm a free agent but I'll probably look for another mission in a few days," Dromm said and glanced at Reaper.

"I'll join you on that," Reaper said. "And make sure to pass on any information we find as well."

"Well, it was great adventuring with you all. I hope we can do it again in the future." Erik smiled as they raised all their cups again, smiling.

"Till the next time!"

They drank deeply from their cups.

"Here's your food!" Tim said as he and another server brought platters to the table and served freshly baked bread, soup that made Erik's mouth water, and a full fish as long as Erik's arm, cooked to perfection.

23
Homeward

E rik watched as Rugrat came back from talking to the owner of the restaurant.

"Got some directions. Come on."

Erik led them out the doorway, checking both before he stepped out. Rugrat looked in the direction Erik wasn't as Racquel followed.

"You two have been together a long time," Racquel said.

"Too damn long," Rugrat said.

Erik snorted as he kept walking and leading them.

"You work like you are one person, like you know the thoughts of the other before you move. It is interesting," Racquel smiled.

Rugrat's stomach moved uneasily. He felt like there was something wrong with her expression and her eyes.

Did I do something? Is something wrong?

It didn't take them long to reach their destination. There was a set of guards outside a building that looked like a teardrop. Curtains covered the entrance, obscuring one from seeing inside.

They reached the entrance to the teardrop as a guard held out a hand.

Erik checked his storage ring filled with mana stones he'd traded his mission points in for.

Should be enough to get us the information we need.

The guard raised an eyebrow and lowered his hand.

Erik led the way inside, parting the curtain and moving to one side slightly.

Rugrat looked past him, seeing a simple counter with a brazier of magical flame above it. A woman wearing a painted mask of a traditional smiling lady, thick blacks, contrasting reds and whites, stood at the desk.

"Hello, we'd like to get some information," Erik said.

"Information is not easy to come by. What are your topics?"

"The Black Phoenix Clan and the Sha Clan."

The woman raised a bracelet, a sound transmission device. It glowed as she talked to someone. "Please follow me." She walked to the right, passing through the opening between counter and wall. She reached a corridor covered in cloth and pulled it to the side.

"Door number eight." She bowed her head as she held the thin mesh curtain.

Looks like formations in the fabric, or special material.

They passed through and the curtain slid back into place, blurring what was opposite and cutting out any sound.

The door to room number eight opened as Erik reached it. They walked inside to find someone in a plain black mask with only holes left for their eyes. Three cushions had been arranged in front of a low, wide table that the broker sat behind.

The door shut as they sat down.

"You are looking for information on the Sha and the Black Phoenix Clans. A most interesting conflict connects the two. What do you wish to know specifically?"

"The details of the conflict, their interests in the lower realms, their morale, weaponry and tactics," Erik said.

"Interesting." The black mask studied Erik.

"Twenty Sky grade mana stones for the details of the conflict, and lower realms, forty for basics on their weaponry, morale and tactics."

Rugrat let out a hiss.

Hell, information is worth more than gold!

Erik handed over the mana stones.

In a flash of light, they disappeared.

"I will start with their weaponry, morale and tactics. The Black Phoenix Clan has several major warships, creating seven fleets of forty ships. They use some updated designs, but they are similar to heavy ore transportation ships that have been outfitted with mana cannons on the exterior. It relies on several kinds of stone for armor instead of iron, to reduce cost. They have powerful fighters who are good for competitions, but they are weaker in head-on confrontations. They have a lot of people, but few resources to spend on them."

The mask paused as the teleportation on the table flashed, and two books appeared.

"These books contain most information on the two groups."

Rugrat took them and stored them away as the man continued.

"Each ship holds a powerful modified mana cannon under their armor: a Phoenix Breath Cannon. Auxiliary cannons angle downwards so they can all be employed at once on a target. They have aerial and ground forces, though their ground forces are primarily used to teleport over to wherever teleportation pads have been placed, usually inside their enemy's defenses.

"Their morale is high since they attained the Violet Cloud Realm token. Several clans and sects are looking on them favorably and have pulled them to their side.

"The Sha use a different kind of ship. They use cannons alchemically powered to fire powerful shells of enhanced iron on their enemy. These metal shells do not do as much damage as a mana cannon, as they do not use any mana, or very little. But they can fire them repeatedly into the enemy. Their ships are faster, thinner, and longer. Many others imitate their design. They attack their enemy head-on, taking down the ship, dropping it to the ground before boarding or attacking them in the air and boarding them directly. Would you like more specific information?"

"How much?" Erik asked.

Rugrat thought he saw the mask move in a smile.

"Three points for the Black Phoenix Clan, ten for the Sha."

"Let us continue with the original information."

"Very well. The morale of the Sha Clans is also high as they also have a Violet Cloud Realm token. The Black Phoenix Clan, encouraged by others, attacked the Sha Clans. The Sha have kept to themselves, but they have an interesting technology. While it is not useful in the Seventh Realm, it is believed that it would be more useful in a lower realm. With the Black Phoenix Clan's provocation, the Sha Clans replied in kind. They have not liked one another for a long time, but recently, after each acquired a token, their annoyance turned to aggression. Each is looking to get an advantage over the other. If they can, then they can claim their territory and their token in the Violet Cloud Realm."

Is that why the marshal's niece came to visit us?

"In the lower realms, the Black Phoenix Clan have no interests. A lone Black Phoenix Destroyer attacked a city state called Vuzgal to capture the dungeon core that was hidden under the city. The Sha have multiple clans across the lower realms. They are a strong force, but neutral in many conflicts. It is only if someone tries to steal their technology or attack their people that they act."

The black mask, who had held their hand inside their sleeved robe, opened it palm up, covered in a black glove.

"Do you wish to learn more?"

"No, thank you."

Erik and Rugrat left, and headed for the nearest totem. It was time to go home.

Returning home, Erik and Rugrat called a meeting with Elan and Glosil. Delilah was seeing to other business.

Elan had his people pouring over the books as Erik and Rugrat summarized what they'd learned in the Seventh Realm and gave Glosil the plans to the corvettes.

"That's all they said on the Sha and Black Phoenix. Rest should be in those books." Erik rubbed his face. They hadn't really stopped yet. Rugrat, sitting beside him and across from Glosil and Elan, covered a yawn. As soon as they got back, they had called the meeting to debrief.

"I think something went wrong. Somehow, the Black Phoenix Clan must have found out that the marshal's niece was down in the lower realms. They might not have known everything, but they sent out feelers. Something must have tripped up those feelers when we were fighting the sects," Elan said.

"Do we trust the Sha or not? That's really the question. We have some similarities with them, and they did reach out to us," Erik said.

"Simply put, even with everything we have, if the Black Phoenix Clan, the Willful Institute and the Stone Fist Sect come at us in one move, we're not going to be able to hold. We might have some powerful tech, but we need people, and we need the alliances," Glosil said. "The Phoenixes could take us out on their own with their ships. If they were willing to spend the mana stones."

"I agree. We can't sit here without anyone on our side or we're going to find ourselves screwed," Erik said.

"So, we need allies, but who do we ally ourselves with?" Rugrat asked, leaning his head against his fingers.

Delfina looked at the people in the lecture hall. She checked her letter again and walked into the room. There were several people in a group talking to one another. A young woman played with a formation. There were several tech-looking types.

Delfina locked eyes with a man sitting in the back of the room.

Well, he's a big one.

Tribal and Japanese tattoos curled down the man's shoulders and along his arms.

And I'm guessing he's not from around these parts, like me.

She scanned the room, seeing a man with a goatee. Several men and women crowded around him as he pointed out things on the plans.

She moved to a seat near the rear row, watching the different people in the room. Several minutes later, a large, heavily tanned man walked in. His guards stood by the door.

The guards wore body armor and helmets that seemed to have been ripped from Earth, but the glowing runes betrayed the fact they weren't in the Sol system anymore.

"Hello, everyone, and thank you for attending. My name is Colonel Kanoa. I am the guy in charge of the Alva Air Force, and I am here today to offer you all a job. Don't worry. I'm not asking you to jump out of birds or learn how to fly them into the teeth of the enemy. Your task will be no less vital and will make sure that more of my people come back and less of the enemy are able to threaten us."

Delfina sat up in her seat as Kanoa cleared his throat.

"For a long time, most of the development of any military application was carried out by Lords West and Rodriguez. We have worked on several military applications, but that places the work of many on the shoulders of a few." Kanoa looked at the group that had been talking together and at the young girl working on the formation in the corner.

"We have a number of people present from different backgrounds.

Ammunition specialists..." Kanoa raised his hand, pointing at the large man with the tattoos. "Formation masters, refining experts, smithing experts, factory tooling directors and managers, alchemists, healers, even an ex-air force tech." Kanoa shifted his hand between people, pointing at Delfina last.

"What I am looking for are people who are interested in taking the applications and technology coming out of Alva and using it to create weapons and technology that will assist our people on the battlefield. Now, if you aren't interested, I would ask you to leave. If you are, or want to learn more, please sign the contract that is coming around."

Kanoa pulled out a stack of papers and put it in front of someone. They took the papers and handed them to the side and backward, sending the contracts out.

Delfina took one and passed the pile onto the next person. She scanned the contract and cut her finger, putting it on the contract, sealing it.

No one left the room.

Kanoa sent one of his guards to collect the completed contracts, waiting until the guard came back before continuing. "Well, let me welcome you to the Alvan Military Research and Development Department. Anything and everything you want to play with, you will be allowed to do so. Whether it is potions to heal or bombs to destroy, it will be your job to take everything we have and tinker with it until it is better."

He walked to the podium and rested his hands on it. "Now, the first projects are not going to be easy. I want you to work on creating missiles that can shoot straight ahead or can track their target and destroy it, as well as better armor and defenses for the birds."

Get to mess with all the tech that's lying around here! Sure, work on missiles, but could I make a car? Heck, might be able to make a plane or a helo too. All this tech just waiting for applications.

Delfina grinned as she unconsciously wrung her hands.

Roska stood on an observation tower, using her binoculars to study the fortress that guarded a hill surrounded by water on three sides. It was nighttime on the water floor, and far away from the town and outposts that dotted the area.

A flare went off on the hillside. The troops within the fortress woke up and ran to the walls. Officers ordered people to their positions.

Unseen to them, a dozen or so people rose on water pillars from the sheer rocks and landed on the wall, climbing up the cliff.

A spell shot out down the hillside, hitting the fortress' mana barrier, causing it to flare as soldiers looked in the direction of the new threat.

Other spells hit the mana barrier, seemingly probing it for weaknesses.

"Good distractions. I'd do the same if I were breaching the fortress head-on," Niemm said from beside her.

"Yes, but can they get the information?"

The attacking special team trainees mimed killing soldiers and throwing them over the wall and into the water below, quickly crossing the open ground to the tall building and disappeared inside.

She changed a setting on the binoculars, seeing through the walls of the buildings as the special teams cleared them quickly and effectively.

They planted a formation and exited the way they had come in.

A flare appeared over the area, signaling a powerful spell. Defenders on the walls turned to look at the buildings that had been destroyed.

They reorganized to head in as shooters on the wall fired at them with explosive paint rounds, raining down hell on the hillside wall.

Other attackers moved between buildings, under their fellows' cover, disappearing.

"They're saying that they're storing the bodies in their storage rings and then the storage rings are in their dump pouches," a team member acting as an observer within the command center said.

"Okay, makes sense."

The defenders were re-organizing, trying to pin down the attackers. Spells hit the barrier of the fortress as attackers in the grass kept up their attacks.

The attackers on the wall opened up with spell scrolls, a flare lighting the sky.

The team that had assaulted the command center rushed out under their fellows' covering fire. They didn't pause, jumping up the wall and over the other side.

The rest of the attackers turned and jumped with them, using gliding spell scrolls to cut over the water, gaining distance before they dropped beneath the waves.

Spells from the hillside stopped, and the few team members hidden in the grass faded away.

"So, what're they doing next?" Rugrat asked.

Roska jumped and turned, ready to punch him. Niemm held his rifle strapped to his side, letting out a groan as they both calmed down.

Rugrat grinned.

"Shit," Roska hissed, feeling her heart calm as she bled off the tension and forced herself to relax.

"When did you get back? Niemm asked.

"Not that long ago. Erik went off to the hospital. I wanted to check in and see how the training is going." Rugrat looked at the fortress. Those inside were undergoing their debriefing and the special teams moved out of the water and the snow grasses to meet up.

"It's going well. They've completed the basic training to test their mental stability and make sure they're team players. Now they are going through training in different scenarios to let them try out some new tactics. First, they train to attack different installations with different objectives. Next, they will learn infiltration and information gathering skills from the intelligence department. Then we'll have them run through some mock missions in different cities before we allow them to carry out missions with us," Roska said.

"Sounds like a ton of fun," Rugrat said.

"Well, it feels good to be up here rather than down there." Niemm nodded toward the special team members that stood in a half circle around the special team member who was running them through their AAR and would give them their next mission.

"How are things with the army?"

"The Reserves got a bunch of training. They were good, but they weren't the best. Some of the officer roles have become part of the reg force. That way they know what is going on, have the latest training, and can pass it on to their soldiers quickly. We've had more people join the reserves. They're going through basic training like any regular soldier, though everyone is going straight to their specializations first. So, people are picked out to take on certain courses; sharpshooter, mortar team member, mage, engineer, whatever," Niemm said.

"The CPD and the Special Teams still only accept people that have completed all the training."

"Training and cultivating. They're going nuts with it all," Niemm said.

"Good nuts or bad?" Rugrat asked.

"Good, for the most part. We've got enough cultivating pods now that soldiers will choose to rest in them, just to increase their body or mana tempering a little bit," Niemm said.

"Bad in the way that they're spending so much time on training that they don't take any free time. There are people that have been ordered, by higher, to take time off." Roska sat back against the lip of the observation tower.

"We have more people than ever in the military, a hundred and ten thousand in Alva's army. Nearing a hundred and fifty thousand in the Vermire Army, though they have a lot of mercenaries in their ranks, so a hundred thousand in total?"

Niemm nodded. "Sounds about right to me."

"Another three hundred thousand in the adventurer guilds, though most of them don't even know that we exist, so..." Roska shrugged.

"How strong are the people in the different armies?"

"Adventurers are all over the place, some First Realm, very few of the Fifth and reaching the Sixth Realm. Say, less than a thousand at the Sixth Realm standard. Ten thousand for the Fifth; fifty thousand at Fourth Realm. The rest are weaker. The Vermire forces, other than Pan Kun and the commanders, could fight in the Second Realm. But they would need to have numbers on their side to win in the Third Realm.

Alva military soldiers are at the standard of the Third Realm. Everyone else is Fourth and Fifth Realm. Those who have been in longer are stronger. Close Protection Details could make it in the Sixth Realm. The Special Teams could venture into the Seventh Realm. How is it up there?"

"Most people are around level sixty-five, guard around sixty-seven. The leaders around sixty-nine, the people in power are usually in the low seventies. Seems that the Eighth and Seventh Realms are closely connected, so people pass between them all the time. Not odd to see people who are level seventy-five walking around." Rugrat pictured the people they had met in the Seventh Realm.

"Journeyman crafters are hired help. People are crazy about the tattoo thing we saw on the Phoenix people. Mana is the way of the future. But they have few with our stages of body cultivation. Assume that everyone has Body Like Iron and have a solid core or are working toward it. The strong ones have attained their mana hearts."

"Damn, that's a pretty big cultivation jump compared to the Sixth Realm," Niemm said.

"They use dungeon cores to create mountains of mana stones and attune them to create cultivation chambers like the first cultivation chambers we had where they flood them with pure mana. Their cities are massive and have several floors of dungeons underground. It's pretty crazy. And they have airships that use dungeon cores flying everywhere. The Black Phoenix are a *minor* clan in the Seventh Realm."

The trio grew silent.

"Well, if they decide to come down here, we'll show them some good First Realm hospitality." Roska promised.

"We just need time," Niemm said.

"Ask me for anything but time." Rugrat replied. "Not sure who said that, but yeah it's true."

24

Moves and Counters

"Ah, Elder Hao, it is good to see you," Cai Bo said as the older man walked into her office and moved to the couches where she was sitting with a pot of tea. Her cup released threads of steam.

"High Elder, is there something wrong? From your message it seemed that there was something of immediate importance." Elder Hao said as he sat down.

"Yes, Elder Hao. I have some disturbing information. It seems there are some people that have still not heard the sect leader's orders. There are those within our ranks who are still thinking about themselves instead of the sect."

"Outrageous, do they have no honor?" Elder Hao said, stroking his beard as his brows pinched together in apparent rage.

"I have been following up on supplies that have gone missing. The results have been most displeasing." She collected her cup and sat back, making no show to pour Elder Hao a cup. "Elder Hao, I should praise you. I always thought that you were a spineless coward, but now I see that you are actually a sneaky rat." Cai Bo smiled as she sipped from her tea.

"I would watch my words if I were you, Elder Cai Bo. While we are both high Elders. You are still my junior!" His voice rose as he pulled on his robes, his face turning in fury.

"Oh, then I will not find out that several shipments of supplies that were meant for cities in the Third Realm were diverted to the Hao Clan's personal warehouses instead? Do I need to name the cities? Two of them fell in the attacks. Maybe if they had those supplies, they could have held on."

"Be careful with what you say, Cai Bo," Elder Hao said dangerously.

Cai Bo's mask slipped as she snarled. "You'd best learn to act your station, dog! Unless you want me to go to the sect leader and report the truth of the matter. Should I tell him about the assassins you planted, killing clans members in the heat of battle to clear the line for your own people and muddy the waters? I am reminded of the *brilliant* tactical genius, the newly promoted third general Feng Hao." She raised an eyebrow. "I find it interesting how such an inept boy was able to lead so many people valiantly in the defense of Goreck City. Don't you? Do you think that Elder Lui would be interested in what happened to General Tong?"

Elder Hao trembled, his face turning red and white.

"Yes, you could attack me, Elder Hao. You might even kill me. But do you think the sect leader would allow you or your clan to survive after the elder that has helped him the most through this entire war is killed in some random meeting? Oh, believe me when I say the information will find its way into his ears."

She sipped her tea as Elder Hao bowed his head, his hands gripping his robes.

"What do you want?" He looked up from his knees and at her.

"Ah, now you get it. I don't care about your clan. I don't care about the supplies. But I will need something from you in the future." She pulled out a contract, placing it on the table and pushed it across the table.

Elder Hao looked at it. "This is outrageous!"

"Oh, I think your complete loyalty for staving off the sect leader from wiping out your entire clan is worth it. Do you think that I have only been paying attention to your clan?"

"You snake!" Elder Hao snarled.

Cai Bo laughed, looking up to the ceiling before she got herself under control. "Ah, it is nice to see under these masks. While you act as an honorable elder you are nothing but a silly little boy trying to steal a few things off the counter. Such a naughty one. I don't care what you think of me."

She sipped her tea and let out a satisfied sigh. "You and your clan will belong to me, and do as I bid. I will not ask you again." Her eyes dropped to the contract and then back to Elder Hao.

He gritted his teeth. He quickly bit his tongue and spat his blood on the contract. As it completed, he threw it back toward Cai Bo.

"Now, what do you want?" he snarled.

Cai Bo used an air spell to carry the contract into her hand, surveying it in one hand.

"Bow."

Elder Hao moved against his conscious control, standing and then stiffly bowing from the waist.

Cai Bo put the contract away, swirling her tea and sipping the remainder.

"On your knees." Her voice was icy.

Elder Hao moved to the side of the table and dropped to his knees, placing his hands on the ground and forcing his head down to his hands.

Cai Bo watched him struggling on the floor for a few seconds, enjoying the thrill.

Maybe Mercy and I are similar in some ways. Though the young girl loves to flaunt her power.

Cai Bo stood from the couch, finishing her tea and putting it down.

"What is it that you want me to do?" Elder Hao ground out through his teeth from the floor.

Cai Bo stopped next to Elder Hao's head.

"You will see, pet. Go and carry out your duties and get me this information." She dropped a scroll next to Elder Hao. "Get out of my sight and act in the same way you would have before this meeting. Do nothing out of character."

She walked toward her desk as Hao snatched the scroll. "I will not forget this, Cai Bo!"

She turned and looked at him, her face expressionless. "I would hope not. Three hundred and twenty years ago, a young general Hao led a campaign against the Floating Lily sect. You used the opportunity to decrease the power of the other clans. You used the Bo clan as your vanguard to soak up the attacks. You used it as an excuse to take over the regions controlled by the Bo because they didn't have the forces to protect themselves."

"You did all of this for my actions three hundred years ago? The Bo clan must be proud!"

Cai Bo's smile was an ugly thing. "You think I care about that group of idiots? The Bo clan was just some middling clan with thoughts of greatness. They were nothing in the eyes of the Sect. No, I grew them to get access to resources, to people of position and power. Those foolish clan *leaders,* are nothing more than wasted talents that bask in their imagined greatness." Cai Bo scoffed.

Hao frowned.

"You don't get it, do you, Elder Hao?" Cai Bo smiled, turning to face him fully. "I don't care about the Bo Clan. I don't care about Hao Clan or this Willful Institute. I was thinking about being the Sect Leader, but now, now we have a Seventh Realm clan asking for our help. Why be limited by a sect that has only reached into the Sixth Realm and can barely get more than a few people into the Seventh Realm?"

Hao paled.

"Ah, I guess you're starting to see it now, Elder Hao. I like dealing with the smart ones. Now don't go telling anyone." She chuckled and waved at him, smiling as she returned to her desk.

Elder Hao walked out of the room. She let out a satisfied sigh, closing her eyes and remembering the expression on his face.

"More to be done." She rested her hand against her face, thinking.

The sect leader was greedy, keeping information a secret, and keeping the dungeon core. What did it matter? The Black Phoenix Clan would learn about it eventually and tear the sect apart. It was only one dungeon core; they had fleets of ships that relied on dungeon cores. The sect wouldn't survive if they decide to do that.

She turned her chair and looked over the city, through the windows.

There was a knock at her door.

"Come in!"

The door opened to reveal Marco Tolentino.

He had lost the fight against Vuzgal. There would have been no way to win if he continued his attacks. Still, he was smart, and knew how to command people. Useful traits. He was a survivor, using the Black Phoenix Clan as a cover and helping them as much as possible. *Not just another young man looking to increase his power and show off to others. This one can think.*

"Marco, thank you for meeting with me." She waved him forward.

His boots rang out on the stone floors as he approached, stopping at her desk.

"Come here." She indicated for him to join her at the windows.

He stepped around and stood behind her, looking down on the city.

"It is a good sight, right? One of the best views in the city," Cai Bo said.

"It is a magnificent sight," Marco agreed.

"Ever the diplomat. You interest me, Marco." Cai Bo turned and stepped next to him, lowering her voice. "It might be a good view in the Sixth Realm, but it is not the same as standing aboard an airship, and it is not the Seventh Realm."

Contraction of the eyes, the vein in his neck that sped up momentarily before he clamped down on his reactions.

Good, good, this one is interesting!

She turned back to the window. "There are three other groups in the city that are as powerful as us. It has remained that way for several decades. The sect is comfortable with that. There are only a few people that make it into the Seventh Realm each year, but it is a thing of *honor.*" She snorted and tilted her head to appraise Marco. "What do you think, Marco? Do you think it is an honor to reach the Seventh Realm?"

Marco opened his mouth and then coughed. "I think it would be a great honor to represent the sect in the Seventh Realm."

"Represent the sect? Interesting, but what if you were to get a position in the Seventh, say in a clan?" Cai Bo mused.

Marco's eyes thinned.

"You have the interest of the Black Phoenix Clan, and I am a high elder of the sect. I think that we can come to some agreement."

"What do you want?" Marco asked.

Cai Bo laughed at his expression. "You look at me as if wondering what I will steal from you?" She shook her head. "I am offering you something that will benefit us both. Your clan will rise in power, probably control the sect for the years to come, while you and your siblings could not only reach into the Seventh Realm, but carve out a position there. What I am offering is to get you into the Seventh Realm, to give your family the power they so dearly want, and you care little about. To give you a path to increase your power."

"What do you get?" Marco asked.

"The same thing as you. I want to increase my power. I have reached the peak of what the Institute has, but there are many above us. If we can get on the Black Phoenix Clan's side, then who needs the Sixth Realm when we can establish ourselves in the Seventh Realm?"

Marco relaxed.

"I know that I am not the first person to offer you something like this, nor will I be the last. The Institute is filled with people that aspire higher than their position. Your own elders must have come to you with their plans." Cai Bo shook her head. "Tell me, right now, how many armies do we control that can fight?"

Marco frowned. "There is the army of ten thousand in the Sixth Realm, two in the Fourth Realm. And then the army in the Third Realm." Marco trailed off and looked at her.

"Hmm, seems that army is controlled by the Kostic Clan, who are vassals of mine. In the last couple of months, they have recovered several cities that were ours and taken others from competing sects. An army of fifty thousand with fighters from the Fifth and Sixth Realm. You know that Low Elder Kostic is a resourceful man. He brought the Stone Fist Sect to our side. Such a powerful ally with plenty of friends that have been eagerly helping us. It is interesting how much information they have on the lower realms."

Cai Bo paused as Marco's attention was rooted on her.

"You see, there are a lot of people looking for these Vuzgalians, but how many of them are in the lower realms? How many of them have an army with Fifth and Sixth Realm fighters and several other sects that are eager to prove themselves? Who has an information network across the lower realms?"

Cai Bo smiled and gave Marco a side-long glance. "You have fought them before. What do you think? Do you think they will roll over after we attack them? Or do you think that they will throw everything they have at us in a war the lower realms will talk about for generations?"

"It will not be an easy battle."

"I agree, and I want to make sure you have the support you need to secure victory. Against their weaponry, their mana barriers powered with a dungeon core, our current weapons will not be enough. Only the Black Phoenix Clan will have the items we need." Cai Bo walked away from the window to her desk and looked at the papers there. "When we find the Vuzgalians, the Black Phoenix Clan might not find out right away, but they will with time. When they do, they will cut us down like rot. The sect leader thinks that once they leave, they will no longer pay attention to the lower realms. He is thinking of taking the dungeon core and the loot of

Vuzgal for himself."

Marco's hand shook.

"Yes, I had much the same thought. Instead of using the dungeon core ourselves, an item that is largely useless to us, would it not be more useful to use it for the benefit of the sect, the benefit of the younger generation? If not connecting us to the Black Phoenix Clan, getting us the resources we need to control the other sects that support us and pierce through into the Seventh Realm. This is a moment of change. A moment that could see you entering the Seventh Realm, if you pick the right person to help you."

Cai Bo turned, putting her hands in her sleeves, smiling at Marco. "While those other elders might have grand plans, they are old. Their cultivation has slowed down. They think of silly games, caring about reputation over results. I care nothing about reputation and only about getting stronger."

There was another knock at the door.

"Come in," Cai Bo said.

The door opened. A large man with flecks of grey and white in his hair walked into the room.

The resemblance between him and Marco was uncanny.

"Clan leader Abe." Cai Bo smiled.

"Father." Marco bowed.

The doors closed and Abe Tolentino reached the front of Cai Bo's desk. He cupped his fists and bowed. "Master Cai Bo."

Marco looked between his father and Cai Bo.

"You raised your son well, Abe. I was very impressed with his results in the Fourth Realm."

"You honor us, Master." Abe smiled.

"It looks like your son is confused." She walked to the window as Marco moved to his father.

"What is going on?" Marco asked.

"You have heard of the rise of the Tolentino Clan in my father's generation?"

"Yes, the revival of the clan allowed us to go from a middling power to consume other clans and become one of the strongest clans within the sect."

"That was due to the backing and guidance of Master Cai Bo. She secretly helped us reach our current position. Only a few within the clan know that she is our secret and powerful backer. My father was a strong man, but he was not well versed in the ways of politics and maneuvering."

"You are always saying how you think she is too weak and that we should not worry what she says."

Abe winced. "Well, can't have the other clans thinking that you are my force."

"You come from the Bo clan and they hate us," Marco said.

"They are a group of fools and idiots with ideas of grandeur. Don't worry, their time will come." Cai Bo's eyes thinned as Marco tensed, adjusting into a fighting stance.

"Bring the Black Phoenix Clan to our side." She took out a scroll and passed it to Abe.

"What shall I say of this meeting?"

"You heard that I was talking to your son, and you came in and demanded that I go through you first. Throw your weight around." Cai Bo waved her hand.

"Yes, Master." Abe bowed, and grabbed Marco's head, forcing him to bow as well.

"So, this is the plan." Elise pulled out a piece of paper and put it on the table. Rugrat slurped down his noodles, putting down the bowl and picking up the sheet.

"Contracting out parts to crafters across the realms, break them into regions so people aren't making all the parts for one thing in one area." Rugrat nodded.

"How is the gear situation?" He looked to Taran and Kanoa. Kanoa gestured his elbow to Taran.

Julilah, Qin, and Matt listened, picking out pieces of food from the table and adding it to their rice as they talked about formations and projects.

"We have thousands of people in the service. The military is eating up all the building capacity it can. Ammunition, food, potions, medical gear, guns... We paused turning over the old weapon factories to build the new railguns so that we can produce enough weapons for those going through training. The mages and mortar teams have given up their rifles to make sure that we have the weapons we need for the other positions that primarily use a rifle."

"What will this do for us?" Rugrat tapped the paper.

"It will allow us to outsource most of our civilian needs and focus on high level gear. We can use people with a lower skill level to assemble the parts. Free up the crafters that have the skill to work on the stronger gear," Elise said.

"We have improved the ability of the factories, but it takes time to tool them, train people and get them operating," Taran said.

Rugrat finished reading the piece of paper and passed it back. Elise waved it into her storage ring as she kept eating her noodles.

Rugrat heard the sizzle of cooking meat. He looked around the food market, the hum of talking as people got their lunch. Steam and flames rose from the stalls as servers rushed around with their meals.

Some bowed their heads and looked away from Rugrat.

He grabbed some meat from the dishes between them with his chopsticks, putting it with his noodles, picking it all up and eating it.

"So, you said that you had something you wanted us to see?" Matt asked.

Rugrat pulled out a wad of blueprints and plans, passing them to Julilah who handed them to Qin and over to Matt.

Matt put them between himself and Kanoa.

"Plans for a fighting airship?" Matt asked as he scanned through the pages.

"Yeah, I got them from General Ubren. She had the plans, and books on airships, cannons, aerial tactics and so on. Something else for your research and development team to look at and think on. Got two Sky grade Dungeon cores that you could play with."

"Two Sky grades! Couldn't you use that to make another dungeon?" Elise asked.

"Yes, but we have a lot of back up and training dungeons already. Won't be much use there, but if we can't use them for warships, use them as the power cores for different machines." Rugrat shrugged and quickly snatched up some more noodles, enjoying the tangy, sweet and salty sauce with the mixed vegetables and meat he had added.

"We can look at them. But it might be a long time until we can work on it properly. We're stretched thin and we don't have the resources," Matt said.

"Well, Erik and I have made a rather sizable donation of materials.

Rugrat pulled out the list of materials he and Erik had been left with after their trades with the rest of the group and after their share of the loot.

2144x Sky realm Iron
4587x Earth Iron
2x Lesser Sky-Grade Dungeon Core
4x Damaged thrust formations
2x Sky grade mana cornerstones
8x Heavy Mana Cannons

They had traded nearly all the mana stones, the points, training materials and potions for this.

Rugrat passed the note over.

"We don't need to use the dungeon cores for just purifying and storing mana. Dungeon cores can change their environment as long as they have the materials. Egbert used them before to make the formations on the different floors. We could do the same with these dungeon cores and just remove the formation. The dungeon cores are great at shaping materials, but we found that you still need to add in the activation medium afterwards with formations," Julilah said.

"We throw down a bunch of metal and they produce barrels. Then we move them out of the way and they start building more barrels right away. As long as we have the blueprints, right?" Taran looked at Matt.

"I never thought about it. The things that I worked on with the blueprints and the dungeon core were always meant to be permanent." Matt scratched his goatee. "But yeah, it should work."

"Well, then it looks like we just found a way to speed up production in our factories." Taran smiled, raising his glass and taking a big drink.

Julilah threw the part across the room, embedding it into the wall. "This is garbage, all of it, useless! The sizing is all wrong! Are you sure they were crafters? Children could do a better job!" Julilah yelled at the trader.

"I am sorry, Miss Julilah! They assured me that these were the highest quality parts. I gave them the required blueprints as well."

Julilah surveyed the traders that had brought the parts to her for inspection. "Only a few of these parts are useful! The rest are not worth the metal they are carved into. They won't fit into the final product."

An assistant walked up.

"What is it?" she growled.

"You have a meeting with Momma Rodriguez, Miss Julilah."

Julilah rubbed her face. "Okay, I will head over. Make sure that you only accept parts that meet with our specifications, people's lives could depend on it."

She left the academy grounds, quickly walking across the city toward the small house that Erik, Rugrat, and Momma Rodriguez called home. She composed herself and knocked on the door.

Momma Rodriguez came to the door wearing an apron.

"Ah, Julilah, please come on in!" She ushered Julilah in and closed the door. "I am just making some fruit crumble. Rather easy, but with all that fruit coming from the Wood Floor I thought it a waste to not put it to work."

She drew her into the kitchen where she had the ingredients laid out.

Did she really call me over to bake? Julilah bristled. Why did people keep treating her like a child? She was one of the most qualified formation masters in all of Alva. But, because she was young, they treated her like a kid. They didn't do it with Qin nearly as much.

"I thought it would be nice to bake while we talk. Here's an apron."

"What did you want to talk about?" Julilah accepted the apron and put it over her head.

"I wanted to talk about Tan Xue." Momma Rodriguez moved items about as Julilah's thoughts fell into a jumble.

"Why do you want to talk about her?"

"I wanted to know what she was like. And if she would want you to get on with your life and live it to the fullest. To learn and teach others in her spirit. Or if she would like you to continue to use work to hide and vent your frustrations, lashing out at others?"

Julilah was thrown off by how blunt she was.

"Would you mix this together?" Momma Rodriguez put ingredients into a bowl and passed it to her.

Julilah took it numbly.

"Been some time since someone has been straight with you, it looks like."

"Y-you..." Julilah said indignantly, recovering.

"Will you stop acting like some damn child? Yes, Tan Xue is dead, a great and wonderful woman who raised you like her own and cared for you deeply. One that got her friends to promise to look after you if something happened to her. She is dead."

Julilah rocked back on her heels as she trembled.

"She died protecting your best friend, protecting others."

Julilah shuddered and lowered her head. Looking at the bowl of ingredients as her eyes filled with tears.

Momma took the bowl from her and guided her to the small table in the kitchen with two chairs covered in ingredients.

She put Julilah down in a chair, brought the other over and hugged her. Julilah collapsed into her, feeling empty with Tan Xue no longer there.

It was some time before the crying stopped and her eyes dried up. She released Momma Rodriguez and wiped her eyes.

Momma patted her on the back. "It's never easy losing someone that we love, but it's harder to move on in a world without them. Tan Xue is gone, but you should never forget her. Do her memory proud. Don't just work on your machines and formations all the time. Take time to meet with friends, to go out and meet boys or girls. You are so young, Julilah. You have your whole life ahead of you."

"But it could end at any moment. If I don't do the work now, it will never be done."

"If you do nothing but work all the time then, other than your inventions, you will have nothing to show for your life. What will your friends say? She was a great formation master, but I didn't know her beyond that. Or do you want them to speak of the tales when you did something risky, something spontaneous. We're not meant to live a life doing one thing. You must experience life fully, or why is it worth living? Do *all* things with determination, zeal and passion."

Julilah calmed down. "But there is so much to be done."

"And there will always be more to do. We all leave this life with unfinished things. There is no stopping that. Our entire lives might be spent in the pursuit of one thing and never attain it, but is it better to try or give up?"

"Try," Julilah said.

"I think so as well."

Julilah let out a ragged sigh. "I'm sorry."

"Don't tell me that. Tell the people that you work with." Momma Rodriguez patted her back and stood.

Julilah grimaced, her mind replaying the last couple of weeks and how she'd treated the men and women that worked for her.

"Come on, I have a need for an assistant!"

Julilah was pulled into the process of crumble making, forgetting all about formations for a while.

Momma Rodriguez checked the topping Julilah whisked together, taking a pinch and eating it.

"Hmm, needs more cinnamon." She pulled out the spice and tapped it into the bowl.

"How do you know the right amount to add?" Julilah asked.

"Oh, I'm not sure. I've been doing this long enough that I do it by eye."

Julilah frowned, her mind returning to the odd-looking parts. "Well, there's only one way to make crumble, no? One recipe?" she asked.

"Each person has their own small twist or technique that they use to change it."

She kept stirring, slowing, and then stopped completely as her eyes widened.

"That's what must've happened. We have our own measures, while standard across Alva, they're not standard across the realms." Julilah smacked her head. "We were thinking in terms we understood, not in ones that they understood!"

Julilah looked at the door and then at the bowl in her hands.

"I have to make a quick note." She took out a pencil and paper, scrawling down a note before getting back to whisking.

Julilah let her mind slip away again as she focused on the crumble, and for the first time in a long time she let the tendrils of strain and stress that had gripped her brain relax.

25

The Sha Move

Commander Chmilenko grumbled as his ships slid into the clouds of Earth Cloud Valley. The earth element surged within the destroyer. He could feel the rest of the fleet, five corvettes, arranged in a star formation around the destroyer.

"Damn that Stassov for running off to the lower realms. It leaves it to me to secure this backwater valley. Mana density is half of what it is at Fallam's Lake. Any dungeon cores?"

"There are some small ones being registered at the bottom of the valley," a man said from his position at the main map table.

"Pushed to the surface with the magma? Make a note of them and we will come back to pick them up. We'll need to patrol the area first. Looks like those damn Sha didn't find out about the opening."

The fleet continued through the clouds, dragging in the surrounding mana and creating eddies in the earth element clouds.

The bridge of *Le Glaive* was silent as Marshal Edmond Dujardin ran his thumb and forefinger over his moustache. He looked over the main deck of the ship that stretched forward to the forecastle and prow. Each were ships of the line, three hundred meters long, one hundred wide and forty meters from keel to top deck. Runners ran under their ships. The design had proved itself so well that other forces had imitated them.

Each ship looked like a warship from the age of sail. Lines of gun ports ran down their sides, the rear of their ships, and the forward sections. Posts jutted out, drawing in power, the sails pulling the ships forward. Each held five hundred massive cannons on each side.

His own ship, *Le Glaive,* ran four hundred meters with eight hundred and fifty cannons on each side.

"The spider has transmitted the enemy fleet's coordinates," Captain Adamus said, standing near the helm.

"Good, about time they showed up. Prepare to teleport," Edmond ordered.

His words travelled through his ship and the other three. Sails retracted. Armored shutters opened, allowing the sails to be stored inside as the ships gathered power, burning through a massive amount of mana stones.

"Teleport in five, four, three..." Adamus started counting down. Power built through the ships, their hulls' formations brightening, drawing in mana from the area. The clouds churned and darkened, the ship's formations lighting them up from within. "Two, one!"

Mana surged through the ship in a wave from the dungeon core outward. The ripples of power cleared a hollow in the new clouds around the ships as they finished transitioning.

Edmond checked the positioning of the rest of the fleet. They were arranged in a single line, with *Le Glaive* in the lead. He used his Dungeon Sense, locking onto the enemy fleet cruising nearby. The enemy sailed without a care in the world, forward and down from their position, accelerating in parallel.

Drive formations flared with power, causing the air to shimmer. The ships dropped slightly before the formations caught them.

Everyone took the impact with ease.

"Barriers are up!" Adamus said. "Run the cannons!"

"Aye, aye, *Capitaine!*" A woman manning the gunnery console talked through her sound transmission device; gun ports opened along the sides of the ships. The loaded cannons were run out, gleaming monsters of metal and formations.

These same cannons might be used on walls of castles, once placed never to be moved again. They were six meters long and able to spew out cannon balls with a nearly forty-centimeter diameter.

"Seems that they have spotted us. They are powering their formations to increase their altitude," Adamus said.

"All ships ready!" another aide said.

"Get us point blank. We might not get another pass on their upper decks. Stagger the line so they can use their forward guns," Edmond said.

The forward cannons shot the same cannon ball, but their barrels were longer, and they were more finely crafted, increasing the power they could display.

The fleet pushed forward and angled down. The ships behind *Le Glaive* fanned out to the left, right, and above.

They forged through the clouds, still unable to see their opponent as their formations surged.

Edmond and the rest of the crew waited in tense silence.

Shadows appeared in the distance. The rising Black Phoenix Clan ships were trying to gain the altitude advantage.

"Have the forward cannons fire by ship when they can. Target the destroyer."

"Yes, Marshal!" Adamus passed the orders on. The cannons of *Le Glaive* fired. The ship bucked as smoke rolled over the bow, passing over the ship as fast as it had appeared.

The cannons on the other ships fired. Edmond watched the cannon balls descend on their targets.

The shared mana barrier connecting the Black Phoenix ships flared as the first hits struck.

The metal rain continued as the forward cannons reloaded.

Captain Adamus took the helm, shifting the entire ship to line up the cannons.

They rumbled again, striking the barrier, making it shudder and shake.

The Sha ships slowed their speed as they closed with the Black Phoenix fleet.

"Prepare for tilt," Adamus yelled. The Black Phoenix Clan were down and to their left. The Sha ships leveled off and tilted to their left. People held onto their stations and the grab bars across the ship.

Spells filled the air. Clouds of dust turned into dirt spears and rained down on the Sha fleet's barriers.

"Seems that their mages have come out to play."

Edmond had a wild smile on his face as he looked through the left bridge windows, seeing the Black Phoenix Clan ships below.

The clouds shifted, rolling the ship, tilting the guns up and then down like waves of old.

The Sky Marshal waited, watching the angle and the range. "Fire!"

Rolling cannon fire buffeted the ship as the batteries opened fire on the enemy destroyer. The barriers flared, and the ship shuddered.

"All guns fired. Reloading!"

"Release turning sails!"

Sails ran up the masts, catching the wind and snapping the ship around to the left as formations added their own power.

The gun crews proved their worth, reloading with lightning speed and fired again.

The second Sha ship tilted dangerously. Black smoke billowed from her cannons, striking the Black Phoenix's barriers. Its sails shot out of its armored shutters as it turned to the left, dragging its momentum around.

Soon the third and then the fourth ship joined, circling the Black Phoenix ship as it fought to gain altitude and push forward, out of the Sha's encirclement.

"Their corvette is converting!"

Edmond looked at the map, watching the Black Phoenix corvette as it unfurled, revealing its primary cannon hidden deep within its core. Its mana barrier evaporated, but the linked mana barrier between the fleet covered the ship as it pivoted and aimed. Formations flashed through the ship, mana funneling into the main mana cannon.

Its attack struck at the same time it left the corvette, striking the barrier of *Le Glaive*.

"Barrier down by thirty percent! Recovering!"

"Another corvette is converting!"

"First corvette is recovering. They're burning their mana stones."

The ship shook as the second corvette fired its main cannon.

"Prepare the fleet to split their formation. Get inside their barrier," Edmond said.

The cannons on the Sha ships fired furiously. The Black Phoenix Clan were gaining altitude. It would be a matter of time until the two fleets were level with one another.

The destroyer rolled to one side, firing the cannons along its side up at the Sha ships.

The mana cannons lit up *Le Glaive*'s barriers once more.

"Barriers at fifty percent!"

The destroyer rolled and fired on another ship.

The two forces battered one another with their cannons, the barriers only getting a short break between attacks.

The Sha flagship shuddered angrily.

"First corvette cannon recharged."

"Make sure we pay some attention to those corvettes and break their formation." Edmond's voice was dry.

"Prepare the cannons! We're about to break inside their formation," exclaimed Adamus.

The sails shifted as the ship changed its course. It cut a tighter circle. The formations made the ship shake as they changed course to come in across the rear of the Destroyer, inside its mana barrier envelope.

The destroyer turned to present its broadside.

The cannons along the port side fired. Without their barriers to protect them, the volley smashed through the stone and metal hull of the opposing ship, every cannon firing right through its backside.

Cannons on the starboard side fired on the smaller corvettes that had been maneuvering to fire back at them.

Two corvettes were smashed under the attacks of *Le Glaive*. One dropped, its formations failing.

The other shuddered under the weight of fire and fell away, dropping toward the ground as it powered its teleportation formations and disappeared in a flash of light.

A corvette fired on *Le Glaive*, striking her armored side. The mana cannon's blast punched through firing positions, igniting the powder stored near the cannons, killing gunners and stabbing deep into the ship.

"The main destroyer is powering their teleportation formations. Their mana barrier is down. The entire fleet is trying to jump."

"Fire on them with all cannons!" Edmond barked, standing and walking to the map. He staggered with the attacks striking *Le Glaive*.

"Turning the ship!" Adamus turned the helm. The ship leaned, and they presented their aft. "Fire aft cannons! All mages, cast attack spells!"

Cannons as large as those in the bow fired. Stone chips erupted inside the destroyer.

Spells illuminated the space between the fleets, both sides mages displaying their strongest attack spells, enhanced through formations to be as powerful as mana cannons.

"Their mana cannons might charge faster, but they don't have the power of our cannons!" Edmond said.

The two fleets leveled with one another. Sha cannons thundered, covering the sides in rolling smoke while Black Phoenix mana cannons created spell formations at their muzzle, their spells lighting up the ships as they tore through the sky toward the Sha ships.

Both sides' barriers colored as the Sha charged in closer, having the speed. Their cannons worked on the Black Phoenix barrier while they fired frantically to gain an advantage.

"Take us in! Expand barrier!" Edmond yelled. "Hold fire. Ready all batteries to fire in series."

The fleet's barriers widened and weakened, reaching out to touch the Black Phoenix ship's barriers. The interactions of the two barriers cancelled one another out.

"Fire and retract!"

Sha cannons rocked the ship, tearing through the Black Phoenix Clan's hull and guns.

While they were inside the enemy's barriers, the enemy was inside theirs.

They battered one another with attacks. The converted corvette fired one more attack into the third ship of the Sha line. They had all been dragged into the furious melee, trading cannon fire and spells.

The destroyer disappeared, leaving spells and cannons to fire through empty air. The corvettes disappeared as well.

"Damn those cowards." Edmond hit the table, using his Dungeon Sense.

"Get me the captains!"

An aide came over with a sound transmission device.

"Reload and affect immediate repairs on your ships. The enemy is some forty kilometers out. We will attack them once we are ready," Edmond said.

A cough came through the sound transmission channel.

"Is there a problem?"

"Marshal, while we can chase after the fleet and bring them down, they could be preparing their own ambush," Louis Gerard said. "The plan was to attack the ships that showed up and harvest the mana from the area.

With the cost of our ammunition, we need the stones to sustain our fleet."

Edmond balled his fist and slowly released it, saying nothing into the channel between the captains.

Adamus moved over from the helm to the main map table. "We're losing the advantage. They're heading deeper into their territory. We follow them, we will use more resources. They'll have to take all their ships to get repaired. It will take them out of the fight for some time. Gerard, as much as I don't like it, he is right. We could jump into a trap. And do we really need to destroy their fleet, or is draining their resources enough for now?"

Edmond looked at him and then back at the table.

"Set up security patrols in the area. See to the wounded and repairs. Retrieve the spider from the bottom of the valley. Send out teams to recover what remains of the corvette we took out. Draw in the surrounding energy and make sure that the ships' mana draw envelopes don't intersect one another."

He said into the captain's channel, "As much as I want to take out that fleet, we will do more damage draining their resources. We don't know how long until they return, so get to work."

Louis Gerard sighed as he leaned back in his command chair, pinching his brows. He had darker skin, with deep brown eyes. His build spoke to long years of training. He breathed in and looked to his XO and the rest of his ship's bridge crew. "Status?"

"We took a few hits to the port side; seventeen dead, forty-three wounded. Repairs are underway. Two cannons were taken out. They're being checked right now to see if we can repair them."

They didn't have the materials or people to make new cannons each time they were damaged.

"Good, have the mana gathering platforms ready. Step down our fighting forces but have an aerial squadron on constant watch."

"Yes, Captain."

Gerard stood up from his chair and walked toward the main map table. Too many in their clan have focused on the arts, making clothes and food, and not enough on making more weapons. If they wanted to win this war, they needed more ships and more victories. *We cannot blindly charge and face the enemy into death each time. The marshal is reckless.*

The fleet spread out. A ship left *Le Glaive*, descending toward the magma. Levitating platforms covered in formation script shot out from the different ships. The masts on the platforms activated, creating a net that drew in the surrounding elements, creating a massive gathering formation that forced the mana and elements toward their mother ship.

The ships' repairs accelerated visibly.

"Lady Velten requests an audience," an aide said to the captain.

Gerard hid his grimace. "Bring her here."

The aide nodded.

Velten's heeled boots *clicked* as she walked across the bridge, looking at the windows and the map table.

She wore her black hair in a braid, a purple stripe running down the left side of her face. She also wore a jerkin with several matchlock pistols within reach of her hands. A rapier rested at her hip. White and silver tattoos framed her face, running down her neck and her hands.

Louis used his sound transmission device so they wouldn't be heard. "And to what do I owe this honor, Lisa?"

"Spread thin across all of the areas we control, fighting for every inch. Yet the Marshal scares up several ships of the line to come out on his hunting trip."

"This will reduce the enemy's energy stores and increase our own. Airships are not cheap to run."

"Nor are our cannons," Velten said. "I heard that the Black Phoenix ran into some trouble not so long ago. A frigate went down to the Fourth Realm, attacked a city-state. A city-state that used weapons like ours. The marshal didn't do anything, and he has not made any plans to deal with this new threat."

Louis grunted.

Velten continued. "We both know it is a matter of time until people figure out how to make our weapons. We have been quiet for many years and the powers of the Seventh Realm have left us alone. Our cannons have their advantages, but we cannot sustain their continuous use. We will run out of cannonballs at this rate, and our smiths can't keep up with production. Already, our quality of cannonballs is lacking."

"He is the marshal, and we are the clans." Louis looked as if he tasted something sour.

"And for how long has he lorded over the clans, kept us suppressed, limiting the number of people that know of his weapons? There are new arrivals, and they have better technology than us. What are we going to do when the other sects buy their technology and come after us? We won't have anything. We need to do what is best for the clans. We need to secure our future. It won't take long for others to catch up to us. We must use this time to establish ourselves and become part of other forces. We are on our own."

"You are talking about treason!"

"No, I am not. I am talking about doing what is best for the clans. I do not care what the marshal does, but we need to do what's best for our people. Didn't he teach us that? And then he treats us like children, while he rushes into battles."

Louis dropped his gaze, looking at the formations that showed the number of sky mana stones increasing at a rapid rate.

Cai Bo quickly recovered as she stepped into the Fourth Realm. *This mana is so thin.*

The group pushed past the traders and others that stood around the totem. The totem guards, seeing their emblems, moved to the side.

They reached the street ahead of the totem and pulled out magnificent aerial beasts, leaping onto their backs.

They flew over what had been the Vuzgal mountain range, seeing the broken city of Vuzgal.

The Associations were angry at how things turned out, but had done little in the way of responding, only forcing the Clan to pay for the damages and losses. Millions of earth mana stones, but what were a few million Earth mana stones to a force that uses airships?

The *Eternus* lay on the ground in front of Vuzgal, along the road that had connected it to the East and West.

Aerial patrols greeted them, checking their identities before they were allowed to land on the ship.

They were guided through the ship and onto the bridge, where Captain Stassov sat. Her crew moved around the room with purpose.

Cai Bo entered the sound cancellation field around Stassov's throne and bowed. "Captain Stassov, what might we help you with?"

Stassov studied her. "Cai Bo, what do you want from this?"

"Either aid to reach the Seventh Realm or a position in your clan,"

Cai Bo said.

Marco, standing off to the side, looked between the two women in sudden alarm.

Stassov smiled. "You are bold. Do you think that one dungeon core will allow you to join my clan?"

"No, but I think that it is enough to make you interested in me. While I am not strong enough now to assist you, I will be with time. With your support, that time will come faster."

"You think rather highly of yourself."

"The sect leader wanted to keep the dungeon core for himself and use it to increase our power. He was waiting for you to leave before he dedicated his efforts to looking for the core," Cai Bo stated.

Stassov hit her armrest and stood. Her aura spread out, forcing Cai Bo to her knees. "He dares! Does he think that I will show him mercy?"

"He is an idiot who only cares about his cultivation. He has reached the position of sect leader and believes that everyone else is too stupid or weak to do anything about his plans. While *he* has not been looking, my people have. We will find you your dungeon core."

Stassov's aura retreated. "Ah, I guess these little outbursts won't phase you?"

"You must've known from the beginning that there was a chance the sect would do something like this. You have researched the sect. By now you must know the locations that we control. If we were to take the dungeon core, you would hunt us down."

Stassov waved for her to go on.

"Something must have happened if you are being forced to return to the higher realms. You could become distracted and information from the lower realms is uncommon. You need someone you can trust, here, to get you that the dungeon core. I will contract myself to you, assuring that I will get the dungeon core, and bring it to you."

Stassov sat down in her chair, holding her head and watching Cai Bo. "I sense there is more."

"The Vuzgalians are strong, and I am not sure we can defeat them. We need an advantage—weapons that will allow us to compete with a force backed by a dungeon core."

"Spit it out."

"We need those airships, or at least weapons with the power of a dungeon core to punch through the enemy's barriers. We also need a way to detect a dungeon core."

"You will work under Gregor and his hunters to build a force and airships capable of defeating the Vuzgalians. All dungeon cores are property of the Black Phoenix Clan."

Stassov looked at Cai Bo. It wasn't a question or a request, it was an order. The silence stretched before Stassov smiled. "I'll have a contract prepared. You will not share any of the information that I give you. You'll remove that sect leader. Any dungeon cores that you or any of your people recover you will turn over to me."

"Yes, Captain Stassov." Cai Bo bowed her head.

"And you—" Stassov looked at Marco. "—will make sure that she doesn't betray me."

Erik and Rugrat passed through Alva's totem and appeared inside Cronen Mission Hall.

"Back to work," Rugrat said. They exited the totem and walked to a totem guide booth.

"Where to?"

"Looking to go to the city Purkesh," Erik said.

"Okay, three mana stones."

Erik passed over the three Sky grade mana stones. A guide came over.

"This way." She walked them toward the totem; they waited in the departure line.

"The Sha Clan use Purkesh as their main base, right?"

"Yeah, they have a permanent berth for their ships. The fight between them and the Black Phoenix Clan has been heating up. Heard they landed a good blow on the Black Phoenix Clan recently."

"Yeah?"

"Took a region from them and bashed their ships up."

Erik passed the guide the Sky mana stones. Their power flowed into the totem. The totem's light enveloped them.

They appeared in a wet city; rain poured from the heavens.

George crouched on Rugrat's shoulders. A haze appeared around him, turning the rain into steam before it could touch him.

"Have a good time in Purkesh. The Sha are in the southwestern part of the city," the guide said, disappearing in a flash of light.

Erik and Rugrat pulled out ball caps as they headed for the guards' gates of entry.

"Purpose of visit?" the guard asked as they walked up.

"A meeting," Erik raised his voice, pulling up his cloak against the rain.

The guard looked at them both. "Two mana stones each."

Erik paid the fee.

Damn, this Seventh Realm is expensive. After buying all the resources he could from Fred and the others, their supply of Sky grade mana stones was pitifully low, as in nonexistent.

The guard waved them forward.

The city looked like something out of Ancient Rome. Grand pillars held up magnificently carved reliefs. Rain fell from curved tiles and into the rivers and drains, leading away from the city.

Round houses, like coliseums, stood in the distance. Bridges curved over the rivers and lakes that passed through the city. Boats were moored up along the riverside, their owners getting away from the rain in the cloth-covered marketplaces.

Erik and Rugrat headed in the direction the guide had pointed them in.

Erik approached a man watching the rain from under his cloth overhang.

"Do you know where the Sha Clan's berth is?"

"Keep going along this road for another five kilometers," the man answered dismissively, and headed into his store.

Erik and Rugrat kept walking.

"He was pleasant," Rugrat observed.

"Ten Realms." Erik shrugged.

They kept walking, asking a few people where the berth was located. The berth was more like fifteen kilometers away, not five.

"That looks like it." Rugrat leaned forward, pulling out the Sha's invitation.

Erik looked at the crest and the gate at the end of the street, the wall blocking off several kilometers of the Sha's clan land.

"You think it'll still be valid?" Erik muttered.

"Well, we're committed now, aren't we?"

"Let's get a better vantage point," Erik said.

Rugrat looked around. "Follow me."

They walked between buildings, dodging under the overhangs of the roofs to avoid the rain.

Rugrat paused next to a building. Erik came up beside him and scanned the opposite direction.

A woman walked into a house and closed the wooden door heavily against the elements.

The building they stood in front of was some fifty meters tall. Erik clapped his hands and interlaced his fingers. Rugrat nodded.

Erik squatted down and Rugrat backed up. He took a short run, jumping up and putting his foot in Erik's hands. Erik raised his hands, hurling Rugrat skyward, then turned around and backed up. He held the brim of his hat to see Rugrat disappear over the side of the roof.

A rope dropped down, slapping the wet stones.

Erik checked the alleyways and grabbed the rope, scrambling up rapidly. He slipped over the roof on his belly. Rugrat was in a crouch, one hand holding onto the rope. Erik clicked his tongue and pulled on the rope. Rugrat released it, lowering himself slowly to his belly while Erik stored the rope.

Rugrat looked into the Sha compound beyond the gate. Erik moved around on the roof to get closer.

"Guards patrolling the outer wall," Rugrat observed.

The rain picked up, dancing across the street, blown by strong breezes.

Inside the square lay a star shaped fortress. Inside the massive outer star formation lay a nine-sided city broken down into blocks of houses and buildings.

Aerial beasts moved within the mini-city. He cast Eagle Sight. A group of airships rose from the ground; two frigates and a destroyer. They cut off, away from the city, disappearing into the clouds.

"That's one hell of a city," Erik said, looking at where the ships had come from.

"Yeah, and we want to talk to the leader of it," Rugrat said. "We see this much on the surface, but I wonder what their dungeons are like."

"Didn't think of that. Yeah, they have to be dungeon masters to fly those ships. They must've altered the ground underneath, likely several cities on top of one another."

They ignored the rain and took their time watching the city.

"We're not going to learn much more this way," Rugrat said. "Shall we see if the marshal is home?"

"Might as well." They checked the ground below and slid off the roof.

Esther sighed, rubbing her face and falling on her couch. "What did you just say, Old Jia?" She stretched out her feet and legs as she grabbed more reports from the piles on the cushions beside her.

"There are a pair of Two-Star heroes at the front gate. They gave the guards a sealed letter, our sealed letter. It was addressed to you or the marshal." Old Jia had an amused look on his face as he held out the letter.

Esther put her reports on the table next to the couch. "Our letter? They've got crap timing." The leather of the couch rubbed as she stood up.

"Fun reading?" Old Jia asked.

Esther gnashed her teeth. "None of it good, and definitely none of it fun."

She took the letter from him and turned it over. "The Clans are restless. This is my handwriting. Huh." She put the note away and opened the letter. Inside there was a small note, gunpowder, and round shot.

She took out the note and opened it.

We accept your invitation to talk. Lord Erik West, Lord Jimmy Rodrigeuz.

Esther's head felt like there were alarm bells going off. She read the note again, passing it to Old Jia, and looked inside again. She pulled out some pellets and rubbed them on her fingers and sniffed them. "Definitely not a formula that I know."

She looked at Old Jia. "Well, it seems that the Vuzgalians really aren't dead."

Erik and Rugrat followed the guard. They passed through a formation that removed the water from their clothes. Sha in the halls frowned at their attire.

Funny wigs. They look like old style judges, or George Washington.

Erik and Rugrat watched everything from under the brim of their ball caps, which had turned darker with rain. George jumped from Rugrat's shoulders and grew to his full size, drawing people's attention to the wolf and his red, blue, and green fur that looked like flames as it shifted.

Erik felt a twinge of pain at the loss of a familiar weight on his shoulders, or the comforting presence beside him.

They passed open doors, showing people bent over their desks, writing. Dozens of Sha messengers grabbed or dropped off letters, papers, and books, placing them on desks and leaving.

It felt like they had jumped back in time. Everyone was dressed like they were living in the Seventeen hundreds, back when the Brits and French were fighting one another in the States.

The guard knocked on a door.

An older man opened it, revealing a couch against the left-hand side of the door.

"Please, come in," Old Jia said.

"Stay," Rugrat said to George. The big wolf turned in a circle and sat next to the door, watching people go past.

Erik walked in first. The office was small compared to most, maybe five meters wide and ten meters deep. Mage lights glowed in the ceiling. Behind the old man and door there was a clothes rack. A fireplace laid to the right side, opposite the couch and the desk covered in papers.

At the back of the room bookshelves took up the left and right walls. A screen pulled from the ceiling covered the rear wall.

At the large, solid desk sat a woman with wavy black hair. Her brown eyes studied them both, her hands clasped in front of her.

Erik felt the creak of the wood flooring.

"Your coats and hats?" the older man asked.

Erik pulled off his hat and his cloak, passing them to Jia. Once Jia had them, Rugrat pulled off his cloak and hat.

They both wore worn boots, combat pants and combat shirts with a brown camouflage pattern down their sleeves and collar. Their two-star medallions were attached to their left sleeve, over their shoulders.

"Miss Leblanc, I assume?" Erik said as he approached the desk.

"Lord West. Lord Rodriguez." She nodded to them both. "I received your message." She patted the letter filled with powder and musket ball. "While I have many questions, I must ask you why you are coming out of the shadows to talk with me."

"Well, I doubt you would be willing to harm two Two-Star heroes. The Mission Hall would be most unhappy, and we want something." Erik gestured at the chair.

She waved to it. He and Rugrat sat down.

"And what would you want?" Esther asked.

"An alliance."

Quest Completed: The Marshal
The marshal, leader of the Sha clans, has extended an invitation to you.
Requirements:
Reach level 60 and ascend to the Seventh Realm
Head to the Sha Clan headquarters
Provide a sample of gunpowder
Rewards:
750,000 EXP

113,042,932,548/128,249,000,000 EXP till you reach Level 86

Niklaus let out an aggravated sigh as he rubbed his face.

Mercy sat back in her chair, tossing the latest report on the table. "Nothing! Not a damn whisper. It's as if they disappeared into the air!"

"If the Black Phoenix Clan find out what we're doing, we wouldn't last till tomorrow. The sect will hang us out on the chopping block if we're found," Niklaus said.

"Then we have to find something and make sure the Black Phoenix never learns about it. On one side there is death, on the other we could reach higher than ever before," Mercy said.

"The Silaz family was killed in a raid on their trade caravan in the Second Realm. Chonglu disappeared. His children are with his wife, who is a high ranker in the Fighter's Association. Lord West's teacher, Zen Hei, is teaching in the Seventh Realm, a powerful figure within the Alchemist Association." Niklaus looked at Mercy. "We don't have any leads left."

Mercy snarled but had nothing to say. Imagining, not for the first time, putting her whip to work against her dear cousin.

Niklaus laughed, waving at the papers that covered the table. "We have nothing. All the people we could ask are out of our reach. Those kingdoms that were defeated in the First Realm have the gall to ask for our support. The force they attacked counter-attacked, taking their lands and a couple of cities.

"They think we're here just to waste resources on them! I should send down the army to teach them a lesson." Niklaus snarled, his fist balling. "While I'm down there, I'll tear their kingdoms apart! I'll show them how to defeat this new Empire and crush their damn dungeon! It wouldn't even be worth the loot!"

Niklaus slammed his hand on the desk.

"What did you say?" Mercy's images of eliciting pain from her cousin were disturbed by his words.

Niklaus froze, composing himself and bowing his head. "I am sorry, cousin, for my outburst."

"They have a dungeon?"

"A small dungeon with a few rooms. There was supposed to be a big regional dungeon that our people from the Second Realm used, but its strength eroded over the years."

Mercy tapped the desk. "What is this new nation's name?"

"Uhh…" Niklaus pulled out a report, sifting through papers. He snatched one up. "Vermire. Vermire Empire."

"Tell me more."

"They have a consortium, a group of crafters that were brought together by the Empire to teach the people. It's based in an area thick with powerful beasts. Originally, it was a series of outposts. They've united under one leader and control the entire area and the lands beyond."

"We should have a closer look at this Vermire Empire. We need to report this to Elder Cai Bo."

Niklaus' lips parted before he closed his mouth assessing what he said next. "Yes, cousin."

26
House of Cards

Cai Bo found Elder Kostic waiting in her office. The doors sealed behind her as her pensive look shifted into a snarl. "A bunch of puppets on string. The entire sect is now looking for the Vuzgalians."

"High Elder, your new mission might not last all that long." Kostic bowed with a smirk. "My clan has been working tirelessly, and I think we know where the Vuzgalians are hiding. You remember the attack that happened in the First Realm?"

"Something about a new nation. All the groups around it attacked it and failed. Didn't our people report that there was no connection to Vuzgal?" Cai Bo sat back in her chair, resting the side of her head on her spread fingers.

"Yes, but that might not be correct. There was an anomaly before the attack. A powerful blast of mana spread through the First Realm. People demanded to know what it was. The new nation, the Vermire Empire, said that a new dungeon had appeared."

"New dungeons can effect various phenomena when they appear." Cai Bo frowned.

"Yes, and it is the site where another dungeon exists. A few of our sects in the Second Realm descend there to get prizes and to increase their levels. It opens infrequently but the city using it was able to turn out experts every few years. Now we know why."

"So, they were secretly using a dungeon?"

"Mercy is from the lower realms. Dungeons in the Second Realm and Third Realm are rare. I did not think of it much either. In the First Realm, most people do not even know of the existence of dungeons, they are so rare. In this location, there are not one but two dungeons?"

"They do clump together." Cai Bo tapped her lips. "But I agree it is strange."

"They have links to the Silaz family. We know that there are Qin Silaz, Domonos, and Yui. Their younger brother, Wren, lives in the Vermire Empire and travels through the lower realms. Chonglu, the man who was lord of Vuzgal for only a few short days, used to control a city near it."

Cai Bo sat up. "Why did I not hear of this before?"

"There were coincidences. We didn't know if it was the same Silaz family, as their trail went cold. If it was, then they might have a connection to the place, but they had left it. Knowing about the dungeon lords, the dungeon cores, it starts to make sense."

"They don't need a city to live in. They could live under it just as easily. Are you saying that the Vermire Empire is actually Vuzgal? That they have a dungeon underneath it that they control to raise their people and make their weapons and gear?"

"That is what we think."

"Do you have any concrete information?"

"No, but we have Chonglu linked to a city that lies on the border with the Vermire Empire. The Silaz family has disappeared, and the person that might be one of them is traveling or doing business in the capital, King's Hill. The people are all from the First Realm. The guards all use basic weapons. The crafters are all skilled and they have started their own consortium."

Cai Bo would be watched if she went down to the First Realm. It would raise questions. She needed time for Gregor and his dungeon hunters to create their weapons, and she still had to work on the Antal clan. If she could bring them over to her side, she would control three quarters of the Willful Institute.

It was an opportunity if she could seize it. Her people were in place. She had an idea of where the enemy was. She controlled the board; if she told the sect leader, then her moves would be limited.

"Who knows this?"

293

"Mercy, General Niklaus, and myself. I have made sure that they will not tell anyone."

Cai Bo drummed her fingers on the desk. "We need confirmation. This is what you will do. Take a powerful spell scroll and activate it in their capital, see how they react. If Vuzgal is the other side of Vermire, we should see movement that shouldn't exist in the lower realms."

"Yes, Elder Cai Bo."

She glanced at a report on her desk.

They had gained much in the fighting, enough to support their current forces and even create some growth. They needed more victories and loot to wage another battle like the one at Vuzgal. *Just what do you have hidden in the First Realm?* Cai Bo didn't dare underestimate the Vuzgalians anymore.

Marshal sat in his command chair aboard *Le Glaive.* He held out a report he had just finished reading. "Our intelligence suggests that the *Eternus* has returned from their long vacation in the Fourth Realm," he said to Captain Adamus, who was talking to a man with a clipboard. He walked to the marshal, accepting the piece of paper. "Another destroyer will be annoying to deal with. Do you think that they will use it to retake the area?"

Edmond finished the letter with a pensive look.

"Sir?"

"Sorry, what did you say?" Edmond said.

"Do you think they will use it to retake the area?"

"They might. They're bold enough. They have two full fleets in reserve. They could use them, but everything indicates that those two fleets are being upgraded and their crews are undergoing rigorous cultivation in preparation for the Violet Cloud Realm. Sorry, but I need to return to Purkesh."

"Has something happened?" Adamus asked.

Edmond turned on a formation in his chair, making him and Adamus open and close their jaws to pop their ears. "The Vuzgalian lords have appeared in Purkesh."

"From the city the Eternus destroyed?"

"Yes, the one that uses similar weapons to our own. I think they are new arrivals, a newer generation of people from Earth. They brought a musket ball and gunpowder with them, and the gunpowder is not a formula that we use."

"Sir, they're from the Fourth Realm."

"They made it to at least level sixty before they came to find me, and they're Two-Star heroes."

"Two-Star? Why would city lords be heroes? Each mission is a massive risk."

"Who knows, but I intend to find out. If nothing else, I might learn about what happened in France."

Adamus nodded.

"I will use the teleportation arrays and head back. Take command of the fleet, Louis. A stick in the mud, is a good commander and leader. Make sure to listen to him. His grandfather taught me a great number of things," Edmond said, standing.

"Yes sir."

Captain Stassov placed down her cultivation scroll as she sensed someone stop near her throne.

A bowed aide stood to one side of the magical circle that pierced the floor and rose around the dungeon core, poised in the Phoenix's Talons.

"What is it?"

The aide cupped her hands. "Commander Chmilenko orders your immediate return to the Seventh Realm," she said in a low voice.

"Has something happened?"

"He was attacked when patrolling the Earth Cloud Valley by the Sha Flagship and several of their warships."

Stassov hid her grimace. "Make the preparations."

The aide left as Stassov activated her sound transmission device.

"Commander?" Gregor answered.

"How goes the search?"

"I have made an ally in the Willful Institute. She is leading the search for the Vuzgalians, but the sect forces are still organizing, and the ships are not complete."

"Do you think you can capture the dungeon core this time?"

Gregor held his tongue as Stassov watched the crew prepare for transition back into the Seventh Realm.

At least we will stop burning through mana stones. She cursed how heavily her attack had cut into her personal resources.

"I would not wish to attack them without airships and the support of the Sects. I don't know what kind of defenses they have, or if they will be in one location or multiple."

"You are that afraid of them?"

"Afraid, no, but I am wary," Gregor said. He had earned the position to not be scared about her retaliations.

Stassov's gaze turned to Ranko, who walked into the room and moved to the map where Goran, the new Ground force sub-commander, stood.

"How long will it take to create the airships?"

"A few months. Their weapons are weak, and the crafters are... usable." Gregor's tone was pained.

"Make sure they cannot command any of our ships and that they don't steal our designs. You have three months, Gregor. Do not let me down. In six months, we must both attend the Violet Sky Realm."

"Yes, Commander."

She cancelled the sound transmission. She felt the thrumming energy running through the Talon and stepped out of her chair and between the spell formations to stand at the map table.

"We are ready for teleportation, Commander."

"Good, make it so."

Mana stones melted into dust as power ran through the warship. Light built through the formations until it flashed and dissipated, revealing a new scene outside their windows. The whirring noise slowed down as everyone moved.

"Teleportation into the Seventh Realm is complete," a navigator called.

"Take us to the shipyards to meet with Chmilenko's fleet.

27

A Meeting of Generations

Those of the Sha clans, wearing their makeup, styled hair, and wigs, glanced at Esther and her two companions, speaking to one another in hushed whispers.

Nothing moves faster in the clans than gossip.

She reached the end of a corridor and passed through a magical formation. The smell of roses drifted through the greenhouse.

The greenhouse was dedicated to roses. Couples walked with their arms linked, taking in the garden. Roses had been weaved across trellises, creating walls of flowers and thorns with hidden corners and private spaces.

Those enjoying the garden stalled in their merry-goings. Others from the depths of the garden were leaving, bowing their heads to Esther and looking at the two men behind her as they departed, guards sweeping behind them, clearing out the people.

Esther's gaze was drawn to the pure white tree standing in the middle of the greenhouse, its red leaves drifting in the breeze, hanging over the walkway around it.

Soft light came in from the glass windows, held together with finely crafted and carved iron filigree.

She walked around the tree and through an archway of red, pink, and white roses.

"Seems pretty French to me," Rugrat said.

Erik grunted.

Esther caught a glimpse of the two from the corner of her eye. Their heads turned slowly from side to side, taking it all in.

There was no awe in their eyes, accepting what was around them. There was a weight to their presence that would come and go. She half-relaxed with them around, but would then notice, consciously or not, that they were moving in a way to cover one another, looking for threats.

The path opened to a round covered area. Two paths among the walls, made of weaved roses, led in as a larger path revealed a vista of rose fields, grown into a design across the ground.

Esther greeted several guards around the intersection with her eyes and waved her hand.

They turned and walked through a small garden and under the covering trellis. Roses grew through the walls and the roof.

A white iron table had legs that looked like growing roses.

Erik had his right thumb in his belt loop as he walked under the covering, looking left and right.

Rugrat came in behind him, holding his belt buckle.

"Please make yourselves comfortable." Esther held out her hand to the table.

Erik picked a chair, positioned it to see the large opening and one of the paths in. Rugrat strolled around, admiring the roses and looking out the doors. He leaned against a banister that separated the covered area in the middle of the garden from the small garden plots around them.

Esther examined the duo as they took in the landscape. Lord West's eyes met hers as she casually let her gaze drift to the manicured garden beyond the large opening, facing the opened front of the hidden meeting area.

They were lords. Now they are people without a city. They're just Two-Star heroes. It is sure to cause a stir that the marshal met with Two-Star heroes for a chat.

"So, how do you know the marshal?" Erik asked.

"He is my uncle."

"You from France as well?" Rugrat asked.

"No." Esther bristled. *You think I'm that old?*

"LeBlanc sounds French though," Erik said.

"My father took on the name in honor of the marshal."

"Who is your father?"

"He was the captain of the Royal guard." Esther touched her father's sword.

"Was?" Rugrat asked.

"He was killed carrying out his duty." Esther felt a stony expression fall over her.

"Sorry to hear that," Erik said.

She saw Rugrat press his lips together and nod as well.

"Thank you, it was a long time ago now."

Silence stretched as they all shifted in their positions.

"How long will it be for the marshal?" Erik asked.

"I do not know. He has other matters to attend to," Esther replied.

"Thankfully, they are all clear," Edmond said as he walked out of one of the rose walls, striding toward the covered garden. His royal guards moved to either side of the opening, one hand on their swords, the other on their flintlock pistols.

Erik stood as he entered under the trellis.

"My name is Edmond Dujardin. Many call me the marshal." He reached out a hand.

"Just call me Rugrat."

"Rugrat." Edmond rolled the word around and smiled, pivoting.

"Erik West. Just call me Erik."

They shook hands quickly, and Edmond gestured to the table. "Shall we?"

Edmond sat at the table in front of Esther, Rugrat to the right and Erik to the left.

Esther pulled out the letter and put it on the table. Edmond opened it and looked through the contents. He pulled out some of the powder and sniffed it, then passed the letter back to Esther.

"So, it must be the early two thousands back on Earth?"

Erik and Rugrat looked at one another. Rugrat lifted a shoulder.

"Yes, it is. Are you from France or Quebec?"

"Ah, much easier without the games." Edmond smiled.

Esther kept watching the duo, making sure not to miss anything.

"Yes, I am from France. I arrived some three hundred years ago. One day, I was fighting the British in Canada. The next minute I am in the First Realm."

"That explains a lot," Erik said, sitting back in his chair.

Edmond cleared his throat. "What of France?"

"Uhh, well, let's see. I'm not that well versed in French history. Earth is at a time of widespread peace. France is a strong country in the world. Guess that since then, there have been two world wars."

"World wars?" Edmond asked.

"Nearly every country in the world was fighting one another from America, Europe, even Asia," Erik said.

"What of the royal family?"

"Oh?" Erik looked at Rugrat. "Uh, there were some revolutions and your royalty turned into a government. Like everyone votes for who the leader of the country will be for a few years, and they run the place. Five years later they can get re-elected, or another group gets a shot at it."

Edmond's shoulders sagged. "What of the war with England?"

The two men looked at one another.

"Did they win?" Edmond asked.

"I don't know. I don't think so. Sure, there is Quebec and there are some French places in the states like Louisiana."

"The British won?"

"Uhh, that's not really accurate, either. There are no British or French in that part of the world. There's Canada to the north and the United States to the south who are allied with one another. France and the United Kingdom, uh, Britain, they're allies too. With one another and with the United States, Canada, Australia, New Zealand, I think like all of Europe?" Rugrat glanced at Erik "There's a lot of places in Europe. I get confused who everyone is."

"We're from the United States, an ally of France," Erik said.

"So, we lost the war?"

"I don't think so. Neither the Brits nor the French really won it."

"The nature of the world. One decade we are allies, the next we are enemies." Edmond sighed.

"Well, since the world wars, some hundred years ago, Earth hasn't had any major wars and alliances don't change that much."

"No war?"

"Well, there is still fighting, in places, but not on the scale that could be called a war," Rugrat said.

"We think of a war as a world war, though," Erik countered.

"You went to Paris on leave, right?" Rugrat pointed at Erik.

"What is Paris like now?" Edmond asked, sitting up.

"It's busy. There are so many cars around. There are people

everywhere. All over the place there are buildings that are hundreds of years old mixed in with the modern," Erik said.

"Cars?"

"Self-powered carriages. France may have been attacked many times in the past and invaded, but they stand tall and proud. You can find people from France around the world. Actually, Melissa Bouchard is from France. She'll have more information. She lived in Paris. I was only there for four days."

"I would very much like to talk to Madame Bouchard," Edmond said.

"We'll see what we can do. She's wrapped up in her work most of the time," Erik said.

Esther stopped a smile from reaching her face, wanting to grasp Edmond's shoulder. She didn't realize how much he had longed for information on his home country.

"Thank you for indulging my questions." Edmond smiled and sat back in his chair, folding his hands over one another. "You escaped the Black Phoenix Clan's attacks, and now you show up here with my invitation. I must ask, why have you come out of hiding?"

Erik sat up. "We want an alliance with the Sha Clans."

"An alliance? Now, I might be rude to say, I know that we can offer you much, but what can you offer us?"

"We can offer you supplies and technology."

"Supplies?" Edmond asked Erik, who indicated to Rugrat.

"Gunpowder, round shot, and cannons."

Edmond chuckled. "I am sorry, but I fail to see how you can produce enough gunpowder or ammunition to support my needs."

Rugrat and Erik grinned.

"That powder in the envelope, we can produce ten thousand times that amount per day. We can create those musket balls at a rate of several hundred. Depending on the measurements and formations on larger cannon shot, we can produce tens of them now."

Esther stilled, listening to those quantities.

"Once we know what you require, we can supply more, faster," Erik stated.

"Even with all the crafters in Vuzgal working, that should be hard to fulfil," Edmond said.

Erik and Rugrat smiled.

Edmond held his chin.

"We both know that the biggest problem with using cannons and muskets is how much ammunition you use. In a fight, you go through ammunition quickly. Hard to keep up with that kind of consumption in a war," Erik said.

"You also offered technology?" Edmond asked.

Rugrat pulled out a piece of paper, pushed it across the table.

Edmond opened the paper and studied the drawing inside.

It was a cylinder tapered at one end.

"What is it?"

"It's called a bullet, or round, and contains a projectile similar to the round shot and the powder in one unit." Rugrat pulled something from his storage ring.

Esther half-drew her sword. Rugrat paused, holding a round between his forefinger and thumb.

Edmond raised a hand, and Esther slid her sword back into its scabbard.

"Doesn't allow the water to get in to mess up your powder, quicker to load. Though they are harder, much harder, to manufacture than powder and round shot and each of them has to be nearly identical." Rugrat put it on the table with the sound of metal on metal and walked back to where he had been standing. Esther cast Scrying Eye spell, seeing through the round and relaxing.

Edmond picked up the yellow and reddish metal round. He looked it over before rolling it in his fingers.

Erik pulled out several rounds from his storage ring and lined them up on the table, placing them where the metal overlapped with a monotonous clang.

Edmond stopped rolling the one in his hand as Erik pulled out more and more, only stopping when he had a small army of rounds standing on the white metal lattice table.

Esther cast her spell again, seeing no difference in the rounds.

"May I?" Edmond asked.

"Please, *monsieur*," Erik offered.

Edmond picked up different rounds, holding them in opposite hands. He picked several at random, rolling them in his left hand, holding the first round in his right.

Erik explained all the different rounds, how they were self-contained, and the different parts.

She hated to admit it, but she felt that the skeptics were right at that moment. It was only a matter of time until their technology was improved on by someone else and used against them. *These rounds, their ability to produce powder and round shot in such quantities, just how are they able to do it?*

"What you hit the *Eternus* with, was it based on these?" Edmond asked.

"Somewhat," Rugrat answered indirectly.

"With our alliance, we seek support in the lower realms."

"Against the Willful Institute and their allies?" Esther interjected.

Edmond gave her a look of thanks.

"Yes." Erik and Rugrat's faces hardened.

"So, for our support, you will supply us with ammunition?" Edmond queried.

"Yes, and open trade routes between our people," Erik said.

Edmond sat there quietly.

Rugrat caved first. "You built this all off muskets. I don't know what your production speed is for gunpowder and shot. I suspect it's low because you can't trust everyone with the secret. If you did, then everyone would learn it. Here, you have met your match and people are not that interested. In the lower realms, it is what is stopping your enemies from taking your cities."

"We're the only people you can trust to make your ammunition and supplies," Erik said.

"Oh?"

"We already have the knowledge. All people from Earth do. While they might not know how a weapon works, they have a good enough idea that a group of them could pull one together," Erik said.

Esther and Edmond tensed.

"How many rifles did you own before this?" Erik asked Rugrat.

"Fourteen, I think. You had more than me?"

"I was at eleven. Firearms, while not common in some places, are known across the world. We had several wars and three hundred years of working with firearms to improve them. You didn't even need to be in the military or the police force to get weapons. Anyone that came over from Earth has the knowledge."

Esther's stomach tensed.

"So, ammunition and trade between our people for our support in removing the Willful Institute. I still know so little about you."

"Oh, we don't want to just remove the Willful Institute. We'll help you with the Black Phoenix Clan as well." Erik held Edmond's eyes.

"You think you can take on the Black Phoenix Clan? Do I need to remind you that they crushed your city with one destroyer? They have tens of destroyers, frigates, and corvettes. Even with the debuffs of the city, and your people's own buffs, you were unable to keep it."

Erik tensed his jaw and Rugrat rolled his shoulders, his hands remaining on his belt-buckle.

"That was then, and this is now."

Edmond looked between the two of them. He grew silent, looking at the rounds that covered the table and the one that he held in his hand.

"Let us discuss terms, shall we?"

Heidi Storgaard circulated mana through her body, leaving the snow behind as she walked into the hall with Gudriksson and her fighters.

People and cots filled the hall.

"Get some sleep, we have watch tomorrow at noon," Heidi said.

"I'll check on those supplies," Gudriksson said.

"Aye, if you need me, I'll be in my quarters."

The group fell apart, heading to their bunks and to carry out their chores.

Storgaard strode through the hall. She didn't miss the furtive glances and whispered words as she passed.

She reported to the command center. Officers and leaders stood around the table, organizing their defense. The United Sect Armies had not just focused on the Fourth Realm. For weeks, they had been attacking Meokar and Reynir, battering their defenses to reclaim their lost honor.

"Report?" An officer on guard duty asked, snubbing Storgaard's once higher rank. With the United Sect Army's attack, her accolades had been stripped from her, and so had her rank.

She heard some snickers and snorts in the room.

"Walls clear. Nothing to report." She yawned, not caring what she looked like.

"Very well. You're dismissed." The man's eyes flicked up as a grin appeared on his face.

Her anger flared at the mockery in his eyes.

She turned as if to leave and whirled around, driving her mana as she kicked the officer in the side. He shot across the room and smashed into the wall.

She looked at him long enough to know he was alive, but unconscious.

"Looks like the watch officer didn't watch his manners." She laughed without humor as she searched the room.

Those at the table glared at her. She just smirked in return.

"Ah, sorry. I forgot to watch my strength." She turned and waved her hand. "Sleep well." She purred.

Come on, Heidi, keep it together. What did that get you? A worse reputation to show off some power? They'll think of some new task or duty for you to take on now.

She was distracted, reaching her quarters and undoing the formation she had placed on the room.

She walked into her apartment. Flames shot from her fingertips, lighting the large fireplace to the left, and the candles that hung from the ceiling, revealing Jasper sitting on the couch that faced the fireplace.

She became aware of two further presences at the door just as they threw something in her face.

The world spun, and she dropped to the ground.

She opened her eyes, finding she was sitting in front of the fireplace on her desk chair while Jasper did paperwork on the couch.

She tried to move, but she had been tied to the chair. Panic set in as she felt disconnected from the mana and elements around her. Her eyes dropped to the formation carved manacles on her hands.

"Jasper." A man behind him tapped his shoulder.

"Sorry. Administration. You know how it is," Jasper said, finishing off the last sentence and folding the sheets away.

Storgaard looked around the room. There was one man by the door. Several sat at her dining table, looking out into the inky black night.

The last was the guard she had seen with Jasper at Reynir.

"I am sorry about all of this. Bit hard to get a meeting these days." Jasper smiled.

Storgaard snorted. "What, because of a lack of trust or because you have them with people who are tied up?"

"Mostly because of the Seventh Realm group that is hunting us. Minor inconveniences."

Storgaard snarled. "I thought it was all strange, you know, how Meokar found out that it was the Grey Peak Sect that attacked their treasury. All of your Adventurer Guild showed up. Guess you were the ones that made it happen right?"

"Yes," Jasper nodded.

"Played by a guild," she scoffed.

"Well, you were a guild not long ago."

"Not one that capable of defeating sects established in the Sixth Realm!" She rocked in her chair. "Did you know what happened to Reynir after your fight at Vuzgal? Did you know that they brought their strongest armies to attack Meokar, and that the other sects turned on us? We lost Meokar, and Reynir, as well as *five* other cities! There is an army out there trying to attack this city right now, readying their strength, laying in the valleys, probably waiting for this blasted winter to end."

"Would you like to remove them completely?" Jasper asked.

"No, no, no. Not again! I will not be pulled into another scheme! I lost my city. I lost my position, the faith of my people, and my leaders!"

"Do you know why we picked Reynir? Why we picked you to be the main target of Meokar?" Jasper asked.

"You motherfucker!"

"We picked you because you were the best of the sects. You care about your people. You hadn't been turned and broken by the systems of sects. You had a future, and you wanted to pursue it. We knew you wouldn't use people as your weapons. While it would increase your power, you should be a better leader than the Willful Institute."

"Thank you so much for thinking of me while you were framing me and my sect!" she yelled. "Unlike you cowards, we don't have anywhere to hide. So why don't you fuck off and stay the hell away from us?"

"We seek an alliance."

"An alliance? Hah, you want us to do your dirty work! Too afraid to kill a few people?"

"She's got spice." One of the women at the table laughed.

"I've got spice. You want to back that up?"

"Calm down. Jasper could take you on while he's filling out paperwork." The woman chuckled and sat back in her chair with a confident smile.

Jasper pulled out a folder and put it on the couch beside him.

"This is the information we gathered on the groups you are fighting right now. It should make the fighting for the next couple of weeks easier. These supplies should help as well." Jasper pulled out a pendant and put it on top of the folder. "Inside is the offer of our alliance. We ask you to support us in the coming fight and that we will do the same with you and open up trade routes with you."

"You think that is worth much?"

Jasper smiled. "Just because we lost Vuzgal, it doesn't mean that we're making less gear, or require fewer materials."

"They are backed by a force in the Seventh Realm," Storgaard said, cooling.

"Ah, the Black Phoenix Clan. Well, hopefully, we can gain a key alliance to deal with them. Otherwise, the campaign will take longer. We are not saying that we will lead a counterattack right away. No, everyone is weak from the fighting. It will take some time to re-arm you all, get your fighting forces into peak condition."

"Which takes supplies, ingredients, materials, mana stones," Storgaard stated.

"Well, it would be beneficial if you had a trade partner willing to sell you items well below market price. There's a list inside the storage ring with our prices. Even if you're not interested in allying with us, we would be happy to trade with you. Getting supplies past your enemies like this will cost a bit extra."

"So, you want our mana stones?"

"No, your broken gear and materials will do much better." Jasper stood. "Pass on the information. If you wish to talk more—" Jasper took out a purple and black candle. "—light this and put it in your window. Truly, I am sorry about all that happened."

Jasper looked at the man behind him.

He pulled out a vial and breathed on it. A powder rose from the bottle and crossed the room to a struggling Storgaard.

"You damn basta-!"

She slumped against her bonds. The next moment, she felt heat on her back as she fought the chair. She found that she was kicking against the floor.

"Storgaard," Gudriksson said, standing over her.

She gathered her mana, relaxing.

"Are you okay? It seems you've been drugged."

"Damn you, Jasper," she hissed, standing up. On the couch was the folder and pendant.

"Jasper?" Gudriksson stood.

"Adventurer's Guild, or Vuzgal. Little bastard showed up here with his people." She looked around the room, moving to the other apartments. She checked everywhere then returned to the couch. "No signs of how he got in here. Sneaky bastard."

She studied the folder, picking it up. She opened it and started reading.

"What did he want?"

"An alliance."

"After what they did?"

"How many times have we used other people, other sects?" she muttered, flipping through pages, shaking her head in disbelief. "I need to talk to Elder Lindstrom."

"You sure? Adventurer's Guild appearing here, giving you a folder," Gudriksson said.

"Vuzgal took on several sect armies at the same time and would have defeated them if not for the interference of a Seventh Realm warship. Even under that pressure they managed to kill several thousand fighters from the Seventh Realm. You think that is an alliance that they would not consider?"

28
Probing Attack

"Do you think they'll try anything?" Aditya asked. He stood at the map table in his office with Colonel Yui and Major General Pan Kun. Reds and yellows filtered over the grand windows behind the desk that looked over the city of King's Hill.

He turned his head to Evernight, who sat at a desk to the side of the room.

"No, they know what will happen. They are doing it to look strong. Others put them up to it to see what our reaction would be. They want new trade rules. We're skipping around them, not paying taxes. Their economy is crumbling and their enemies and allies on the opposite side of the Beast Mountain Range, are reaping the benefits," Evernight said.

Aditya held his chin. "We have been throwing our weight around since the fight. If we do it for too long, then others will shy away from dealing with us. Let's ease up."

Glass shattered, and Aditya was thrown forward over the table. He crashed to the floor. Papers flew everywhere. Glass covered the room.

"What the hell was that?" Aditya yelled.

Evernight ran to the window frames.

Pan Kun reached down to pull Yui up.

Aditya reached the window. The mana barrier covering the Lord's manor stained with a magical attack.

On the other side was the other half of the attack.

The stone had been cracked and cratered close to the gate.

For the first time since he became the leader of the Vermire Empire, the constant line of people wanting to talk to the lord, or to the administrators was no longer there, washed away in the destruction.

The entire street had been cleared. Houses on the other side, ten meters away, had caved in.

People clambered out of the destruction and chaos, sporting confusing looks, covered in blood.

Another explosion ripped through the city. A spell formation appeared in the sky seconds before it detonated, tearing through the streets, buildings, and Vermire citizens.

"That was the southern marketplace!" Aditya shouted, looking at the dimming light. *It's dinnertime.*

Pan Kun and Yui used their sound transmission devices to send the Alva and Beast Mountain Ranges military into action.

"Close down the border and totems. No one in or out. I'll deploy my people to find people with storage rings. They'd need to have a storage ring to get something like that into the city. Put the Vermire military on high alert," Yui ordered.

"What can I do?" Aditya asked.

"Reassure the people. Get them to follow the military's instruction. Have the police figure out more information. Be ready. This could be their opening attack."

Storbon glanced at his team as the light of totem teleportation dissipated.

"Welcome to Purkesh," their guide said, preparing to leave.

The team walked up to the guards into the city. Paying a fee, they got inside.

Storbon and the group headed for the nearest aerial tower.

"Not bad digs," Rugrat said as they lounged in their private apartment. Marble table, with gold-covered metal workings rose from the floor to support them or flowed into the white and light blue doors. Crown molding ran along the ceilings, showing an impressive artistic skill.

"Not bad at all," Erik said.

Their sound transmission devices went off. They sat up and accessed the message.

"Lords, this is Jurumba Special Team Four. We're in the Seventh Realm. There was an attack on King's Hill yesterday. We are arriving at your location shortly."

Erik and Rugrat leaned forward.

"You think?"

"Don't matter what I think. We need to hear it from them. No sense in making assumptions."

They waited in the quiet. Rugrat got up and paced, stretching his body.

A knock at the door made them both turn.

"Who is it?" Erik asked, standing slowly.

"I bring a message. Several people have arrived and wish to meet with you. The leader says his name is Storbon."

"Let them in," Erik said.

Several long minutes later, there was another knock at the door.

"Sirs." It was Storbon.

Rugrat reached out with his mana and opened the door.

Two members of the team remained outside. The others glanced around the room on their way in. Everyone activated their sound transmission devices.

"Place is clear. Now, what happened?" Erik said.

The group fanned out through the rooms, closing the doors in the apartment.

"King's Hill was hit. We don't know who it was, but the spell scrolls were strong," Storbon said with a heavy face.

"Someone from the higher realms?"

"Nothing conclusive. Could be from the First Realm, but they'd have to have connections into the Third Realm. We'd guess, and that costs a pretty mana stone."

"Black Phoenix Clan, Willful Institute, Stone Fist, one of the other sects that attacked us?" Rugrat shook his head. His eyes met Erik's. "We've made a few enemies."

"What's happening now?"

"Beast Mountain Range has been locked down. Alva's army is ready to move. Elan is using his network to figure out who's behind this. Information points to the Willful Institute. Mistress Mercy. The Willful Institute group that gave the First Realmers weapons and gear are all dead."

"Someone trying to get information from them went against the contract that was made?" Erik asked.

"That's the running assumption. We're in the dark."

"Okay, I presume Delilah and Glosil said something?"

"They sent us to find you, give protection, and act as your relay. Delilah said that we need allies and supplies more than ever now. Glosil agreed."

"Are we getting any traction with our other efforts?"

"A few groups have shown interest. They thought they knew who we were and what we could do. Then Vuzgal happened. Now, they don't know if we're strong or weak. If they ally with us, they're going to stir up a nest of ugly and we aren't up against people that will forget who they allied with."

"Any of them telling our enemies?" Rugrat asked.

"Not yet. Elan thinks they want to test us first."

Erik sighed, rubbing his face, and turned to Rugrat.

"Nothing we can do, Doc. We need the Sha, and we need them sooner rather than later."

"And how do we do that? Even the marshal is having a hard time getting his people to agree to anything with us. It's been five days."

"If they can pin down the BPC, give us some support in the lower realms, that's all we need," Rugrat said.

Erik kneaded his neck. "You're right. We need to clean up these problems in the lower realms."

Louis Gerard supervised the bridge. Through the windows, he could see the Earth Cloud Valley, and the ships coasting forward in formation, sails across their hulls drawing them forward.

Floating mana gathering formations spread around every ship like scattered flowers. They drew in mana along their petals, compressing it and sending it in a concentrated beam to collection formations across the ships. They looked like a dandelion connected by light.

Louis glanced at the dungeon core as the stream of light turned into a pillar of light. A check showed the Sky Realm cornerstones across the ship growing, filling the storage spaces with mana stones.

"Looking thinner," Lady Velten said, walking over the bridge to stand next to him.

"What do you want now?"

"I come bearing gifts." She pulled out a letter.

Gerard took it and read the contents, his brows pinching together. He turned on his sound transmission device. "This is true?"

"I couldn't make it up. Seems there are new arrivals and they're interested in trading gunpowder."

Louis read the note again, burning the information into his mind. He cast Flame, setting light to the paper, and waving the drifting ashes away distractedly. He needed to learn more. If they knew how to make gunpowder, then they could, no should, know how to make the Sha's other weapons as well. The time had come; someone had caught up to them. If they destroyed this group, they were just one of many new arrivals.

If these people had more developed natural sciences, as the marshal called it, they could flip the Realms.

"What do they want in return?"

"Protection, supplies, mana stones."

"And he's entertaining them, trying to gather support." Louis ground his teeth. "There was a time when he would have demanded their fealty or threatened them. Now he looks to play his games and show favor." Louis was disgusted—angry. Not even those in the same clan would get favorable terms while he and his were forced to carry out their jobs without a word against his power.

Damn tyrant.

"Do you see now?" Velten asked.

Louis glared at her, turning his gaze to the window of the ship. "Gather me more information and I will think on your proposal."

Freedom must be fought for. He repeated his family's mantra, the mantra of his clan.

Glosil sat with his coffee. He put down the latest reports and gazed out of his window at the first barrack's training square. Blaze was out there harassing Alvan Reservists.

Glosil stood up, taking his coffee with him. His guards followed him as he left his office and wound down the stairs to the floor below.

He arrived as Blaze finished with his reservists.

"All good?"

"Yeah, just had some people that were sneaking off to a few taverns last night instead of sleeping. They're getting rowdy with nothing to do but train. I told the training staff to increase the difficulty. Make it so they're too tired to care about anything but sleep. That should do the trick." Blaze growled.

Glosil grinned.

Blaze cleared his throat, hiding the upturn at the corners of his mouth. "So, what brings you out of your office?"

"Just…" Glosil took a deep breath and let it out. "You know?"

"What's got you feeling so good?"

"The Dragon and Tiger Corps have been filled up, one hundred and ten thousand soldiers under arms. Not all of them are fully trained, but that is nearly two times our numbers from Vuzgal. The reservists have been training constantly and our defenses here have been worked on over years."

"Feeling more confident?"

"A little." Glosil admitted.

"What about the reports on the United Sect Army? Nearly a million under arms?" Blaze opened his clasped hands.

Glosil looped his thumb into his belt and sighed. "Something like that spread over four or five realms."

"About one hundred thousand of our people in the reserves part time, another two hundred that could be called up." Blaze continued. "Our people are mostly low level. It takes a lot more resources to train a soldier than it costs the Sects to pick out fighters from among their ranks. Our standing army is around ten percent of our population. They have more like twenty or thirty percent."

"I know but, when we started, we were a small backwater village, and now we have the strongest military in the First Realm."

"I'd say in nearly all the Mortal and Earth realms," Blaze snorted.

"Your reservists are going to swell in the coming days. The corps will look to training internally. A lot of people had to skip some training to take on their current role."

"So, I get anyone else?"

"Training of reservists and reg force will be together. Those that have other things to do will be with you. Those that don't can take more courses and apply to join the reg force."

"Time to build up their individual strength and firm up our foundations."

"Correct, we've built our numbers quickly. Now we need to build their strength."

It was Blaze's turn to let out a long breath as he stood straighter. "Shit, I almost feel sorry for them."

"Who? The Sects or the troops?" Glosil asked.

"Both."

The two men's eyes met with a similar gleam; laughter bubbled out of their throats.

Soldiers nearby increased their pace, fleeing from the duo.

29
Machinations

Esther watched the group with Erik and Rugrat entering the grand hall. Chandeliers hung from the ceiling, bathing the late night in a warm light. Golden frescos and statues decorated the room. A massive red carpet covered the polished floor.

Marshal sat close to the windows, his back to the new arrivals as he played on the piano. Esther and three of her guards fanned out around him, watching his back. He had sunk into the song, bringing it through highs and lows, speeding up to bring the notes together, weaving them with one another in playful delight.

His eyes were closed, playing from feeling as his hands danced.

Esther studied the guards that had appeared. They looked well trained, positioning themselves off of instinct, moving naturally and working as a whole. Erik and Rugrat flowed with them. They must have trained together to get such coordination.

No elemental tattoos, though. Do they not cultivate the elements to increase their strength?

The more she studied them, the greater her interest.

Edmond's hands rose from the keys as his last notes lingered in the hall. He ran his hand over the top of the piano before standing.

"So you have come with amendments to your offer?"

He stepped away from the stool. An attendant pulled out a platter, putting a cup on it and pouring tea.

"We will open up trade and technology with you," Erik said, "and promise not to sell to anyone else, but you have to keep the Black Phoenix Clan engaged in the Seventh Realm. Whoever supports us in the lower realms is welcome and they will find compensation, but we will not make it part of the contract," Erik said.

The clans were using this to force Marshal into a corner, wrest more power away from him. He needed to do this slowly or he would lose more power and sway in the clans. Esther hadn't realised so many would work against him. She had heard the rumors, but the clans were more divided than ever as the younger generations were affected by the power they were born with instead of achieving it on their own.

Marshal sipped his tea, taking his time. "Has something happened that I should know of?"

"Nothing that will affect you. We just have to move up our timetable," Erik said.

"I accept your new offer. I will see that we come to some agreement."

"Do not keep us waiting too long, this is the lowest offer that we will give you," Rugrat said.

The light from the information book dissipated. Cai Bo waved her hand, collecting the dust into her storage ring as she sat at her desk with a pensive gaze.

Elder Kostic stood on the other side of her desk, waiting.

"There is something there. I can feel it." Cai Bo filled the silence. "Those formations were strong enough to be in the Fifth Realm. Their entire military has sound transmission devices. Your niece says only kings and queens have them in the First Realm."

"Fourth and Fifth Realm traders walking the streets. Why would a trader that can go to the higher realms work in the First Realm?" Kostic said.

She leaned back in her chair, interlacing her fingers. "All we have is assumptions. Nothing connects them to Vuzgal—yet. I feel it, though. I feel that this is the place."

I need something definitive.

"Kostic, do you think you could identify people from Vuzgal in this

Vermire Empire?"

"If they show their faces. Maybe?"

"There might be some of them in the open but not all of them." Cai Bo went quiet, thinking.

There is only one card to be played.

She pulled out a pen and paper, working on a letter.

"Kostic, you will take this letter to Gregor. I am requesting him to send one of his dungeon hunters with you. Hopefully, with their Dungeon Sense, they will find out if the Vuzgalians are there."

She finished the note and gave it to Kostic.

"Yes, High Elder." He bowed, leaving.

Cai Bo was still turning over her plan in her head, looking for other ways to attack, when her door opened.

Marco entered the room. The doors closed behind him and the sound canceling field dropped into place. His strut calmed as he stood in front of the desk and bowed. "Master."

"Stand up. How is the ship building?"

Marco rose, grimacing. "The ships use a lot of power to operate."

"You have the mana storing formations to create Earth grade mana stones."

Marco held his tongue.

"Speak."

"Yes, we can make mana stones, but they do not produce them faster than the ships consume them if we're in flight."

"We can always get more mana stones. Do not use the ships and let them increase their stocks of mana stones. What of their fighting capabilities?"

"The barriers are stronger than what we have and it can move relatively quickly. The buffing formations are a step above our own. Our cannons have been added to the ships. Expert Mana cannons. With the airship they should be stronger than on their own."

"Tell your father to trade everything he can for mana stones. Have people noticed the disappearance of dungeon cores?"

"I don't think so. As you ordered, Gregor and his hunters have been clearing through dungeons that were too hard for us to complete or were hidden. As we thought, upgrading a dungeon core takes other dungeon cores. Increasing a grade will be extremely hard but going from a lesser to common stage isn't as hard."

"Worth it?"

"Depends. We need more space to work with. If we are in a cramped space, the dungeon cores fight over the same energy. Increasing the grade is useless. In that situation it is better to combine them, increasing the overall range of the dungeon core and its rate of absorption and conversion."

Cai Bo checked the time. "I have a meeting to attend. You can go back to being the arrogant young master that has connections to a Seventh Realm clan."

"They have grasped our greatest weakness, but instead of wiping them out, as we've done with everyone else, you want to not only trade with them, you want to support and defend them!"

Lord Vasquez slammed the polished wooden table.

The Marshal sat at the head of the long table. Lords and ladies of the different clans sat along the sides. Several seats were empty—lords and ladies taking on other challenges.

Others grumbled with agreement and jeered as Vasquez launched into another speech. Marshal glanced through the windows overlooking the surrounding gardens several floors below Purkesh. Mana lights kept up the facade of being above ground.

Out of the seventeen clans, he had six on his side. He needed three more to win the vote.

"We should capture them, find out where they are located, and destroy them before they can threaten our power!" Vasquez finished off with a flourish.

"Your grandfather was a great leader of men, Vasquez." Marshal's words rolled across the polished table. "Two clans, represented at this table, and Harrod joined the Sha Clans because of their interest in our technology. Do you think we should have killed them to make sure that the next group that makes our weapons chooses to hide them instead of using them to join us?"

Vasquez opened his mouth.

"Rumors that we kill those who have attempted to steal or replicate our technology have only hindered us. Now there is a choice ahead of us, a simple one. Do we trade with this group and get the supplies we need to continue fighting the Black Phoenix Clan, or do we let this opportunity pass? When they do reach the Seventh Realm, they will treat us with the same off-handed manner."

Those around the table stirred.

"They came from the Fourth Realm. There is no way that they can reach the Seventh Realm that quickly, all the more reason to destroy them," Lord Farouq said.

"And where would we find them? How would we know that some of them would not escape, take their time to plot and attack us? That is not even taking into account that they are not the only new arrivals. There will be others, and with them there will be more technology." Marshal looked at Robert, who nodded.

"Either we can welcome them, and assist them now, so they will assist us in the future, or we do nothing and they too will do nothing."

Lord Velten cleared his throat.

Marshal's gaze slid over, clenching his teeth.

Lord Kankoa Velten was a slight black man. His beard was braided, pulled into silver rings. Marshal lifted his eyes, seeing Milo LeBlanc, his nephew, smirk behind Velten.

"We have heard rumors but have seen nothing to show what these people can do. If they are worth allying with. I simply ask that they show us their capabilities." Velten pressed his finger to the table.

"If our supplies are so low, should we not rely on our own people to make up the difference? For years the formulas for gunpowder have been hidden under *your* control and now we find out that we cannot keep up with current demand." Velten opened his hands. "I am simply asking that you allow us to help with your burden. Remove the restrictive contracts you placed on gunpowder makers. There are many willing to work as long as they do not become enslaved in the process."

"Those contracts protect us all. It is hard and thankless work, but it has kept us safe for hundreds of years," Kameela said in a bored voice, leaning on her armrest.

"Hundreds of years ago is not today." Velten's smile had a bite.

"Harrod, powder numbers," Marshal said.

Harrod checked his notes. "We have powder stored for a full load in the Violet Cloud Realm, and we have enough powder and shot for three months of fighting the Black Phoenix Clan."

"We have nine months until the realm opens. The fighting with the BPC has increased and we need more gunpowder makers. If not, we need this trade deal. We need this trade deal anyway to make sure that they don't sell to anyone else," Edmond said.

"Which puts us at a weaker position!" Vasquez slammed his fist on the table again.

"If you continue to act as a petulant child, I will bend you over my knee and spank you as I did seventy-three years ago!" Marshal growled, locking onto Vasquez.

Vasquez clamped his mouth shut.

Edmond breathed out through his nose and looking directly at Milo. "I will agree to changing the contract. I will not have anyone outside the clan making the powder. They will do it in our facilities, and they will never sell it or give it to anyone that is not of the Sha Clan."

Milo's nostrils flared, crossing his arms and smiling in victory.

"That should suffice for now," Lord Velten said. "Of course, that is, if they can perform."

Erik, Rugrat, Edmond and Esther were under the rose covered trellis again. This time Edmond served them tea, having finished his summary of the meeting.

Erik searched for the guards around them, but saw none. He was trying to distract himself. "So we need to hit the Black Phoenix Clan to show that we are strong enough and useful enough to be an ally?" he asked.

Edmond winced at his word choice. "I wouldn't put it that way."

"But that is the way it is."

We were just attacked, and now we need to mess around in the Seventh Realm to get a seat at the table.

Rugrat accepted a cup from Edmond and leaned back and raised it to his lips, which were pressed together into a white line.

"Okay, but I'm going to need information and time."

"How much time?" Edmond put down a cup in front of Erik and started to pour his own cup.

"Two months, just in case."

"Okay, I can do that. What information are you interested in?" Edmond set down the pot, picking up the saucer and cup, checking over his shoulder.

Esther walked closer to the table.

"Locations of the BPC, everything you have on them, blueprints of their ships, who do they trade with, who fixes them up, who do they hate?" Erik picked up the cup and took a sip. It smelled like strawberries and chocolate, the hit of stamina recovery a nice touch.

"This contains all of their known locations." Esther pulled out a packet of information. "Here is a list of known contacts and the different materials they supply." She pulled out a much thicker folder.

"Do you have their security procedures when someone enters their compounds and different areas? Who can access different areas?" Erik asked.

It's a crazy idea, but it should secure our contract and force the Sha to fight the BPC.

"Yes, it depends on the city or area," Esther answered.

Erik pulled the folder over with the location information for the BPC.

"What are you thinking?" Rugrat asked, using his sound transmission device.

"I'm thinking we hit them right where it hurts, hit their ships and shipyards."

"Bold."

"Go big or go home."

30

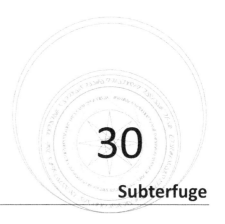

Subterfuge

E rik and Rugrat found themselves in Alva, in the changing light of the mana drill.

Aditya, Chonglu, Delilah, Egbert, Elan, and Glosil sat around the table.

"So, the attack wasn't from anyone in the First Realm, and it wasn't from the Black Phoenix Clan. If they thought this was where we fled to, they could have sent several mages powerful enough to level the city in a single attack," Erik said.

"A hundred and fifty-three dead, nearly four hundred wounded; I'd say they did a pretty good job," Aditya said through gritted teeth.

"Nothing that you could have done," Rugrat said.

Aditya grunted, not believing the same logic.

"Elan, anything?" Erik asked.

"Not regarding the spell scroll. The flow of information we had at the beginning of this conflict has been locked down. Mercy and Niklaus have been appearing in public more often. It looks like Niklaus is gearing their army up. Groups have left the Institute. A lot of them have been dungeon diving. They're trying to hide their identities and what they're doing. It happened right after Cai Bo met with Stassov. I think that she is a dungeon lord or hunter and passed it on to the rest of her sect."

"What's our play?" Erik asked

"Wait and see," Glosil answered. "We're still training people, arming and armoring them all. We don't know who attacked us; we have ideas, but nothing concrete. We continue on, shift some of the Special teams from assassination missions to sabotaging the BPC ships. We'll move up CPD's to take their old targets."

Erik sat back in his chair. "We just wait?" He held up his hands.

"Our biggest problem is equipment right now. We don't have the materials to create much high-level gear. Those resources you brought back, while substantial, are a drop in the bucket. We've been replacing front chest plates for armor because we don't have the metal to do the back plate, it takes four ingots to do each plate. Even with all the metal you brought back, that's only enough armor for five hundred troops. We have the skills and the ability. We just don't have the materials."

"If we look to upgrade all of our stuff each time then we'll never be ready."

Glosil intertwined his hands and rested them on the notepad in front of him. "The way I see it, the Willful Institute, or someone else, will find us eventually, or we'll have to attack them city by city to clear them out. When we have the people and the supplies, we can start with the assassinations, cut out their command and control and strike. If we attacked their command now, they could shore up their weaknesses and get new leaders."

Erik sighed. "Retain the element of surprise. When they think they have us on the ropes, we hit them."

"Correct. In the meantime, we need those supplies. We need everything and anything you can get from the Seventh Realm."

"Alva uses more resources now than ever before. We're working with the Trader's Guild to see if we can get some traders in the Sky Realm, but you're ahead of most but our military types. A few hundred million experience is hard to find," Delilah said.

Erik looked at Rugrat.

"We'll go between here and the Seventh Realm. With the Mission Hall, we can get a good supply of resources. Keep us close, easy to find us."

Niemm and the reformed Special Team One sat in a restaurant, watching the entrance to the Black Phoenix Clan's compound. It covered a large hill. The tall wall hid several shipyards, underground mines in the dungeon below, processing and refining stations, and living quarters on the other side.

"Well, we're not going in through the front door," Setsuko said, picking at her teeth with a toothpick.

"They might have started off as miners, but they're an airship clan now. Those guards are strong enough to make me excited. Mana barriers, weapons... We have some idea and none of it is good for my retirement plan," Kinnon said.

"Well, you know the one thing these big clans and sects all forget?" Niemm's gaze rested on a smaller gate where a carriage rolled up. The guard checked their information and allowed them past the gate. "They forget that you need people to maintain your big toys. Forget about the maintainers, focus on fighting."

"What are you thinking, boss?" Kinnon asked.

"You all been keeping up on your crafting homework?" Niemm snorted at their expressions and tilted his head to see the gate. "Everyone forgets the crafters, the nuts and bolts, the people that keep everything running."

The elevator stopped before a corridor of mirror-smooth stone, lit with actual flames—flames that stretched ahead to a heavy-set gate.

Head Asadi's guards walked out of the elevator, Cai Bo trailing behind.

Fighters wearing the armor of the Willful Institute opened a gate, bowing from the waist as the head and his guards passed.

Three more gates and a cavern stretched ahead of them.

There lay eighteen airships at various stages of completion. The ships didn't look anything like the Talon. They were crude ships of war, all the creature comforts stripped away to turn them into mobile cannon platforms.

Three of the ships reached the size of a corvette, the rest nearly a quarter of the size.

We call the smaller ships corvettes and the bigger ones frigates, but they'd just be armed fliers in the higher realms. Cai Bo hid her sneer. When she had control over the sect or joined the Black Phoenix Clan, she'd change it all.

The airships had cost considerable resources, supplied by the Willful

Institute, to keep them a secret and to staff them with their people other than their Black Phoenix Clan captains.

Airships lay in berths in different states of construction.

One corvette had most of its decks, but its hull was missing; metal and stone extruded, growing. Crafters and mages swarmed the ships, speeding up the process, laying down pillars, walls, creating formations.

There were three ships at that stage.

The ships varied from there down to a dungeon core suspended in mid-air. Materials dumped into the berth were molded, altered and shaped, creating a pillar to support the dungeon core. The metal and stone of the pillar spread out, creating the ship's superstructure, dragging materials in the berth through the air and piecing them together slowly.

"Eighteen corvette class airships with Earth grade cores," Asadi observed, looking at all the ships and the thousands of people that were working to complete the projects.

Cai Bo grimaced. She had seen real warships, and these were little more than armored floating mana cannon batteries.

Gregor walked over. His dungeon hunters stood around the cavern, or hidden within the ships near the dungeon cores. Only two of his hunters had come with him.

While the Willful Institute made the ships, Gregor's hunters controlled the cores and, by extension, the ships.

"How has your search been in the other realms?" Gregor looked at Asadi, who glanced at Cai Bo.

"We have been hearing some rumors from the lower realms. I have my best people working on it."

"They will show up eventually, Cai Bo." Asadi put his hand on her shoulder.

She bowed her head. "Thank you, Sect Leader."

She rose, seeing the bare ghost of amusement in Gregor's eyes. One of his hunters had gone with Elder Kostic down to the First Realm to find the truth of this Vermire Empire.

"It won't be long until our ships are ready to fight. We must find more dungeon cores to increase each ship's power and more resources to create the different components needed. I have work to get done. Let me know when they are found or when you have more materials for me." Gregor inclined his head slightly, turned, and left.

Asadi activated a sound canceling formation. "Have you been able to look into that matter I asked about?"

"Some of the clans have recovered more materials than they reported in their victories." Currently, the loot that they gained in battles across the realms supported the clan. They might have lost at Vuzgal, but the United Sect Army had not stopped, retaking all the Willful Institute Cities and many more. "I looked into their actions. It seems that their greed wasn't stamped out completely."

She pulled out a book and passed it to him.

He opened the first few pages, reading it. He closed the book with a snap. The barest hint of a smile pulled at the corner of his mouth.

"Very good. Very good indeed."

She had tried to manipulate the information on other clans as much as possible to increase her power base.

Everyone was doing the same thing. Not one clan wasn't a part of it. Hiding in plain sight was the best way to make sure that one wouldn't look too deep.

Head Asadi pulled out a token on a necklace and held it out to Cai Bo.

"This?" She stepped backward. *Well played old man. You haven't lost your touch.*

"It is a small thing for all you have done for me and the sect. I do not forget to reward those who help me." Head Asadi smiled, pushing the token to her.

He was an idiot who ruled with his own personal power, thinking that it would maintain his position, and others fell for his charisma. Personal strength was great, but using the strength of others, that was real power.

She cupped her hands and bowed, feeling the weight of the square piece of metal carved with flowing runes, the links of the chain piling up in her hands.

"I have great hopes for you, Cai Bo. Do not shirk your cultivation."

Cai Bo raised her head in genuine shock.

Asadi laughed like a doting grandfather.

"Thank you, Head Asadi!" She bowed even deeper.

"Come, come." He gestured for her to continue as they walked the berths.

He dismissed the sound canceling field around them and waved over the crafter in charge of the ships.

"Head Asadi, we are making great progress. The armor is of the highest Journeyman grade in most areas. We have mounted Expert level mana cannons to every position and have our own formation masters working to inlay the spellcaster's buffing formations."

He rattled on about the thick armor of the ships, their upgraded mana barriers, everything that was developed to handle the attacks of Vuzgal weapons and repay it with destruction.

Cai Bo sunk into her thoughts, weighing the Institute against the Black Phoenix Caln.

The Bo clan was weak and useless, as was the Hao clan. The Tolentino Clan were the most loyal and had the greatest value, with so many powerful youths. She would take this opportunity to embed some of them among the Black Phoenix Clan, if possible. Based on the battle and the results, she could make her move. Pain gathered in the back of her skull as her Willful Institute contract started to take effect.

For the betterment of the sect! I will lead them to victory or make a grand alliance! The pain abated before it became unbearable. She would need to watch herself. The contract stopped her from actively working against the sect, but it did not stop her from killing the sect head or lying to others.

As long as she believed her actions were the best ones for the sect, the contract wouldn't harm her. Thus, the dance continued.

Delilah rocked with the carriage as Aditya stepped inside, closing the door behind him. He nodded in greeting and sat next to Chonglu.

"I guess this is not just a ride to watch the promotion ceremony?" Aditya chuckled.

"Snatching the minutes that we can get," Delilah said. "Alva has reached over a million people and the Vermire Empire has been rapidly expanding, with some four hundred thousand people."

"With the cities, it is hard to get a completely accurate understanding. I think that it is closer to six hundred thousand."

The carriage pulled forward, starting off.

"Chonglu?" Delilah indicated for him to continue.

"We have a problem with supply, specifically the supply of high-quality resources. With the loss of Vuzgal, we lost a major inroad. Our traders are working to bring down more resources, but war is spreading across the realms between the Adventurer's Guild and the Willful Institute. Most of our supplies are being turned into weapons and ammunition for the Guild. That does not leave us with much here. We are also supplying the Adventurer's Guild's dependents. Near two hundred thousand guild members, with that number again in dependents. Some have joined Alva, but most are in the different dungeons."

"What about the lower levels of the dungeon? They have high grade supplies."

"They do, but they are limited. If we use them all they will not recover. Egbert is increasing the size of the dungeons as much as possible. We have more people joining every day," Delilah said.

"So, what can we do?" Aditya asked.

"Elise and her traders are doing everything they can to get us the supplies that we need. In the meantime, we'll ration out the resources we have and recycle the things that use high quality resources, but aren't needed."

"What of the defensive network here?"

"That is a priority, and will get all the resources it requires to be fully functional," Chonglu said.

"You think they will find us?"

"It is our duty to protect the people and allow them to live their lives freely. With this we assure their security. To do any less would go against our duty as leaders," Delilah said.

"Yes, Council leader, I cannot agree more. The actions of the surrounding kingdoms and nations have made me look at defense more than ever before.

"For now, we can ration our supplies, but in the coming months we will be running low. We might have to move resources toward supporting the military," Chonglu said.

"You said that the traders are working to help on this front?"

"They are, but they are wary of going to the higher realms. Many of them are shying away from using the associations. Seems everyone is looking for us. One slip up and we'll be found out."

"Crafting dungeons?"

"They have been a great help and are relieving some of the issues, but they don't have the capacity we require. The dungeon tokens have been the greatest aid, allowing us to buy different items that can be broken down and refined into basic materials."

"Is there no other way?" Aditya shifted in his seat.

"The traders are our best bet, them and the Special Teams. The Teams are on operations and do not have the time to go looking for resources," Delilah said.

"There is another possibility and route," Chonglu looked at Delilah.

She scowled and looked out of the carriage window at Alva.

"Erik and Rugrat have access to the mission hall in the higher realms and might have found a cache of supplies. If they retrieve the supplies, we can have a small influx. Then if they set up a few trade agreements, and we power level a few Close Protection Details, they can carry out the trades and give us a new route for supplies."

"Why go to the Seventh Realm direct? Why not go to the lower realms?"

"Everyone is looking for us." Delilah kept looking out the window, watching people walking along the sidewalks. "In the lower realms they all know that the Willful Institute and the United Sect Army are looking for us with the backing of the Black Phoenix Clan. They are recruiting people all over the place and have taken city after city. With their need for supplies, they are buying everything up. All the traders are dealing with them in the lower realms. That is why it is so difficult for our traders. Thankfully, most of the dungeons we control in the higher realms are being used to produce some kind of material."

"Going direct to the Seventh Realm, Erik and Rugrat can trade with people that are the same level as the Black Phoenix Clan," Chonglu said. "They will not beg and scrape to get into their favor. They might not know of them or care about them. Erik and Rugrat could also post a request at the mission hall and get the materials we require anonymously. There are billions of people in the Seventh Realm and supplies that are rare in the Fourth Realm are common in the Seventh."

Delilah studied Aditya. "We have gained a new enemy in the Black Phoenix Clan, and we need better materials to make weapons that can deal with them."

"What about these airships?" Aditya asked.

"There are some ideas among the crafters on how to create an airship, tempered with the knowledge of the Earthers'. While they seem like grand and great projects, in reality, they might not help us as much as we would like. You would have to talk to Glosil and Matt to learn more."

Aditya nodded. A shadow passed over the carriage as they entered the first Alva training camp, passing under the gate.

The camp had expanded several times, creating a three-by-three square before the other training camps had been created.

The carriage came to a halt, and Aditya opened the door and stepped out. The others followed.

They arrived next to several stands that had been erected, taking over most of the parade square of the first training barracks where the first Alva soldiers had been trained.

Delilah accepted the guidance of the CPD, arriving at a reserved set of seats.

She smiled and nodded to people as she passed, Aditya and Chonglu trailing behind.

They took their seats. Other members of the council were there as well. They chatted quickly and quietly as the stands filled up completely. Some stood in the corridors leading to the parade square on the first and second floor.

Scrying orbs glowed, linked to scrying screens across Alva for people to watch the ongoing ceremony.

A bugle called out two sharp notes. Silence descended upon the stands as they looked to the bugler.

Erik, Rugrat, Kanoa, and Glosil walked out from below the stands and stood in the center of the parade square.

Glosil stood forward from the other three.

"Colonel Yui!"

"Present!" Yui stepped out from the left side of the parade square.

"Colonel Domonos!"

"Present!" Domonos stood beside his brother.

"Major General Pan Kun!"

"Present!" The trio stood at attention to the side.

"Come forward!" Glosil ordered.

The three marched out, Yui taking the lead and the other two following him. They halted in front of their fellows, turning as one they remained at attention, and snapped off a salute.

Those waiting returned the salute, and Glosil relaxed.

"Colonel Yui Silaz, Colonel Domonos Silaz, step forward!"

They did so.

"Today is an imporant day for both the Dragon and Tiger Divisions. From this day forth, the Dragon Division will become the Dragon Corps."

Erik pulled out the Dragon Corps flag. On the flag lay a gold and blue dragon.

"The Tiger Division will be known as the Tiger Corps." Rugrat pulled out the Tiger Corps flag, with a gold and red tiger upon it.

Kanoa stepped forward and pulled out a small box next to Glosil.

"Commanding these units, Colonel Domonos will be raised to the rank of Brigadier General." Glosil shook his hand and removed his old rank pins and replaced them with new ones from the box in Kanoa's hand.

Domonos and Glosil saluted before he walked to Erik, and saluted before he was given the flag.

Erik saluted him, and Domonos returned to where he had stood before.

"Colonel Yui will be raised to the rank of Brigadier General as well." They repeated the process and Yui returned to stand with his brother and Pan Kun with his new corps' flag.

"Major General Pan Kun," Glosil called out.

"Sir!" Pan Kun walked forward and saluted.

"Today it is my pleasure to honor the Alvan Reserve forces. Pan Kun, you are ordered to assume command over all Alvan Auxiliary forces, to bring the unit formerly known as The Beast Mountain Range Army up to the standard of the Alvan Reserves, and to train and command the Alvan reserve forces in totality."

It was a big decision, and it would bring all reserve units under the command of Pan Kun, including the Adventurer's guild and Alva citizens that had signed up as reservists.

"Do you accept these orders?"

"Yes, I do, sir."

"Good. To carry out your duties, you will be awarded the rank of Lieutenant General." Glosil changed his rank pins and saluted.

"Two army corps, an air force, and a reserve nearly as big as all three," Aditya said to Delilah's side.

"Their job to defend us. Our job to make sure they have the tools to do it," she whispered back.

Aditya nodded. "Too right."

31

Resource Gathering

"I still don't like it," Erik said, finishing tying up his shoes on the porch of Momma Rodriguez's house in Alva.

Rugrat shrugged, his fork scraping on the plate, getting every last bit of the cobbler.

Momma came out of the swing door. It smacked shut against the door frame as she carried two packed meals in a paper bag. "Here, something for the road."

"Thank you, Momma R," Erik said, accepting the packed lunch and storing it.

"Thanks, Momma." Rugrat took it, holding the paper bag under his plate while bending down to hug her from the side.

She patted his back and rubbed it, took a deep breath, and stepped backward.

"Erik." She turned and opened her arms.

Erik smiled and leaned down, hugging her, taking care to not squeeze too tight as she gripped him as fiercely as she had Rugrat.

She pulled the plate and fork from Rugrat's hand and picked up Erik's plate from the table. "You two be safe now."

Erik stepped off the porch.

"We always are, Momma," Rugrat said as he followed Erik.

The two men walked away, half turning as they waved.

Erik saw the wetness in her eyes as they turned the corner. He smacked Rugrat on the back. "Let's go steal us some supplies."

They pulled on cloaks and hats as they got closer to the totem. Rugrat placed his cowboy hat on his head and whistled. George glided from the sky, shrinking and landing next to Rugrat, folding his wings away.

"All ready."

They arrived in Cronen Mission Hall and headed for a map shop. Erik opened the door. Its hinges squeaked as a bell above the door rang.

The place had maps on the walls and in glass boxes. There were shelves filled with maps and a large globe to the left of the door, right in the middle of the large glass front window.

There were several people checking maps. Others consulted the three workers behind the desk.

Someone walked down a set of stairs right ahead of the doorway. Covered from head to toe, it was hard to determine if they were a man or a woman.

A formation lit up above the stairs.

Map Consultation - OPEN

Erik passed the covered person and walked up the creaking stairs with Rugrat following.

The stairs turned, and Erik jogged up the last three steps. There were three rooms ahead. Two were closed, the one on the far left was open.

A man sitting behind a desk rolled up a scroll and put it in a storage ring. Erik knocked on the door, pushing it open more.

"No map fragments or pictures that illustrate where one might find an item. I only deal in true maps. I am sealed by the Ten Realms to not talk about what you tell me." The man cleared his desk with a bored voice. He looked up at Erik and Rugrat. "Are these terms agreeable?"

"Yes," Erik said.

"Good, I, Follox Habberd, swear that I will not tell anyone in the Ten Realms the content of our conversation from the time you close that door to the time you open it."

Erik looked at Rugrat and tilted his head to the door.

Rugrat closed the door after George. The duo sat in front of the table grid, George sitting beside Rugrat to get scratches.

"One mission point per consultation." Follox tapped a slot for their heroes' medallions.

Erik put his medallion into the recess. It flashed with light.

Broke again.

Follox waved to him.

Erik pulled out Ubren's map and passed it to Follox. He looked at the map and cast several spells on his eyes. Putting the map down, he spread it out with his fingers.

"What would you like to know?"

"Anything and everything."

"I am guessing whoever had this was part of an airship crew, a fighter. They went to Azraadale frequently. They would go to the different outposts from time to time, spending most of their time in the cities. They also liked to make several detours. They seemed to like this detour in particular." He circled a mountain and tapped it.

"How can you tell?"

"The detail here is much greater than everywhere but the cities. The other detours were infrequent. But this person went regularly to this mountain and to this cave. Interestingly, the information on the cave cuts off at this point. They stopped recording information." He zoomed in. "You can see the changes in the trees here, but in other areas, the trees are in different seasons, meaning that they have not been visited in a while or are randomly visited. Compare that to the routes they took between the cities and the trees. You can see that this mountain was a frequent place to visit. Right there, I guess that is where their stash is. You'll have to watch out, though. It's right on a border between two clans. Three mana stones and I'll sell you an updated map for the area."

"How can we get there?"

"Fastest or safest?"

"Both," Rugrat said.

"Fastest, Azraddale, then cross over this clan line. That is why whoever owned this had to be a fighter. They patrolled this area randomly, got a bunch of detailed information on these outposts. Two forces, a clear divide. Had to have an airship. They were going over the trees and the changes between areas aren't that spaced apart, so they did it frequently."

Follox sat back in his chair, blinking slowly. "Your safest route is to go to the other clan." He tapped on another city. "Iro, then take this route to the mountain. It's on this other clan's territory. Shouldn't have a problem. Good thing you have an aerial beast."

Erik and Rugrat thanked the man and left the store.

They headed toward the nearest totem, making a stop at one of the seedier and cheaper looking inns along their route.

"How long would you like the room for?" the innkeeper asked.

"A month please," Erik said.

"Okay with your twenty percent two-star status, that would be ninety Sky grade mana stones."

Erik gritted his teeth. "Thanks." He passed over the stones.

The innkeeper checked them before passing over a formation. "Room five on the left."

Erik and Rugrat went down the corridor, away from the front desk and reached room five. It wasn't much; just two beds and a cramped private bathroom.

"Don't get out your blacklight," Rugrat said under his breath.

Erik pulled on gloves, lifting one bed and stacking it on the other.

"Yay, bunk beds." Rugrat pulled out a teleportation formation and put it over the dust that created a rectangle where the bed had been.

"Let's hope this stash has enough mana stones to make it worth it." Erik sighed.

Rugrat powered up the teleportation formation, checking it and feeding it more mana stones.

"All good to go here."

Erik held down his hat. It threatened to escape his head while he, Rugrat, and George exited the defenses around Iro's totem. The late-night shrouded the city in darkness.

Cold wind from the surrounding mountains created eddies in the sky and whistled through the streets, pulling at doors and window shutters. Passers-by used water and fire spells to keep themselves warm and dry.

Snow capped many of the houses. Formations, drawing in ambient mana, melted the snow as it landed, funneling it into the city sewer system.

The land was rough and broken. Stone jutted up in great big slabs, with houses built right up to them, giving them a tribal and nomadic look and feel.

Erik checked his compass. He saw signs for a dungeon road as people hurried up and down stairs leading underground.

"Looks like a subway system," Rugrat commented, seeing where Erik was looking.

"Let's check it out."

They moved with the press of people, the wind dying down and the warmth flooding back as they heard the rushing noise of movement.

"Like a subway system," Erik said. When they reached the bottom of the stairs, people took out sky mana stones, placing them on turnstiles, giving them access to several platforms that stretched out across the city.

A train shot past on a through-line, its undersides glowing with formations.

"More of a train carriage," Erik said as the train disappeared, leaving a rush of air.

"No train tracks, just well-maintained grooved stone roads," Rugrat said.

They moved to an area covered with boards. A scribe removed some information on a board and updated it.

They walked up to a woman at a counter. "Where are you looking to go?"

"We want to go to the southwestern gate," Erik said.

"Platform sixteen." She pointed down the grand train hall.

"Thank you." Erik and Rugrat walked through the hall filled with the noise of people. Restaurants, tea, and other shops covered one wall between the stairs that led to and from the surface.

Erik dropped his mana stones into the turnstile. It powered up and turned over, allowing him to pass through. Rugrat followed with George jumping up on his shoulder and back down to the ground once he was through.

People ran toward trains as they were about to leave or stepped off them as they just arrived.

"Different, but similar," Rugrat said.

"Yeah, at the end of the day we're, well, most of us are, humans. I wonder what happened to the other races?"

"Might be something to find out in the higher realms." They reached their platform and the waiting train and stepped up into the carriage.

While it had big road tires, the insides were laid out like a normal train car.

Erik and Rugrat took their seats. George sat between them as the train started to move. The doors remained open to the platform.

The train built up speed, following a well-worn road that led the big metal and rubberized wheels as they went faster and faster. Erik saw light ahead, the carriage shifting on the uneven grooves in the ground.

They came out in a burst of light, looking out over a massive cavern with several floors of dungeon revealed below. A river ran through the landscape. Nestled up to it was a harbor and spiraling town.

Compound walls where ingredients were grown and cultivated dotted the landscape. Struts of stone held their road to the ceiling as they disappeared between rock formations that supported the ceiling and protected the dungeon below.

The train stopped at several stations before their stop was announced.

Erik tapped Rugrat, who had fallen asleep.

He looked around, wiping his eyes and standing up with Erik. He stumbled with the sudden braking, holding onto a pole as the carriage shifted and slowed, coming to a stop.

Erik and Rugrat walked out with George. Soldiers piled out of the train, organizing on the platform before marching off.

Erik and Rugrat joined the rest of the people ambling for the stairs to head up out into the cold. Their clothes were worn and their expressions dreary as they trudged on.

Others headed to stairs leading to the dungeons below.

They braced against the wind. Erik and Rugrat held their hats as they came out again into the windy city.

"All right, let's go find that flying platform," Erik said over the wind.

"Looks like the formations here aren't the best," Rugrat said, slush covering the sidewalks.

"We've had worse."

They walked toward the gate.

"Where are you going?" a guard asked from inside their warmed hut.

"Mission Hall business." Erik moved his cloak to the side to show his medallion.

The guard made a noise of interest. "And you confirm that your actions will in no way harm the interests of the Ubreick clan?"

"Uhh, no. Wait, are the Ubreicks and the Ubrens related?"

The guard leaned closer, checking both sides. "If I were you, I wouldn't say it so loud. They used to be the same clan, but we split a long time ago. Though they keep sending over raiders and bandits, saying that they are not affiliated. Bandits and raiders don't last long here. You find any, let me know."

"Okay," Erik said.

The man grunted and sat back in his seat. "You're free to go. Good luck."

"Thank you."

Erik met up with Rugrat and George on the other side of the gate.

"Now for the next part." Rugrat patted George as George grew to his full size.

"What are you feeding him? He keeps getting bigger," Erik said. The snow around George evaporated in the heat.

"I dunno at this point. Buffalo for a snack maybe?" Rugrat said.

George flapped his wings, throwing snow around.

"All right, all right, we're getting on." Rugrat threw a saddle on to George's back and secured it. He jumped up front, and Erik jumped up behind him. George's back was large enough that they could sit behind one another comfortably and Erik could have his own handholds. He did *not* want to have to hug Rugrat from behind.

"All right Georg-ey boy, let's get to it."

George scraped his feet on the ground and started forward, gaining speed on the ground before opening his wings and creating a blast of fire, sending them upwards. Using a mix of fire spells and his wings, George shot into the skies.

"Oorah!" Rugrat yelled, holding onto his seat handles with his left and his hat with his right.

Erik pulled off his hat, storing it as he pulled up his scarf and put on glasses against the wind.

They kept toward their destination.

Rugrat rode with the turbulence, dipping down and then shooting back up again. The wind howled in his ears.

George had to fight forward. They were close to the mountain now; the area was thick with water, metal, and earth elements.

"I can't see shit." Erik used his sound transmission device. It was the only way to talk.

"I can sense it up ahead. These elements are nasty, just under an elemental storm. Casting spells in here would be wild. George's spells are fifty percent strength with all this. Dropping each time we get closer."

George breathed out. A gout of flame cut through the sky ahead and exploded, creating a path. He rushed through the opening. Rugrat held onto his hat, seeing the outline of the mountain finally.

He checked the map strapped to the inside of his wrist, looking at the marker.

George was getting tired from all the flying and forcing their way past the elements.

"George, just get us close buddy," Rugrat said.

George didn't reply, but forged on as they met more turbulence. He created a blast of fire behind himself. Using it like jets, he cut forward, lowering altitude for speed. They rocketed across the sky. George fought the air trying to toss them free, to raise them to the heavens or drop them to the ground below.

The elements shifted again. Rugrat could see the looming mountain that extended above them.

"We're real close, George!"

Suddenly, they were through the elements. George flapped his wings in a panic. They were too close and too fast to the mountainside.

Rugrat, Erik, and George used spells to slow their speed. It wasn't enough.

Rugrat's mana blades shot out, cutting down trees in their path.

"Jump!" Rugrat yelled.

Erik and Rugrat threw themselves off George. Erik used fire spells, trying to slow before they crashed into the snow, bouncing on the ground. Rugrat yelled out as he felt his legs snap like dry twigs as he flipped forward, the bones rubbing against one another as he ground his teeth together to stifle the screams. He hit his arm on a rock and felt something break, a popping sensation in his ribs. Something hit his head, darkness overwhelming him and bringing relief.

"Fuck." Erik coughed on the sound transmission channel. His right arm was broken in several places, but his body was already repairing itself. The bones grated on one another. Fingers twisted and regrew. His hand had been shredded.

He glanced down at the limb of a tree that had gone through his left armpit, between his ribs and into his lung.

Erik screamed behind his lips as he shifted face down in the snow.

Pull yourself together. Assess, fix; Rugrat needs you.

His left arm was still holding the back of his head. Moving his fingers sent a string of complaints through his forearm and elbow.

Erik drew out a revival needle from his storage ring, not moving more than necessary, spitting out gritty, dirt-filled snow.

By feel. he put the needle into his neck and injected it. "Damn." Parts started to snap back into position, mending together and fusing.

He cast a quick Fuse Bone spell to his broken arm to keep most of the pieces in place.

"Come on, come on." Erik rolled on his broken arm. He let out a suffering groan, feeling the bones shift as he rested on it. He moved his arm, putting himself into the recovery position, careful to not move his raised left arm.

"Divine Ground." A green healing spell formation appeared underneath him.

He used his mana to grab onto the tree limb, and pulled it out of his side in a quick motion.

"Nrggh!" Erik grunted sideways into the ground, rubbing his face against his arm, using the pain from the grinding bones to keep him there.

Erik coughed as blood wheezed out of the hole. He used a water spell to hold the blood back. The holes started to close. Erik carefully moved his right arm; it was completely repaired.

"Rugrat, you there?" Erik asked on the sound transmission device. "George? George!" Erik yelled.

Erik screamed and pounded the ground with his right hand as his ribs started to regrow. He held on as they connected, turning into a deep itch.

He pushed himself up and to his feet and slowly lowered his left arm. There were a few painful twitches, but he was good otherwise.

Erik cancelled Divine Ground and pulled out a Life Detect scroll. He tore it apart, watching the ripple.

"Rugrat, George! Yell out if you can hear me!"

He found George's form farther up the mountain.

Erik controlled the mana around him. Floating into the air, he took off toward George, shooting across the snow.

The scroll detected Rugrat on the other side of George.

George was mewling; his wings were torn and broken around him. His fur was matted with blood, his legs broken.

Erik hissed at the sight. A thread of fear turned his stomach. He saw Gilly in his mind's eye, broken. Erik punched himself in the leg, snapping out of it. He started working, setting the broken bones. George's wings were a mess. Erik injected George in the neck with a revival potion.

George quieted, but he was still unconscious.

"Nothing life threatening." Erik breathed out in relief, storing him in his beast storage device.

He flew over to Rugrat.

The big man had crashed into a boulder. A spider-web of cracks ran through it from where he had struck.

His left leg was twisted unnaturally, covered in cuts. His left arm and legs were broken by their unnatural angles, and his head was covered in blood.

Erik dropped next to him, scanning Rugrat.

He got Rugrat on his side and injected a revival potion into his neck for the brain bruise he'd seen forming.

Rugrat groaned, his head lolling side to side before falling silent again.

Erik paid no attention. He used Fuse Bone on Rugrat's arm, rib, jaw, skull, and leg fractures, getting them mostly in the right place so they wouldn't cause further damage and his body could start healing itself.

Erik didn't want a bone fragment piercing an artery and causing internal bleeding. He noticed something in the corner of his vision and turned to see figures approaching from the edge of the Life Detect scroll's range. "Beasts. Got to get moving."

He pulled out healing and stamina needles, based on the body cultivation needles, and strapped them to Rugrat's good arm, activating them. The drill-like needles drove through his arm and into the bone, activating their healing and stamina regeneration formations.

Rugrat groaned. His eyes opened, finding it hard to focus with his exaggerated eyelid movements.

Erik checked the area. The approaching beasts were following their trail of destruction through the trees and mountain.

He grabbed Rugrat's shoulder, shaking him and getting him to focus. "Rugrat, you're okay. Just take a rest in the beast storage crate."

Rugrat muttered something, but his face was swelling up, his jaw roughly fused together.

Erik stored him in the storage crate with George, then checked his map. He pulled out a spell scroll and tore it. The spell wrapped around him as he stepped into the air, flying toward the marker on his map, up the mountain.

He stayed close to the ground; too high, and he would enter the turbulent elemental energies.

He weaved through a copse of trees and tore another Life Detect scroll.

The beasts had reached the crash site.

Erik dropped to the ground. He pulled out George and smeared a salve under his nose to keep him under. There was no sense in letting him suffer the pain of his body pulling itself back together. Erik applied two healing and stamina formations, the drills tapping into his bones.

He switched to Rugrat, who had passed out. Erik applied another revival potion to the neck so it would reach the brain faster.

Erik saw movement in the distance. "Great, just what I need."

The beasts were fighting one another at the crash site and there were other beasts moving toward them.

Erik pulled out his rifle, checking it was loaded and secured it, before pulling out and putting on his helmet.

He stored Rugrat and kept moving, heading toward the marker on his map.

He felt a presence shooting toward him from above and behind with his domain.

Erik flew backward, grunting about the change in direction. Air blades cut the ground where he had been headed, slicing through snow, rock, and dirt.

An angry screech echoed over the mountains as a bird with blue, purple, and white feathers shot past Erik. The beast's passage plowed a path in the snow over the mountains.

Erik fired at the beast, but he was too slow. As fast as it appeared, it shot back up into the heavens, entering the low-lying elemental storm clouds.

The bird of prey must have had a wingspan of a hundred meters. It looked like a Roc of legend to Erik.

Erik ran ahead, gathering his power. Flames appeared around him as he added to the spell scroll. He cut low and fast over the ground, using his reactions to dodge trees and boulders, spreading out his domain.

He felt a surge of mana.

The flames and the mana under his control surged. He threw himself to the side. Blade of air obliterated rocks and trees. His speed drew up snow from the ground as he whistled across the earth.

He swerved to avoid a boulder as the Roc slashed out.

Erik's barrier took the impacts. He was smashed toward the ground, fighting to stay in the air. He took the hit with his right arm, protecting the beast storage crate on his left hip. He needed to find cover—now. If he stopped here, he would be torn apart. One hit to the beast storage crate and it would collapse, killing Rugrat and George.

He gritted his teeth, rising. He grabbed his rifle with his left, using his domain to see the ground ahead, dodging across the mountain.

Now! He turned, flying with his back to the mountain, firing up at the Roc.

He yelled as he dumped his magazine. Rounds hit and exploded.

The Roc let out a screech, its feathers torn apart, red splotches trailing from wounds.

Erik kept flying, pouring in more power, hoping to use the distraction.

Filling its voice with power, the Roc unleashed a cyclone of cutting wind, water, and ice, striking the ground, tearing apart trees, raising dirt, and turning boulders to gravel.

Erik's sudden increase in speed meant the attack missed him, but he felt the chilling wind ripping at his loose clothing.

Faster!

Erik tore out his empty magazine and dropped toward the ground. He called the earth up into footholds and called on the power in his muscles as he touched the ground, using his explosive movement technique. He surged across the ground, cutting air resistance, creating an explosion behind him each time he stepped down and using the last vestiges of power in the movement spell scroll.

The Roc's cyclone attack collapsed.

Erik didn't look back, focusing on his terrified sprint, tearing through the landscape. The Roc's scream followed him as it dove closer.

He smacked in a fresh magazine and pulled on the charging handle. He dodged to the left, grazing past a copse of trees and over a boulder that exploded. A chunk of rock hit Erik and threw him off his path.

Erik felt the rush of wind as the Roc's claws missed him and slashed the ground.

The beast flapped its wings and rose with an angry shriek.

Erik struck snow, rolling. He covered the storage crate with his left arm and held his rifle in the right.

He came to a stop, seeing the Roc banking sharply.

"Piercing Shot." Erik braced himself, raising his rifle and fired.

His rounds met with the Roc's wing, punching through it. The force of the cold wind and the tight bank and several large holes turned the Roc's wing useless. It spiraled, shrieking in anger and surprise, cutting off its scream attack.

Erik adjusted his aim and fired again. His rounds stitched bloody holes in the side of the Roc. It dipped and then dropped from view, crashing into the snow.

Erik felt a flush of experience filling him. He reloaded and stared at the barren landscape, now with browns of dirt and furrows left by the Roc's attack, marring the Mountain's pristine whites and greys.

He pulled out Rugrat and George from his storage crate.

George's wounds were still repairing, and he was stable.

Erik stored him again and pulled Rugrat up onto his knee, one hand on his rifle as he pulled out a squeeze bottle and released the powder under Rugrat's nose.

Rugrat coughed and sputtered, turning away from the powder and out onto the snow.

"Shit, damn, ourgh!" Rugrat shook his head and instantly regretted it, working his jaw.

"We're on a mountain and the residents aren't happy about it. Just had a Roc try to kill us. Downed it back there," Erik said.

"The hell is a Roc?" Rugrat slurred his words, sounding like his mouth had been numbed at the dentist. He pulled out the Beast and put on his helmet.

"A really big, pissed off bird." Erik switched to his sound transmission device, using Medical Scan.

"Jaw's a little fucked. Your bones—I fused them. They'll move themselves back in place, but don't trust your legs. You're a stumble away from breaking them again."

"Great, worst case of osteoporosis you ever did see."

Erik stood, scanning the area.

Rugrat looked at the two needles sticking out of his arm and grunted. He injected two more revival potions into his legs.

"What's the play?" Rugrat asked.

"Get to the cache. You good?" The spell reached out farther as Erik saw beasts and giant humanoids moving toward them.

"Little bit more fucked up than normal. George?"

"He took a bad hit. He's still out of it. The faster we get to cover, the sooner I can work on him." Erik reached out and helped Rugrat stand.

"Oorah." Erik and Rugrat gathered their mana. Rugrat jumped into the sky. The mana contorted to him as he surged ahead.

Erik raised dirt and stone pillars through the snow and pushed off. Pillars pierced through the ground to meet his feet, crumbling under the force as they raced up the mountain.

He pulled out spell scrolls, attaching them to his shoulders and his sides, their pull tabs easily reachable.

"Group of Giants ahead. Got blue skin." Erik jumped up instead of forward, rising next to Rugrat as he tore a flight spell scroll on his hip. The spell wrapped around him as he flew with Rugrat.

"Watch out." Rugrat grabbed Erik and moved to the side. A spear of ice shot past them. Erik felt the passing chill as it carried on.

Rugrat released him, grabbing the Beast.

There were five giants, five meters tall. Their eyes and hair were white, their bodies a mix of white and blue runes. Hides covered them and they held spears that looked to be carved from ice so cold it had turned to glass.

Rugrat fired as the thrower straightened. A tombstone appeared as they landed back three feet from where they had been standing.

Erik sprayed the remaining ice giants. The sudden death and pain made them run for cover behind boulders.

"Come on," Erik said.

They kept flying, racing for the cave.

Erik used another Life Detect scroll, seeing the giants coming out of hiding and checking on their dead.

Other beasts moved toward them.

They turned toward the mountain, finding a sheer face covered in sharp rocks, formed by the winds and ice.

"There it is." Rugrat pointed to a ragged opening in the mountain. The edges around the cave were jagged, like a rusty broken dagger. There were hints of it once being smooth, crafted even, and wide enough for a corvette or larger ships.

Markings worn away with time and weather lie around the large cave.

"You got a Life Detect?" Erik asked.

"Yeah, one sec. You out?" Rugrat pulled a pull tab, tearing the spell scroll.

"No, give me a sec. Need to reup my rips." Erik grabbed new scrolls and attached them to his armor.

"Cover me," Rugrat directed.

They hovered in the air near the wall and the cave entrance.

Erik reloaded. "Got you covered."

Rugrat pulled out spell scrolls, attaching them to his armor.

"Watch out!" Erik grabbed Rugrat, flying out of the path of air talons that cut several feet into the stone where they stood.

Rugrat unlimbered the Beast again.

The Life Detect reached into the heavens, revealing their attackers as Erik separated from Rugrat and dropped to the ground, the floor rising to reach him.

"Rocs! Run!"

The birds screeched. Their screams battered the edge of the cave and followed them as the birds tore up the ground and aimed at them

"Behind me!" Erik pulled out a stack formation. He twisted it with a click. The formations lit up, a mana barrier snapping into existence.

The attacks struck the barrier. Erik was tossed backward, the barrier coloring rapidly. Like a ball of glass found in flame, the attacks diverted around him, hitting the walls.

Erik reached around to the back of his carrier, latching the stack formation to his lower back, using spells to keep himself level.

The scream attack dissipated.

"Dead end!" Rugrat yelled. Erik dropped to the ground, turning to face the cave entrance. The cave was four hundred meters long and just under one hundred wide, too narrow for the Rocs to fly in. Stone rose to brace Erik's feet and back, increasing in thickness.

"The entrance has to be here somewhere! Use your inorganic scan to see where its hidden."

Erik pulled out his rifle and aimed down the cave, seeing the Roc's at the end.

Rugrat slapped his hand against the wall. The spell formation appeared over the stone.

Erik fired as another scream rang down the cave. Wind and ice tore at the tunnel walls in a tornado turned grey with stone as it carved the walls apart.

Erik's shots hit the stone washed up in the attack.

They broke on the barrier, eating away at the walls surrounding them.

"Damn you! Rugrat, rifle!" Erik threw his railgun to the side, hooking it in place.

Erik turned. Rugrat unclipped his rifle, one hand against the wall with his eyes closed. He threw over the Beast. "Loaded, on safe, blunt rounds."

Erik caught it, flicking off safe and casting piercing shot.

He fired on the right Roc. Surprised, the beast was struck in its expanded chest. A puff of red came from its body before it fell backward off the edge of the ledge.

The second shot hit a large boulder thrown up by the middle Roc's attack. Stone fragments turned into shrapnel, shredding the bird.

The third Roc canceled their attack and started to move. They jumped as Erik's shot connected with their wing.

He heard a screech and then nothing.

Erik held the Beast against his body with his left hand. The stone on his back dissolved, pulling off the stacking formation. He opened the formation and tossed in several Earth mana stones as the Roc at the entrance shrieked.

"Rugrat!" Erik's voice rose.

"I think I have something," Rugrat said.

"You think or you know?" Erik yelled. "Mag!"

Rugrat pulled one from his vest, tossing it.

"Explosive!"

"Got it." Erik caught the mag and shoved it between his chest and his plate carrier.

A Roc appeared at the entrance to the cave, wings flapping to land.

Erik fired, missing. The Roc screamed, another attack tearing up the cave.

"Jammed!" Erik smacked the bottom of the magazine and hauled on the charging handle. He tossed out the round, released it, and slammed the forward assist as he aimed again. The barrier broke at the Roc's scream.

Another made to land. Erik struck the screamer. The round hit it in the head, dropping it.

The new Roc closed their wings to land. The sudden change screwed up Erik's aim.

The beast screamed; it was stronger than the one before. It slammed into the new barrier like rolled paper meeting a blowtorch. The barrier closed in, shedding power.

Erik fired at the bird, his rounds striking the mess of stone, ice, and wind blades.

"I have it!" Rugrat yelled, his elemental chains attacking the Roc's from every direction.

Erik heard the clinking of chains as the scream died down. Chains of elements with blades at the end attacked the Roc.

"Use an earth moving spell there." Rugrat waved his hand at a section of wall he had been scanning. A mana blade appeared, cutting an x into the wall.

Erik fired on the bird. Distracted, it didn't notice the round until it was too late. The chains slackened and disappeared.

Erik turned and ran toward the x on the wall.

He flicked The Beast on safe and passed it to Rugrat.

"Four rounds left. On safe blunts!"

"Got it." Rugrat caught the rifle and reloaded.

Erik felt the heat from his stack formation, the smell of warmed metal.

"Get your barrier stack up. Mine's toasty!"

Erik reached into the wall and commanded it. Stone shifted, creating a corridor as wide as a man. "On it!"

Stone parted ahead of Erik. He reached up, pulling out a charge, sticking it to the ceiling. He repeated the process and pulled out a spell scroll with his other hand.

He heard Rugrat shooting and screams through the cave.

"Erik! Barrier won't hold long!"

"I'm working on it!"

The stone was sky grade. Erik felt the strain through his body, as if the mountain were pressing down on him. He pushed ahead, reached out. There was no more stone to shift.

Erik tore a spell scroll, creating a luminous ball that floated out, revealing a hangar of sorts. "I'm in, Rugrat!"

"Coming, dear!" Erik saw Rugrat charging through the tunnel. He was thrown forward with the force of another scream attack.

"Fire in the hole!" Erik grabbed his clacker, squeezing it.

The charges detonated, closing the man-sized tunnel, spewing stone and dust, collapsing.

Rugrat was on the ground, aiming the Beast between his legs at the collapsed stone.

There was no movement. There was a scream, and the rubble shook.

Erik dropped the clacker and tore the spell scroll, aiming it at the rubble.

The spell fused the stone together. It was rough, unlike the smooth wall, but it closed the gaps.

The luminous ball cast a pale light over the hangar. Erik studied it in greater detail. Grabbing his rifle, he tore a spell scroll on his chest. The Life Detect spell spread out.

Rugrat got up, and they checked the area.

"Nothing alive," Erik reported, lowering his rifle but keeping his hands near it, ready.

They looked up at the airship hangar. There were three slips big enough to fit corvette airships.

"Ladder." Rugrat gestured with his rifle.

Their footsteps echoed through the stone hangar. They crossed the large open space in front of the slips. It must have been to allow ships to turn around and move to the slips after the narrow cave entrance.

Erik went first up the ladder, holding his rifle with his right hand. He leapt up the ladder, taking the last few rungs slowly. He led with his rifle looking over the hangar.

There were several warehouses across from the slips. Exposed stairs led to a command center that would have looked over the corvettes.

Erik moved away from the ladder, scanning.

Rugrat stepped up behind him.

"Good."

They moved forward, Erik watching the right, Rugrat watching the left, one behind the other.

Erik led them to the first warehouse on the right. They pushed open the doors. Checking inside, they found racks on racks of storage crates.

They cleared the warehouses. Some were healing rooms and living quarters.

They checked the command center last.

"All clear. Looks like we're the only ones here." Erik lowered his rifle, walking to the dead formation consoles.

"One of these should open the doors out of here," Rugrat said.

"Why don't we wait a bit? I don't want to run into those Rocs."

"Must be a supply depot, a hold out if there was a war. Get a good position on the enemy and don't need to go back to the cities to resupply." Erik felt tired. "I need to check on George and I should make sure your bones are setting properly."

"All right," Rugrat's voice was tight.

Erik used a section of floor to pull out George. The healing rooms didn't have a place big enough for him.

Rugrat hissed. George's wings had been healing, but the damage was heavy. His fur was torn up in different places.

"I have him knocked out. We'll set his legs and then work on his wings," Erik said.

"Tell me what you need."

They shifted bones into place and repaired ligaments using fuse and healing. It was painstaking work; the wings were badly mangled.

Erik took out several formations to light up the area as the illuminating spell scroll faded.

"Okay, we'll make a supporting structure for his wings." Erik cut into George's wing. Using a length of wood and ties, he secured the wing bones in place.

"Sorry, buddy," Rugrat said. He drew his knife as well.

They splinted George's wings, using fuse bone spells. A section of his wings had been torn off. George's strong body was working overtime to repair the damage.

"All right, he's a strong boy. Shouldn't take him long to heal. I'll keep him unconscious, so he doesn't get stressed or move in a way that hurts him and undoes everything."

Erik used a clean spell, removing the blood from his hands and clothes.

"Okay," Rugrat said.

"Now, your turn," Erik said.

"Yay, me." They went to the healing room.

Erik numbed Rugrat. He'd set the bones, but in his hasty work, some were crooked and others he'd just fused the shards together.

Erik opened up Rugrat and sliced off the shards, cutting bones that hadn't set properly and fusing them the right way.

"Don't I need that?" Rugrat said, staring at the ceiling.

"Ah, you'll grow it back."

"How the hell you got your license, I'll never know."

"Easy, it was Army issued, and they let me practice on marines," Erik shot back, distracted, pulling out another piece of bone.

"You know your hips went into your gut? Nasty."

Rugrat reached between his legs cupping his pants.

"Your nuts are fine." Erik rolled his eyes, checking his handiwork before sealing Rugrat's knee.

"You know I gotta check."

"You find anything?"

"Yeah, my nuts."

"Not your nuts, I mean in this place."

"Not yet. Still, running my Inorganic Scan, takes time to spread out that far. It spreads over a larger area, there's more that my brain has to handle."

"Great, so could take a few decades?"

Rugrat flipped him the bird.

Erik grinned and moved to Rugat's feet.

"You got another pair of boots?"

"Yeah, why?"

"Cause you'll need them."

Erik used the boot to keep Rugrat's feet together. Conjuring a mana blade, he cut into Rugrat's feet and got to work, taking them apart.

Erik finished working on Rugrat's feet. "I'm all done here. Change your boots. I'm going to check out the other storage crates."

"Cheers," Rugrat looked at his bloody boots. They had been shredded. "You do good work."

He pulled his foot out of his shoe, wiggling his toes through the shredded socks, studying the holes in the top and bottom.

"Good thing I brought extra socks."

Erik grabbed his rifle from another bed, heading out of the healing room.

He went to the right-most warehouse and started opening the storage crates.

"Replacement mana cannons. Formations in this one. Unrefined sky iron in here. Animal feed, potions, food for humans. Ah, weapons."

Erik talked to himself as he worked, a grin on his face. He pulled out the storage crate filled with sky and earth grade mana stones and poured them from the storage crate into his personal ring. "It feels good to have money again."

Rugrat appeared some time later to a warehouse that had been pulled apart. "Having fun?"

"There's enough resources here to create a whole new corvette, I'd guess," Erik said.

Rugrat whistled.

"We've got both of the dungeon cores, though we didn't get a tenth of the resources needed to build one and those were stone and iron ships. We could make a pure iron ship from all this. I guess they were going to use the stone from the mountain to create their ships."

"So, what's our play?" Rugrat sat on a storage crate.

"Let's contact the Special Teams first." Erik flicked through options and tried to connect to Niemm.

He frowned and started going through the other members he knew were in the Seventh Realm. Then he tried to contact Fred and others.

"I can't get a signal," Erik said.

"Let me try," Rugrat said.

"Crap. We must be too far inside the mountain to send a signal. There has to be stealth formations here as well. We're blocked off."

"Okay, well, no worries. We've been on missions where we can't contact support before. We'll gather the storage crates, put down another teleportation formation here. Let me check the area." Rugrat closed his eyes and Rugrat felt a pulse of mana run through his body. "I think I have something. It looks like a hidden teleportation formation, and there's a recess in the wall with formation etchings on it."

We'll go and check on where that teleportation formation goes, then take whatever's on the other side and bring it back here. We'll teleport everything to Cronen, store it there, get the teams to help us, get carriages and take it all down to the First Realm."

"Okay," Rugrat said.

"Get as much into your storage devices as possible," Erik said. They had brought the biggest storage devices they had.

They emptied boxes of iron ore and mana stones into their storage devices, but it was a small dent in the supplies.

They placed a teleportation formation and checked on George. He had healed enough that Erik felt safe bringing him back awake.

They removed the splints and Erik healed the incisions they'd made in his wings.

He used a waking powder.

George shook, pawing the air, lying on his back. His eyes rolled, lethargic, but they became brighter. He leapt to his feet, growling and looking around.

"Easy boy, easy. You're okay. We're okay," Rugrat said, holding out his hands and walking toward him.

George's head whipped around. He jumped and used his wings, skittish and watching the hangar.

He calmed down as Rugrat patted him before turning his head to accept the scratchings.

"Let's wait a little bit, get some rest before we test that teleportation formation," Erik said.

"Sounds good to me." Rugrat said. "Sound good to you, boy?"

They ate their packed lunches, letting their bodies recover completely, and waited until they were feeling refreshed before they entered the second to last warehouse. Rugrat tapped a piece of wall. It shattered, revealing a small square recess on the other side.

"The pendant thing," Erik said.

Rugrat pulled it out and pressed it into the wall.

Formations glowed up the wall, running down to their feet, outlining a teleportation formation. They made sure they were inside the formation and Rugrat pressed it again.

"Ah, oh shit," Rugrat said. "Get off!"

Erik saw a red splotch of his blood on the pendant.

The formation activated in a flash of light.

32
Stepping on a Snake

ow Elder Kostic and his guards fought to keep up with the demanding pace the Dungeon hunter had set since leaving Zahir for the Beast Mountain Range. They crossed through the forest with ease. Beasts scurried back into their burrows as they passed.

They slowed as King's Hill became apparent in the distance and the Dungeon hunter closed his eyes, grimacing in concentration or at being in the First Realm.

His eyes opened with a shudder. "This place." The Dungeon hunter looked around with new eyes. "Vuzgal must have been their second base." The words barely came out in a whisper. "We have to return. I didn't find the main dungeon core, but there are several embedded into the ground. They create some kind of formation across the area."

"Across the city?" Kostic asked as the dungeon hunter turned his mount.

"The entire range."

Kostic opened his mouth, trying to sputter out a few words.

The Dungeon hunter didn't wait. He snapped his reins as his mount took a running jump, leaping up the trees and spreading her wings wide as he cast several spells to increase his speed.

Kostic turned with his guards as they fled back the way they had come, forgetting the fatigue from the hard days of riding.

He saw a flash of light, followed by the sound of rolling thunder. Through the treetops, the Dungeon hunter's mana barrier fell under an attack from five sparrows.

Explosions rocked the forest around Kostic, tossing him free of his mount as the trees exploded around him.

His vision focused, an unknown time later. He felt dazed, his body in pain as he coughed blood.

Kostic got up, finding his right leg broken. He tried to pull himself up a tree, watching as one of his guards started running. The ground was torn up in dust devils that cut through the running man. His momentum carried him forward, tripping over the ground and smashing into the roots.

Kostic coughed and looked around, hooking his arm around the tree supporting him.

He peered into the sunlight. *They must not have seen me. I wonder if the hunter made it away. The sect will come down here and destroy every last Vuzgalian.*

He pulled out a sound transmission device.

Pain bloomed in his stomach. He dropped the device and fell against the tree, his hooked arm coming out as he turned to see several people walking through the forest.

They wore the faceless armored helmets of the Vuzgalians, and their firearms.

One man squatted out of arm's reach.

"Elder Kostic, what is the Willful Institute doing down here with a dungeon hunter?"

Kostic tried to gather his power for one last attack only to find that he had been shot in his mana core.

The light dimmed from his eyes, and he slumped to the ground.

"A Black phoenix clan member and Low Elder Kostic." Glosil smacked his leg and grimaced.

Everyone in the command center had come to a halt, making half-hearted gestures to their work. They'd all heard Elan's report to Glosil.

"Bring all units to readiness. This is not a drill." Glosil moved to the map table at the rear of the room and pulled out his sound transmission device.

Lieutenant General Yui ran into the command center. Glosil waved him forward. Elan called Delilah, quickly informing her of what had happened.

She was quiet afterwards, Glosil pushed on. "They will know that we killed them soon."

Delilah cleared her throat. "Okay, Commander, what do we do?"

"In my mind, the Willful Institute will lock down their leaders as soon as they can. If we don't act on Operation Clean Slate, we won't have the opportunity in the future. It's clear the BPC are helping the Willful Institute, and we need to make sure they don't interfere. I think we should have our teams in the BPC Shipyards carry out their mission immediately and have the teams located in Henghou and other key United Sect Alliance cities strike at preset locations."

"Erik and Rugrat?" Delilah asked.

"I sent them a sound transmission as soon as I got the report. There's been no reply yet," Elan said.

Delilah was quiet on the channel.

"Erik and Rugrat said that we were to take charge of our destiny, that there might be times when we have to fight without them. Have the message passed to the assassination and sabotage teams that they're to take out their targets immediately. I wish them luck and Alva awaits their safe return."

Roska wiped her brow, adjusting the rag that covered her hair while watching the side gate to the Willful Institute dungeons.

The gate opened to admit another convoy of carriages.

Roska stretched. Just another of Henghou's citizens down on their luck and only able to glance inside the grand gates of the sects that controlled the city.

"Looks like more loot coming in," Davos said from his unseen observation point.

The Willful Institute in Henghou had been gathering loot from across their recaptured cities.

Their coffers have to be feeling the pinch from the fighting.

Roska wandered the street, blending in. She grabbed some stamina potions for a few pitiful mana stones, switching it for an Alvan potion.

They didn't taste like much, but it was better than the smell and flavor of the cheap stamina potions.

Another convoy, this one twice as large as the one that had entered and with markedly fewer guards, left the side gate.

Roska's sound transmission device pinged as she moved to the side to listen to the message.

"Black Phoenix Clan is working with the Willful Institute. A scouting party was found and eliminated in the Beast Mountain Range. All teams are to execute sabotage plans if possible and return to Alva ASAP. Operation Clean Slate and Retribution are okayed."

Roska felt a shiver run through their spine. *Fuck, they found us.*

She called the rest of her squad spaced around the city as she used her Dungeon Sense.

"All right, everyone gather up on my position. We're going to hit some of these convoys and bomb the hell out of the pl—ah, shit."

"Boss?" Davos asked.

"Relay to messengers. I am picking up eighteen dungeon cores located in a line under Henghou. Shit!" She bit the inside of her lip. *I should have scanned earlier. Those have to be weapons of some kind. Maybe ships.*

"Change in plan, not just another observation mission. Meet up at rally point Alpha. Our mission is to find out what those dungeon cores are for, recover as many as possible, and destroy anything else in there."

Cai Bo turned as Gregor slammed the door open to Head Asadi's office, finding her and Asadi discussing over a map. "The dungeon hunter I sent to the First Realm has died."

"Cai Bo?" Asadi said, venting his rage at being burst in on, unsure what to say.

Gregor cleared his throat. "He was following a tip by Low Elder Kostic, who is probably dead as well."

While he cared little for Cai Bo, bringing her and the different clans under her control into the Black Phoenix Clan's fold could bring him accolades with the clan and a great wealth of resources in the future.

Asadi looked at his desk, his eyes moving from side to side. His lips pressed together as he looked up, standing proud. "Elder Cai Bo, is General

Niklaus ready to move?"

"Yes, Head Asadi."

"What of the other Sects?"

"They require more time."

"How much?"

"No more than five hours."

"What other forces do we have under our control that are ready to move now?"

Gregor stood to the side, listening and waiting. *The sooner we begin, the sooner we can get out of this mess.*

"We have two armies that could be ready to move within the hour."

"Good. Have Mercy and the other armies attack as soon as possible. We need to capture totems to transport our forces through. Once we confirm that the Vuzgalians are there—"

"No First Realm fighter would be able to kill my hunter," Gregor snarled.

"That may be the case, but we do not want to shame the other sects and lose their support if it is not the case. How long will it take for the airships to be ready?"

"Three are ready to go now, including *Perseverance*." The flagship was Gregor's personal toy, slightly larger than a corvette with a nearly complete dungeon built to hide its inner workings and the empty bay that rested in the heart of the ship.

He had sent her word to Captain Stassov as soon as he had found out his hunter had died, but she might not be able to get away from the Seventh Realm at such short notice.

"The others?"

"Give me a day and I can get three more. Give me two days and I can add another four. If I scrap the other warships, it will take less."

A messenger burst into the room. "Head!"

"You dare!" Asadi growled, gathering his power.

The messenger dropped to his knees, smacking his head against the floor. "Several elders and seniors have been assassinated across the realms."

"What?" Asadi's power drained away.

The messenger pulled out letters and held them above his head. "There are more reports coming in!'

Asadi plucked them from the man's shaking hands with a spell and spread them out in midair, creating a wall in front of him. "Have our people lock down their cities immediately! Have all the seniors and elders return immediately!"

Cai Bo scanned the pages, impressed.

Oh, very well played Vuzgal. You are a worthy opponent, but the sect you attacked is mine! The sect is in a time of chaos. This will be a great opportunity to solidify my power in the sect.

She knew now that it was Vuzgal. This kind of planning had to take place over years. They had been resilient enemies, to be sure. They would not dare to lead this kind of attack; it would lead to a life and death battle with the Willful Institute.

None of the other sects would be willing, but Vuzgal has already lost their city. The Vermire Empire must be their base of operations, and this is their retaliation.

33
Retribution

Special Team Two met inside a basement rented through the intelligence agents and connected to the Blue Blossom Sect.

Roska and the rest of the team quickly and expertly pulled on their armor, not caring about the blue blossom armor they'd forged. They wore Alvan armor.

"We need to do this fast. That means spell scrolls." She put on a helmet and took out a mage staff. Along its side she had affixed spell scrolls with pull tabs.

"So, blast a tunnel down there, get inside, and blow it to hell," Kristoff said.

"You got the idea. Ready?"

The last bits of gear were slapped and pulled, checking they were in place.

Davos had set up a formation plate and knelt on top of it.

The team gave a thumbs up and got onto the formation plate.

"Do it, Davos." Roska grabbed two levers sticking out of the formation that moved two magic circles.

Davos turned and inserted the power core of the formation.

Roska pressed down on the left lever, and they sunk rapidly through the ground. The right lever guided them through the stone.

They hurtled through the ground, weapons drawn and ready.

They came out of the ground into a hallway with carriages heading down a winding slope.

Yells called out before they dropped through a carriage, the underside of the formation drill tearing it apart as they dove into the ground again.

The team members released spells, pulling the stone back together as Roska sped toward the dungeon cores.

"Get ready!" Roska yelled.

Light spilled in again to the sound of heavy work. Roska held onto the levers as it dropped through open air.

"Hold on!" she yelled as they grabbed onto one another, falling some twenty meters.

The drill and team slammed into a half-built ship, tearing through compressed stone and metal. She couldn't hear the yells of the crafters over the scream of the drill, but she felt them.

She glanced around. Her team had landed with her and were pulling on their spell scroll tabs all in one go.

Roska felt her stomach tighten harder than when they'd fallen through the ceiling. *Eighteen warships!*

Her eyes caught on the nearly completed warships to her right, and then she was through the outer armor of the ship, speeding deeper, cutting through the ship.

Davos was with her, holding onto her side, his rifle in the other hand.

They cut and dropped. As they dropped again, a spell struck the bottom of the formation, breaking it and hurling it backward.

Roska let go of the handles, falling away from the drill as it crashed through consoles and the crafters working on them. Davos must have jumped off too, as he fired on the spell caster.

One of Gregor's hunters.

The hunter's barrier remained steady as he readied a spell.

Roska waved her staff, unleashing a bolt of mana that crashed into the man's barrier, and sent him into the throne he had been sitting in. Her eyes caught the dungeon core hanging above the seat between formations, and she unleashed another attack on the man.

"Covering!"

Davos ran up to the man. Roska cut off her attacks while Davos shoved his rifle into the mana barrier and fired.

The man's barrier and tombstone appeared at the same time.

The deck shook as Roska turned, spell ready. The rest of the team fell down her path of destruction into the ship.

"Davos, get control of that dungeon core. Activate all the weapons we can. Hit the ships on either side. You two stay here. The rest of you, on me!"

"What are you going to do?" Davos yelled as she ran for the door.

"Steal some dungeon cores, hopefully! Make sure to get out before shit goes bad. Use the dungeon core as Egbert taught us!" Then she was through the door.

She let Kristoff go ahead of her. Hooking the staff on her back, she pulled out a rifle.

They ran through some open paneling and jumped from the ship, landing on the pier next to it. The pier was filled with materials being prepared for the ship.

They fired on the fighters rushing down the pier, cutting them down.

"Use your smokes!" Roska dropped smoke into her hand from her storage ring and threw it out across the pier, quickly hiding them from view.

The team crossed the open area as a whirring noise came from behind, followed by the sounds of a rolling barrage. The smoke drifted away from the lifting warship as it smashed into the ceiling and fired onto the most complete ships and the ships beyond Roska's and her half-team's reach.

Good old Davos, thinking ahead.

The team ran up a gang plank and into another ship, using mana blades and explosive charges to cut through to the heart of the ship.

Kristoff walked out into a wave of attacks, hitting his barrier and smashing him through the wall.

Another team member tossed in several grenades, shooting out a wave of hot gasses and deforming the wall they were leaning against before they charged in again.

The hunters, blind and deaf, rolled around on the floor. The rest of the room had been shredded.

Roska and the others killed the dungeon hunters.

"Cap, don't want to hurry you along, but there're a lot of fighters coming toward us," Davos said.

Kristoff lowered his hand, having taken control of the dungeon core.

"No weapons active on this one."

"Davos, you got a mana stone charge?"

"Yeah, I got one. Damn."

"Plant it, ditch the ship, and get the hell out of there. We'll do the same. Kristoff, we got engines working?"

"Barely."

"I'll take what I can get. Get us moving."

"Yes, Cap."

"You two get the charges planted," she said to two of her newest team members.

"Yes, Cap." They ran off toward the ship's mana stone stores.

The ship rose, scraping against the pier with its half-formed engines screeching its way up the side.

"Damn, Kristoff, you think you can be any louder?"

"Thing's a tub of metal with only three working movement formations."

Kristoff grunted, focusing on his task.

Roska grabbed a working screen as the ship freed the berth. It was still scraping along the pier, but gaining momentum as they slowly started to gain altitude. She tore her spell scrolls along her staff and on her vest, using the screen to place them.

"Brace!"

The ship smashed into the one beside it. Stone and iron screeched against one another like nails down Roska's spine as the ship plowed into more ships trapped in their berths.

"Davos?"

"Under attack here. They got some of the other ship going. We're heading out."

"Meet back in Alva, fast as you can."

"Yes, Cap!"

"Charges are set. Found some people on the ship still. Working our way back to you," one of the team members she'd sent out reported.

They crashed into another warship; their altitude dropped.

"Took out a movement formation."

"Hit the next one and we'll bail," Roska said. The two team members she'd sent to set charges entered the command center as the ship was tossed to the side with an explosion.

Roska smacked into the wall before the ship crashed into a pier and dropped into an unfinished corvette's berth, crushing the little work that had been completed on it.

"I think that might have ruffled some feathers," Davos said, loosening the tightness in Roska's chest.

"All right, let's get the hell out of here. Kristoff, grab that core." Roska got up, pulling another team member to their feet. Right had become down.

"Got it!"

"Follow me." Roska dropped between doorways to the unfinished corvette. Cutting apart a few panels, they reached the dungeon core and fused it with the one in Kristoff's hand.

"Let's go."

Using the dungeon core, Kristof compressed and uncompressed the ground around them, dropping them downward at an alarming speed.

"Do it," Roska said to the two who had planted the mana charges.

They used a clacker, activating formations they'd tossed into the mana stone bunkers.

While the outer armor of most ships was strong, the armor around the mana stones was rarely so. The power source was completely stable, unless it fueled something else.

Formations consumed the mana stones rapidly, creating other spells which would create other spells until the spells were so tightly packed as to corrupt one another, all within a tenth of a second.

They felt the explosion as they dropped through the ground.

"That is going to hurt some."

"Once we're deep enough, we'll use teleportation spell scrolls. Head to rally point Echo, and we'll totem from there."

"How do you think the teams are doing in the higher realms?" Kristoff said.

"Well, they've had months to work on their surprises. Let them worry about it. We need to get the hell out of here," Roska said, shaking herself. She couldn't relax just yet.

Gregor yelled and kicked a burnt and twisted piece of metal, looking at the smoking ruins before him.

"Cousin," a hunter said.

Gregor wanted to punch the man but held back with so many sect eyes around. "What?"

"Five hunters were killed, and three dungeon cores were stolen. All the ships were damaged. Nine of them will have to be completely rebuilt."

Gregor ground his teeth, hearing the pinging of cooling metal. The ceiling had caved in at different sections. "Combine the dungeon cores. Get me as many fighting warships as you can. Strip the others. I want them ready before the end of the day."

"Yes, Sub-Commander."

Gregor snarled and walked over to Cai Bo, who stood nearby. "Have your boy, Marco, send a message to Captain Stassov reporting everything here."

"Yes, Sub-Commander." She bowed.

Gregor watched her go. She was a devious one, but she reminded him of Stassov—ambitious and willing to do anything necessary to win. It was why he followed Stassov. Cai Bo would make a better sub-commander than Ranko. He had lost his nerve after Bela died. *Otherwise, I might have some damn help here.*

He found another piece of metal to kick, denting it as it sailed across the broken pier. There were plenty of metal parts scattered around.

"And get that minion of yours, Mercy, or whatever her name is, to launch her attack. They act quick, these Vuzgalians. I don't want our route blocked!" he yelled after Cai Bo.

Aureus completed basic training with the Intelligence department, getting a mission in River Guard, one of the cities outside of the Vermire Empire. The city boasted a large river harbor, a totem, and a permanent and sizable city guard that doubled as the king's army.

Jian got along well with Delfina, spending most of his days taking lessons from the Alva teachers. With him safe, Aureus was able to take on the mission, which mostly consisted of being in the right places, talking to the right people, and listening to their woes.

He stepped outside the tavern, raising his hand and blinking against the light. Thunder sounded in the distance, but the skies were clear.

The discharge of mana washed over the city, unused to high level spells.

Aureus pulled out his sound transmission device. "Massive spell at River Guard. I'm moving in for a closer look."

Event
The city of River Guard is under attack! Pick a side!
Defend River Guard Attack River Guard

"River Guard is under attack!"

Aureus ran across the street and jumped, grabbing onto a piece of wood sticking out of the building's muddy side. He threw himself onto the roof.

He ran across the tops of building, jumping from one to another, working closer to the totem.

He slid to a halt at the sight of mounted sect members charging through River Guard's streets. Stone tiles dropped to the road below. His eyes locked onto the sect members' emblems and the banners that flew from their forward riders.

People cried out, jumping back into their homes. A sect fighter cut out with a spell, killing a group of guards, and destroying several homes with casual ease.

"There are Willful Institute members coming through the totem," Aureus reported to command.

He looked up. Sect fighters pushed out in every direction. The city guard might have numbers, but they were useless in the face of this level of power.

A whip snapped out, catching a man at the neck and hurling him backward. Aureus followed the whip, finding a woman in their midst.

"Mistress Mercy is with them."

"Go to ground and hide. Report when you can," the agent on the other side ordered.

"Understood."

Someone spotted him and one of the Willful Institute fighters hurled a spell at him. Aureus jumped from the roof. He landed on a fleeing carriage. Tiles and beams shattered above him and rained down as the driver whipped his beasts faster.

Aureus rolled off and into an alleyway, gaining his feet and running away from the sounds of shouting. River Guard was lost, but it would take them time to capture the city and gain use of the totem.

Major General Lukas checked the map in his command center. It was linked to the Alva dungeon cores, showing him everything that moved in the city of Shida in the Beast Mountain Range.

An alarm went off as an aide stood and turned, spilling his papers on the floor.

Event
The city of Shida is under attack! Pick a side!
Defend Shida
Attack Shida

"Sir, there's been an attack by people from the higher realms at the totem! They're wearing Willful Institute armor."

Lukas looked at the map, seeing markers disappear around the totem. He turned, seeing the light in the distance. "Arty arty arty!" People ran for cover, repeating his warning as they ducked into the building and under cover. He turned toward the explosion rolling across the city.

The wave of sound passed quickly.

"Send in our Alva teams. Lock down all totems and gates! Take us to full readiness."

Another alarm rose in the room, one that sent shivers down Lukas' spine as his sound transmission device vibrated.

He took it out, listening to Glosil's voice.

"Willful Institute forces have taken Totems across the First Realm around the Vermire Empire and claimed them as their own. There are reports that they are gathering to prepare for an assault. Go to full readiness and be ready to evacuate your people. We could come under attack at any minute. Report any attacks and lock down the Empire."

Lukas breathed heavily as he turned his head to the questioning gazes of his officers. "The Willful Institute is coming. You all know your jobs."

Motion returned to the room.

Lukas raised his sound transmission device, contacting the Alva command center. "We had an attack at Shida. Appears to be Willful Institute trying to secure our totem defenses."

"Understood. Have you removed the threat?"

He checked the map. It showed only friendly markers moving among the totem defenses.

"Yes." Lukas bit off the words, clearing his throat at the lost soldiers. His map updated and new markers appeared in the cities around Vermire Empire as more Willful Institute forces flooded in. "For now."

Delilah looked around the command center. The map constantly updated with information; it showed Zahir City laying in destruction after the passage of Mistress Mercy and her army.

"Council Leader," Glosil said, pulling her back. "You need to make a decision!"

"Do you think this is their attack?" Delilah said, her hand shaking as she pushed her hair to the side.

"I don't know for sure. What I do know is that Mercy will cut a bloody trail from River Guard to King's Hill if we don't stop her. There are armies amassing on our borders. If we do nothing, then the people of Vermire Empire will be slaughtered, but we may survive. If we defend, then there is no guarantee we will be able to save them."

"But we are the patron saints of lost causes," Delilah said, her voice firmer as she looked at the map. "Commander Glosil, defend Vermire. Defend Alva and save our people. Evacuate the cities in the Beast Mountain Range to the secondary dungeons under the Empire as fast as possible."

"Yes, Council Leader." Glosil came to attention with the other officers at the table and saluted. "Domonos, work with Pan Kun to hold and evacuate the cities. Yui, take your Tigers and man the defensive network. Egbert," Glosil yelled to the ceiling.

"Yes, Commander?"

"You and Davin are on call. Be ready to assist as needed." Glosil turned to the men and women of the command center. "Raise the bunkers and clear our lines of fire. Let's give these bastards an Alvan welcome!"

Domonos and Yui ran as they talked into their sound transmission devices.

Delilah watched the markers shift as soldiers used teleportation formations to cross the Vermire Empire. Guards and police officers started evacuating cities.

Bunkers rose from the Beast Mountain Range, the ground altered with earth spells. Soldiers cut down swathes of trees and brush with their attacks, picking up the debris in their storage rings.

In just seconds, the Beast Mountain Range was altered.

"My queen!" A portly man, the lord of River Guard, ran out of his castle with his entourage toward Mercy and her group.

Mercy's whip shot out, laying a bloody line across the man's chest.

The man cried out, falling backward. Three more bloody lines cut his fine shirt before he reached the ground.

A tombstone rose above him as people behind him cried out and ran.

Mercy whipped those within range as she walked with her group across the square. None of those with her moved to attack. No one wanted to stop her enjoyment or draw her ire.

After there were no more living toys, she took in a deep breath, pushing back her hair.

"Cousin, two other cities are under our control. Three more should be controlled within the hour."

"What about the confirmation we needed? What about my uncle's killer?"

"We do not have that information currently. Scouts are pushing into the Beast Mountain Range. Our strike force is preparing to head to Zahir next, the city that our Uncle Kostic passed in."

"I wish to be a part of this force," Mercy said.

Niklaus swallowed his words. "Of course, Cousin." He paused as they walked through the gate of the castle. People fled through every other exit afforded them. Mercy's whip snapped out, killing a slow servant.

She let it trail behind her, leaving a bloody line on the stone that turned to marble as they stepped into the interior of the castle.

"The scouts have our confirmation. There are bunkers coming out of the ground. We got glimpses of them before our aerial beasts were cut down."

"So, it is them?"

"It appears it is the Vuzgalians, yes."

Mercy whipped the doors ahead, blasting them apart to the empty throne room.

"Good," she hissed. Her whip smashed the throne apart and revealed the city cornerstone.

You have captured the city: River Guard

"Have our forces gather. We attack Zahir next."

Storbon stood on the formation. It activated, the light passing over him. Two Black Phoenix Clan soldiers watched him, spears at the ready.

Another guard studied the small console to the side.

"Move forward."

Storbon stepped off the formation and passed the guards.

"Next!"

Storbon left the inspection station. Behind, there were several squat buildings. Storbon met the gaze of the other team members coming out of the buildings or through the scanners.

Magically powered carriages ran on a track, going from the tool sheds and workshops along the main dock-way. Crafters grumbled in the early morning sun, talking to one another. Storbon headed for one of the workshops and joined the lines leading up to the quartermaster. Some of the crafters rubbed the last of sleep from their eyes. Others chatted with their friends and neighbors.

The lethargic line moved enough for Storbon to reach the quartermaster, a tired-looking woman behind a metal screen.

"Formation smith," he said.

She nodded. Turning around to storage crates, she pulled out a tool belt and put it on the counter.

"Thanks." Storbon grabbed the tool belt and headed out of the building.

A carriage load headed off to one of the slips as new carriages moved up. Crafters boarded once it rolled to a stop.

Storbon walked to the carriage for berth four. There were hundreds of crafters loading into the carriages or coming off them as they finished their shift. He was late reaching the carriage. There were no seats left, so he stood crammed in with others. Storbon saw one of his team members sitting in his carriage.

They spotted one another. Without making any gesture they looked away.

The carriage rolled forward. A few jumped onto the stairs and clambered up before the carriage left the station.

They quickly sped up, moving past fabrication facilities and alongside supply wagons. They ran across the shipyard, the berths on their left, the workshops on their right.

The shipyards never slept, maintaining and repairing the Black Phoenix Clan warships.

Their carriage slowed and paused at a dock. People jumped off, heading from the gantries into the airship.

The carriage filled up with more people coming off shift.

Storbon shifted his toque, moving the scarf around his neck.

The other team member got off early, heading to their entry point.

Storbon was one of the last, near the rear of the airship.

He got off with the press of people.

The guards checked the formation-pressed card he had been issued, scanned him again, and waved him onto his ship. Storbon pulled on his tool belt, walking up the stone gantry to the BPC Destroyer.

He walked through the ship, passing BPC guards at strategic locations, finding the foreman of his section.

"Storbon, picking up some overtime?" the foreman said, sitting behind a desk.

"All I can."

"Not many prospects for a formation smith like you, only Journeyman and no clan." The foreman sneered, checking his sheets. "You're working on the sewage systems."

"Got it," Storbon said, turning to trudge away.

He felt the foreman gather his power. Storbon flexed his feet, taking the spell and hitting his head on the doorway on the way out. He cried out, cutting his head with a conjured mana blade.

"Those of the younger generation have no respect for elders. You forgot to bow. Now get out of my sight!"

Blood covered the side of his face. Storbon held his head, stopping his body from healing the wound, and staggered out of the room. He headed toward the sewage department. He checked the area, then moved his hand. The cut on his forehead sealed in seconds.

A clean spell removed any trace of blood.

Storbon walked into the sewage department, hiding his smile.

Two crafters sat working on formation plates. They glanced up from their work as the door behind Storbon closed.

"Hey boss," Jurumba said.

"How's it going?"

"Pressure's been building all night. It's about ready," Jurumba said.

Storbon passed the two team members. They pulled off their scarves and handed them to him.

He walked to a formation plate and used a cutting knife from his tool belt to cut into it, finding several such scarves on the other side.

"Well, I think it's about time we found new jobs," Storbon said. He pulled out packets from his jacket and other parts of his clothing. His toque joined the pile of rags. Sown packets and others piled in his hands. He switched with the other two, working on the formation plate and keeping watch. They stripped out sections of their clothing, growing the pile.

Storbon checked the time. He used a cutting tool, forming a dense mana blade on the edge as he started to cut through different plates.

The door opened as Jurumba was stripping down. He squatted behind a half-wall, appearing to be working.

The new team member stood up as two guards and the foreman walked in, closing the door.

"What's the hold up? I'm getting complaints about showers not working and toilets smelling." The foreman stormed in and clipped Storbon on the head. Storbon let himself hit the wall with a grunt. "Huh! You think that you can drag your feet?" The foreman kicked him.

The other team members moved against the wall behind the BPC guards. One of the guards grinned as he watched Storbon. The other was looking at the squatting Jurumba.

"I'll put you in the shit water myself if you don't fix it today!"

"Hey, you! Stand up. What are you sitting on?" the guard looking at Jurumba said.

Storbon gathered his mana and stood up. He grabbed the foreman's leg, tilting him backward, and punched him in the face, smashing him into the ground. The guards' eyes went wide as twin mana blades cut through their necks.

The foreman was dazed, looking at the dead guards. The team member caught them and lowered them to the ground.

A mana bullet put an end to the foreman.

Storbon turned and worked on the panels quickly. An eye blistering smell came from the gap. He pulled up his shirt against the smell.

Jurumba pulled over the rags and tossed them in.

The alchemy treated fibers would react with the water, creating an explosive solution.

The other team member collected the bodies in a dead guard's storage ring. He put his hand over the hole and released the bodies.

"Ourgh!" he complained as water splashed on him, and he cast a clean spell.

The door opened.

"Ah damn!" a woman yelled, holding her nose. "I heard a noise from the next compartment. Everything okay here?"

Jurumba held the back of his head. "Yeah, just hit my head from the smell. Idiot over there pierced the tank."

"Yeah, okay." The woman closed the door. Storbon heard her gagging as he fought to control his throat while he sealed up the tank again.

Jurumba leaned against the wall outside the door as Storbon and the new team member went through the storage rings. They tossed anything flammable into the vat, created several formations from the metal in the room, powered them up with Sky mana stones, and tossed them into the tank. Storbon checked on all the sewage tanks. "Okay, looks like we're ready to go." He attached heating formations to the outside of each of the tanks.

"Shall we get going?" Jurumba stood.

"Yeah, let's get the hell out of here."

They left the room, passing a few guards.

"Where's the foreman at?"

"Dunno." The crafter they were asking shrugged and went back to work.

"Dammit, he better not be sleeping on the job again," the guard said as the trio walked past.

The guard held his nose. "What's that smell?"

"Sewage tanks," another crafter offered.

The team members walked through.

"I heard that the Black Phoenix are cutting our pay again, say that they're going to force us into restrictive contracts," Storbon said to Jurumba.

"Screw that, I'm getting off the ship before they lock us in here."

The team members continued their conversation past groups of crafters who paused to listen.

"I heard that the foreman in section F-Thirteen found out early and skipped out on work so he wouldn't get locked in," the new team member said.

Crafters put down their tools, talking to one another, and headed off to look for the foreman, who apparently knew the truth.

Storbon and the trio walked off the ship. The guards didn't care about crafters leaving, just the ones boarding.

Storbon was the last into the carriage.

They found seats together, watching as crafters started to come off the ship. They walked up to the guards. "Hey, is it true you're cutting our pay?" one crafter yelled.

"What are you talking about? Get back to work! Are you going against your contract?" a guard yelled, drawing his weapon.

"Look, these clans already want to get us into more restrictive contracts! You think that because we work for you, you own us?" another crafter sneered.

The carriage lurched forward. Some of the crafters ran over and jumped on, wanting to get away from the growing tension. The two groups were pushing one another, yelling over one another, their words blocking each other out.

Storbon and his team members got out of the carriage with the others when they reached their stop. They moved to some empty smoking tables and sat, looking like others who had just gotten off work. Most were smoking incense, what Erik and Rugrat called a cigarette, which increased their stamina.

Other team members walked over, looking at them, taking up table space or squatting and talking.

Niemm sat down opposite Storbon.

"How are the fabrication shops?"

"Ah, you know, they're not bad. Lots of good honest work, if you have the people." Niemm grinned.

"Honest people?" Newly promoted captain Yao Meng sat down to Storbon's right. "Gah, you smell horrible."

"Thanks," Storbon muttered.

"Hey, lads." Gong Jin patted Niemm and Yao Meng's shoulders.

Yao Meng pulled out an incense stick and lit it. Others did the same. The little sticks created a relieving habit.

Six Special Teams filed into the rest area.

Storbon checked them all twice. "Looks to me like we're all here," he said to Niemm.

"Same here," Gong Jin said.

The crafters' mood seemed to shift. People were arriving from the ships, talking about the pay cut. The crafters were getting riled up as more crafters left what they were working on.

Niemm pulled out an incense stick and held out a formation lighter. He squeezed it three times as an explosion tore through the side of one of the warships.

"Huh, guess this one's out of fuel," Niemm said around his cigarette, pocketing the lighter.

Crafters and guards stared at the black clouds rising into the sky. An alarm blared through the shipyards. Crafters turned and ran for the gates.

"See you at home," Niemm said.

The team leaders nodded and broke apart. They found their teams and rushed toward the gate with the rest of the panicked crafters.

The guards couldn't hold them back and got out of the way.

Ships rose into the sky, powering their formations in alarm.

A ship ballooned and exploded outward, cracking in half as it fell toward the ground.

A wave of heat struck the fleeing crafters.

Storbon got to the other side of the gate. People rushed out in every direction. Residents of the surrounding compounds watched in horror as Black Phoenix Ships exploded. Tea houses and restaurants closed their doors.

Storbon and his team ran along the outside wall.

The Destroyer from berth four pushed into the sky. Smoke appeared around the ship. "Drop!"

The team dropped to the ground as the smoke ignited.

The force of the explosion washed over the compound and the buildings on the other side. Ships attempting to fly were tossed wildly away. Secondary charges erupted deep inside, crippling them as well. Metal and stone smashed through fabrication shops, through the shipyard, and even broke sections of the wall.

"Move!" Storbon yelled. They got up and kept running as crafters were still trying to regain their feet.

A section of smoking ship soared over the wall, crashing into the street, skipping and smashing into another building.

Storbon and the group kept running. They reached a tavern, knocking on the door. The door opened, and they rushed in to find several Alvan intelligence agents.

"Out back."

They moved to the rear of the tavern. Their gear was ready for them between rows of casks.

They quickly stripped out of their crafter clothes, pulling on their storage rings and trader's clothes.

Other teams made it into the tavern and grabbed their gear.

The tavern owner came downstairs with the rest of his people and pulled up a carpet to reveal a teleportation formation.

They finished changing into trader's garb and stepped on the teleportation formation in teams and disappeared.

Storbon came out into a cave of a dungeon.

"Get those wagons ready!" Gong Jin growled as carriages and beasts were pulled from storage devices.

The intelligence agents appeared, checking the beasts, filling the carriages with storage crates from the tavern.

"All here." Niemm tossed an incendiary bomb on the teleportation formation and activated it.

He stored the formation and nodded to Storbon.

"Okay, let's roll out."

Storbon and the Special Teams took up their roles as the caravan's guards as they exited the cave and headed toward the closest dungeon city and its totems.

Captain Stassov read the letter Marco Tolentino had brought to her from the Sixth Realm. She lowered it and looked through the windows of the bridge at the park around her.

Screens showed the *Eternus'* position within Chmilenko's main fleet. She saw a destroyer, two frigates, and seven corvettes as they headed to reclaim the Earth Cloud Valley.

She tapped the letter against her armrest as a commotion rose from the communications officers.

"What is it?" she growled as the noise grew.

"Sorry, Commander, but it appears there was an attack on the Etoa

Shipyards."

"Who?"

"Seems to be the Sha. Reports say their ships are mobilizing to attack. They're lifting off from their three shipyards."

"What is the damage?"

"Eight ships were destroyed outright. Seven others were badly damaged. The shipyard is a wasteland. Thousands of clansmen were killed. Craftsmen are refusing to assist in working on the ships. The yard and the ships are feared lost."

The timing was too perfect. An attack on the same day the Willful Institute's ships were revealed and their elders started to show up dead? It was too much of a coincidence.

It has to be the Vuzgalians.

She debated telling Commander Chmilenko for the split second the thought entered her mind. No, that kind of information was best kept secret.

She indicated to one of her personal guards.

The guard walked into the sound canceling formation and dropped to one knee with his hands cupped.

"Get me a corvette sized phoenix breath weapon and enough mana stones for five shots. Take it to Gregor."

"Yes, Commander." The guard departed.

34

Seize the Route

Iva's totem was a hive of activity as people were ushered through quickly and efficiently. Gong Jin came through with the rest of the Special Teams.

Roska was there to meet them, waving them off to the side. "Get geared. We're under attack!"

The teams dropped their Seventh Realm gear, changing as she relayed to them everything that had happened since they blew up several BPC ships.

"Other sects?" Niemm asked.

"Nothing yet, but we should expect them soon. We're at full readiness. Bunkers are up and we're evacuating all Vermire citizens."

"So we're fully exposed?" Gong Jin asked, tying off his boot.

"Yup. They have also been busy bunnies. Built two dozen airships. We screwed them up, but nothing like what you guys did to the BPC," Roska said.

"How strong are we talking here?"

"They were all earth grade dungeon cores, smaller than the corvettes Erik and Rugrat got the plans for. Weaker, but more of them."

"What's the mission?" Yao Meng asked, slapping his carrier closed.

"Slow down the enemy. We're being given different areas. We move in, use the teleportation pads, disrupt the enemy, slow them down, give our people time to evacuate. Mess with the enemy as much as possible. Ready?"

Everyone pulled on the last of their gear. They had their railguns out, checking them.

"One ready," Niemm said.

"Three ready," Gong Jin reported.

"Four ready," Storbon sounded off.

"Five ready," Deni sounded off.

"Six ready," Tully said.

"Seven ready," Han Wu reported.

"Eight ready to rock," Yao Meng added.

"Okay, off we go!" Roska led them toward Alva's old entrance. They ran through the city. "Teleportation pads are taken up with the regs moving to the cities and bunkers. We're getting the air express!"

The streets were cleared of everyone but soldiers.

Roska led the teams to the elevators at the side of Alva. The elevators shot up, taking them above the city, but the trip took a while.

They passed several floors, arriving in the large air force hangar. The doors were open to the left, revealing the Beast Mountain Range.

Sparrows shot out of the opening, taking to the skies. Kestrels lay ready and waiting.

"This way!" a man yelled as he jogged out, leading them onto the flight deck where the kestrels were waiting.

"Each team gets a kestrel. Team One on the left. Team Eight on the right!"

"See you on the other side!" Gong Jin shouted. They raised their hands in farewell as the Special Teams split for their rides.

Gong Jin ran up the iron-plated wooden cargo hold of his kestrel.

Mercy saw the city of Zahir revealed as she and her force tore down the road connecting it to River Guard.

Zahir, once known as Chonglu, closed their gates; guards stepped up to their walls.

Mercy's army cleared the road, driving people off by force or leaving those too slow to make excuses to their gods.

The Willful Institute fighters spread out as they breached the farmlands around the city.

"Take them down! Leave none of them alive!" Mercy yelled.

The ground exploded under the riders. Arrows and spells fired from the walls. The First Realm attacks were nothing but inconveniences to them.

She slowed her pace. The mounted forces around her spread out, charging Zahir.

"Use your spell scrolls," Niklaus ordered from beside her.

Fighters thundered across the ground. Their spells rose to meet those that rained upon them.

Spells of the Fifth and Sixth Realm tore free of the ground, released by the heavens, smashing the city between them. With no barrier to protect against such carnage, attacks tore through the walls, blowing houses apart.

Mercy pulled out a spell scroll that caused the air to shift around it.

"Pull back from the walls!" Niklaus' voice came out in a rush, his veins throbbing in his neck as Mercy held out the spell scroll, aiming it over the city.

The fighters turned and started to come back, leaving the dead and wounded.

"Take them down. Kill them all!" Mercy yelled, tearing the spell scroll.

Shadow passed over the sky as spell formations appeared, unleashing flaming meteors that crashed through walls and houses, exploding into boiling stone.

Fires rose as the meteor rain increased, coming in faster and faster.

"Prepare to sally!" Mercy raised her whip. She would have her blood. For her uncle, she would claim a city and their people. *So weak and they think they can attack my clan!*

"Mercy," Niklaus hissed.

Mercy turned on him, her eyes wide and wild, drawing her whip to put him in his place at last.

"We have our orders from Elder Cai Bo. Push forward to Wild Reaches!" Niklaus reminded her.

Mercy stared at him, her hand tightening on her whip, tasting blood in her mouth from grinding her teeth. How badly she wished to leave a bloody line on that face, to feel the deep thrum of her heartbeat, the heady feelings of power over his powerlessness.

She snarled and tossed her head, easing her grip.

Niklaus turned in his saddle to the other leaders and the fighters.

"The city is won. The loot will be claimed later. Push forward and take the Wild Reaches Outpost!"

Trumpets called through the battlefield; the slaughter unfolded. The Willful Institute fighters turned into two arrows around Zahir and passed what remained of the city.

"What?" Delilah asked. Silence had fallen in the command center.

The aide gritted his teeth, resenting having to say it twice. "Zahir is gone. The Institute used spell scrolls. They breached the walls and hammered it with a Sixth or Seventh Realm spell scroll. They're going around it to Wild Reaches."

"Have Han Wu head them off. We need to slow them before they reach the trading outpost. The bunker line needs time to form. Have the sparrows move in support. We need to stop their head-long charge. What is the situation in the other cities? Are there other sects and groups appearing?" Glosil said.

"They are waiting and massing. They have taken over the cities completely and cleared the roads. There are no other sects at this time."

"I don't doubt there will be more in the future."

"Commander, what about Zahir?" Delilah asked.

"Zahir is gone. We have to push on," Glosil said.

Delilah felt her guts twist. "There were thousands of people in that city."

"I know, Council Leader, but they are dead. There is no bringing them back and we have hundreds of thousands to protect."

His words snapped her out of her thoughts and back to reality. *Did you think that because you were the leader of Alva that the realities of the Ten Realms somehow stopped?*

"We need to accelerate evacuations. I'll help there. Commander, do what you need to do."

She held his eyes, an understanding between them.

"I will protect Alva until my dying breath," Glosil nodded.

"As will I." Delilah shared in the nod.

They turned to their tasks.

The kestrel turned expertly. Han Wu looked outside. Forest opened to reveal artillery firing positions. King's Hill formation plates had been placed around the city and farmers were being herded into the city. Formations flashed in large squares as people were led away. Alvan soldiers, regular and reservists, marched through the streets.

The mountain had transformed. Cuts appeared on the surface to reveal the air force's bunkers as well as railgun cannon positions.

None of it was as clear as the bunker-line. The trees had been cleared over a three-hundred-meter-wide circling path that looped King's Hill.

Hills formed on one side of the line, bunkers piercing through, creating depth.

The Kestrel they were in shot across the forests, faster than the patrolling Sparrow wings that flitted over the Beast Mountain Range. They lost altitude for speed, coming in just a few meters above the trees, shaking them in their passage.

They passed over Wild Reaches. Like King's Hill, the outpost was revealing its true strength.

I just have to buy them enough time to defend themselves and pull back their people.

They cut an angle that allowed him to see the smoke on the horizon from Zahir. They passed defensive towers, built to connect and defend the Beast Mountain Range. The woods thinned as they passed to the civilized side of the mountain range.

Their speed cut expertly as they banked, the pilot guiding the Kestrel to lose speed as fast as they had gained it.

They turned, the pilot bringing them to a halt, holding the Kestrel facing the direction they had come from. It was still flapping as the rear ramp floated above the top of a hill.

The gunner moved to the side and waved him forward.

Han Wu got up and ran down, jumping from the ramp. He landed on his side, scanning as he slid down the hill. He came to a stop, pulling up his rifle up as he checked the area.

The rest of his ten-man team followed him, fanning out at the base of the hill.

The kestrel took off once the last man was out. Its wings beat on the forest, climbing higher and then away.

Han Wu checked his map. It didn't show any markings other than some random beasts in the area.

He checked the progress of Mercy's three hundred strong war band.

"Let's get going. We need to get ahead of that crazy bitch."

Han Wu and the team moved into the forest, heading for the first marker on their maps. They split into two groups of five as they reached the marker, a section of road.

"Egbert, trap formations, please." A flare of power appeared under the road and dissipated.

"Okay, traps are up and active! We have aerial and artillery support. We're just here to slow them the hell down, so get ready to move. If we're really in the shit, call Egbert. The whole of the Beast Mountain Range is his dungeon now."

They spread out on a forty-five from the road, using what cover they could find, pulling stealth tarps over themselves as they lay in wait.

"Captain Han Wu, this is Major Wazny. I'm your aerial support. You need us, just give me a call."

"Wazny, good to have some eyes in the sky. Could you be ready for a strafing and bomb run? I want them to walk into my traps dazed, dumb, and confused. Might not even realize me and my people are here."

"Be happy to do so. Tell me when and give me a map ping."

Han Wu sent him a ping.

"Got it."

"Now for the waiting game."

They didn't have to wait long.

"Aerial attackers!" a sect mage yelled.

Mercy sneered at the birds in the sky from between the trees gradually encroaching on the road.

"Check your barriers. Keep moving!" Niklaus yelled.

The birds came in low and fast, their twin weapons leaving deep pockmarks on the barrier's surface.

Spells appeared around the birds, trying to take them down. Metal cylinders fell from the birds, striking the barriers.

Trees were torn apart and scattered, clearing the forest and skyline.

Mercy had to fight to control her mount from the destruction.

A barrier failed under the bombs; several struck the ground. Mercy saw the white and red light, then shadows and blurry figures, the images burnt into her eyes.

She blinked it away as the explosions died off. She turned to where she had been facing; craters pockmarked the ground, a chaotic path.

"They're coming back around!" another soldier yelled.

"Beware of the aerial forces. Report their presence to the forces behind us!" Niklaus ordered one of his aides.

"Let's go!"

They charged forward as another wing of aerial attackers appeared. The first group of Willful Institute fighters were washed away by an attack under their feet, taking out their barrier.

"Traps!" Mercy heard Niklaus shouting, rearing her mount as others surged ahead.

Explosions rained from above and spells from below.

Mercy saw flashes in the forest as her guards hauled her along.

35

In Distant Realms

n the Fourth Realm, several elders of powerful sects and sect leaders of weaker sects ate and drank jovially in a grand hall. The hall spilled out into an overly large balcony overseeing one of the largest cities reclaimed by the sect's alliance.

The small talk rose again among sect leadership as High Elder Hao of the Willful Institute reported on the events in Vermire, the hiding place of the Vuzgalians.

"In the First Realm? Are you sure, Hao?" one of the sect leaders said.

"It is highly unusual, but who would think that a sect in the Fourth Realm would sink so low as to hide in the First Realm? It was why it has taken us so long to find out where the Vuzgalians retreated to," Hao hissed, allowing frustration to flavor his words.

"Where you lead, the Stone Fist Sect will follow, Elder Hao," Elder Elsi said.

"Thank you, Elder Elsi." Hao inclined his head.

"A force in the First Realm. Do you think that they will be that much trouble? They have fallen this far." Another elder laughed and shook his hand. "My forces are ready!"

"They are slippery eels, and you can see how they attacked our elders even while in hiding. I fear they might have plans for your sects as well," Hao lamented.

The sect elders hid their displeasure at his veiled threat.

"I hear that it was the Blue Blossom Sect that did that. I heard that they found some interesting prizes from the Black Phoenix Clan. We are all brotherly allies here. Should we not share in the rewards as well as the costs?" A young elder smiled.

Hao's grimace didn't have time to form. It spread into a grin as he held out his hands to embrace the sect's representatives in front of him. "Captain Stassov bestowed a great gift upon my sect. It is true. We cannot share it with others, but we have been training night and day and have finally learned enough to convert your dungeons to cultivation dungeons. No longer will you need to hunt the beasts inside. You can absorb the mana that is refined there to increase your cultivation and the cultivation of your sect members with pure mana. It will allow you to increase your cultivation speed by ten, or even twenty times!"

Hao raised his glass to the other elders. They smiled and raised their glasses.

"Let us remove this thorn in our side and bring about a great change in the Ten Realms. With the sects gathered here, we can change the face of the lower realms and reach the higher realms together!"

The elders agreed with their voices, but their eyes were cold.

A group of vipers, but all I need are their fighters.

Hao moved to the side, Elsi trailing him.

"About that other matter," Hao said to Elsi, using mana so only the other elder could hear him. "I have talked with Elder Cai Bo, and she believes if you can assist her in some matters, she will not only draw in the Stone Fist Sect to the Willful Institute but cement the bonds of the Elsi Clan and the Hao Clan as one of the strongest clans within the Willful Institute."

"Elder Hao." Elsi smiled.

"We are staunch allies. Should we not show the rest of the realms that we stand united?" Hao smiled.

"I couldn't agree more, and please tell Head Cai Bo that I am willing to help her in whatever capacity she requires. You will forever be my elder in my eyes, Elder Hao." Elsi cupped his hands in salute.

The airship warehouse disappeared around Erik, Rugrat and George as they were plunged into darkness.

"George, light," Erik said.

George grew brighter, revealing a cracked, worn stone floor. Water dripped in the distance and there was a sound like cracking icebergs, but deeper and sharper.

"Luminous Ball," Rugrat said, tearing a spell scroll and storing Ubren's pendant.

The ball reached up to the ceiling as Erik saw what was making the noise.

Stone Golems walked out from the wall, cracking away from their resting places.

Erik fired on one. It collapsed as he stepped forward. Rugrat shot behind him.

"Stone golems here!" Erik yelled, back-to-back with Rugrat.

"Same here!" Rugrat's fire spears heated Erik's back as they were cast, ending in cracking explosions in the distance.

He downed his third golem when the first started to reform.

"It's putting itself back together!" Erik said.

"You need to take out the formation core in its chest. Otherwise, it'll repair itself! Grenade out!"

Erik felt the grenade explode at the edge of his domain range. The mana energies in the room increased as stone golems dropped from the ceiling or clambered from the ground and walls.

He fired into a stone golem standing up. His rounds shredded stone, carving a line through them. The golem was unaffected by the attacks.

"Sky Stone. Good thing I'm Sky Iron." Erik threw his rifle into his storage ring and drew in the power from his surroundings. Elements surged into his body, through his veins.

He opened his eyes, passing through the darkness without needing the illumination spell. He sensed mana. He sensed the elements, and he resonated with them.

His skin cracked and broke, turning as black as charcoal. Stone protrusions cracked along his joints and magma flowed through his veins.

The elements in Erik's body cried out, elements and mana circulating as one source through his being.

Erik flashed toward the enemy. Cracks of explosions powered him as he used an old technique, but one that had never failed him. Power fed through his body, into his fist.

The stone golem's hands smacked him from either side. They shattered as Erik's fist struck. It was like a cannonball had shot through the golem. Stone shards spewed out the back of the golem, revealing a small glowing formation.

Erik fired a mana blast from his hand, hitting the formation, destroying it, and sending out ripples of mana that blasted two other golems to the side, missing parts of their bodies.

Rugrat shot a Golem closing in on Erik. Striking the formation with pin-point accuracy released the contained mana, causing it to shatter.

"Once you know where the formation is, it's a lot easier to deal with!"

George's breath melted the stone. A swipe from his paw removed the formation cores and destroyed them.

Erik flashed forward. The stone of the golem opened around his hand, revealing his core. Erik tore it out, throwing it and shooting it with a mana bullet. The core exploded, taking down two more golems.

Erik ran into the melee. Attacks hit his armor and his body, cutting and bruising him, but his regeneration kept up as he forged on.

A golem stomped on the floor. A pillar shot out, hitting Erik. He caught himself in the air. Flames danced around him as he reached out. Stone shot up and into his hand. Magma traced up the forming handle and into the spear as he adjusted it, landing and throwing in one motion.

The spear passed through two stone golems, shattering and scattering them.

Erik pulled out a potion, drinking it.

Elements' Rage
Increased attack power of all elemental spells by 12%

Erik reached out, running forward. Stone shards raised from the floor to his hands, forming twin hammers.

A golem threw his hand at Erik, turning it into stone needles.

Erik's hammer formed into a shield, ringing with impacts. He stepped to his right. Stone jutted out. It shot out as he jumped to the left, dodging around another golem that was shredded with the needles. Erik hit the ground. A spear of stone and flame rose from the ground, piercing the golem's formation core.

Erik's shield turned into a hammer once again. He jumped up and over the forward golems and toward the ranks of golems behind them.

He smashed his fist into the ground. A crater rippled out, transforming into stone spears and impaling the nearby golems.

Erik threw his hammer. The hammer head shredded away to reveal a stake which stabbed into the golem that had been shooting him with stone shards. The spears around Erik exploded, destroying the formations, creating a wave of explosions that cleared the area.

Erik created another hammer in his hand, his head swiveling to find a new golem.

"Think that's all of them." Rugrat walked over with George.

Erik saw dozens of magical chain-pierced golems behind Rugrat's back.

They showered the ground with shards of stone.

"Easier to let the magic do the work for you, huh?" Rugrat grinned.

"The hell is this place?" Erik used a night vision spell, seeing through the darkness.

"Not sure, but I'm interested in what's behind that gate."

They were in a roughly square area about a hundred meters in every direction. The teleportation formation was at the back rear wall in the center. Ahead, there was a gate made of iron.

Erik released his hammers. They let off smoke as they cracked the ground.

The gate showed several formations that needed to be turned to the right position to allow entry.

"Rugrat?" Erik pointed to them.

"Give me a second." Rugrat put his hand to the metal.

"Oh, this is tricky. Resists my scan." Rugrat tapped the gate in different places, walking around. "This is like one of those Japanese puzzle boxes. You turn one thing, press another thing, then pull another. Complicated."

Erik moved to the walls around it, using his elemental resonance with the material.

"Well, when the gate is too strong, why not test the wall?"

Erik channeled into the wall. Energy rolled from his body as the wall shook, sky stone shifting into a tunnel.

He broke down the stone, compressed it and fused it.

He felt the air on the other side releasing, stale and old.

"One entrance." Erik waved to the tunnel. He wiped his brow.

"You know I could have figured it out," Rugrat muttered.

"This was easier and has less chance of something trying to kill us."

Erik pulled out his rifle, reloaded, and took point. Rugrat and George followed him.

The tunnel opened into the back of a rack of supplies. Erik kicked the storage crates out of the way and smashed through the shelves.

He shrugged off the dust, walking into the storage room.

"Well, hot damn," Rugrat said.

Erik whistled. The room was twenty meters by twenty, but it was filled with storage crates stacked on shelves up the wall and several shelving units that ran down the length of the room.

"Okay, let's get an inventory and get a teleportation formation down. You want to check the walls, see if there is anything hidden in here, and check around the room with the golems?"

"You think?" Rugrat asked.

"Not sure, but she hid this cache in the shipyard. If I were her, I'd have multiple caches so if anything happened, I'd still be able to get something."

"They're going to freak in Alva with all of these supplies. Should be able to arm and armor everyone with gear made from sky iron."

Erik saw his blinking notifications and accessed it.

Skill: Healer
Level:118 (Master)
You are a Master on the human body and the arts of repairing it. Healing spells now cost 20% less Mana and Stamina. Patient's stamina is used an additional 30% less.

116,928,732,843/128,249,000,000 EXP till you reach Level 86

36

Arrival of the Sects

Egbert stood on the highest mountain of the Beast Mountain Range, overlooking Alva. To the south was King's Hill. To the east lay the Wild Reaches Trading outpost and Zahir.

Egbert surveyed the land covered in sprawling forests.

The outposts stood out among the trees, civilization finding their way. Roads cut through the forests, connecting them.

Beyond the Beast Mountain Range lay the flatlands, the plains. Blocks of forest and farmland butted up against one another, villages dotted amongst.

The cities lay beyond the plains. Egbert could feel them, the dungeon reaching to encompass the entire Vermire Empire.

"A lot has happened in the last few years," Egbert said to Davin, who was floating in the air beside him.

"Lots of pies and treats," Davin said.

Egbert laughed, but it was short-lived. He turned again to the east, to the invaders, the dagger that stabbed into Alva's heart.

Dungeon cores linked the entire area. To Egbert, the Vermire Empire was his domain. Nothing moved without his knowledge.

He saw Han Wu and Gong Jin's teams as they fought in the forests. The Institute fighters pushed ahead, using spell scrolls that tore through the forests and lit up the skies, trying to deter the Alva Air Force as they peppered their mana barriers and dropped bombs that caused the trees to shake and the ground to tremble.

Egbert felt spells complete as he switched his view. He scanned across the Wild Reaches Outpost. Soldiers wearing the armor of the Vermire Empire mustered on the walls. Groups moved from house to house, making sure no one was left behind. Families gathered their belongings, hurried to tunnels and teleportation formations underneath the city.

Bunkers had risen around the outpost, dirt and stone falling from their flat roofs.

Open market squares were turned into artillery positions.

The fountain in the middle of the city had been removed, replaced with a stack enhancing formation plate and stack formations.

Egbert's vision pulled back farther, along the road that pierced through the wilderness connecting the outpost to King's Hill.

Tree lines had been cleared and bunkers stood in clumps, covering one another and creating a defensive network in the middle of the Beast Mountain Range.

Egbert checked the bunkers as he felt the mountain shift.

Spells opened stone as artillery cannons and the newer rail-cannons shifted forward into position.

"Activating mountain formations," Egbert reported to the Alva command center.

The formations through the mountain he stood upon activated.

A mana barrier spread from the mountain, reaching out. Sheets of mana barriers illuminated the sky, stretching upward from the bunker line, from King's Hill, from several smaller mountains. Several barriers connected to one another, with larger ones encompassing them, creating depth and of barriers that encompassed kilometers.

"Beast Mountain Range Barrier is active," Egbert said.

He felt a disturbance at the edge of his reach. "I have several armies moving toward the Empire's outer cities and tower line."

Egbert's vision changed. He looked at the gathered armies on the march. "They are made up of several sects."

He gripped his fist. Runes covered his body, each glowing brilliantly. His bones had gone from yellow to brilliant white, the power of the dungeon core and pure mana cleansing his body, empowering him.

They marched in blocks numbering in the thousands, filled with their strongest warriors and fighters. The sects had come to wipe away the stain on their honor. The Beast Mountain Range was a large place, and they had come with ample forces to lay siege.

Aerial beasts swirled above like vultures over carrion.

"Hundreds of thousands march," Davin said.

"Do not discount our own forces. We have one hundred thousand regular soldiers, twenty thousand in the air force, and another two hundred thousand in the reserve forces. It has been a long time since such armies have clashed."

"Not including the Adventurer's Guild."

"Or discounting that we have been working on our defenses here for years and concentrated our efforts in a way that we could have never done in Vuzgal."

"But they learned our weapons and tactics there." Davin cocked his head to the side.

"Even if you know the weapons your enemy uses, it doesn't mean that you will be able to beat them." Egbert swiveled his head from the black tendrils reaching toward the Beast Mountain Range.

"They have entered the Empire." Davin pointed.

Egbert followed his mottled red arm, seeing the armies spreading out as they reached the outer towers and cities that ringed Vermire Empire.

Egbert's vision swam as he looked closer, spells aiding his sight. Alvan Artillery and mortar batteries were being set up in farmer's fields, many kilometers away from the cities. Alvan soldiers filled the walls and the towers that created a linked outer defense.

The towers lay along a ring road that encompassed the entirety of the Vermire Empire. If one had been to Vuzgal, they might notice a similar design as they acted as barrier cornerstones. They had one central commanding tower and five surrounding towers that sprouted from the wall. Now, bunkers appeared at the bases of these walls and instead of archers, machine gunners stood at the archer slits.

Simple, but they will exact a bloody toll from any that wish to pass.

"War comes to the First Realm once again." Egbert reached up, pressing his robe against his chest, feeling the dungeon core and mana stones that had grown like ice through his bones. He felt his dungeon core resonate with the other Alvan dungeon cores. His eye flames turned green as he saw more than the forests, fields, and mountains. He saw the dungeon cores, the formations that had been carved into the very ground. It turned all of the Vermire Empire into one formation, controlled by the hundreds of dungeon cores dotted around, centered on Alva that glowed with power.

"Make a hole!" Acosta yelled as she walked through the tower. Soldiers moved to the side as she walked past, continuing to hurry to their positions. The bunkers had been raised and were manned. Mobile mortar launchers on gnome machines had been deployed back from their position, guns grounded and elevated to bear.

The United Sect Alliance will be here any minute.

She made it into the tunnels before an alarm rang through the compound.

"The alliance has been spotted. Make ready your positions. Clear command channels." Captain Acosta's voice rang through the compound.

Acosta ran, reaching her command bunker. The door sealed behind her and locked. *We've got too much to cover with not enough people.* The plan was a simple. They wouldn't be able to hold the cities or the outer towers indefinitely, so they would hold and defend for as long as possible to get their people out and slow the enemy. Then, they would abandon both, and fall back to the next line of towers, then to the outposts, then to the bunker-line before King's Hill and Alva. There they would have the numbers and density on their side to hold.

She used the periscope, locking onto the United Sect Alliance forces that rushed down the road toward the towers.

Spells barely left scorch marks where they hit the mana barriers. A river of humanity spread through the forests. Her attention tore toward rippling trap spells cutting through sects riding up the road. Flashes landed among trees, mortars and artillery shells meeting sect fighters in a rain of metal.

Sects reached the range of their guns. Machine guns and rifles hit barriers like grit being tossed into water, creating ripples. They didn't penetrate, but were adding color to the barriers at an alarming rate.

"Artillery is shifting fire to cover our flanks," a sergeant called out.

Acosta turned, watching the wall of artillery fire that played out between them and the next tower. It was thin and sporadic, but the sects charged through the sporadic fire.

"Damn them!" Acosta gritted her teeth. Their powerful barriers were protecting the sect riders above and below. "Clear our damn skies!"

Acosta checked her maps. The sects had spread out and pushed for any possible opening, not looking to engage but to drive forward into the heart of the Beast Mountain Range.

The first groups made it past the towers on speedy steeds. Weapons fire traced around them, sparking barriers, but it wasn't enough to kill them all.

Tombstones dotted the ground, but it didn't stop Acosta cursing under her breath.

Lukas heard the marching of soldiers and baying of trumpets across the silent walls of Shida. The city was draining of people, heading underground.

"Seems that they've come," observed Badowska.

"We'll just have to send them back disappointed." Lukas watched as trees parted and fell, revealing the sects that had widened the road for their army's passage.

They marched forward over the surrounding farms of Shida, an indomitable force.

"Ready yourselves!" Lukas yelled through his sound transmission device. "Mages, artillery, prepare to fire on my command."

"Yes, sir," officers from the Vermire and Alva army reported together.

"Now the die is cast. We can only see what happens," Lukas said.

The advancing army, filled with mixed sects, each created their own square of fighters, expanded to cover the front of Shida.

Lukas watched a farmhouse, his marker, studying the armies as they approached. Spells lashed out, destroying small picket fences. A blast of water magic struck the farmhouse, causing it to spew forth in stone, wood, and straw.

The debris hit the ground, sucked into the dirt with spells until there was nothing in the way.

Casual strikes cleared the fields of crops, crushing them and turning them into paste at the feet of the oncoming army.

Lukas scanned the advancing line, feeling the wire of tension running through his people. Nagging worries plagued his head, and he focused on the farmhouse.

A warrior with a hammer yelled, half jogging two steps forward.

White air elements gathered around his body, creating a fog focused on his hammer as his steps carried him farther before he struck out.

The air shattered in a wave of force, tens of meters away from the farmhouse. Straw was stripped from the roof, the walls caving inwards as the structure shifted to the side and lost its hold upon the ground, spraying across the fields.

The warrior laughed and looked at his fellows, who grinned and taunted.

Lukas' fists curled, turning white before he forced them open, his lips slowly parting into a wolf's smile.

Silently he waited, watching. The first boot landed on the barest outline of stone and wood where the farmhouse had lain, dirtying it with mud.

Others stepped upon the farm's foundations.

Blasts of magic cleared their path through debris. Lukas didn't flinch.

"Sir?" Badowska whispered.

"Hold." Lukas' word lingered, his hand reaching out to the side.

He looked at his opponents, at their layout.

He grabbed a nearby Alvan man and brought him close, his arm across his shoulders as his left pointed forward.

"You see that group there, the ones on the mounts studying our walls?"

"The one on the tiger mount with blued armor and green fabric?"

"He's your target."

He moved down to the next soldier.

"See that man there with the white hair, black and silver robes standing near that man with the sect emblem?"

"Yes, sir."

"He's yours."

Lukas identified several groups and people, giving each of his best shooters targets. He closed his eyes, recalling the battlefield in his mind.

The forward observer spoke to the other observers, relaying orders to the artillery crews.

"Sir, we're set."

He opened his eyes and breathed in deeply, checking the ranges by eye.

"All units, prepare yourselves! Artillery, open their barriers! Fire!"

Lukas swore he could feel the artillery cannons thumping across the city.

Vrrshhzzroom. Shells pass overhead. Many in the armies looked up in search of the sound.

"Hold, wait for it," Lukas growled, affixed to the scene in front of him.

Barriers flashed into existence as the shells struck, piercing through.

The shells exploded above the armies. Scathing iron rain tore through their ranks, killing and wounding hundreds.

"Mortars, fire. Machine guns, fire!"

Those around the scene of destruction paused, but those at the front only increased their pace, ramping up into a jog. Formation squares merged, turning into a black tide with flashes of iron as they ascended the hill Shida rested upon.

Their forward lines were greeted with tracer fire, creating long whips as they traversed from left to right.

Mortar rounds popped off in mid-air, flattening those below as if stomped on by God's foot.

Some mana barriers popped up. Artillery cannons rotated on to position and fired, tearing through the mana barriers and those underneath.

Mana cannon crews pulled out their weapons and fired on Shida's mana barrier.

Machine guns converged, shifting their fire over.

The combined sect army was too large for the guns and mortars to kill them all. They rushed toward the bunkers into the teeth of the Vermire Army's repeaters. They didn't have the range or lethality of the machine gun, but they made up for it in their weight of fire.

Lukas watched the battle, pulling in the forward observer.

"Get me that one!" He pointed at a group flashing their flags. "Priority target for anyone with flags or instruments!"

"Sir," the observer called out his orders.

"Badowska, have the right and left flank ready for spill over."

"Yes, sir."

Lukas stood there, studying his opponent.

"Egbert, are we able to activate the trap formations yet?"

"Not yet, sir. The other sect armies are just starting to engage the other outer cities."

"What is the situation at the towers?"

"Glosil is preparing to collapse in the forces at the towers."

"Understood. Inform the commander that Shida will hold the sects here."

"Activation of debuffing formations in ten seconds."

Lukas studied the forces that were pushing into the teeth of the repeaters and the bunker's defenses, reaching the archers.

"All mages, stand ready. Prepare spell scrolls!"

Mages stepped onto the casting balconies across Shida's walls. Enhancing formations glowed under their feet, filling them with power. The air around them shimmered with power, moving with them.

"Debuffing formations active!" Egbert said.

Lukas saw lines of power visible through hundreds of meters of stone and dirt. It ran around the border of Shida, extending forward like galloping horses, zig zagging and creating runes as it surged down the hill and across the farmland, under the feet of the sect armies, and into the forests beyond.

The sect army stumbled, finding their stats reduced by thirty percent in the blink of an eye.

"Mages, attack!"

Spell formations snapped into existence along the wall. Energies gathered, altered, and discharged.

The walls roared with lion roars of flame as they crackled overhead, leaving a wash of heat that dried sweat and stung the eyes.

Lukas breathed in hot air as the fireballs added their destructive might to the tapestry of attacks.

Mages on the opposing sides cast counter-spells, destroying the fireballs in mid-flight.

Spell formations appeared in the skies above the battlefield, the Alvan mages working in concert.

Lightning struck the ground, creating an arcing river of silver spreading like roots of a tree through the sects' ranks.

Spell formations appeared above Shida, striking their mana barrier.

Mana cannons fired from extreme range, shooting mana bolts. Spears of blue light flashed and spread across the barrier with a hammer's thunder.

Illusions appeared in front of the bunkers, confusing the eyes and obscuring the gunners' views.

"Have the mages on the walls guide the fighters in the bunkers and remove those illusion spells!" Lukas barked.

Smoke and fire appeared on the battlefield as crops sparked alight.

"Check our supplies. Make sure that those guns don't run dry. We hold them here."

Aboard *Perseverance*, the command center was a hive of activity.

Crafters moved out of Gregor and his hunters' way.

"Leave." Gregor said.

The crafters looked at one another before evacuating the command center.

Hunters closed the doors and Gregor stepped forward with several others. They opened a panel in the front of the bridge and dropped into the empty space underneath.

Gregor pulled out components of the Phoenix Breath cannon. He and his hunters worked silently in the hidden depths of the ship, assembling the cannon that ran through the heart of the warship.

It didn't take long for them to assemble the cannon. Gregor climbed out. A hunter that had remained in the bridge stepped forward.

"Asadi wishes to report on the happenings at Vermire."

Gregor's upper lip lifted in a snarl. He turned away and looked at the different formations displaying the outside of the warship that had come out relatively undamaged from the raid. "What of the other warships?"

"Seven others will be capable of fighting. They will need another day before they are completely ready."

"Tell Asadi we will move in one day. Have him send Cai Bo to report what is happening in the First Realm. Invite the sect elders to the different ships they will man."

"Sir." There was a note of disapproval in the man's voice.

"Do not worry. They are a sect. Even our clan does not reveal all of our secrets to one another. People who are in power in a sect are not going to want to reveal secrets that beget them power. Then they will be wise enough to not share with others, unlike youngsters and braggarts. Invite Asadi to board the ship in four hours." Gregor turned his attention to the dungeon core held above the command chair in the rear of the bridge.

The bridge, like the ship, was small and cramped, and built for one purpose—to take a beating and keep fighting. It was built to defeat Vuzgalians.

Mercy's mount reared as another trap went off nearby. She smacked the beast relentlessly with the side of her whip, cutting its white fur.

"You will calm yourself or I will end you," she hissed into the ear of the beast, her hand twisting the reins.

The beast cowered in fear, dropping its wide eyes down as explosions tore through another mana barrier, killing dozens.

"Marco orders us to reinforce Zahir to the West just outside of Vermire," Niklaus yelled.

Mercy saw several fighters charging ahead crumple. She fired out a spell with other mages into the forest, trying to catch the hidden force that had thinned their ranks.

She ground her teeth, following Marco's orders. He was no older than her, but he commanded the army, while she commanded just part of the vanguard.

"Pull back!" She grumbled.

Niklaus wheeled his mount around. He rode through the ranks, whistling as he rode. The whistling spread through the ranks.

Mercy and her force pushed to return. Her guards forced fighters out of the way with their mounts.

The tide of fighters shifted, turning away. She heard an odd whistle. She caught a glimpse of Niklaus as the ground around him and his guards was thrown up and bloody holes punched through their group, taking out the mounts and the soldiers.

Niklaus and his mount fell in the dust.

She looked away, kicking her mount forward, through the soldiers, not caring if they got out of the way fast enough or fell to her beast's hooves.

"Faster!" she yelled to her guards. The force broke, fleeing back to Zahir.

The sound of cannons and machine guns filled the air around her tower, taking the reaper's harvest of the sect's advanced raiders that passed her position.

The last of the guns fell silent. Tracers hit the dirt around the fleeing attackers, beyond their range and heading for the Outposts.

"This is Commander Glosil. All towers prepare for immediate movement back to second line. I say again, all towers prepare to pull back."

Acosta grabbed a sound transmission device to talk to her people in the tower. "Secure your shit. Prepare to move in thirty seconds!"

Casings were cleared, ammunition and smoking barrels replaced.

In the distance, Acosta could see their group of minders watching them, just out of range. They were meant to pin them into their tower so they couldn't break out.

We've been planning to defend Alva ever since we moved in.

"Everyone ready!" Sirel reported.

"And in only twenty seconds. Looks like that training is paying off!" Acosta pulled the sound transmission to her and held onto a nearby grab bar.

"Pullback underway!" Acosta reported and signaled to an aide.

Acosta's stomach lurched as the tower compound, associated bunkers, and wall dropped underground.

She caught the look of surprise on the watchers' faces as the ground sealed above the compound.

They stopped. The roots of the buildings and the bunkers were all on one solid stone and metal sheet that fused with a platform beneath.

"Hold on!" The aide sounded a little too excited, in Acosta's opinion.

Acosta moved with the sudden acceleration along formation lines.

Stone and dirt parted ahead of them and closed behind them like they were inside a cresting wave.

Their acceleration slowed and stopped with a jolt.

"Stand to! Check your maps for enemy disposition!" Sirel barked as the defensive shrouds opened and weapons extended outwards, now kilometers ahead of the raiders that had made it past their first position.

Acosta checked the updating map, showing the towers in their new positions, creating a denser defensive line.

"Ascending!" the aide said as they rose through the ground. The sky appeared above them again as they locked into place.

They tore through the ground to the surprise of the United Sect Alliance.

"Fire at targets as they appear!" Acosta yelled, feeling the tower compound's guns rumble in her bones.

Cannons and mortars fired into the sky as machine guns scanned the area.

Welcome to Alva, you fucks.

Glosil walked around the map. People moved between stations, connecting him to every leader across the entire battlefield.

His eyes flashed between points, soaking in all the information.

The towers had been bypassed with the United Sect Alliance using teleportation formations, bringing in reinforcements to keep their momentum.

"Estimates have it at two hundred thousand sect fighters. They haven't brought any of their supply train. They're fighting and using the supplies they brought," Elan said.

"Less chance for us to break their supply lines as we did in the Fourth Realm. Don't have to slow down or deal with their hangers on." *Not like they can't carry most of their supplies in their storage devices.*

"They stopped all the battles in the other realms that they were engaged in."

"Well, it's good to know that they care about us so much," Glosil said dryly, pausing in his walking and standing next to the map with his hands interlinked behind his back.

"Are our formations ready?"

"Not yet. They take a lot of power and have minimal effects. Mana gathering formations are active, which should cause them enough problems. Hold off for now. We need to conserve our power."

Elan listened to his sound transmission device. "Blaze sent a report. The Adventurer's Guild are gathering their forces."

"I don't want them to attack until the united sects are committed. We must end this here or it will never end. I want them to split into three forces: one in the northeast, one in the northwest, and the last in the south. What is the status of the Dragon Corps?"

"Lieutenant General Domonos reports that the Dragon Corps are deployed and ready in the bunkers."

"Tigers?"

"Broken into company units as you ordered, and ready and waiting at preset deployment locations. They await your command."

Glosil rested his elbows on the table, holding his left hand with his right, supporting his chin. He was transfixed by the markers of the Tiger Corps' companies dotted around the Vermire empire and the sect forces around them.

"Whoever led this attack didn't want any fuckups. Push us hard and move aggressively to get down teleportation pads to leapfrog forces forward. Speaks to Marcos' tactics." Glosil shook his head. "And what is it that the Willful Institute has that the other sects don't, Kanoa?"

"The dungeon cores?"

"Yes, but more importantly, they have fought us before and have a better idea of our capabilities." Glosil rested his hands on the table. "They're trying to put us on the back foot from the start. If they think of us like the Sha, then they think that we have supply issues. Could that be their strategy?"

"What?" Kanoa asked, finding it hard to keep up with Glosil's rapid thoughts.

"Trade the lives of their lower-level soldiers to deplete our resources and engage us directly with their strongest forces."

A chill settled in the room as people stilled around the table.

"You think?" Elan asked.

"Was it not you that reported that the Willful Institute think our fighters are on a lower tier than theirs?" Glosil stalked the table, his eyes latching onto Elan.

"Yes, but—"

"We must remove the lens of Alva from our minds and look at this as sects! Power of the highest ranks matters more than the power of a thousand at the lowest! The Willful Institute, how rapidly have they increased in size since Vuzgal? How many thousands have joined their banner? How many mouths must they feed? How many resources must they fork over? What is the use of these sect members if not to clear the path of their seniors whose loyalties are secured, their families generationally integrated with the sect?"

"So they're using this as an opportunity to thin down the number of people in their sect?" Kanoa asked.

"The machinations of sects are complicated and messy. This is a war for us, but a show for others. They cannot back down; they cannot lose. If they do, then they enter a path of decline. Now the battle is joined, and the sects have entered. Even if in a token force, they must send over more as we are a true opponent. Even if we fall, we threaten their rule, their stability."

"They have to clear the stain upon their honor."

"And we will entice them. We'll draw them in." Glosil's words sent a stir through the command room.

"Sir, what do you mean?"

"This is not just a war. This is an opportunity, Kanoa." Glosil looked over the map again. "They came to our backyard and expect that, because of a stain on their pride, we should roll over and die for them." Glosil chuckled, a wolf's smile spreading. "They think this is a small outpost. A place we have taken refuge. They do not know it is our true home, the heart of our power. No, we will draw and lure. We will fight and withdraw. We can lose the towers. We can lose the cities, the plains, the forests. Our power doesn't come from the land we own. It comes from our people. As our people grow, we grow. Here, today. We make a stand to say that we stand together stronger than any sect."

Glosil looked up, his expression solemn, his eyes sparking with brilliance. "We break them here. We break their main army in the First Realm. The United Sect Alliance will collapse. Have Lieutenant General Domonos take control over the Wild Reaches Trading Outpost personally. That is where they will hit again. They've driven a wedge. They'll want to see how far it goes. For today, they attack Alva, and we will make them pay a bloody price for stepping upon our lands!" He grew quiet, all drawn in. "For tomorrow, our children might live upon them. Have the forces in the first tower line pull back to the second line. We can't let them gather to push our weaknesses. Send a message to Yui. If he sees an opportunity for a counterattack, he is to act upon it at his own discretion."

37
Long Game

ai Bo walked beside Head Asadi as they boarded *Perseverance* with a collection of elders and his personal guards. It was the largest ship within the berths, an ugly beast made of metal sheeting like a patchwork-quilt. Sections were blackened by the damage from the earlier raid.

Crafters rushed across the ship, creating the necessary components to speed up the ship's completion.

The bridge was in the center of the largest corvette, nearly the full size of a proper corvette. Every creature comfort had been pulled out for more armor, bigger mana barrier formations, and mana cannons. Seer formations were active, showing the focused activity within the shipyard. Entire sections from scrapped corvettes were being cut out and placed on the new corvettes to speed up completion.

In the middle of *Perseverance's* bridge, Gregor stood with his hunters around the dungeon core.

Stations around the dungeon core spread out into five sections, each with different roles on the ship, and also the ground, aerial, and sect communication areas. They were each manned by proud elders of the leading clans.

Cai Bo checked the reports from a messenger.

She walked to Sect Head Asadi. He stood at the map table but turned toward Gregor, who was talking with his hunters inside the magical formations under the dungeon core.

Head Asadi turned from admiring the dungeon core as she approached. "Ah, Cai Bo. What news?"

"The united armies have reached the Vermire Empire outer cities, circling around them in places." She touched a map to the map table, updating its information.

"Ah, the bunkers of Vuzgal. You have done well in tracking them down." Asadi turned to Elder Yasin.

"And these locations?" Gregor said, joining the table and pointing.

"They have set up a number of defenses. They have a defensive circle of towers that connect the cities, another that connects the outposts. Marco's first move was to rush the towers and pass them. We have teleportation formations inside their outer ring of defenses. Forces are massing for attacks on the outposts and secondary towers. A force from River Guard penetrated through Zahir city, opening a line of advance to the outpost line, clear of towers." Cai Bo traced out the corridor. "The Vuzgalians are focusing their aerial forces there to stop our advance. With the combined pressure along their lines, they are being forced to consolidate."

"Teleportation pads?" Gregor said.

"It appears so," Cai Bo said.

"Striking them with our mobile forces without a supply train and teleportation pads should prevent them disabling our rear," Asadi said. "We will press them on every front. They only have fighters from the First Realm and the people that escaped from the Fourth Realm."

"Don't look down on them. They're stronger than most forces in the Sixth Realm." Gregor stared at the table, unconsciously stretching his spear hand.

Asadi nodded, but didn't comment.

"We will be ready soon," Gregor said, and turned from the table.

"Cai Bo." Asadi kept her close as the other elders returned to their jobs.

"Head Asadi?"

"The faster we can drive into the heart of these Vuzgalians defenses, the better. We need to keep them on their heels. Once our forces are gathered, drive them forward into the second line as fast as possible. Once we have a breach, keep pushing with the formations. Make sure that Marco doesn't fail."

"Yes, Head Asadi. I will pass along your orders."

He nodded and waved her off.

She moved to a station that was to be hers and sent sound transmissions, sending out orders and gathering information.

38

Fleeting Shadows

ll of the tower's forces have pulled back to the outpost line," Badowska said.

Attacks crashed against the city barrier, washing out what Lukas was trying to say. He looked at the walls. Undead under the command of Vermire Army—the new name for the Beast Mountain range Army—more than quadrupled the soldiers on the walls.

Artillery cannons and mortars peppered the advancing Sects forces.

They brought stronger barriers.

The wall of sound washed over them.

"Pan Kun ordered us to remain as a thorn in their side unless something changes."

"So, dig in and hold. We can do that." Badowska's face split in a savage grin.

"All right, have our people pull back as well. We don't have the numbers to defend against an attack from every direction," Lukas said as attacks dashed against the city's mana barrier.

"Sir," an aide acknowledged.

Lukas paused. Shida had only grown since becoming part of the Vermire Empire.

There were no Beast Mountain or Vermire soldiers in Shida anymore. They had all been pressed into the Alvan army, a single army.

Finally, Alva has been revealed. Lukas looked beyond the walls, seeing the spells crash against his barriers.

The Sects used long range spells and cannons to cover their advance. Mana barriers were a thin cover against the reply of Alvan artillery.

"Aerials!" someone yelled.

The sky lit up with tracers arcing into the dark of night to meet Shida's greatest foe. Aerial fighters.

The sky blossomed with flak rounds to meet the fliers as they dove through the city's mana barrier, tearing their spell scrolls as fast as possible. The spells tore up the city indiscriminately.

Lukas raised his arm against the lightshow.

The fliers cut out over the ground, fleeing the enraged Shida.

"Get me a damage report. Make sure that we rotate units on and off the line. Morning is not long off. I know they have the cultivation, but I want them mentally alert for what is to come."

"Sir!" Badowska agreed.

A new day. Lukas moved to the reports that littered the desk. He passed over them to look at the map showing the full united sect force in all its glory.

"They came with enough, five hundred thousand to seven hundred and fifty thousand." Speaking the number out loud, he couldn't comprehend it. It sent a shiver down his spine. It was as if they were not just holding back fighters. They were holding back the tide, and the ocean threatened to wash them away with the slightest oversight or weakness in their barrier.

"They are definitely Vuzgalian," Marco growled, rubbing his face.

"Was it the weapons or the bunkers? Or does the fact that the entire place is one great big formation and has mobile defenses give it away?" Eva Marino asked.

"That was part of it. They're organized." Marco looked out of his command tent at the forces attacking the second line, the outpost line. Dawn was breaking over the Beast Mountain Range as the towers and outposts stood tall among the forest.

Just what could we do if we had a force that organized?

Marco cleared his throat and drew his attention to the map. "Their formations are grinding us down again, costing us nearly five times the mana to do anything. Have we made any progress in disrupting them?"

"Nothing has worked thus far." Eva chewed on the inside of her mouth.

"So, an army of Earth and Sky realm forces are unable to defeat an army from the Mortal realm." Marco snorted as the sect commanders from other forces inside the tent glared.

"They are using weapons from the Sha that don't require cultivation, just supplies. They are without honor." Eva's glare told Marco to not antagonize the other sects.

What a poor situation we are in. Elder Cai Bo is the only one that sees we will be left gutted in the fighting.

"The mana in this place is so thin that only beasts and invalids could call it home," Marco said.

Marco used a sound transmission device to not be overheard. "Teacher Marino, we must weaken them. We stepped on something, something we were not expecting."

He held Marino's eyes as she cocked her head to the side.

"Do you think?"

"This is greater than Vuzgal. Entire castles that drop below the ground and move kilometers underground? Just what are we standing on?"

Marino didn't refute him. She looked at the map and grimaced. "What are we to do? We are committed. Why would they have a base in the First Realm, the worst of them? And you are saying they are not connected to the Sha?"

"They have similarities to the Sha, but I think we are seeing a new group of people. New to the realm." Marco said.

Eva's eyes bored into him, making him continue his point.

"These weapons have similarities to the Sha, that much is clear. But only in degrees. Their armor, their formations, their main weapons are different from what the Sha use. I have learned that much from the Black Phoenix Clan. They might have ties to the Sha, but the complexity of their weapons is much higher than anything the Sha created."

"Even if they are new arrivals that does little to help our current situation."

"No, it doesn't, so we must look at the situation here. We can bring down supplies from the higher realms, giving us a continuous supply of power. They are locked in, unable to move. We need to deplete their mana reserves. Have our forces attack the mana barriers with everything that they have. Use the mages over the spell scrolls. We don't have the resources to spare going all out with our spell scrolls."

"They will bleed us for every step and never engage decisively unless we're at a complete disadvantage," Marino muttered, looking at the table as well.

"The mana gathering formations here are stronger than the ones in Vuzgal. This has to be the place, their last fall back. And they made it to last," Marco agreed.

"Should we slow the advance?" Marino asked.

"A good idea, but ultimately useless. We will burn more of their mana stones, but we know what happens when we give them even a few days to prepare defenses. The sects have become used to successive victories. This will not be an easy fight to win. We must push through or lose our momentum."

"There is a Mistress Mercy demanding to see you," an attendant said.

Marco canceled the sound canceling formation. "Is Niklaus with her?"

He looked toward the doorway. Niklaus, while he was from the lower realm, had proven his worth in Marco's eyes. He'd been suitably impressed with Niklaus, not only for taming his wilder cousin, but leading successive victories across the lower realms.

Mercy had the eye of Cai Bo, was wild and undisciplined. The attendant shook his head. He wouldn't have let her in normally, but thinking of Master Cai Bo, he grimaced. "Let her in."

He went back to studying the map. "Here, see those forces? Order them to slow their advance. Get them to recover and consolidate their forces. They are pushing ahead too fast. It will allow them to get their weaker forces out front. It might be an idea to draw in the forces of the surrounding kingdoms to supply us with bodies."

Marino nodded and started to send the right messages.

"How are we looking at the Wild Reaches Trading Outpost?" Marco asked.

"Word from the front lines is spotty. Vuzgal aerial beasts were thick in the area, but they have since moved away. They are supporting the retreat of the cities. Still, there are traps across the roads and in the forests and unknown fighters hiding in both."

"Progress?"

"Has come to a standstill."

"It must be those ghost groups again." Marco snarled, thinking of his supply lines in his attack on Vuzgal. He had lost more supplies in those attacks than supplies he had used to advance on Vuzgal.

Mercy burst through the doors with her guard trailing behind. Her clothes were stained with mud. She snatched a glass from a passerby, downing it and thrusting it back into their chest.

"Get me another," she decried, stalking over to Marco and the map.

"What is the situation at the outpost and on the road?" Marco asked as she approached, holding his tongue as his eyebrow arched at her actions.

"Those fools, they couldn't do anything. Even Niklaus, that traitor, demanded we retreat! When will we take that outpost?"

"Mercy," Marco snapped.

She stared at him, working her jaw.

He saw the thoughts flicking through her head; working out what their strength was, wondering if she could win in a show of power.

Marco released his mana, dropping her to her knees, forcing her into a surprised kotow.

He grimaced, releasing the pressure, feeling dirty for showing his power to suppress one so weak.

He used mana to transmit his words to her ears without others hearing.

"Do not think to play petty games here, girl. You might have Cai Bo's interest and your uncle might be dead, but do not forget your position," he growled and let the mana speak fade, talking aloud. "You have dealt with a lot. Go and rest in the rear." He rounded on the table, his back toward her.

I will make sure to report to Cai Bo first so that she doesn't use the situation against me.

"Tell our people to use the rolling spell tactic we developed at Vuzgal. That should flush out their people."

A thought rose as Mercy stalked out. "Mercy, go to the surrounding kingdoms. Get their support through whatever means necessary. We'll need their fighters."

The others in the room had a perplexed look. He let them wonder as Mercy half bowed and quickly departed. He didn't need to turn to see the snarl on her face.

"We move to the front line. I can't see what is happening back here."

"Are you sure that is best?" Marino dropped her voice.

"The closer the better."

"And their cannons?"

"We'll just have to use less conspicuous tents so they don't know where we are."

Gregor sat on his throne, his vision filled with dungeon screens and magical formations. The reams of information were old, comfortable companions.

That should be it. He checked the information on the Phoenix Breath weapon, reviewing the connections.

He nodded to himself, waving away the screens and standing.

"We go now," he said to the assembled elders.

They checked with Head Asadi, who gestured for them to continue their preparations. The ship's formations flared to life, shimmering with power as the berths lit up one by one.

Gregor looked through the screens, seeing the warships' formations power up.

"Prepare for transfer."

Gregor altered formations with a thought as mana built within the ship.

Mana cannons went through their last checks. Mana stone storage rooms were checked and secured.

Crafters moved away from their labors, the ships filled with the strongest mages, and best mana cannon gunners. Aerial fighters filled the warehouse-like decks under the armor's surface and clung to the top of the warship's casting decks.

It took time for the power to build, consuming mana stones at an incredible rate. Formations went from bright to blinding, then everything *shifted* as if everything were fundamentally wrong with the world and then it snapped back to reality.

Perseverance and her seven sisters appeared around the Willful Institute controlled totem in Henghou.

People looked up in awe at the warships as guards pushed back those trying to pass through the totem.

The totem activated as the first two warships disappeared. Gregor felt the transfer. Spending most of his life in the Seventh Realm, he hadn't felt the sensation many times.

Henghou disappeared as they appeared over River Guard.

Pilots used their formations. The air shimmered around the ship, moving the ship's bulk as it cleared the totem, and looked at the transfer point outside the city walls. Sects used teleportation formations to join the forward forces attacking the second defensive line.

Gregor grimaced. The last alterations had taken longer than he'd expected. Afternoon was quickly approaching in the First Realm and the Vermire Empire had held their own against seventeen different allied sects which had deployed over five hundred thousand fighters and conscripted nearly two hundred thousand from the surrounding nations.

Gregor looked at the map table that Cai Bo and Head Asadi examined. He could see the cities holding out at the edge of the Empire's reach. They pinned down much of the attacking force.

The second defensive line was tighter than the first, with shorter breaks between defenses and greater artillery cover. They were holding firm for now.

Gregor used his Dungeon Sense, a paltry thing now that he was linked to an Earth grade dungeon core. He could feel several dungeon cores. *Too weak to matter.*

"Use your sense," he snarled, waving at one of his hunters.

They did so, still linked to the Sky dungeon core on the *Eternus*. He pulled out a map and put the different locations down.

A formation of dungeon cores. Not even the Sha would be so wasteful. Most of them are mortal mana cores as well.

"Do you think they broke apart the dungeon core into smaller ones for this formation?" he asked the dungeon hunter.

He pursed his lips. "I don't think so. This place must have been built over time. They would have been discovered otherwise, or else they would have only a few months to create this. I think these dungeon cores were placed before. A lot of them are of a smaller grade. But if they are all controlled by one person. They will have a much larger area under their control, but it is weak."

"So they're hiding the Sky dungeon core." Gregor nodded. His hunter's thoughts agreed with his own. "We need to break through their second line and drive in hard, give them less time to get smart or try to run. Even if we can just get these dungeon cores, the clan will be pleased."

Aureus felt a sudden shadow fall over the city. He looked up to the sky, feeling his skin prickling almost painfully. "Shit."

Two more corvettes appeared above the city's totem. They moved around the massive frigate, casting its shadow onto the city below.

"This is Agent Aureus. I have spotted one frigate class airship and five, no, seven corvettes above River Guard."

The ships accelerated. Cheers rose from the Willful Instituted fighters in the city below.

"Hey, you there. What are you doing?" a Willful Institute fighter yelled. He was with a group of other fighters sent to round up the people of the city.

"I didn't do anything wrong," Aureus said, backing up as the trio approached. Aureus checked the two tubes strapped to the underside of his arms.

He raised his arms to the side.

"What are you doing lurking back here? You a spy?" the same man asked as he walked forward confidently.

"Not even worth that much experience, I bet," the man on his right with a spear said.

"My momma told me to never waste free experience," the man in the middle grinned and gathered his power to attack.

Aureus raised his arms and leveled the tubes at the spear fighter and the silent one.

The formations in the tube activated with a silent burst of mana.

The modified railgun barrels fired, striking both attackers in the chest. They sputtered, falling soundlessly as Aureus drove power through his bones.

The talker glanced at their falling bodies.

Aureus used the time to rush forward, grabbing the man's sword arm and neck.

"Thank you for the armor. It will help me greatly."

The man struggled. Aureus' hand closed like a vice, crushing the man's windpipe. He struggled but eventually stilled, adding a third tombstone to the alleyway.

Aureus checked the surrounding alleyways, storing the bodies in his storage ring.

He moved to a door, using a slip of metal to throw the latch and head indoors.

Glosil watched the markers and movement on the main map table. His eyes, along with everyone else's, fixed on River Guard as the seventh ship appeared and moved toward Beast Mountain Range.

"Kanoa, how confident are you in those new missiles being developed?"

"They don't have lock on capabilities, but they go in a straight line just fine, and they pack one hell of a punch."

"Enough to take out an airship?"

"Should be able to."

"Gather your air force. Have your best unit armed with the missiles. Their mission is to hit those corvettes. Egbert!"

"Sir?"

"You will support the air force." Glosil's eyes flickered over positions on the map. "These towers here, pull back our forces there. How are our Special Teams?" He looked at Niemm, who had several healing needles stabbed into his arm.

"They're ready for whatever you need, Commander."

"Elan, you command the teams and the close protection details. They're moving up stronger units through the rear. I don't want them to have a free ride to the front."

"How, sir?" Elan asked.

"Hit and run, sir?" Niemm asked.

"Hit and run. When you have targets, call them out to Egbert."

"Yes, sir!" Niemm smiled evilly.

Others carried out his orders as Glosil watched his map. This was his role, to see the entire battle down to the working parts and from on high.

"Tell the forces at Vermire to expect a flank. Looks like there's a breakaway unit heading for them. I want numbers on the people still in the cities and outposts. Get me supply rosters, too. Whoever lets my guns go silent will be out front with a fucking spoon!"

Glosil's eyes latched to the area outside Wild Reaches, looking for support, for extra resources, more fire support.

"Get the Special Teams out of there now! Damn you, Marco. Have Domonos support with artillery."

"Are you sure?" Kanoa asked.

"Does it look familiar to you? It is new, with spell scrolls or stronger mages, but he's using spells to carve a new path to Wild Reaches as he did at Vuzgal."

He debated sending out Egbert and the dungeon's attack formations. *Be a waste and reveal our hand. Need them to commit and use them to the most effect to break them.*

Cai Bo looked over River Guard. Aerial forces rose from the city and around the airships as other aerial beasts and their riders took off from the airships, patrolling the skies.

"We will head toward Wild Reaches to support the ground forces. Make sure your people keep up," Gregor said at the map table.

"Have our forces advance," Asadi said to Cai Bo.

"Yes, Head."

Cai Bo sent the orders, noting the annoyance hidden in Asadi's features. He had the honor of having the warships manned by the Willful Institute and being the only person that Gregor would talk to.

He is used to control. She smirked, keeping her thoughts to herself. All the ships were manned by the Willful Institute, but no one other than members of the Black Phoenix Clan controlled the dungeon cores.

Cai Bo held onto the grip bars of the map table as *Perseverance's* formations accelerated, its mighty bulk pushing forward. She glanced at Asadi and back to the screens around the bridge.

She stretched her hand, the thrill of plans within plans as she sat in the background, controlling all.

Ships created eddies in the surrounding mana, causing the air to distort as the dungeon cores sucked the mana in the area dry.

"Pull back!" Niemm ordered through the sound transmission channel.

Han Wu looked up through the broken trees, through the smoke of the previous fighting. Mud covered his smoke-blackened face. He saw the spells appearing above their heads, all around them, behind them.

"Gong Jin, brother, there're more spells behind us than in front."

"Mount up!" Gong Jin said.

The special team members pulled out their panther mounts. Getting on their backs, they turned and charged forward.

"Armor!"

They opened the corner of their carrier, turning the formation there into place. Power rushed through their bodies.

Han Wu reached down and turned the formation on his mount's armor.

They surged ahead, roaring as they raced through the broken landscape.

Han Wu let out a whoop, grabbing a Gatling gun and hooking it into his panther's back mount. He slapped the pin into place and hooked the ammunition box on his mount's side to the weapon, cocking it.

Spell formations from above and below started activating. Their mounts dodged and weaved at speeds fast enough to strain their bones.

He reached to the right side, twisting and turning the mana barrier stack formation, activating it.

Spells rained down around them as they rushed through the destruction.

They surged out of the woods. The forward lines of the sects rested, downing potions, preparing for the fight to come. Casters behind them unleashed spells as others tore apart spell scrolls.

"Fire!" Gong Jin and Han Wu said at the same time.

The Gatling guns whirled and unleashed a solid line of tracers that spotted the mana barrier in front of the frontline. It dissipated under the attacks as rounds shredded through the fighters on the other side.

The Special Teams turned, firing as they went.

"Spell scrolls!"

Han Wu reached for the scrolls attached to his vest, aiming and tearing them all.

Spells appeared through the ground, activating. Dirt and stone over kilometers dragged together into golems; air blades cut into the enemy. Illusion clouds of smoke sprouted among their ranks.

Anarchy ruled the sects, surprised by the sudden attack.

The Special Teams turned and charged into the forest, away from the path. Some had presence of mind, aiming their spell scrolls at the group, or into the forest.

Trees shredded as they passed.

Han Wu raised his arm against a lightning spell that tore through a tree. Parts of the tree as large as his finger stabbed into his side and arm.

The Special Teams spread out, going as fast as their mounts could carry them.

Han Wu's body pushed out the shrapnel as he fired spells at the spell formations in the sky, trying to disrupt them before they activated.

Han Wu saw a fireball explode in the sky. He curled over his mount, trying to cover them as the weight of the detonating fireball flattened him.

His head rocked forward, smacking his Gatling gun. The world turned dark.

39

A Wild Phoenix and Dragon

ai Bo paid no heed to the elders around the map table in *Perseverance* as they approached Wild Reaches Outpost. The forest around the small town had been flattened, its mana barrier colored with the impacts of spells.

They held on, repelling every attack. They'd passed the ruins of Zahir. The burnt-out city was nothing but a stain on the ground below now. It hadn't been part of the Vermire Empire, just had the fate of being in the way.

Teleportation formations had been placed forward of the city, marked more by the enemy's continued bombardment.

"The harassing forces have been removed and the sects are progressing quickly. None can stand in front of our Willful Institute's fighters and the might of our United Sect Army!" An elder laughed. "Head Asadi, they must be despairing at your arrival! Marco takes after you in his youth. It remains to be seen if he will mature to be even half as powerful as you!"

"It is just as I planned. They fight hard, but this *Empire* must be their last position. I never thought a place in the First Realm would have anything useful. It is the end for them. There is nowhere for them to go now." Asadi did not argue with the praise or correct them on who came up with the strategy.

Cai Bo smiled quickly, remembering what Head Asadi had said. "Your tactical genius has only grown over the years, Sect Head."

"Ah, enough of that." He chuckled at her praise.

"We have aerial forces heading toward the fleet."

"Head Asadi, I will leave ground and Aerial combat to you, but we must reach King's Hill as fast as possible," Gregor said.

"Understood." Head Asadi nodded. "Could the cannons assist against the Wild Reaches Outpost?"

Gregor paused and took out a spell scroll. "Give this to your casters. It should break their barrier and throw them back. Make sure your army is ready to follow or it will be wasted."

"I thank you for your gift, Hunter Gregor." Asadi passed it to Elder Tolentino.

"Thank you, Head Asadi." He bowed and accepted the scroll and left the bridge to go onto the casting deck.

Asadi looked at where the aerial forces came from. "Destroy them. Take them out of the skies. Tell the ground forces to increase their speed. Prepare to advance. We don't have time to waste on these small towns and outer defenses."

Cai Bo glanced at the bunker-line. It remained there, quiet and untouched, a clear challenge to their advance.

Mages on the ships lit up the skies with spells as the ships continued their laborious forward momentum, arranged in an arrowhead formation with the *Perseverance* in the center of the diagonal lines.

Aerial fighters between the ships grouped together to engage the Sparrows that cut through the skies, engaging the ground forces laying siege to the Wild Reaches. Thousands were in movement, a complicated and dangerous dance.

Forces started to shift, preparing to make use of the spell scrolls' distraction.

"Look alive! They're getting ready for another push!" Domonos used the command chat, looking up from his map and through an arrow slit at the enemy beyond.

His eyes caught the warships heading for his Wild Reaches Trading outpost.

"Make sure you stay in cover!" Domonos yelled and switched channels. "Hey, arty, can you do anything about these airships?"

"Artillery Cannons can shift to support, but they will reduce coverage between defenses."

"Railguns?"

"They're out of range right now."

"All right, give me what you can. I don't like them up above me."

Domonos watched as attacks hit the warships' mana barriers, lighting them up.

They're interconnected, not even showing a bit of flex.

Artillery cannons left cyan smudges on the barriers that eased between impacts.

Domonos hit up the main command chat. "Looks like the ships' mana barriers are interlinked and stronger than they were at Vuzgal. Artillery cannons are smashing them up, but nothing is making it through."

"Stronger than *Eternus*?" Glosil asked.

"I think they would be individually. Together, they don't have much flex."

Domonos watched as a spell scroll—by how rapidly the spell came together—activated on the bow of the largest airship in the middle of the arrowhead. The beam of light burned through Domonos' eyes; the world went silent and filled with a wall of noise.

The earth rumbled around him, tossing him backward. He felt himself go through a wall and covered his head, as it seemed like the whole building dropped on top of him.

He groaned, using healing spells on his eyes as he threw the stone off, hearing Glosil and Yui's voices.

"Shit, they used a spell scroll through the barrier and the wall!"

The outposts' mana barrier evaporated overhead as Domonos turned to see the destruction behind him. The wall had been blown apart, the cannon having traced to the side, destroying most of the wall.

Domonos got up and grabbed an officer. "Take some soldiers and get command of that area now!"

"Sir."

"All units, this is Domonos. Prepare for a counterattack. Conqueror's armor, unlocked. Use Defender's Might."

Domonos opened the corner of his carrier and turned the formation. Power flooded his body as he pulled out a needle and stabbed it into his leg.

Defender's Might
Increase all stats by 5%

He felt the power fill him. He checked his rifle and looked at his guards, then connected to Glosil. "Commander, the wall has been hit. I have a fifty-meter section open to the enemy. I have people working to get my soldiers out of the rubble and organized. I have activated the armor and buffing potions."

"Understood."

Domonos switched to the leadership channels between the different outposts. "Wild Reaches has been breached. You will all do your duty and hold your outposts. You are on independent command. If you cannot hold, then pull back to King's Hill. Reorganize and then move to support the bunker lines."

He cut the channel as he strode from the command center, looking at the men and women inside. "You two—stick to me like glue." He pointed at two aides. "The rest of you move to direct your units in person. We will rebuff their attack before falling back to the bunker line. Get the wounded out first."

"Sir!" The room came to attention and then relaxed into motion.

Domonos indicated to Zukal.

"Why do I feel I'm not going to like this job?"

"Because I need someone at the rear making sure that nothing goes wrong. And we shouldn't be seen in the same place, dear." Domonos grinned.

Zukal snorted. "Shit, you need to get a proper wife one of these days. I feel like I'm your minder most days."

"Isn't that the role of a good second in command, to make the commander look omnipotent while running around cursing him?"

"Ah shit, who told you my secrets?" Zukal asked.

The two men shared a terse laugh.

"Good luck, brother."

They shook hands and went their separate ways.

Domonos pulled his helmet on.

"Sir, what's the plan?" his Close Protection Detail leader asked.

"We need someone to hold that breach." Domonos pointed at the hole with his rifle, releasing his panther from her beast storage crate. "And, well, I don't know if you see any other units around that have our kind of fire power and skills?"

"All right, girls and boys, you heard the officer. Time to earn our danger pay."

"Choi, what's your situation?"

"Ready and waiting, sir."

"Good. I need you and your people at the breach now. Support the line and deny the enemy."

"Yes, sir. We're on the way."

"I'll be waiting."

"Got it, sir," Choi drawled.

Domonos let his protection detail's leader take point as they approached the area. The wall covered three streets. Soldiers were all over the place, recovering the wounded, and pulling out people, getting them moved to the rear.

The panthers moved through the rubble with their jungle senses, leaping and prowling forward.

The dust from the attack dissipated, revealing the carnage.

Domonos ground his teeth but forced himself to look around, to take in the big picture, trusting his people to do their jobs.

Machine guns in the bunkers tried their best to reduce the strain as mages cast spells onto the enemy ranks.

Domonos ducked as a mana cannon smashed into a section of wall, taking out the mage and the casting balcony that jutted out of the wall.

"We have any updates on the mana barrier?" Domonos asked his two trailing aides.

"It looks like the mana barrier formation has been destroyed. The grounding formations in the city have been weakened so we have spotty barrier protection."

"Okay." Domonos swung off his mount.

"Get down in the dirt. They'll be coming soon!"

Mana cannons fired, crashing into the walls.

"Order the walls abandoned," Domonos yelled to the other aide.

The Close Protection Detail threw around stone blocks as big as them to create firing positions, spells altering the ground.

"Sir!"

"What do you want us to do, sir?" the first aide asked.

"Dig the hell in. You know how to use a rifle. Well, today you'll be putting it to work."

"Yes, sir!"

Domonos used fuse spells, creating a position to lie down behind. He pulled out an ammunition can, hooking up the belt feed to his machine gun. He hadn't pulled an M8 Railgun because he had accepted his fate to be in the rear. Now he wished he had a little more firepower. "Ah, you'll be just fine for the job, won't you?"

"Sir, we have arty on the line. They're ready to support if we need it. Firing from the bunker line and the mountain," an aide said. Even several meters away, the sound transmission made him sound right next to Domonos.

"Get them to bear fifty meters ahead of the destroyed bunkers. I want them to sweep one hundred meters to either side and straight for three hundred. Got it?"

"Yes, sir. Rounds no closer than fifty meters ahead of bunker-line, one hundred meters traverse either side, three hundred long."

"There you go; get them to hold and wait on my command."

"Yes, sir."

Domonos looked down the hill. He heard the yells overcoming the sounds of machine gun fire as his CPD fired. He rested the barrel of his machine gun on the stone wall and looked over the wall to see the enemy pushing the hill.

He aimed and fired at a fighter jumping onto the top of the bunker. The man fell unnaturally as Domonos raked his tracer fire over those behind him, the ground spitting up dust as they collapsed.

Domonos aim followed his tracers, casting explosive shot. His rounds exploded upon impact.

A mana cannon spell fired past his position, tearing through the partial remains of the wall and into the sky beyond.

Mages cast spells at the firing positions. Domonos ducked but kept firing as a stone was hit with a mana blast, turning it to powder.

"Artillery says they're ready and waiting, sir!" His aide came back to him.

"Okay, once they're five meters past the bunker line, call it in, one of you!"

A spell enchanted arrow blew away part of Domonos' cover. He shifted his aim to see one of his guards cut down the rogue archer.

One aide called in an artillery spell as the sky howled with dozens of small meteors that smashed into the ground.

A spell went off to Domonos' side, tossing him away. He crashed into stone, tumbling as he held onto his rifle.

He came to a stop, checking himself. Only minor bruising. He checked his rifle. The box had torn off at the tear off point, but it was fine.

He tore out the ragged link, scanning and slapping in a fresh magazine.

"*Get* your asses back in fucking position. Even if I die on this fucking hill, you will hold it for the wounded," Domonos growled at the guards he saw moving toward him.

He looked for his own position. It took some time to find it in the broken landscape.

Staying low, he ran back over. "Hey, my two aides, where are you at?"

"I'm good, sir,"

There was nothing else.

Domonos saw a fighter running up toward him. He fired, dropping him. He peeked into the anarchy of weapon fire, spells, and death as he ducked down again and ran. Spells rained down where he had been seconds before.

"Looks to me like they're five meters past; call in that artillery!"

Domonos held his rifle in one hand, half-crouched, and scaled to where the spell had hit.

He stilled, seeing his aide. He hadn't known the young man's name. He looked up at the sky with the blank expression of the dead.

Domonos grimaced, storing him, and putting the dead aide's storage rings in his pocket.

The sky howled and rumbled with the artilleries' delivery of iron rain.

Domonos pulled out an ammunition can. He hooked it up to his rifle and used the straps to wear it like a backpack.

He felt the wave of force from the artillery as it pushed forward.

"They're telling me that they can't keep it up for long sir, and the air force is coming in."

"Domonos, it's Glosil. You're going to have air force come in and harass the enemy fleet. I don't know if you can see it, but they're moving in on your position and their guns are charging up."

"And our rail cannons won't be accurate on the airship until they're past my outpost."

"Correct."

"Got it, sir."

Domonos checked the map on the inside of his forearm, moving it around, checking the units around the outpost.

The soldiers pulled back from the bunkers, blowing them as they went. Those at the lower ranks pulled back first, so the stronger, higher ranking members could cover them and peel back, leaving their strongest fighters at their withdrawing front.

Surrounding units and people coming back from the bunkers grabbed wounded as they went.

Acosta ran over with her people, spreading out to thicken up their fighting line.

"Hey, boss," she said. Stones shifted under her as she sat next to Domonos and looked over at the artillery beyond.

She ducked back down and Domonos pulled out a map, putting it on the side of the crater.

"They're gathering their people in front of us. They know they have an opening here and I think they want to use it." He tapped on the map and circled it.

"I would agree with you on that, sir."

"We've got the air force on the way. Apparently, they're going to do something about our airship problem. At the same time, the ships are moving and they're going to get into range of us before Kanoa's people get in range of them. We're going to deny them this section of wall, but we have to be ready to peel back. We're not holding, just delaying."

"Seems a bit like what we've been doing this entire time."

"We have a lot of ground to cover. We might have released powerful beasts into the forests to harass them and filled it with traps, but we can't hold all these places. At the bunker line, we'll have the forces in place to defend and hold."

"Unless that ship opens its mouth and spits out more mana."

"You are a ray of sunshine on my rainy day, aren't you, Acosta?" Domonos put his map away.

"Hey, you're the boss. I'm just one of those ornery NCO types. Didn't Zukal warn you about me?"

"No, he warned me that you could outdrink any of the other protection detail leaders. That's why he put you up for promotion."

Acosta snorted, and Domonos smiled slightly.

"All right, so hold this wall, but not too hard. Got it, boss. I'll check in on my people."

She scurried off, dirt and stone tumbling down as the artillery fell away.

Domonos coughed, trying to clear his dry throat. "Stand to! Stand to! Here they come!"

He pushed forward, using the rubble; he checked to make sure that the pack was feeding, shifting rock around to clear his line of sight.

He tried to move the spiky rock against his knee.

Movement pulled his eye. Mana cannons fired. They struck bunkers, tearing them apart, and spells struck the walls. Those lying down across the breach waited.

Domonos was hit with rocks, the impacts affecting him little as he shook them off like pebbles.

The sects' fighters yelled, their weapons raised as they surged forward, over the bunkers and up the hill.

"Fire!" Domonos ordered.

Railguns, machine guns, spell scrolls streamed down the hill, cutting through the enemy.

Sect members collapsed under the weight of fire. They found craters, defilades in the ground and returned with attacks of their own.

Domonos heard something… *different*, feeling the mana surge upward.

He looked from the battle, seeing the airships and their cannons.

"Move it. Incoming!"

The cannons released their attacks.

They crashed into the wall, into the ground. Gunners were thrown to the side. People were tossed like leaves in the wind.

Pandemonium lived there as the defenders turned and ran. Officers called for their people to retreat.

Domonos tore spell scrolls on his carrier, aiming at the hill. Stone golems rose from the ground. Some were destroyed by the cannons. Others rushed down to the bunkers and out of sight.

Domonos looked at his people, shouldering forward through stone tossed their way.

They just ran. As people dropped, they were picked up. They used spell scrolls as they could.

They got away from the wall and the immediate range of the guns.

Domonos didn't know how he survived. He turned at the next street, covering his people, firing on the sect members making it over the wall.

He glanced at his people.

Those with missing limbs were helped away from the battle; their body cultivation starting the healing process. The stamina drain would be too much, turning them into a liability in the short term.

He made sure they were all behind him.

"Form lines of security as you fall back!" Domonos yelled. "Rear security, move back in three! Two, one... Move!"

Domonos turned and ran. His heart in his throat eased as those still able to fight behind him covered him.

He pushed past them, finding a second rear line had formed and tucking into the third line.

"Rear line! Pull back! Help any wounded. Wounded to the rear immediately!" Domonos yelled.

The lines moved, and he found he was at the rear again, counting in his head.

One

"Rear line, move back!"

He turned and ran. Everything in his body screamed in alarm as he passed the second line. He dropped as he felt the passage of mana over his head striking a building.

Domonos got his feet under him, running forward through the falling rubble. He saw movement through an alleyway. Seeing a Willful Institute insignia, he fired through the alleyway at the charging sect forces, cutting down several.

The city seemed to be coming apart around them as they ran for the teleportation formation hubs.

"Watch your flanks! They're in the city!"

He grunted, pushing up into a lunge.

Why the hell does my knee hurt?

Domonos rubbed it, pausing, thinking about the rock stabbing into his knee when he'd been shooting from the wall.

He ignored it, walking on.

Get your head together.

Others would never get to complain about lying down in an uncomfortable firing position again.

The landing crew looked away as Wazny's Sparrow landed aggressively, throwing up wind and debris.

Beast masters moved forward, grabbing the sparrow and pulling it toward food troughs filled with alchemically enhanced food.

Wazny turned a formation, the canopy of his cockpit opening.

The rest of his people came in to land on other pads.

"Talk to me, Delfina," he said, seeing the small Spanish woman with her clipboard.

The formation underneath him and his sparrow activated, speeding up their recovery. He looked at Dalton, who was checking the different birds.

"We're loading you with the new penetrator missiles."

"They ready? I thought you were still testing them out."

"Well, you did the test runs with them. They shoot in a straight line, and they make a big boom. Dalton!"

The big man finished checking the other sparrow's cockpit. He quickly talked to his people and ran over. "'Sup, boss?"

"Tell Wazny about the payload."

"New missiles, sir, straight shooters. No fire and forget yet. They have three stages, acceleration, penetration, and detonation. They have four earth mana stones chained together for the payload. Unfortunately, they won't work with your current bomb drop system; modifying your rigs will take hours. We're going to jerry rig them to your birds. You'll have two missiles each. They'll mess up a corvette, but they'll be rigged outside your bird. You get hit by a missile, good chance it'll blow."

Wazny took a deep breath, looking over the other pilots who were eating and drinking, closing their eyes, readying themselves.

His gaze dropped to Dalton. "Thank you for letting me know, Chaos."

"Didn't want you going out there not knowing what you're holding."

"Can you make sure every pilot is briefed?"

"Yes, sir."

Wazny nodded as he saw mages using earth spells to grow out the tree cockpit around the sparrows to hold the missiles.

"We're going to be holding a new pull tab. You rip it, the missile will kick off," Delfina said.

"Okay." Wazny pulled out a stamina tube, what some of the Earthers called a chunkier yogurt tube or melted freeze pop.

Delfina nodded and went back to work as Wazny tore open the tube and slid his hand up the packaging, swallowing the mushy creation robotically. His mind filled with images of what had just happened, the fighting in the skies, the losses of his people.

He closed his eyes and sighed. *Later.*

Wazny finished off the tube, taking a swig of water to get the paste out of his mouth.

"All right, Major, you're ready to go," a weapons tech said.

"Thanks." Wazny turned the canopy formation. His canopy grew together again.

He looked around and checked on his pilots.

The beast masters, loaders, and weapons techs moved to the side.

Wazny lifted his thumb, checking on the people to his right and left.

He saw their thumbs and faced the marshaler with his glowing batons.

Wazny nudged his sparrow forward. They moved toward the flight line, turning to face the entrance to the mountain hangar.

Kestrels shot out ahead and curved away as they headed off on their own missions.

The light next to Wazny changed from red to green. Wazny's mount rushed forward, extended her wings and then, with a powerful flap, they were airborne. Formations on the floors and the ceiling created warm air, raising them up and forward quickly. They soared out of the entrance. Wazny banked to the left, checking through his canopy, seeing other sparrows spitting out of the mountain hangar, carrying their twin missile payload.

"All right, that's enough sitting on our asses. We've got a direct delivery for those Willful Institute airships. Mission is to take out the corvettes first and then take out the frigate."

"Major Wazny, didn't want you to get all of the action."

Sparrows and kestrels lowered from the heavens, forming up around Wazny's unit.

"Major Storbeck, good to see you."

"We'll take on the aerial forces around the airships. You take them out."

"I'll owe you a beer after this one."

"Hell, I'll buy the next round if you can take out one of the bastards." Storbeck laughed.

Wazny checked his wings. The Alva Air Force spread around him and his attack sparrows.

"Listen up! We're going to hit the corvettes and move deeper into their formation to strike the frigate, if we can. If we can't, spread out and dump your missiles into the other corvettes or into the enemy below. Don't hold onto your missiles!"

The forward sparrows and kestrels began their dive, picking up speed as they dropped toward the airships.

"Keep above the airships and watch for spells. All their cannons are located on the sides and underside."

Wazny stopped transmitting, his stomach clamping up. He checked the two missiles and dove with the aerial beasts around him.

The Institute's fleet was laid bare below them. The Aerial riders started to climb as casters on the top of the ships cast spells or ripped spell scrolls.

Sparrows opened up with their machine guns and railguns. Streams of tracers struck the mana barrier, covering the entire fleet and aerial beasts.

Spells lashed out at the descending aerial forces, hitting the stack formation barriers around the different pilots.

Barriers were used up and destroyed, sparrows killed, dropping and cartwheeling below. A kestrel was hit in front of Wazny, dropping down and away. Two people jumped from the craft, then a third and the fourth. Wazny sighed as the kestrel smashed through several trees, broken upon the ground. Destructive formations sparked across the Kestrel and flames spread.

They were taking losses, but speed was their ally. The first wings passed through the mana barrier. They must've torn every spell scroll they had as tens of spells appeared among the enemy aerial riders and their tracers connected with the riders' personal barriers.

The air force's formation broke over one corvette. Several dropped bombs. The ship staggered, and the mages were washed from the ship's upper casting deck. The thick metal and stone compressed layers armored the ships against the attacks.

The air force wings broke into three formations, two heading left and right toward the other corvettes, the third aiming for the frigate, *Perseverance*.

The first missile-toting sparrows got their shot on the bombed-out corvette.

Twin streams of flame appeared under their sparrows. The missiles glowed with a drill spell on their front, stabbing into the upper deck of the corvette.

They chewed into the upper armor layers before detonating.

Sections of the ship blew out from the sides as more missiles pierced the ship and detonated. Formations flared and failed as the corvette dipped, the linked mana barrier fluctuating. It held for a half second before several key somethings exploded and the ship dropped out of the sky like the metal brick it was.

"Head for target two, everyone," Wazny ordered.

It had taken two wings' worth of missiles to take out the first ship. There was no way that he could take out the frigate with his remaining missiles.

They banked away to the left, aiming up on their second corvette.

Aerial forces charged through the air force, targeting the missile wings.

A lucky spell hit a missile head on. The missile, sparrow, and pilot disappeared in a fireball.

"Go evasive."

Wazny and the other pilots jinked, trying to throw off any aim on them as they neared their target. Wazny dove, tearing the buffing spell scroll that wrapped around the two missiles. The corvette threw out spells across the sky to destroy the missile laden sparrows.

Wazny saw a sparrow to his left fire their missiles, only to get smacked with air blades, cutting them up and dropping them out of view.

Wazny checked his aim and raised a bit, targeting the command center. He fired his missiles and activated the conqueror's armor on his sparrow.

The missiles shot off across the deck of the corvette and hit the raised command deck, breaking through the windows as Wazny flew over the rear of the ship.

The bridge exploded. The whole ship's formations went dark as it dropped and then accelerated wildly, pitching forward. Other missiles slammed into the corvette, throwing it around before it snapped through trees, crashing into the ground, and sending up a wave of dirt.

The aerial beasts and defensive spell work were thick around the frigate, sure death.

"Wing three, dump your missiles into a corvette and pull back!" Wazny ordered. "Storbeck, we're dry. Let's get out of here."

"Storbeck is dead, sir. This is Imotep. We acknowledge!"

The remaining sparrows banked, firing on corvettes in range. Some hit, releasing gouts of flame through the outer decking, leaving scorch marks and warped metal, but little else to mark their passing.

The Alva Air Force activated their buffing spells, diving once again, picking up speed as they passed over Wild Reaches Trading Outpost.

He could see some fighting in the streets as streams of Alvan soldiers rushed for teleportation formations, then disappeared.

Wazny looked back at the enemy fleet. The remaining corvettes moved into a triangular formation around the frigate, no longer looking fresh as bomb and machine gun fire pock marked their hulls.

Perseverance rocked again, formations flashing and failing.

Gregor gritted his teeth. "Turn the cannons on the defenses. Bring the airships in closer for mutual support."

"Mages and aerial forces are to deal with incoming attacking aerial forces," Asadi ordered. "Have the ground forces push forward with everything they have. Draw in reinforcements from the units attacking the second line if we need to. The sects attacking the cities go on the defensive and pin in the Vuzgal forces there. Any spare fighters should be shifted to the front. Where are our reinforcements?"

"We have all of our forces in the field. Most are being organized at the cities where we came in from the higher realms," Cai Bo reported.

"See if you can hurry them along. Have Marco keep the attacks up on the second line." Asadi fell into silence for a moment.

He turned to Gregor. "We have two options. We can ground down their defenses, use our weapons to drain them of power, or push inward as fast as possible."

"We are a sitting target. We require mobility. If we take out their central dungeon core, they will lose their power. We head for King's Hill. We will find their dungeon core and tear it out. You will act as a distraction out here."

Asadi nodded as a dungeon hunter stepped up to Gregor.

"The cores?"

"Our cousin was killed on the second ship. A group of hunters is going to recover the core. The other ship, our cousin survived and is bringing the core here."

"Good, this place is so thin in mana I doubt that we are even in the realms anymore. Having another core will be welcome."

"Head Asadi, might we send recovery teams to the ships to recover the mana stones?" Cai Bo asked.

Gregor overheard them. The woman was painfully dutiful, a loyal Willful Instituted High Elder unless one knew the deal she had struck to gain power to control the sect or enter the Black Phoenix Clan.

"A good point. Elder Hao, send people to recover the mana stones immediately. Use only trusted people. Having that many mana stones in one's reach would tempt anyone."

"Yes, Sect Head. I will see to it personally."

Gregor would be glad to be done with all these vipers and back in the higher realms dealing with his own clan.

Derrick stepped out of the totem. There were no walls around the First Realm city's totem. People looked over in wonder at the group of ten that stood there wearing expert and journeyman level armor with the Adventurer's guild emblem on their chest.

Guards that had been patrolling nearby walked over.

"What is this place?" Derrick asked, walking to greet them.

"This is the capital of the Shikoshi Kingdom, my lord," the guard said politely.

Derrick pulled out his sound transmission device. "In position. Send the others."

"Queen Ikku, right?" He looked around, spotting the castle in the distance.

"She—" The guard frowned as the totem flashed again. The square filled with fighters wearing the same Adventurer's Guild Emblem.

"Forward march!" An officer called out. The square of people marched out in time, splitting apart.

The totem flashed again, and another square of guild members appeared, marching out.

"Well, we best have a little talk with her."

"Wh-what for?" the guard asked.

"She attacked our home and we're going to need your totem for a while." Derrick grinned and waved his beast storage device as he and his personal guards pulled out their aerial beasts.

"No rest for us guildies."

Erik returned to the hidden storeroom through the teleportation formation as Rugrat hit a section of wall with his hammer.

The stone broke, revealing several small storage devices. There were several such holes around the storeroom and even more in the room outside where they had fought the stone golems.

"I think that should be it," Rugrat said.

"Nice, once we have this all shifted to the storeroom we can head back to Cronen." Erik stacked storage crates on the teleportation formation.

Rugrat inspected the storage devices from the stone and put them into a pocket.

Erik finished stacking up crates.

"I'll get the other ones. See you on the other side," Rugrat said.

"Okay." Erik activated the teleportation formation.

He re-appeared in the airship warehouse. He moved all the boxes that were on the teleportation formation, shoved them against the wall, and dragged them out into the exterior corridor. He sat down on a crate, looking at all the storage crates in the room.

The teleportation formation flashed. Rugrat appeared with the rest of the storage devices from General Ubren's hideaway.

"Damn, that's a lot of boxes," Rugrat said as he picked a couple up and tossed them to Erik. Erik caught them and put them around outside of the warehouse, catching the next one tossed over.

"We'll head back to Cronen. We should get a signal there to call in the Special Teams to help us take all this to the lower realms. That, or we go to Alva, grab some people who can make it to the Seventh Realm and have them cart everything back. You filled up on mana stones, right?"

"Yeah. You sure we don't need metals or anything else?"

"We need the stones to get to the First Realm and pay for the passage of everyone using the totems and the teleportation pads. Speed up getting all of this to Alva."

Rugrat threw over the last storage crate, clearing the teleportation formation.

"Should we take some of them with us?"

"We take them with us, and we don't have a ride. We'll have to leave them in that seedy hotel or carry them across Cronen. People will start asking questions."

"Yeah, makes sense. Well, back to civilization? George, boy!"

George snaked through Erik's legs, getting to the teleportation pad, only the size of a medium dog.

Erik stepped on the teleportation formation as well.

Rugrat activated it.

They appeared in their rented room again, the smell of wood and wet filling their noses.

Erik and Rugrat's sound transmission devices buzzed wildly.

"Damn, we're popular." Rugrat laughed and listened to the message.

"This is Storbon. We found several airships hidden under the Willful Institute City Henghou. The assassination program and the seventh display operation have been activated."

"Shit," Erik said under his breath.

The next message played.

"This is agent Stonewash. The Willful Institute have attacked the First Realm. They are mobilizing Mercy's army in the Third Realm and are gathering the sect's support. We're heading to the First Realm to support."

"Grab the formation," Erik said.

Rugrat stored it away. Erik threw the room door open. They ran through the hotel and out the door at the yells of the hotel clerk.

They ran through Cronen for the nearest totem. They butted through the line, getting yells as they stepped onto the totem pad.

"Shit!" The Alva totem was in use, as was Zahir's. He flicked through other totems in the First Realm.

"We'll go down random and teleport," Rugrat said.

Erik activated the totem.

It felt like the air had thinned. The two stumbled for a half-second with the lack of mana density.

"Let's go." Erik and Rugrat ran past the people that were gathering to stare at the totem.

They leaped up into the air, not hiding their abilities as they jumped onto roofs.

George expanded to his full size. Rugrat and Erik jumped onto his back, accelerating over the random city's walls. Erik saw the sea in the distance and lush jungles below that had been tamed with a series of cities, towns, and outposts.

"Find out where we are," Erik said as he tried to contact people in Alva. He wasn't connecting to any of them.

"We're far, man. Let's try the formation."

They dropped down into the forest. Beasts scattered in their presence.

Rugrat threw down the teleportation formation.

They plugged in formation links.

"They must've shut down the network. Access only," Erik hissed.

"How far are we? We either random jump around the planet to get close to Alva, or we fly," Erik said.

Rugrat pulled out his map. "There are thousands of totems, even across the First Realm. We're a few hours from it if we buff George," Rugrat said.

Erik looked at George. He growled and tossed his head at his back.

"Thank you, boy," Erik said.

He pulled out a pill and tossed it in the air. George snatched the pill in his jaws. The potent fire element energy spread through his body, causing his fur to flare with power.

Rugrat and Erik swung up on George's back. With a roar, he leapt into the sky. His wings flared with flames along their length. They grabbed onto their handles and ducked against the wind, tapping their magazine pouches, checking their rifles.

Erik closed his eyes, forcing his imagination and mind to calm, conjuring images of destruction, leaving a stunned group of guards and bystanders.

Lin Lei walked out of the totem into the First Realm and up to the nearest guard. Her guards followed her as another group laid down a teleportation formation.

The totem guard stood straighter. "Second group to appear through that totem today. Never seen it used twice in one day."

"Heard it was a flying beast, wolf or something," another guard muttered.

Lin Lei frowned. "Sorry about this." She reduced her power and punched the nearest guard, denting his armor as he was thrown backward, landing on the ground.

Event
The city of Ransal is under attack! Pick a side!
Defend Ransal   Attack Ransal

The guard grunted from the ground. Lin Lei cast a healing spell on him and took out a scroll and threw it to another guard.

"Give this to your leader." She turned and walked away.

A guard yelled and threw a spear.

Her sword flashed out of her scabbard, one slice shattering the spear before she kept walking.

"Don't go causing trouble now." She walked back to the other group, who raised up defenses around the totem and had the teleportation formation set up.

"Keep up the good work," she said to the lower realm guild members manning the defenses. They were from the Second and Third Realms. With high level gear they could easily deal with the First Realm forces, but they'd be hard pressed to fight the United Sect Armies at Vermire.

Lin Lei stepped on the teleportation formation with her guards, taking out her sound transmission device. She looked at the totem, now just inert stone.

"Ransal under attack. Totem is deactivated. Moving to next target."

Across the First Realm, teams of Guild members appeared, punching guards and healing them, passing notes and setting up around the totems.

Domonos helped a wounded soldier through the teleportation formation, dragging him toward the medics. They grabbed the limping man.

The room was in movement, soldiers withdrawing from dozens of outposts to the bunker-line.

They held as long as possible, but they were a small army against a sea of sects. Holding the outposts would only lead to them losing their lives.

"Sir!" A medic grabbed onto his armor.

Domonos focused on him, realizing he had been calling him for some time.

"What is it, trooper?" Domonos growled.

"How long has your armor been active?"

Domonos thought about the outpost, the last retreat as the fighting turned to spells and melee weapons.

"I don't know," he said.

"I thought as much. You're getting some pod time." The man pulled him by the carrier.

"I have troops to command!" Domonos tried to pull his hand off his carrier.

The medic turned on him, putting his face in Domonos' helmet so fast Domonos reeled back. "We have a chain of command for a reason, sir! You don't trust your people to do their jobs?"

Domonos sputtered. The medic growled and shoved his head forward farther.

"I have lives to save, sir. So, shall we compare dick size or are you going to listen to me? Get your fucking ass in a fucking pod so I can get you fighting again."

Domonos was stunned into silence.

"Good!" The healer hit Domonos in the neck with a Conqueror's potion.

Domonos grunted as the medic moved him bodily by his carrier and pointed.

"You follow that group there. Couple minutes of pod time, you'll be at a hundred percent and can use your armor again in the future. You have until you reach the pod to put your shit in order. Am I understood?"

"Yes, medic."

"Good!" The medic signaled to the medics controlling the group who had activated their armor, pulling Domonos in their direction.

Domonos hissed as his knee elicited a wave of pain. He looked down at the piece of metal sticking out of it and leaned on the medic supporting him so he didn't have to use it.

"Ah shit," he muttered as he joined the group.

"You'll be fine." The medic tore the metal out of his leg.

It burned like a hole through his leg as they shoved a healing powder into the wound, repairing bone, and mending muscle and skin.

"Give it a minute to set." The medic ran past him into the fighting.

Wounded came in, were assessed, and put on stretchers. Those with their armor active created dungeon beasts, and civilians grabbed the stretchers and ran them through to the hospitals.

"Pri-Alpha!" a medic called out.

Domonos gritted his teeth with a hiss and stood. His pants were a bloody mess but the hole in his knee was gone.

"You two!"A man smacked Domonos and another with active armor. "Get this man to the hospital as soon as possible!" He pointed to a man he had been working on.

The two bent, picking up either side of the stretcher. The medic kept working, checking the IV line.

The medic used a carabiner to stick the IV bag he'd attached to the man on Domonos' carrier.

"Go!"

Domonos and the other soldier picked up the stretcher. Enhanced with the armor, they shot off.

"Alpha coming through!" the soldier up front yelled.

Walking wounded, even missing limbs or half dazed, got skinny for the wounded soldier as they screamed past.

Other runners used beast storage devices to move wounded quickly.

They sped out of the teleportation hub and into the hospital.

"Alpha!"

"Over here!" A civilian waved them over. They rushed to them, slowing down for the wounded.

They entered a large open warehouse-like building with a large A above the open door. The interior had been turned into a massive hospital. IVs hung from wires on the ceiling. Formations were carved into the ground and the ceiling to assist. Medics rushed around, administering spells and concoctions as needed. Surgery was going on in the open under medic's careful watch.

"Here," a medic called out, wearing his gown gloves and glasses. There was a team waiting around the bed. They put the stretcher down on a waiting cart.

"Three, two, one, lift!"

They shifted the soldier to the bed. A medic released the IV bag from Domonos' carrier. She hooked it up to the hanging wire. The head medic read the notes scrawled on the soldier's head.

Another medic indicated to the door.

Domonos and the other soldier walked toward it.

"Alpha!"

They pushed to the side as another stretcher came in.

"Here!" A medic called out. A team prepared around another open bed.

Domonos and the soldier walked out. They crossed the alpha's and bravo's priority wounded warehouses. There were several Charlie warehouses, all filled with cultivation pods.

People who had lost a foot instead of a leg went here.

They arrived at the front.

"Raise your arms!" A civilian on their left wrapped a bandage with a healing needle around their arm. A civilian on their right did the same with a stamina needle.

They whirred and stabbed through their skin and into their bone, activating.

Domonos grunted and moved forward. Like others, he moved forward quickly and into the raised pod furthest from the entrance. He activated the pod. It began closing and tilting as he pulled his helmet off, storing it and pulled on the waiting mask.

The pod lowered and an aerosolized stamina potion flowed through his mask. He breathed in deeply, feeling his mind clear. The fog that had rested on his brain lifted. Mana flowed into the pod as well.

He tilted his head, looking at the map on his inner arm, using the opposite hand to manipulate it.

"Zukal, it's Domonos. Talk to me. How are things looking?"

"Aren't you supposed to be in armor recovery?"

"I am. Now, sitrep."

"Shit, all right. Yes, sir."

40

Break in the Second Line

Glosil studied the map, scanning the breaches appearing around the outpost line. The enemy forces were being redeployed, utilizing formations to leapfrog past the second line of defenses.

"The Adventurer's Guild is shutting down the totems as we speak. They are shifting fighting forces into the closest cities," Elan said.

"Withdraw the second line to the bunker-line. We'll draw them in against our bunker walls, kilometers from their controlled totems." Glosil circled the bunker line and then planted his hand on it. "Hold them in place here." His eyes turned further afield.

"Once the special teams, the Tiger Corps, and Close Protection Details can get formations into the cities under the United Sect Alliance, we can hit them in the rear," Glosil half-muttered, his eyes working between the different layers of defense and the enemy positions.

The enemy-controlled totems had a burst of activity after the warships had come through, but it had slowed to almost nothing. Every available fighter had been pulled from battles across the ten realms to join the fight. Several other sects, after seeing their gathered power in the lower realms, had elected to join the United Sect Alliance.

They spilled through the opening left by the Wild Reaches Trading Outpost. Coordinated fire from artillery had thinned the coverage elsewhere. Under Zukal's command, they had slowed the press of the sects but hadn't stopped it.

Like an infection, the Sects pushed through the opening in the defensive line, spreading out and attacking other towers, widening the breach. The towers dropped below the ground once again and fell back to the bunker line.

The sects' teleportation formations shifted forces from across the second line right to the front, pushing into the heavily trap-filled area between the outpost line and the bunker line.

Marco's rolling spell barrage tactic allowed them to advance with minimal casualties.

The cities were under constant threat at the outer edge of the defenses, a thorn in the Sect Alliance's side as they had to keep forces there, exchanging attacks with the cities. The fighting had largely calmed down, the Sects taking up defensive positions to make sure the cities couldn't affect a breakout and flank the enemy.

"They have marshaled their forces well. I guess a few months of working together will let even the sects understand how to work together." *Still, it is a massive force with many commanders. Good if they have a simple objective, hard if they have multiple.*

Lieutenant General Yui and his remaining forces of forty thousand waited in teleportation rooms under Alva, ready to be sent out. Glosil was tempted to unleash his forces now, to open up the cities and effect a breakout.

No, I need them to create a smoke screen for the guild, the last nail in the coffin. Some of the teleportation formations had been found and destroyed as the enemy advanced, but Alva had been laying down teleportation formations for years. Many of them remained.

Glosil could feel it all balancing on a wire.

Outposts were evacuated first, stripped clean of anything that might help the enemy, charges primed. As the last defenders left, they blew the outpost, turning it into a crater, denying the United Sects a forward base.

He watched the towers dropping below. The enemy surged between the gaps left behind to find the ground littered in trap formations.

Artillery crews targeted where the towers and outposts had been, waiting and watching as the enemy filled the open spaces. They relaxed for too long as the waiting cannons opened fire once again. The enemy had brought stronger mana barriers than what they had at Vuzgal, but they couldn't expect to hold up against too many direct hits by the artillery cannons.

Rail cannons blazed, striking out at the enemy warships. They broke barriers and shredded armor. It was so thick to take several hits, having to rotate the ships to spread the damage and present the barriers on their other side. They traveled just fine, if they were looking forward or backward.

That damn shared mana barrier is a bigger pain in my ass than I feared. We're wearing them down, but not fast enough. Egbert doesn't have the mana to use the formations again. The air force has been taking a pounding, and we don't have any more missiles left.

He looked at a bar on one of the main screens displaying Alva's power reserves. In the city, it was snowing mana stone powder from the rate of mana stones that were being burned through. Even with the drill no longer operating.

He was abuzz with adrenaline, not born of anger or excitement, but fear. He danced on that wire, everything in the balance. His body was numb, but his brain was alight with plans and counterplans, running through situations.

"Keep the barriers on the towers, bunker line, north mountain and the cities active. All others, shut them down. Have all commanders look to conserve power. Only medical cases to be transmitted through the teleportation formations. Keep the formation board clear."

A section of the command center had been given over to the teleportation operators. Their job was to teleport people to the right place across the First Realm.

"Domonos reports that he's heading back to the front with others who have recovered from their injuries," Elan said.

"Good." Glosil patted him on the shoulder and squeezed. "Zukal did a fine job. Those two are one hell of a team."

The fighting had gone on for over three days. Now, the morning of the fourth day peered over the mountains, casting new light and shadow. Nearly eight hundred thousand sect members and conscripted First Realm fighters crashed against Alva's defenses. Another two hundred thousand lay dead or wounded.

Nearly three hundred and fifty thousand Alvans manned the walls, reservists both from the Beast Mountain Army and those that had stepped up and Dragon Corps. Forty thousand of the Tiger Corps lay in wait and a two hundred thousand Guild members prepared to move.

Marco stepped onto the teleportation formation. In a flash, the distant warships were now above him, their barriers taking hits intended for the teleportation formations underneath as the sects boiled forward.

His guards guided him to a set of tents set on a spell-raised hill. The ground had been cleared with spells, forces marshaled and sallied forth into the thinning forest ahead.

He stopped before the tent, looking over the thousands that poured forward. Formations dropped, allowing more to move up. Light flashed overhead, striking the warships' barriers. One failed, rounds hitting the side of the ship, shredding armor plating as the ship rotated. New barriers flashed with impacts as the damaged formations started to repair.

Hits struck the massive barriers covering the deployment area. As one would fail, secondary barriers underneath would take over, creating layered defenses for the first barriers to be repaired and used again.

Marco turned from their preparations and looked at the bunker-line in the distance. They, too, sat upon a spell-created hill, jutting out of the dirt and stone.

A shiver ran through his spine. He gripped his hands as he tried to dissipate the feeling. *Just what carnage waits on that hill?*

Towers from the second line appeared behind and above the bunkers, scarred from battle. Repairs were affected immediately. He couldn't see anything along the line, but he had the feeling of standing in front of an ant hill. Even if he didn't see it, he sensed the furious, controlled effort that ran through those bunkers like life blood ran through the human body.

He walked into the command tent, finding Eva there already.

"The Sects are pushing forward through the formations. As you ordered, I am getting them to spread out along the line. The towers are all heading back to the bunker-line. There are sect leaders that want to use our formations here at Wild Reaches to push forward."

"Report it to Head Asadi. I think it is in our best interest to push a united front forward. If we're bunched up, we'll be targets for the enemy's artillery. We cannot let the Vuzgalians concentrate their forces anymore. This is where they will fight." He dismissed King's Hill in his eyes.

"Not at the city?"

"No, the defenses at the bunker line are much stronger than anything at the ci—" A sound transmission device interrupted him. "Head Asadi?"

"Hunter Gregor has found the location of the dungeon core. It is located in a small mountain to the northeast of the city, inside the bunker-line and under the mountain the Vuzgalians aerial fighters are flying from."

The map in front of Marco altered, showing a marker on a non-descript mountain.

Glosil watched the map, his eyes flickering between different points, *feeling* the flow of battle. Every order created action and reaction from his own people and the enemy, a mental dance with the greatest risks on either side.

"Something has changed." He waved toward groups of fighters grouping together, shifting from different areas along the line to create a dense field of fighters. "These are Willful Institute units, correct?"

"Yes," Elan said.

Holding back their strongest forces. Marco would bring them with him to have a strike force to slot in as he needs. Unless he has a better target in mind.

He looked at the bunker line, and at the warships pushing forward once again, but who had altered their heading.

"Get me Pan Kun!"

"You're live." An aide activated a sound transmission device in the table.

"Sir?"

"Loop in the special teams on the line, Yui, and Domonos."

They registered moments later.

"They have either discovered our dungeon core or they know about Alva. Pan Kun, you command that section of the bunker-line. Storbon, Roska, Han Wu, you are to support Lieutenant General Pan Kun. Lieutenant General Yui, carry out your attack once you're prepared. Lieutenant General Domonos, hold your line and force a confrontation. Prepare your forces to break out and flank if you need to." Glosil turned to look at Elan. "Any wounded that are sent back to Alva and those willing to fight will man the defenses here."

Glosil pulled out another sound transmission device and called Gong Jin, Niemm, and Yao Meng. "Begin your operations immediately. Cut them off."

Ripples spread through the map, changing the balance. Glosil studied it. *The dice are rolled. Now to see where they might land.*

Niemm rolled over the wall. Yawen and Setsuko shot the two nearby guards before they had time to react without a sound.

Event
The city of River Guard is under attack! Pick a side!
Defend River Guard Attack River Guard

He checked both sides as the rest of his team crossed the wall and spread out toward the gate's tower.

Niemm held back, letting others go ahead. He listened for any notes of alarm before raising his fingers in an okay signal for the rest of the team. "All clear. Get the company ready to move," Niemm said, seeing flashes in the tower.

"Understood," Setsuko said from her perch.

Niemm moved to follow the groups who had made entry to the gate's tower, which served as a place for the guards to pass their time between shifts letting people in and out of the city. The roads were silent without traders.

Bodies lay along Niemm's path as they worked their way through.

They reached the bottom of the stairs.

"Yeah, and then I said..." The guard opening the door walked in, talking to his friend.

He must have noticed the group on the stairs just as the first rounds punched through him and the door silently. The first man rushed forward, lowering his rifle. There were a series of grunts and yells. The rest of the team pushed up and through. The first man had a cut on his arm as he raised his rifle, three dead at his feet.

Niemm spotted the other team coming down the stairs on the other side of the gate. He signaled them toward the gate.

Two hooked their rifles to their carriers and ran to the gate, the rest covering.

"You three, help those on overwatch." Niemm tapped different people. They hustled up the stairs as the gate groaned. The team members did the work of twelve men, opening the gate with ease.

The ground seemed to writhe as the Close Protection Detail's shed their covering illusion sheets; moving through the gate, their officers and section leaders commanded them.

Several rushed forward on their mounts to support. Others lay down teleportation formations.

Niemm saw movement in the distance. Aerial beasts, newly arrived through the city's totem, flew off toward King's Hill.

Niemm pulled back into a corner of the stairs, out of the way. "Lieutenant General Yui, this is Team One actual, message over."

"Go ahead, Niemm."

"We've made entry to the target. Company is moving in."

"Good to hear. Once you have that totem, coordinate with the Adventurer's Guild. We'll do our best to keep them off you."

"Understood, sir."

Major General Lukas ducked into the corridor that ran inside Shida's walls. He blinked, adjusting his eyes to the darkness. Flashes of light, spells against the mana barrier, seared through the arrow slits, shadowing silent gunners against the opposite wall. Soldiers ate and talked, working on their positions to make them comfortable. Casings scraped across the floor by gunner's boots and stored in storage rings.

Brass magnets. Lukas frowned, remembering how Erik and Rugrat snorted at one another when they saw someone doing it on the range.

The conversations ran silent, and soldiers made to stand at his and his guards passing. They were waved back down.

Lukas reached a section of wall, looking at the enemy lines.

Four lines in every direction. Looks like they've been learning.

The enemy camps were dug into the ground, trenches instead of the large compounds they had used at Vuzgal.

He didn't blink, taking it all in as the early hints of light on the horizon brightened.

Lukas studied the enemy lines in the distance and scanned the sparse hallways of soldiers.

"Issue stamina rations to every soldier to be taken immediately. I want them alert and ready."

"Yes, sir," an aide said.

Lukas waited and watched. His eyelids and face felt like it was caked in salt, itching and rubbing with every blink. He used a clean spell and rubbed his face quickly, not wanting to take his eyes off the enemy.

He nearly jumped when his sound transmission device went off.

"Lukas here."

"We're in position. You mind opening up the show for us?" Lieutenant General Yui said.

"Yes, sir!"

Lukas flipped over to the general channel. "Stand to. Stand to!"

The city moved. Those that had been in their bunks or in secondary positions ran to the walls, streaming through the streets.

Those that had been joking and finishing drinking their stamina ration were grim faced and focused as they pulled on helmets, running to their positions, checking their weapons with ingrained reflex, adjusting their tripods. They moved ammunition boxes around to be ready in a moment.

Lukas jumped to the command channel. "In five minutes, I want a show of force. Every mage we have casting spells, every gun firing for three minutes of fury. Friendlies are moving up to their rear. Hopefully, they can do something about their barrier. It's our job to keep the enemy confused and their attention on us."

The replies filtered back, and Lukas checked his timepiece.

The minute arrived.

Shida *erupted* with fury.

The hallway was deafening with the buzz of machine guns. People could only mouth what they were saying and smack one another, using hand signals more than voice.

As one gun sent off a peel of tracer fire, another fired off of it, leaving a cross-stitch of tracer rounds across the enemy positions.

One could feel the taps of the machine guns, the pounding thump of mortars sent skyward, and bass rumbles of artillery cannon.

Spells added their light display, the thunder and fires of magic.

Barriers over the four entrenched positions lit up with the display. The sects, not to be outdone, retaliated with their own attacks. The barriers of Shida lit up angrily once again.

Lukas' eyes burned as he focused on the command area of the nearest entrenched position. *Come on, Yui. Come on.*

They had been watching the camps all this time, figuring out where their leadership hid, where their supplies were stored.

The excitement of the shooting withered as Lukas' unblinking eyes watered against the air whipping through the arrow slits.

Several shells struck the entrenched position one after another. The barrier shuddered and then collapsed.

"Shift fire onto presets!" Lukas yelled.

Cannons, machine guns, and mortars gears whirled onto preset firing locations and fired. They raked mages casting positions, the headquarters. Mortar and artillery shells changed to Earth type shells to collapse the trench lines.

Another barrier was pummeled out of existence, receiving the same treatment as Shida bared her teeth, accurately and deadly reaping their unprotected enemy.

"Moving in on the southern entrenched position. Hold your fire!" Yui ordered through the Shida command channels.

Weapon fire went silent. The cannons and mortars shifted to assist the others.

Between the smoke and dust, Lukas saw the Tiger Corps advancing, firing and covering one another as they ran across the muddied ground, churned up by the boots of thousands.

They marched forward, using grenades and spells on the trenches, pushing forward.

They hit the east and west next. Shida's guns left them little to take In the north. Finally, Shida fell silent, silent in a way it had not been in four days. Her barriers recovered, not showing the impacts of spells as guns smoked and pinged in the chill of the morning air.

Event
You have successfully defended Shida.
Rewards: 32,500,000EXP +20% defensive bonus to Shida defenders.

Lukas didn't know when or where the cheer came from, but it rose through the city as he left the wall, calling his mount. His guards raced to follow him as he rode for the city's totem.

He rushed up the main way when he saw the first of the Adventurer's Guild riding out of the totem.

"Clear the streets and unlock the gates to allow the Adventurer's guild out. Set our people to repairing the formations and the city. Get their weapons clear and send them to get some sleep!" Lukas yelled to his aide who had joined him at the side of the street, yelling over the sounds of the mounted beasts, like rolling drums, as aerial beasts took to the skies.

"Are we going to send forces out with them?" the aide asked, eager.

"No, we remain here and defend. Those are our orders from Lieutenant General Pan Kun. We will hold and support the forces attacking the rear of the Sects."

Lukas pulled out a map, looking as friendly forces poured forth from the once occupied cities around the Vermire Empire.

Strike groups of the Tiger Corps executed attacks against supply points, forces sieging Vermire cities and medical aid stations.

The sect members might get better healing than if they hadn't been captured.

A thick ring of the Sects had formed around the bunker-line. Lukas knew there were more people than in all the other packets combined in that line.

One thing at a time. We've cut them off. Now, we bleed them.

41
Bunker Line

Marco looked at Eva Marino. As the barrier above shook, dust dropped down and shook the mana lights scattered around.

"The Sect Head denies our request to teleport our forces to the airships. He says that they have limited power and cannot deal with the strain. He also disagrees with our assessment of the fighting around the supporting cities. He asserts that we should be able to rebuff the attacks of the Adventurer's Guild and Vuzgalians."

So instead, I have to drop them into the field of battle, right into the fight where the enemy's cannons can destroy some of our strongest barriers, then wait for them.

"Get the rearmost forces to secure their positions. All we need now is for the enemy to charge up our backsides." Marco's sound transmission device buzzed him.

"Marco, focus on breaking this line. We cannot be stopped here. Use everything."

"What do you mean, High Elder?"

"I mean that *every* totem in the First Realm has been blocked off. We cannot get any more supplies or forces from the higher realms."

"How could they?" Marco was dazed with just how ambitious the undertaking must have been.

"It doesn't matter," Cai Bo snapped. "If we can take their dungeon core, we will no longer be debuffed and we can turn this around. Lead the forces attacking the dungeon location. Distract them so Gregor can get inside, and it won't matter what little tricks they use."

"Yes, High Elder." She closed the sound transmission, leaving Marco in silence for half a second.

Marco quickly relayed what he had been told, Eva's face only darkening. He sighed "And you look like you are not looking forward to telling me what you have to do next."

Eva gave him a thin smile.

"With the lack of mana in the First Realm, and the distance that they are teleporting over, the cost to our mana stones is going to be immense. The other sects are asking us to supply a greater portion of the mana stones."

"Marco, you know that lines will form if you continue to frown like that and you will scare everyone else?" Marino said, adjusting the mana formation on her hip.

Marco cleared his throat and his thoughts. "As soon as we started to surround their outer cities, they fled. It was the same with the outposts. This line of bunkers is a spread-out defensive line around King's Hill. It must be their last defense before the city itself. We know that they have a small population. This may allow them to focus their forces."

Marco looked at the bunker-line and the forces on the ground. "Get word to the commanders of the different fighting forces. Tell them that I will part with some of my rewards, but they are to force the line. If we pause here, if we falter, we die."

Everyone in the room looked at Marco. He felt the weight of their gazes, their questions.

"The Vermire Empire has reacted to every action we've taken. They drew us in, causing us to send in our forces as soon as they grouped up to the advancing front to gain momentum. Their retreat drew us in and they pincered us with small units supported by the Adventurer's Guild that attack our walls." Marco looked between the duo, his raised arm level with the floor as the building shuddered once again.

"We thought Vuzgal was their home. We thought it was their seat of power. How many dungeon cores have we found littering the grounds of this empire? How many of our people have had their strength decline with formations that cross *tens of kilometers*? They haven't retreated. We have not forced them. They have tactically withdrawn. What in the *fuck* did we just stumble into? And who the hell are these people?"

The violence outside was louder than ever with the drifting silence.

"Since we have nowhere to retreat, then we must take a play from their book. We must advance. Call all the forces in the cities that are currently under attack. Have them teleport their people to the front while they still can."

"We're abandoning the cities?" Eva said.

"No, we're advancing on the enemy." Marco sneered.

Eva grimaced, and Marco agreed with her sentiment.

The United Sect Army was a mass threading between cleared trees, funneled by roots and uneven terrain toward the bunker-line, their yells like thunder even at this distance.

"Fire!" Pan Kun yelled.

The Alva and Vermire army replied with their own thunder. Barriers across the Army snapped into existence. Artillery units pounded on barriers as machine gunners left lines of tracers and rounds at chest height and mages called down destruction.

The United Sect Army replied with their own mana cannons appearing among the trees, their mages' attack spells.

Barriers collapsed as machine guns traversed their zones, reaping a bloody harvest.

Pan Kun frowned as the enemy mages shifted the earth, creating trenches.

In minutes, they had a chaotic network of trenches under the cover of the charging forward sects.

"That is going to be a problem." Pan Kun turned his periscope, reviewing the battlefield.

Sects continued to push their people up, using mana cannons and spell scrolls to cross the gap. They seemed to have realized trenches were effective, creating paths in the ground to attack from. They had an extensive network of them already.

"Keep using the earth golems and earth spells to harass them. What's the situation with the airships?"

"They're advancing, sir," Nasreen said, connected by sound transmission device "They will arrive within ten minutes."

Pan Kun swung his periscope, finding the ships in the distance. One frigate and five corvettes.

Spells lit the sky with puffs of smoke as mages destroyed incoming artillery shells.

His helmet's sound transmission device flipped.

"Pan Kun, it's Yui Silaz."

"Report?" Pan Kun asked.

"We have secured the surrounding cities. My forces are gathering with the Adventurer's Guild to hit the sect's rear. At this time, we have sealed off the First Realm."

"The airships are bearing down on us. The sects got smart and went to ground. They've created trenches and are extending them toward the front lines. They're using cannons, spells and spell scrolls."

A mana cannon's blast struck above Pan Kun' periscope, blooming on the mana barrier's surface.

He no longer flinched, and kept watching the movement in the dirt. Mortars kept the sect fighters hidden.

"Sir, the airships are in range," Nasreen said.

"Shift fire to the airships. Give them something to think about."

Weapons that had gone silent without targets turned their barrels skyward and released their pent-up energies.

"We've just engaged the airships. I just hope they piss off. If they're in range of our guns, we're in range of theirs."

The airships turned, presenting their broadsides. Spells fell upon the bunkers, sound and light washing out the world as their powerful mana cannons fired on Pan Kun for the second time.

"We'll be there as fast as we can."

"I hope that's sooner than I know it will be, because our mana barriers won't be able to take this pounding for too long."

Pan Kun wheeled his periscope around, watching the movement in the dirt increase.

"Got to go, brother. Stay safe."

"You too."

"All right, you fucking pricks." Pan Kun stepped away from the periscope and onto an enhancing formation, opening a channel to his mages, his engineers, his Close Protection Details and the Special Teams.

"Hit that damn fleet with everything you have!"

Spell formations flowered and angled into the air, glowing so brightly as to burn the image into bystanders' eyes.

Mana transformed into spells, rising to meet the deluge of attacks on their barrier.

Magics distorted the air, crisscrossing one another, striking one another at times. Barriers were slugged back and forth.

"Focus your fire on the big one!"

The fire tightened. The barrier shimmered and shook around the fleet, but the bunkers were spotting as well.

Pan Kun roared, channeling more power into his fireball spell, arcing up into the sky over the bunker.

His body hummed with power, the formation under his feet lighting him from below.

The interconnected barrier spotted and then broke. Attacks hammered the side of the main ship. Personal barriers snapped up around the ship, protecting it before they were torn away. Hits tore away the metal of the ship's side, raking it and holing it in places.

"Our barriers are spotting!" Zukal yelled in Pan Kun's ear.

The frigate applied power, turning abruptly. The corvettes turned awkwardly as fresh cannons entered the fight. The ships moved around, making it harder to get sustained hits on them.

Sects charged out from trenches closer to the bunkers than Pan Kun had expected. They ran toward the bunkers, diverting more fire from the ship.

Attacks rained down on bunkers, focused and precise.

"Niemm, Storbon, I need your team's support! Glosil, we need something to deal with those airships!"

"Moving!" Niemm yelled.

"Egbert."

"Yes, sir. Davin and I are moving."

"The attack formations?" Pan Kun asked.

"We've burned a mountain of mana stones to keep all the barriers operating, the teleportation formations, pods, healing," Glosil ground out.

"But who needs them when you have a devious undead and Fire Imp on it? Kick their fucking asses around their ears!"

Cai Bo stood on the deck of *Perseverance* at her communications station.

Gregor and his hunters were having their own conference around the throne.

"Even the strongest defenses on the ground are no obstacle for a force in the air!" An elder laughed back at the map table.

Asadi stood tall in the middle. He smiled slightly. She thought she saw him frown as nearby movement drew her eye to an aide with a pale expression. Cai Bo waved for them to speak.

"Aerial forces moved to the rear to assess what was happening. They report that the Adventurer's Guild has appeared in force and is marching for our rear-lines, supported by Vuzgalian fighters. The outer cities have broken the siege. Attacks are occurring across our rear lines."

She saw a rail cannon's rounds strike the fleet's combined barrier, causing it to flare angrily.

A red and prismatic streak caught her eye, dropping from the sky above. Her brows pinched together, and she bit back a retort.

The lights shifted as she pointed at the streaks.

"What is that?" she asked her guard.

He used spells on his eyes. "It looks like a skeleton and a small creature with wings covered in flames." He sounded confused.

A spell appeared around the red blur.

She used a spell on her eyes to focus on the chubby, winged creature.

It expanded, horns growing from his head. A crown of blue flames appeared between his black horns, his wings as big as the mage standing beside him as ropey, rippling muscles covered his frame.

The ancient demon reached out with an imperious clawed hand as it and the skeleton passed the veil of barriers covering the warships.

Spell formations wrapped around his arms, appeared behind his back, burning into the air itself as the world shook around him.

A beam of power launched from his finger; it was too fast to track. Cai Bo's attention snapped to the corvette underneath the demon.

There was no apparent damage.

"What?"

She pulled her gaze away as a miniature sun bloomed in the heart of the corvette, expanding the ship, before the sun collapsed and flames shot out in every direction. The corvette tore apart, filling the air with the sound of thunder as the trees under the ship burnt to ash, having no time to set aflame.

The ground peeled back and shredded, the forest tossed away. The aerial forces were nothing more than toys in a god's tantrum.

The red streak dimmed in power. The demon returned to his chubby appearance.

He jumped on the back of the mage like a tired toddler.

The mage turned his head.

Cai Bo shivered at the skeletal head of pure white, the runic tattoos filled with magical power.

The mage shot across the sky; aerial forces rose to meet him.

A staff appeared in his hand.

He waved it in the sky. A spell formation appeared at its end, twisting the air, creating a cone around him. Air blades cut out at the aerial riders as he weaved through their formations. Spells from casters on the deck of the corvette attacked him.

He surged forward, appearing on the deck of the corvette.

He cut out with his staff, killing a caster on his right. He dodged a mana blast from his right. Lightning tore free from his staff, hitting the attacker in the chest.

He danced forward among the spells slung across the deck of the ship.

Clouds gathered from across the skies, darkening as he continued to glow with power.

The skeleton exploded outward, two spells passing through where his chest had been, striking opposite casters as his bones reconnected.

"Ah, so kind of you to set out a welcome mat!" He stepped onto a spell enhancing formation in the middle of the ship. Blue runes outlined his body, contrasting with the flowery shirt under his glowing mage robes as his dungeon core overpowered the ship's dungeon core.

Egbert's runes grew brighter as he wrested control over the corvette.

"You're mine now," he said in a quiet voice.

The cannons dimmed, no longer supplied with mana.

He held his staff to the sky. Lightning descended, crashing into his staff. It glowed brighter and brighter, blinding.

He slammed the end of the staff into the ship. Lightning raced through the ship in a tsunami of annihilation. Formations exploded. Metal and stone buckled. Mana stones ignited. Lightning poured out of the ship, cracking and buckling it and detonating the trees below.

He stood in the middle of the deck, raising himself up to stand.

Smoke came off his body as the glow dimmed.

Machine guns, rail cannons and artillery cannon fire raked the three remaining corvettes and frigate, ripping into their thick armors. A corvette shuddered and shifted, trying to re-establish the combined barrier as Gregor yelled. The ships pulled in close together, their dead brethren dropping to the ground.

Metal and stone sheared off the exploding ship's sides.

The skeleton jumped back into the air and threw a pile of bones which spread out into an undead flying beast that roared into the sky, carrying its master and the fire imp back toward the bunker-line.

Cai Bo watched them leave in stunned silence, the tremor in her hand calming.

"That fucking skeleton again," Gregor growled, smashing the arm of his throne.

The ships pulled in, scarred and ragged, reforming a much smaller mana barrier against the attacks. Gun decks had been holed

"Activate the Phoenix Breath. Alamar, I'm leaving you to command the ship. Listen to Head Asadi. Fire on that bunker-line until you break it, then push forward and fire into that mountain. Carve me a damn path to their dungeon core." Gregor stood, pulling out his spear, his hunters gathering their weapons.

They left the ship, leaving one hunter behind, who reached up and touched the dungeon core, passing several screens.

"I have control over the ship. Once the other ships restore the mana barrier cover, we can fire. We need them to protect us as we charge and fire the weapon. It should break through the bunker's barriers. Make sure your people are ready."

Asadi turned his gaze to the others in the room, the elders concentrating their efforts. Now was their opportunity!

Marco turned from his position behind the tree line. Sect fighters pushed up into the trenches to get close to the bunkers and charge out.

The ground had been churned into mud, even with multiple hardening spells.

He checked his map and looked off into the distance, staring at the mana barrier that covered the non-descript hill.

He opened a sound transmission channel. "Elder Kostic, we have found the enemy's true base. I need your help in rallying the sects to attack the new position. I am told that the *Perseverance* will support us directly."

His eyes followed *Perseverance* as its mana barrier reappeared. Two battered corvettes limped along with it, the barriers snapping to one another.

Their sides had been raked in just a few minutes of fire, opening gun decks, and smashing stone and sandwiched Earth iron. This close to the Vuzgalian mountain could alter their aim and ammunition in seconds.

"I will direct what forces I can to assist. We are running low on mana stones for the teleportation formations."

"Understood."

Marco closed the channel.

"Teacher Marino, gather our forces. We move for that hill!"

She nodded and worked her sound transmission device. The flow of people into the trenches slowed. They reformed under the yelling and commands of their sects and hurried away from the bunker-line and King's Hill in the distance.

Perseverance's hull cracked and opened, drawing in mana to its heart, the Phoenix breath cannon.

Its mana cannons fired on the hill. The Corvette joined in. Powerful and ancient spell scrolls were used one after another upon the hill, tearing up the ground around it, its barrier a combination of splotches.

The corvettes presented their sides. Mages and mana cannons unleashed their torment.

Bunkers tried to fire on the ship, but to engage the warships, they'd have to disengage the advancing sect fighters.

The enemy aerial forces came on their sparrows and kestrels. The sects' aerial riders greeted them, turning the skies into a fierce melee.

Marco and his people mounted their beasts, moving with the surging armies that followed in the path of the fleet.

Perseverance's plating had peeled back to reveal the weapon that ran down its centerline. Formations along the outside of the warship glowed a fierce blue light as the cannon gathered power, lighting the ship from within.

The Phoenix Breath Cannon fired. A lance of power that startled the world itself struck the hill's mana barrier, causing it to fluctuate.

The bunkers had reinforced barriers and tons of power, but their formations could only take so much before they warped, melted, and broke.

The barriers over several bunkers cracked and fell apart. They were blasted away, leaving a path of ruin through the bunkers and ground underneath.

The cannon's light died down, revealing a smoking ravine in the bunker-line

"Move!" Marco yelled. His limbs felt like rubber watching the three warships push forward. Sect aerial forces screened them from attackers as they powered up their formations. The Phoenix Breath Cannon charged as it altered its point of aim.

The swirling streak of power struck out again, aiming at a valley between mountains, near the northern mountain the Aerial forces of Vuzgal commanded.

A barrier snapped into existence, taking the impact even as trees, stone, and dirt were carved from the ground by the cannon's bleed-over.

Delilah covered the wounded soldier with her body as Alva shook. She checked the patient, administering a concoction. He sighed in relief.

"Egbert!"

"We are being attacked by the main ship's main cannon." Egbert sounded... *tired.*

"Will they—?"

"I think so."

"The attack formations, the barrier?"

"The attack formations don't have the power needed to activate and sustain them. Qin and Julilah are working with the dungeon core to keep our defenses going. We are burning through what remains of the mana stones in the bank's vaults."

Alva shook with another impact.

"Contact the council leaders. Pass my order. All civilians are to be evacuated to the lower floors immediately."

Glosil checked his gear. Civilians, soldiers, wounded that had barely

returned to service were organized into a militia of Alvans. The force included farmers, smiths, alchemists, healers, factory workers, restaurant owners and people from all walks.

He had left his command center to stand on the front-line. Three times the Cannon had hit Alva, and three times it had stood.

The sects had pushed through the ravine, spreading out on either side to attack the nearby bunkers. Most rushed beyond the bunkers, toward Alva under the cover of the three remaining warships. They used teleportation formations to shift their forces forward again, bypassing fighting whole sections of the bunker-line.

Attacks from the Adventurer's Guild and Tiger Corps harassed the rear of the sects, wearing their forces thin. Drawing them into direct battle. They were making progress, but it wouldn't be fast enough.

The bunker-Line reaped a great many lives, but they could not stem the tide.

The fourth cannon blast had cut through Alva's barrier, burning through nearly all their remaining mana stone reserves. It had drilled a path through the valley, deep into the heart of stone, carving a new way down toward Alva one-hundred-meters wide, and made of molten ribbed stone.

Glosil looked up at the mana storing formation. It was in a sorry shape, letting out a dim light over the city. Shadows stretched through the once bright dungeon.

Momma Rodriguez swung a mace in her hand. Her eyes caught Glosil's and nodded to him.

Glosil wanted to tell her to hide in the rear, but he also knew how futile It would be. He nodded back and turned to face where the cannon had struck.

"Barrier spells!" Glosil tore a mana barrier spell scroll with hundreds of others.

Barriers like bubbles tore free of spell scrolls, interlacing and ballooned outwards, covering the dungeon core tower and spreading over the surrounding towers and buildings.

A new source of light cut through Alva's wall, crashing into apartments, through trading squares and roads, and a park before striking the layered mana barriers. The barriers burst in a mist of light, passing through dozens before the beam failed.

A rounded molten scar ran through the city, the force throwing stone and mana dust clear.

Debris and released energies battered the mana barriers as they looked upon the destruction wrought by the single attack.

Buildings tipped and collapsed in piles or smashed into one another.

The mid-afternoon sun peeked through the hole, creating a slope from the surface down to Alva. Light distorted, shifting and moving.

Glosil heard it in the distance, the sound of thousands calling for the death of their enemy, rushing down the new ramp into Alva.

Glosil moved forward. His soldiers moved with him.

Magma traced through his veins as his skin hardened around his hands and his rifle. His domain flowed out, his body thrumming with power.

"Man your positions. Move to advance. Do not let them into our home!" Glosil yelled.

Gunners moved to rooftops, setting down formations and pulling out their mounted machine guns, loading and preparing, pointing at the ramp.

Glosil jumped over a section of broken apartment. He landed on the other side, leaving a crater as he ran forward, accelerating, throwing up dust as he jumped off the twenty-meter-tall section.

He heard breaking stone behind him

Several soldiers barreled out of the building, their bodies transformed by their elemental energies, their mana pulsing as they raced forward.

Glosil skipped from rock to rock, over buildings and through them. The noise from the oncoming army grew, amplified as they reached the mouth of the ramp leading down into Alva.

He fired his rifle, a bolt action, one of the first ever made by Erik and Rugrat. The round glowed white as it whizzed through the air, striking a runner, piercing through several others before it stopped.

Glosil worked the action with the training of someone born with a rifle in their hands.

White lines stabbed through the oncoming enemy tide. They hurled spells back, hitting where Glosil had been.

Machine guns opened on the ramp, kicking up stone and dust as they cut through the tide of fighters rushing to meet the Alvans.

The machine guns weren't able to kill them all. They could only thin out the numbers.

Glosil tore out his old magazine and slapped in a fresh one. He dodged to the side, never looking away from the enemy. A spell passed where he had stood, striking through a wall as he calmly shot the attacker, changed to explosive shot and hit a group of fighters. The round detonated, killing them.

More rifles and spells hit the fighters that were nearing the end of the ramp. Soldiers and Alvans on the flanks started to arrive with the forces that Glosil had led forward.

Glosil continued to fire, holding his position. Others reinforced him, creating a line in the fallen remains of the city.

"Prepare to meet them!" Glosil barked as the enemy closed within twenty meters. An arrow hit Glosil's armor, pushing him to the side. He stored his rifle and flicked a shield out of his storage ring, a thick sword in his right.

Buffs landed on him and the forward fighting forces.

Glosil downed a potion. Power filled him. He lowered his stance. "Come on then, you bastards! With me, Alvans!"

Glosil roared and a new wall of noise met that of the sect fighters. Glosil accelerated, smashing his shield into a fighter and tossing them backward. He slashed out with his sword. A ribbon of white followed its path, cutting through three other sect fighters.

He kicked the ground. The stone opened into wells below the sect fighters and closed, cutting off their screams. Moving forward, he slammed into a man with his shield. The wave of force threw him and several others backward into spikes he raised from the ground. Blade and shield flowed as one.

He might be the commander of Alva's armies, but he wasn't going to let even the lords beat him in fighting ability.

A roar tore free of Glosil as his blade was freed from years of training, laying open fighters, defending his charges.

He shifted to the right. "Fire!" he roared. Soldiers fired into the enemy, cutting back their advance.

Glosil took in the battle. They had stalled the advance for now. Machine gun crews opened up into the opening of Alva.

"For Alva!" Glosil yelled and slashed out with his blade.

"For Alva!" The cry tore free from soldier and civilian throats as they charged forward.

A soldier charged forward with a spear, her movements gathering power upon her spear before she drove the flaming vortex forward, blasting through several ranks.

"Keep it tight. We let none past! I want a fire base on that building there, another one over in that courtyard!"

Glosil fought, directing with his sword as soldiers rushed to obey.

The *Perseverance* turned. Power built before the Phoenix Breath fired again, striking a complex of bunkers, the beam cutting across their front.

Cai Bo was in the section of the bridge filled with watchers.

She looked at the hidden city, a massive metropolis with an academy in the distance. The release of mana cracking the hill had been a shock. In the center of the city, a pillar of light dropped from the ceiling and from the floor through a large tower covered in formations that could only house the dungeon core.

"Seal the ship. Bring the cannons online," Asadi said. The ships started to converge.

"What is *that?*"

Cai Bo heard the half-whispered question, following the watcher's eyes to the red and blue streak that crossed the skies.

Perseverance locked together as Cai Bo moved to the console, watching over the man's shoulder as he adjusted the formations to get a better picture.

Cannons opened fire on the bunkers, supporting the forces on the ground. Other screens showed the tide of sects pouring down into the hidden city.

Cai Bo and the watcher were transfixed on the image as it resolved, showing two men on a powerful firewolf.

"The City Lords," Cai Bo muttered.

"Cai Bo?" Asadi asked, half hearing her.

"The City Lords have appeared. They're flying straight toward us!"

"What fools. Cannons, shift us and fire on them! Have the aerial forces move to engage!"

Erik stabbed Rugrat with another potion, storing the empty needle away.

"Fucking oorah!" Rugrat growled.

Erik felt the concoctions he had loaded into himself, raising his power to new heights. The wind tore at them both, George's speed reaching an entirely new level. Erik and Rugrat had fed him monster cores and given him concoctions to maintain his peak condition for so long.

Erik surveyed the Beast Mountain Range. Zahir released smoke into the sky. Farms and villages had been torn apart by the passage of armies. He could see riders, soldiers, and guild members pushing hard through the forests.

The outposts and cities lay in ruin. The once invisible bunker-line, merely an unwanted but necessary plan, was visible to all. Trenches ran through the ground, leading to the bunker lines.

Erik's chest tightened seeing the fighting raging across the bunker line, seeing the opening in Alva, the glow of the dungeon core and city over the heads of the sect fighters that flooded forward.

Tracers and spells tracked across the skies.

Erik's breath caught in his lungs. The bunker line stood; the air force led destruction in the skies. Artillery and mage attacks fell in concert.

What kind of self-centered prick am I to think that they need us to fight? They worked together in fluidity. War had come to Alva and Alva worked together. They were together.

Even if we were dead, Alva would fight on. A weight lifted from his shoulders. The twist of his stomach loosening, he sat up straighter.

They don't need us on the ground. Alva has this.

Erik's gaze captured the flying warships. The main warship fired, the weapon cutting through the barriers over a section of bunkers, leaving an open scar upon the land.

His nostril flared as he felt his fingers go numb, his heart beating in his ears.

"Rugrat."

He pointed at the ship.

"Don't they need us down there?"

"They have it handled. 'Bout time we used all this power."

They looked at one another.

Erik gripped his shoulder. "It's an honor, brother."

"Ride or die! Hold on, George!"

They altered their course as Erik and Rugrat released their control over their bodies and their mana. Their domains spread out around them as Rugrat's buffs fell on George, who expanded. Blue and white flames appeared on his coat as he left a trail of flames behind. Erik felt sweat on his brow as George roared and the sky boomed with their passing.

"Incoming!" Rugrat raised the Beast, casting spells upon it, and fired.

Erik reached his hands out to the sky, feeling the elemental energies around him.

Aerial riders from the United Sect Army saw them, pausing before they charged, casting their spells.

Flames poured from Erik's hands and trailed behind him, his chest tightening as tears rose in his eyes.

The flames roared with a familiar cry, forming into several flame-created versions of Gilly.

Rugrat fired; his rounds passed through open air between aerial riders, rushing toward them. The rounds detonated into chains, stabbing into surprised beasts and riders.

A half-dozen flame dragons exhaled and shot ahead of George, just as Gilly had raced with him so many times before.

Spells impacted the dragon's sides, weakening them as their flames burned into the aerial attackers and they crashed through the aerial fighter's ranks.

Erik stood up behind Rugrat. He used his left hand to hold on to Rugrat's shoulder as he raised his M8, connected to a belt fed ammunition crate on his back.

Erik fired bursts into the oncoming aerial fighters. None even got close under their fire.

George released a wave of fire lances as they blasted through the aerial riders' formation, then jerked to the side.

"Reloading!" Rugrat yelled, tossing his magazine away and slapping in a new one.

Mana cannons and casters shot at the group. Their attacks spackled across their barrier as George wove through the sky, dodging the worst attacks. A stack formation attached to George's harness beeped as it failed, another snapping into place in a half-second.

They pierced the frigate and corvette's barriers, moving higher. Mages covered the frigate's upper deck.

Erik held no mercy as he hosed them down, his rounds punching through the decks below and exploding.

Rugrat's rounds tore chunks out of the armored upper deck.

Erik used his Dungeon Sense. "Core is in the middle of the ship!"

The last of their stack formations failed. George howled as he shifted his body, moving so Erik and Rugrat wouldn't be hit with a mana cannon blast, taking the hit to his wing instead.

"Jump!" Rugrat yelled.

George shrunk in size and Rugrat grabbed him as the wind tore at them.

Erik looked toward the deck of the ship and pulled his arms and legs in.

Erik and Rugrat howled through the sky. Spells buffeted the duo.

Erik yelled wordlessly, turning against the momentum he had gained. His and Rugrat's bodies transformed, taking on their elemental properties, only increased by the effects of the concoctions.

Erik crashed into the deck of the ship, denting it with his fist—a wave of fire that tossed the surrounding sect mages.

He swung up his rifle, firing from the hip into a group of mages. The ship shuddered again from Rugrat smashing into the deck, releasing a blast of mana. Chains tore free from the ship, attacking the mages.

Erik advanced and fired.

Rugrat came up behind him and smacked his shoulder. George was resting on his shoulder, focusing on healing himself.

Erik threw out a punch. The mana and flame imbued fist, smashed into mages, tossing them backward.

Erik raised his arm as a lightning spell hit him. He channeled the power through his body, redirecting, adding to it, and unleashing a torrent of lightning through the deck, tearing it up and shooting out at the mages as he was hit with a fireball. He walked through these attacks, his natural resistances turning them into little more than minor stings.

Erik could see over the lip of the ship; his people were being pushed back on all fronts. Erik grabbed the deck at his side. Metal wove around his arm as he tore the armored deck plating fused to the ship free, covering himself in metal. His domain saw through the metal as Rugrat fired. His rounds exploded above Erik, the force slamming him to the ground as the fighters without any protection were torn apart.

Erik threw the pitted and smoking metal sheet away. He rolled over to get on his feet as an archer fired a string of arrows at Rugrat's back.

Rugrat turned and was hit in the side of the helmet, tossed backward. The other arrows following him unerringly.

Erik pressed on the ship. The metal rippled like water, surging around Rugrat and up into a wall, the arrow and three more striking it.

Spikes appeared under the archer's feet as they dodged.

Rugrat hit the deck and fired, the round punching through the archer. "Prick."

Rugrat pulled off his half-destroyed helmet. His body was already healing the burn and shrapnel marks. A clean spell removing the blood.

Erik slung his rifle to the left side of his armor and grabbed the metal and stone armor, melding it together into a hammer.

"Here, don't lose this!" Rugrat tossed Erik his blacksmithing hammer.

Erik grabbed it and whirled it around. They turned to face a group of fighters charging out of the wreckage of the upper deck. "Cheers! I'll draw their attention!"

Erik ran into the melee. He threw his metal hammer. It exploded into super-heated metal shards, tearing up some and throwing others back. He dodged a spear and pulled on it, yanking the spear user forward, crumpling their helmet with a jab of Rugrat's smithing hammer.

Sparks came off his body, forming into alchemist's flames, into beasts of fire. They tore into the ranks of fighters.

Erik dodged a blade. Rugrat's round passed the space behind Erik's back, killing a rogue with her daggers. Erik grabbed onto the mana, the very fabric of the First Realm, pulling himself up. His hammer strikes sent a fighter flying, and he took a sword blade across his shoulder, cutting into his ammunition box. The box exploded, throwing Erik forward and into the ground.

A spear lanced through his leg.

Erik slapped the ground, and the metal slapped him back, tossing him away.

He tore off his broken helmet, pulling out a shard of metal that had stabbed into the back of his skull.

He dropped it to the ground and yelled. Metal tore free from their restraints, creating a spear in his hand. He threw it, detonating the mana within the construct.

Bottles appeared in Erik's hand. He threw them out. Metal leaped from the scrap around him, creating spears. Flames appeared at the rear of the spears. They shot out in every direction at the approaching enemy.

The spears struck, some missing their target as the bottles shattered, covering the deck in a miasma of colors. Poison deadly to Body Cultivators who had Bodies like Sky Iron. Fighters collapsed, holding their throats.

Rugrat fired at any outside Erik's poison. "Loading!" He snapped a magazine out, the next in and loaded before Erik could blink. Rugrat was emotionless, his body, his rifle and rounds glowing with power as they changed in mid-flight, detonated in mid-air, or behind cover, or sprouted chains or mana blades.

He sowed destruction in his wake.

"George," Erik said. The wounded beast jumped to Erik. Erik grimaced seeing the condition of his body, so low on stamina from the flight. His wounds were grievous. Erik gave him a stamina shot, the strongest potion he had.

George jumped on Erik's shoulders, curling around his neck, and closing his eyes. Erik reached out to the realm's power and drew it into his body, a feeling of godhood, of power throbbing through his body, filled him as his wounds closed at a rate visible to the eye.

Even if we die today, we die for Alva. I was blind. Alva doesn't rely on two men anymore. They have won, they have lost, and they have persevered. I'm just a soldier and it's a soldier's duty to protect his people.

"This we'll defend." He repeated the army's motto, standing taller as the air around him distorted. His body transformed elements, spreading from his elemental core through his bones, muscle, and skin. Those three words resonated with him, deep into his core, engraved into his very bones.

Cai Bo looked at the two lords. The air shuddered around the man holding the hammer. Metal shot from across the deck, combining with flames and earth and mana, forming a shield on his other arm.

"Alva!" The voice resounded through the ship, through the mountains, across the forests and battlefields. "Today is the day that we feared, the day we knew would come. The enemy is at our gates. They stand upon our lands. Soldiers! Guild members! Alvans! Today is the last day of the Vermire Empire and the first day of the Alvan Empire!"

The air around Erik shimmered as he rose into the sky, standing upon the air itself. "Fight with me! Alva!"

Metal and stone were stripped from the deck around him, flying forward, forming a hammer in his hand. Dragons and tigers roared around his body. Flames that had gained sentience surrounded the head of his hammer as he brought it down on the outer deck of *Perseverance.*

The frigate dipped as the hammer blow smashed through several levels.

Mages attacked Erik, but Rugrat's shots blew them backward.

Erik dropped out of view as Rugrat threw his hand out and jumped down.

Explosions covered the surface of the deck.

Cai Bo looked at the other elders. "Who does he think he is? Some lord of the lower realms!"

"An upstart. I will go deal with him personally!" another elder grumbled, shifting his sleeves and moving for the exit.

"We are being pushed back on all fronts," an aide said.

Cai Bo looked at the screens, and she heard it in that quiet. It was a whisper at first, but from the throats of thousands, one word: "Al-va, AL-va, AL-VA!"

The chanting grew across the bunker-line, across King's Hill, and from the forests.

The images from the bunker-line distorted as warriors glowed with power, with elements crashing through spells.

"They're dual cultivators," Cai Bo muttered, remembering what Captain Stassov had said.

She surveyed them all, watching mounted forces sallying forward.

"What did you say Cai Bo?" Asadi asked.

Cai Bo collected herself. "Captain Stassov said that Erik and Rugrat were dual cultivators, that they had fought dual cultivators in the castle. I don't think it was just the city lords. They're *all* dual cultivators."

"Continue firing on those bunkers. Get Marco to reinforce the forces entering. We must take that core!" Asadi growled.

Erik hissed. The metal of the different decks cut up his clothes, his armor, and through his skin.

He finally hit solid decking. He looked around the cannon deck. He hit a cannoneer throwing them backward.

The deck yelled as fighters rushed Erik just as Rugrat arrived.

Mana lances shot out, stabbing, and exploding through the deck. Mana stones ruptured and formations released their stored energies, tearing the deck apart.

Erik was thrown to the side. He hit a cannon with his side, denting it, cracking his plates and several ribs. He grunted, raising his shield as an attacker cut at him from the side with an axe.

The shield stopped the axe, but the force tossed him to the side.

Erik drew on his flames, they sparked into existence as a mage cast a water spell, stabbing through the spell and hitting Erik, throwing him across the deck. Erik hit the back of a stairwell where more men were rushing down.

Erik pushed himself to his feet. He spat out some teeth shards, his body repairing as he stumbled before turning into a hopping run, and then a run. He yelled in frustration, in anger, in pain.

He compressed air and flame on the front of his shield and braced. The two interacted, creating a shockwave that blasted into the enemy, turning into air blades.

Erik ducked under a spear jab, throwing out his hammer, crashing into the attacker's chest. He turned his body, raising his shield to turn a blade. The user's technique cut through the shield and into Erik's bones, biting there.

Erik turned the blade and summoned metal. A shard stabbed through the back of the fighter.

Metal, flame, and earth shot toward Erik in motes of light. The shining metallic wasps turned into nails that shot out, taking out a group. Red grew into blue balls of flame, dropping down through an open stairwell. The deck shuddered with attacks.

Erik panted as he shifted his armor, coughing.

"You look like shit," Rugrat said, his own wounds sealing, leaving only blood on his clothes.

Erik groaned, forcing himself upright, giving him the middle finger and finding his arm wasn't working right.

"Fuck." Erik pulled out the offending section of blade in his arm and tossed it to the side. He wiggled his fingers and flipped the bird. "Better?"

Rugrat snorted and coughed. They looked like battered shit. Rugrat grabbed his rifle, his hands blurring as he altered its structure.

Erik reached down and grabbed the hammer from the flame-whitened wall and rested it on his shoulder. He gave George another stamina potion and drank one himself, followed by a mana potion.

He sucked in air, checking on Rugrat, who drank another potion.

Erik cocked his head to the side. "More coming."

"Well, let's get out of here before they arrive."

"You take George and I'll take point."

Rugrat picked up George from Erik's shoulders, looking him over before putting him around his neck.

Erik looked at the transformed Beast. The rifle had lost its buttstock and most of its length. A chunkier barrel and heat shrouding stuck out of the receiver.

"Ugly, but it'll work."

"Just like you." Erik grinned and swung his hammer. A fireball smashed into a fighter that entered what was left of the cannon deck.

Rugrat snorted. Erik turned and smashed through a wall, following his senses toward the dungeon core.

The bridge of *Perseverance* was quiet as the deck shuddered with another attack. They could see the fighting above their heads, deforming and breaking their ship.

"What is the situation on the ground?" Cai Bo asked an elder who was staring up the ceiling and shaking.

She snapped her fingers, bringing back his focus.

"It..." He checked the map. "We were making progress in the bunkers and into the hidden city, but the enemy has revealed experts everywhere, dual cultivators, people with the power of those in the Eighth Realm. They must be buffed to that point because they can't sustain it for long."

The sound of twisted metal filed the command center. Spells shot for the opening in the ceiling. A dozen feet away another opened, spells crashing into that breach now.

Cai Bo gathered her power, pulling out her fan as she saw something drop from the first breach.

Explosions rippled through the deck, killing dozens as gas filled the area.

"Poison!" an elder yelled. Cai Bo used her wind spells, sending the poison back toward the breaches. Other breaches opened and more small formation charges fell onto the bridge.

Cai Bo waved her fan, throwing the charges away and into the stations. The explosions rippled through the stations, killing dozens.

The two City Lords dropped from a breach. One fired his small stubby weapon, dropping several fighters in one move. The other hurled a spear at the dungeon core. Other spears rose from the ground and shot outward.

Elders diverted the attacks, casting spells to harass the duo, who dove for cover.

Erik hit the deck, spells burning through the section of station he had been hiding behind.

"I think we found the right place!" Rugrat said.

Erik threw out his hand, hurling grenades in the direction of the attacks.

They went off as Erik ran around the station he was hiding behind. He tore iron from the ground, revealing formations underneath, and created a new shield to cover his body. He was struck again, hurled through another station.

"Ow!" Erik rolled to a stop, looking at his ribs and the damage down his hip to his leg. He got up with his battered decking-turned-shield, feeling the wounds healing across his body.

An older man holding a staff slammed it on the ground. A stream of light pierced through the smoke and struck Erik's shield.

The attack threw Erik back. He reached out and grabbed the ceiling, pulling it down.

A surge of power shot out from the man's body.

Erik pushed forward as the resistance from the staff's attack decreased.

An arrow struck his back plate, and he smashed through another station.

A woman standing in the air slashed down at him with her sword. He felt the blade slice through his back armor as she charged forward.

Erik jumped up. She stabbed her blade into his stomach.

His hammer smashed into her head, slapping her down through the floor and several others. Another spell struck Erik and launched him across the room, past the dungeon core.

Chains appeared among the elders and remaining fighters, stabbing into them and exploding.

Erik flexed his mana, stopping his movement. He tore out the blade in his stomach, turned it, and threw it with an explosive spell as he ran. It struck a personal barrier. Debris rained against Erik's side as he charged through stations toward the dungeon core.

Two elders met him. Erik accelerated, their spear and axe barely missing his head. A wall of twisted metal blocked him from the axe thrower's view. He turned into another spear thrust, his shield of stone turning to magma and latching to the spear, pulling his attacker wide. Erik delivered a finishing blow to the elder's head. The axe thrower attacked where he had been, leaving him open as Erik destroyed his own wall of metal, transforming it into daggers that stabbed into the elder's side, wounding but not killing.

Using Finger Beats Fist, he stabbed forward, the momentum from the elbow only enhancing his own energy as he stabbed into the elder's side, causing them to stiffen.

Cai Bo's fan slashed through the air, hitting Erik in the chest.

The elder he had struck coughed blood and collapsed with a tombstone above him. Several elders tried to call upon their spells around Rugrat. His domain suppressed them as he fired on them. They dropped to the ground with perfectly placed shots.

Head Asadi waved a saber. A blue light split into several blades, cutting Rugrat and throwing him backward before he slashed out at Erik. Erik blinked forward toward Cai Bo.

Erik tried to dodge, but his speed was too high. He felt the blades slice through his skin. The blades lost their cutting power but still blasted him off his feet with the sheer force of the fighting technique.

Erik turned and released a mana blast in Asadi's direction, hoping to distract him. An airblade took three of his fingers from his right hand. He could feel his regeneration slowing as he dropped to the ground on all fours.

"Armor!" Erik yelled. His armor had been sliced and opened in different sections. He reached up and turned the socket formation in his carrier.

He shuddered with the power, his body regenerating as he stood. Cai Bo's attacks sliced his skin as fast as it could recover.

Elders and their guards rushed Erik. He flashed forward. The hammer he'd lost flew into his hand as he tossed out grenades and concoctions.

The grenades peppered him as much as they did the elders and guards, but his body cultivation was at least a stage higher. While he came away with scrapes and cuts, they suffered grievous injuries.

They traded attacks. Rugrat glowed with power as he fought his own group. Chains of mana appeared around him.

Erik dodged an arrow. He hit an elder as he grabbed another elder's sword, pinning the archer to the wall. He shuddered forward and punched out. His senses, his domain, his actions flowed as one.

Each attack struck the weaknesses of the fighter, sending them staggering with grievous wounds or creating tombstones.

The power was immense, but this level of strength was tearing Erik's body apart.

They carved a path through the enemy. Rugrat fought Asadi directly. Asadi used spells from his smaller domain to compete with Rugrat, who had a larger domain, but weaker techniques.

Each of Asadi's attacks could kill.

Asadi slashed Rugrat across the shoulders. Thankfully, they had left George on the floor above.

The two titans hammered one another with such power that the ship was breaking apart around them.

Cai Bo's attacks slashed at Erik's openings. He no longer tried to dodge everything if it would allow him to kill one more.

Erik cleared the elders as Cai Bo attacked. Rugrat fired on her before she could get to Erik. That split second distraction was enough for Asadi to land an attack on Rugrat.

Rugrat looked at his stomach as he dropped backward, his domain collapsing.

Cai Bo was on the floor recovering. Asadi panted, turning.

Erik's armor was so broken it fell from his shoulders.

He looked at them both and focused on the dungeon core behind them. Power coursed through it, fueling the ship, its formations, its cannons and their continued to fire on Alvans.

Erik grabbed the formation socket at the corner of his armor and drove it through his armor plate, through his skin, and into his chest.

Power, connected to all the armor-wearing Alvans across the First Realm, flooded him as he *saw through all.* His body collapsed with the sheer amount of power that he drew in.

Erik surged forward. Asadi's sword created images in the air, cutting into Erik's arm and leg as he collapsed. He slapped the floor with his foot, denting it, and tackled the dungeon core.

Dungeon Core
Grade: Greater Earth Grade Linked: Perseverance
You have come into contact with a dungeon core. With your title: Dungeon Master, new options are revealed.
Do you wish to:
Take command of the Dungeon Remodel Dungeon Destroy the Dungeon

"Command!" The very realm vibrated with his words. The power in his body wasn't enough—Asadi's blades were coming for him.

Another man he hadn't seen, wearing the armor of the Black Phoenix Clan, charged him from the other side. He channeled the power of the ship. Flames shot from his hands, turning into beasts in greater clarity than ever before. They seemed to be breathing as they rushed toward the two men. They crushed Asadi's sword-light, sweeping through his domain and lanced through his body.

The other man yelled, pushing forward farther as Erik turned, avoiding his attack, and punched the man. He sent flames through his fist as the man shot back, cracking a wall as he revealed a tombstone.

Erik shuddered, holding his chest. He had moved quickly, but not quick enough to avoid the blade altogether.

The man had cracked the formation stabbed into his chest, burning him as it overloaded.

"Rugrat," Erik gasped as the power dimmed. He hadn't noticed it, but his body had been completely transformed, from his head to his feet by the elements.

Now the changes were starting to collapse as Rugrat directed the power of the ship.

Rugrat coughed, pale as he directed his hands to the side. Lightning tore through the wall and into the open sky, piercing the other corvette and detonating it. With a sucking noise, flames returned from the ship.

Rugrat's head lolled as he looked at the ball of flames in his hand as it resolved into a dungeon core.

Erik was powerless to move, his body fighting to repair all he had done.

It took everything he had to input the commands to destroy the dungeon. Storage devices appeared around him as the light blinked.

Erik dropped to the ground with a grunt.

He saw Rugrat over the churned dirt and craters, the bunker-line a few hundred meters away.

Erik struggled in the dirt toward Rugrat.

Perseverance, or what remained of it, slammed into the ground, cracking and sending out a wave of dust.

Erik groaned, pulling himself forward. Only his left hand and right leg worked properly. He finally reached Rugrat lying on the ground, taking out a stamina potion. He tilted it over his mouth, only to have it kicked away.

Erik opened and closed his hand as the stamina potion seeped into the ground.

A shoe kicked him over.

Cai Bo stood above him, holding the dungeon core.

"Rather impressive, Lord West," she said. Her features were marred with cuts on the side of her face. Her robes cut to reveal her armor underneath, her fan open at her side. "You would have been a useful pawn."

"You forgot one thing," Erik coughed.

"What's that?" she asked.

"George is a *great* boy," Erik stated.

A lance of fire shot into her back and through her front. She started to turn as black smoke released from Erik's pores, catching her in the face.

"And I tempered my body with poison first."

Cai Bo coughed, dropping her fan and the dungeon core, staring at the wound. She slumped to the ground, resting against the side of a crater.

Erik pulled out a needle, applying several to Rugrat and then some more to himself.

George came over dragging his leg, his wings tight to his body.

"Good boy." Erik dosed him as well and looked around. The battlefield had been cleared under the airship.

Cai Bo could hear fighting in the distance as Erik pulled his leg together. He pulled out a bandage and slapped a length of metal to it, securing it with duct tape.

He looked up at the sky, on the last dregs of energy.

"Why?" Cai Bo coughed.

Erik turned and grunted, stabbing his taped-up leg into the ground, pushing himself to all fours. He gave Rugrat two more needles and stuffed storage devices into his dump pouch.

Cai Bo coughed again. "Why?"

Erik coughed, applying a healing armband to Rugrat and one to himself. Wounds showed through his armor and clothes, soaking his armor. His red stained teeth spread in a wide smile.

Rugrat gasped and groaned, reaching out to a station to haul himself up.

"You could have escaped, could have left them to it. Why did you give them so much power?"

"I didn't give them anything but an idea and a path. They did the rest. You know, I thought it would fall apart without us." Erik smiled as his body healed, and tended to Rugrat. "I thought we were the center of it. What an idiot. I thought that we were a guiding light. Two blind idiots. We helped them in the beginning, but they made it a reality. They're not reliant on us anymore. Like kids growing up, I guess."

Erik planted another needle into Rugrat. He grunted and grabbed Erik's shoulder, his eyes fluttering into focus as he groaned.

"You see, weird thing about Marines." Erik coughed, stone wrapping around his leg. "They don't die. They just go to hell and regroup."

Erik laughed, stumbling. He spat out blood. "Come on, buddy."

He grabbed Rugrat, getting him to a sitting position.

Cai Bo laughed, a cruel bubbling thing. "Don't worry. Gregor will grant your wish."

Erik turned on Cai Bo. "Where is he?"

"He's a dungeon hunter. Where do you expect?"

Cai Bo's smile hung from her lips, relishing in the fear on his face.

"Come on," Erik growled, picking up Rugrat. She heard his footfalls as he started running, gathering mana to speed up as the wolf hurried after him.

Cai Bo's strength fled her as the darkness consumed her.

42

Fight for Alva

Gregor held the dungeon core aloft, recovered from one of the other corvettes. He and his hunters descended through stone, dirt, and formations. The ground fell away, and they dropped through the ceiling of Alva.

For the first time, he saw the city. It was massive, filled with lightless towers. Several camps were located among the city's sprawl. Orderly roads led to the center.

A huge, powered tower reached toward the ceiling, drawing in the last vestiges of power from the mana storing formation that covered the ceiling.

No wonder they have been able to sustain their barriers for so long.

He glanced at the hole carved into the city in the distance. Flashes illuminated the fierce fighting.

They are too dispersed. They shouldn't have but a small force at the dungeon core. Did you think that you were the only people that knew how to use a dungeon core to cut through the ground?

The hunters dropped, drawing out their mounts and gliding toward the dungeon core, silent as shadows.

Tracers flashed out of the stand-alone building that housed the dungeon core.

Shit. Guards!

Gregor dove for the ground, his beast pulling her wings in to move faster.

The tracers hit one of the other hunters' barriers, lighting them up in the sky.

Gregor banked from side to side as the machine guns on the tower attacked them.

"Illusion mist!" Gregor yelled out. A spell formation appeared over the tower, spewing smoke.

The other hunters used similar spells to cover the tower in a smoke screen.

"Close with them to melee! They have only their ranged weapons!" Gregor yelled, hoping that these fighters were not like the ones he had encountered in that park in Vuzgal.

Spell formations surrounded Julilah and Qin. Glass-like apparitions flowed around their command formations, rising to form waves and then collapse, shifting into set patterns and melting away.

Julilah and Qin were in the middle of this maelstorm, in the heart of Alva's formations. It was the heart of it all, second in control only to Egbert, who was recovering in the air force mountain from unleashing his attacks upon the enemy warships.

They heard the rumblings of weapon fire in the building.

Qin raised her hand, revealing the situation outside of the tower.

"Egbert, the headquarters are under attack. The Black Phoenix Clan is here," she said. Qin threw the view to Julilah as Juliah managed the power output to a series of bunkers, altering them, fusing the formations together to increase their barrier's strength.

"We have to use the power from the ships," Julilah said.

As the ships had crashed into the ground, their dungeon cores removed, the mana stones stored in their mana vaults were no longer isolated. Through the mana gathering formations they could draw in their power, allowing them to burn the sect's mana stones to defend Alva.

"Shunt all the power to the barriers, cultivation pods, and medical. Shift control over the dungeon formations to the fire floor's dungeon core. Egbert, you need to take over from us," Qin said as she and Julilah moved formations. The circular formations under their feet moved and altered, like several safe tumblers. Formations on the wall lit up with different colors and shifted, stopping for a matter of seconds to send out spells and then changing again.

The headquarters danced around the two expert formation masters.

Qin saw Erik and Rugrat smash out of the wrecked *Perseverance*. They landed on ground that rose to meet them as the air exploded behind them. They shot forward, increasing speed.

Beasts of flame appeared around Erik, dancing white, blue, and red, lashing out at sect members in their path.

Chains sprouted from around Rugrat, pulled by blades of mana.

They ran over the burrows of the sects, trench lines that grew opposite the bunker-lines. Mana cannons, archers, and mages hurled their abuse at the bunkers, which returned fire with tracers, spells, and artillery.

The last corvette turned, their cannons dialing into the duo as they rushed into the breach of the bunker-line.

They carved a line through the enemy controlled ravine. Roska and Storbon's Special Teams jumped from the bunkers on either side and into the opening. They fought back-to-back, breaking the main attack, pushing into the teeth of the sect's charge.

They pushed forward inch by bloody inch, craving the path with blade, fist, gun, and spell. Their actions blurred. Qin's eyes were unable to follow them, even as she monitored the movement of hundreds of formations.

Her eyes fell on the shifting corvette as it turned to bring its side to bear. Mana cannons fired on the bunkers, rotating to shoot on the ravine.

"Re-routing mana to attack formation F-three-seven!" Qin yelled.

"I'll route power. You target," Julilah said.

"Got it." Qin moved the surrounding formations, altering the attack formation that had laid dormant. It would burn through their reserves and the mana they were drawing in from the warships.

Erik and Rugrat ran through the enemy, a whirlwind of destruction. Erik's footsteps left craters in the ground as their rifles shredded through barrier and sect member alike.

Erik grabbed the elements themselves. Stone sharpened around him into spears that shot forward through the sect members.

Rugrat jumped and landed on George, whose breath melted barrier and ground. Rugrat's rifle fired with unerring accuracy. Clumps of chains rose from their impact points, tearing through the surrounding ranks as he threw out grenades from his storage ring. George flew so low that his claws raked fighters underneath him.

Still, to the horde it was little. The openings they created would be filled in a matter of minutes. Thousands of the strongest fighters had pushed past the bunker-line, using teleportation formations to draw forward others.

If we had more mana…

They couldn't even keep the strongest formations running because the mana was so thin, and they used too much power. Too much had been used in their training, in supporting the city, the barriers, the cultivation pods, and the healers.

There has to be something more, something else that we can do!

Qin's eyes burned, a heavy dull pain running through her body from overusing her mana cultivation.

She closed her eyes, stemming the tears as the building shook around her.

She pulled up an outside view. The guards fought for all they were worth. Four hunters lay dead outside the tower, but so did a half dozen soldiers. A man with red armor and a spear led the charge. She watched him kill another soldier, using a spell to counteract one cast in his direction.

"Formation is charged," Julilah said.

"Prepare to destroy all control formations and input blueprint to the dungeon core, full disconnect," Qin said, her voice firmer than she felt.

"Okay." Julilah's voice faltered. She knew what was coming; they both did.

They gave their lives to give us the time we needed.

Qin activated the attack formation.

In the Beast Mountain Range, between the bunker-line and King's Hill, the ground smoked and burned. Red lines like magma appeared on the ground as it shifted. A formation activated, its power burning through the ground. Power leaked from the formation, burning through stone and dirt, visible from above before it locked into place.

The ground cracked from the sheer mana being channeled into the formation. A low hum grew louder and louder.

A mirror copy of the formation—a spell version—pushed up out of the ground and tilted, shrugging off the stone and dirt atop it.

The spell formation paused. Outer rings locked into inner rings in an aperture the size of Qin's fist. Each layer extended like a telescope, the smallest aperture at the front, facing the remaining corvette.

"Now, *this* is a mana cannon. Activating."

Mana washed away from the Alva Empire, mana stones turning to dust in moments as a geyser of flame shot out of the carved formation and into the spell formation's outer rings. The power condensed, passing forward until it shot out in a blue beam as wide as Qin's fist and as blue as the Aegean Sea.

The spell formation rotated, and the geyser erupted once more, then shifted and fired a third time.

The first impact struck the corvette's mana barrier, warping it and *shifting* the metal and stone edifice. The second bolt struck with a vengeance. The dark barrier melted away as the weakened blast splashed against the side of the ship and drilled a burning hole through its hull.

The ship's formations lost their glow as the third blast arrived. It passed through the ship from the left rear flank. The ship dropped toward the ground. As the ship cracked and came apart, a sliver of the compressed blue blast—plasma cannon, some of the Earther's had called it—passed through the upper deck of the right-forward section of the ship.

It fell from the sky, crashing into the teleportation formations, sect members, and trenches below, throwing up dust.

Several explosions went off aboard the ship or underneath, clearing the last of the airships from Alva's skies.

There was a noise, much closer than the screens, as Qin was pulled from what she saw.

Qin and Julilah altered formations as fast as their hands could move. Julilah pulled out a blueprint and held it as the sounds of fighting entered the building.

Julilah input the blueprint into the dungeon core.

"Preparing to divert control." Qin opened a channel to the team on the second floor full of low Journeyman level formation masters, too young to go to the front-line. Delilah and the entire council had joined in the fighting at the molten entrance.

Wounded soldiers rushed toward the dungeon core.

"We're switched!" Qin said as the formations lost their glow. The translucent formations that hovered around her and Julilah washed away into darkness.

The dungeon core illuminated Julilah.

She input the blueprint and then grabbed the dungeon core.

She looked at Qin. "Never really wanted to be a dungeon lord."

Qin let out a sigh of relief. With the dungeon disconnected, the surrounding area was no longer part of the dungeon. If the dungeon core were taken and the dungeon destroyed, nothing would happen.

Qin's lips pulled into a cold grin that her mannerism tutors would have disagreed with. People who had seen her as a fragile waif, unable to control her own mana, would be stunned.

She was no longer that girl. She had become a woman, an Alvan, head of the Formation Master school, a teacher and crafter that had built a weapon that felled a dungeon warship.

She pulled out a formation stack, opening it with a twist and flick. Julilah pulled on her helmet and released the dungeon core to float in mid-air.

Qin flicked the stack closed and hooked it onto her back.

Erik healed me, saved me. Gave me this life. In more ways than one.

She twisted formation sockets in her arm bracers. A red glow appeared around her fist. For the first time since the first Alvan villagers had entered Alva, the formations in the dungeon headquarters went dark. Only the light of the dungeon core and the enchanted armor Julilah and Qin wore illuminated the space.

The wall of the tower exploded. Qin raised her fists. The stone hit her personal barrier as a man in yellow and black armor rushed forward.

Qin punched forward, remembering her brother's training. The stack on her back glowed, channeling its energies through her arm brace. Julilah's firebolt and Qin's elemental fist crashed into the man, sending him back out through another new hole in the side of the building.

Hunters attacked the building, gaining entrance as Julilah and Qin fought side by side.

Qin's barriers failed as the hunters attacked.

"Kill them!" a man yelled.

Six of the black and yellow armored hunters charged in. They cut at Qin and Julilah with furious abandon.

Julilah defended against several spells, dodging a spear only to get hit with a hammer in the side, slapping her into the ground. She punched the ground, rising and missing the swing of a sword aimed at her.

She landed on her feet and punched. Smoke covered Julilah, and she cried out as she smashed through the headquarters' wall.

Qin faced a sword hammer and spear user who worked together as one. She took a hit to her leg, forcing her to use air spells to keep herself moving. A blade cut her left arm as she hit the man back. He left a furrow in the ground, but shook off the attack and rose to his feet as the spear hit her in the stomach. The armor stopped it, but the blow pushed her back against the wall.

Gregor, with his red armor and spear, rushed past the hunters, his attack defeating Qin's panicked defense. His spear ran up her hip, through her ribs, and took off her right arm.

She hit him with her left, the force draining from her body as she did so. The formations compensated, pushing him back slightly and throwing her out of the dungeon headquarters. She hit the cold ring street around the dungeon headquarters.

She coughed as the formations in her armor fought to heal her, to keep her alive.

She tried to pull on her mana, but her wound bled mana, just as it did blood, passing out of her control like trying to catch a river.

The pain ran through her, unlike anything she had ever felt before.

"I did not save your life to have it lost again." The voice was calm and collected, but it resounded like thunder in her ears.

Someone picked her up. Needles stabbed into her as healing spells fell over her. Qin felt her body sealing together. Fatigue, bone deep and lethargic, spread through her bones as she landed on a nearby roof. A wave of wind fell over her as she felt the heat from George's flames.

"George, get them to the healers," Rugrat said. He paused, listening to his mount's thoughts. His voice took on an iron edge. "You keep them safe, boy."

Erik was there, too. He wore new armor, but his clothes showed the burns and cuts of his fighting. His blazing blue eyes saw through her as he gave her several needles and a healing needle.

He cradled her and put her on George's back like saddle bags. She didn't feel the pain anymore. Julilah groaned as Rugrat helped her up behind Qin.

"You are the future of Alva. Protect it. Build it." Erik put a hand on both of them and stepped away.

George spread out his wings as Erik pulled on his gloves.

"Hah, the old blood gloves." Rugrat checked his rifle, holding the *Beast* with two hands.

"Couldn't waste your gift." Erik rolled his shoulders.

Chains rattled, striking away spells that neared the duo.

"Let's go deal with these fuckers, shall we?"

Rugrat fired at the hunters as they charged upwards, spells carrying them up toward the headquarters.

The building was starting to come apart as Rugrat's chains tore free spells. Even near misses contained enough power to destroy the building and those nearby.

"See you down there." Erik took off at a run.

Erik cut his hand, the blood drinking gloves turning a deep red, almost black, as they tightened and throbbed with power. His skin transformed as he drew on the elements within. He roared as flaming beasts sprouted from the sparks on his skin, creating a swirling shroud that defeated any attacks.

He crashed into the ground and leaped forward, digging his toes into the stone and feeling the power in his muscles as he drew in mana, pushing it through his body. Spells struck him head-on. He took the impacts and raised his hands. Rubble formed into a shield.

He saw through the shield, his domain resonating with the power of his elemental core.

The shield of rubble was torn apart in a few seconds.

Erik used an explosion to reach the side of the rubble shield, his enhanced reactions allowing him to dodge the sword. Erik's fist slammed forward, cracking armor and sending the hunter pinwheeling away. A new tombstone appeared over his head where he lay. Blood dripped from Erik's hands.

Erik raised his arm. A fire attack hit his arm.

He grinned, making the fire mage shiver as Erik serpentined forward, punctuated by rapid-fire explosions. He tilted. An arrow skimmed underneath to tear a groove in the ground and explode. An explosion under his feet threw him above a wall of iron nails. Another explosion sent him toward the ground. "Golem!" His words spoke to power as golems as large as cats jumped at the hunters.

Erik kicked off the ground, out of the way of attack spells.

Erik seemed to blur between targets under the acceleration of the explosions. Golems of flame, stone and earth created chaos among the hunters.

Rugrat was unperturbed, firing calmly, taking out a hunter about to complete a spell. Another fought a golem, another taking cover from Erik's attacks.

Gregor held the dungeon core in his hands. He sneered and tore the dungeon core out of the air.

Formations started to fail, and the stored power stopped feeding the formations across the beast mountain range.

The barriers!

Erik covered his storage ring.

"Kill them!" Gregor yelled. He threw out mana stones, the dungeon core drawing in the power as it traced lines through his body and armor.

Rugrat fired, killing one. Erik pulled out a mobile Gatling gun, killing two before Gregor lashed out with his spear. Erik smashed through the wall and into a building; the building rebounded.

"Earth pillar!"

Erik shot back into the room. He saw Rugrat dodge the spear, a chain rising over the remaining hunter's sword and arm, jerking them forward as Rugrat tilted his gun to the side. Muzzle break met armor as he pulled the trigger and rode the recoil backward.

Erik punched at Gregor, who used his spear like a serpent, attacking Erik's openings. Mana drained from the cuts on his arms and his legs.

Rugrat growled and stored the *Beast,* rushing into the fight. He lashed out with his fists, mana blades and chains going ahead of him, attacking Gregor's domain. Gregor swung his spear, fending off attacks, thrown back by their attacks and coordination.

Gregor's flames didn't have the coordination of Erik's, but they dwarfed the power of both their attacks.

"Such fools! I thought you just champions when I first fought you, I did not think that you were Dungeon Lords! Letting little girls control your core! How weak are you?" He laughed in their faces.

Erik and Rugrat's faces were impassive as Erik collapsed a section of wall behind Gregor and struck out with his fist, his other arm raised to cover his face under the swirl of flames. His fist turned into a finger, releasing the coiled power running through his body. Gregor turned to the side. The power melted a groove through his armor plates.

Erik used an explosion and shouldered Gregor. Erik's blast tore through a wall, a pinhole sized attack that stretched on unseen.

Gregor slapped the ground and jumped into the air.

"No, you don't!" Rugrat yelled. His mana channels glowed with power as chains shot from the ceiling of Alva to crash into the man.

Erik connected to the dungeon cores from the lower levels as well, drawing in the power through his body.

The second time burned even more than the first as he sent out a punch, hitting Gregor. He deflected the attack, but Rugrat's blade cut through his left leg.

"If you want the core so badly, have it!"

Gregor threw the dungeon core and tore an escape spell scroll, shooting away.

Erik and Rugrat made to chase when their senses fell on the dungeon core.

"It's going to blow."

Erik and Rugrat looked at one another; Gregor fled for all he was worth. The core was breaking like ice in a vice.

"It'll take the floor out." Rugrat grabbed it to fly off.

"You won't get far enough. We need to divert it. Activate the drill!" Erik yelled, putting his words into action as he reached out with his domain, altering the formations in the floor. Mana and elements were dragged to the dungeon headquarters and diverted downward. They ran toward the dungeon headquarters.

Rugrat used his domain and himself as a conduit, bleeding some of the cracking dungeon core's power into the drill.

Erik and Rugrat looked at one another, their bodies glowing with power.

We have to divert the power, even if it is only a small bit!

"Clear the drill tunnel!" Erik yelled, his voice passing through all levels of the dungeon.

The dungeon core exploded. Shrapnel stabbed into their bodies, breaking the dungeon headquarters. The wave of destruction spread outward.

Erik screamed, opening up all of his mana gates. His Mana Gathering System reached out to the swirling chaotic elemental energies around him.

They took it *all*, turning their bodies into another component of the dungeon, diverting the power into the drill.

Their bodies *burned* on that precipice, stripped apart, and sustained as they cried out around the corona

They would have given up against the pain if it were not for their brother beside them, if it was not for the Alvan people. If it was not the right thing to do.

This we'll defend. This we'll defend. This I'll *defend!* Erik recited the Army's motto again and again into his head, burning it in as deep as the power that seared through him.

Erik and Rugrat fought the chaotic maelstrom of mana released by the dungeon core, forcing it inward, downward.

The Metal floor saw a new dawn. Whites and blacks mixed with blues and yellows reflected off the mirror-like floor. The power rumbled over the dungeon core as it activated, drawing in mana and activating, creating a drill of black energies that drew the power burbling free of where the Living floor's dungeon core had erupted.

The fields of the Earth floor washed backward. The Fire floor gained a new light as the leaves on the Wood floor rustled and whistled. The deep black waters of the Water floor showed blue in their depths as smoke rose from the mountain.

Alvans across the floors looked at that pillar, shuddering with its strength. Beasts stilled at its passage.

The entire dungeon worked as one system. Formation masters grunted and fought the formations that controlled the mana drill, now turned dungeon core drill.

Parts of core struck those on each floor. Blue, purple, white and clear shards struck the dungeon cores, absorbing into one another, redoubling the power they drew upon and the power of the drill.

Sound returned to Erik.

"Oorah!" Rugrat yelled out, his howl rivalling the lowering tempest of power.

The power suddenly fled, the last of it directed through the drill hole, a blasted blackened thing. Pieces of dungeon core studded the area, stuck in buildings, in Erik and Rugrat.

Erik stumbled on the broken stone. The remains of the headquarters and buildings for three blocks had been smashed apart as if by a giant, but they stood.

"Oorah." Erik lost his balance and fell into the clattering stone. It was warm against his cheek. The smell of dust and stone filled his nose. Through the dungeons, he could feel the accumulated power decreasing, spent with the drill's use.

Erik grunted and waved his hand, pouring out mana stones.

Rugrat stood like a drunken pirate. He stumbled as he poured out the Sky grade mana stones. Formations activated around them, liquifying the dungeon cores and repairing.

Erik coughed, sending up dust from around him.

The darkness threatened to take him as Rugrat pulled out a beast to support himself, his legs bowing outward.

The shards of dungeon core burned in Erik's body like hot irons that failed to lose their heat.

The fatigue and the other pains masked the feeling.

Erik groaned and rolled onto his back. He breathed heavily, agonizing over his next move to sit up.

He threw out more mana stones. They dissipated, the dungeon cores and formation masters directing their power into Alva's defenses. He heard the fighting in the distance.

He thought he felt a rumble in the ground as he sat up. There was almost an instinctual feeling to draw in the power of the mana stones near him.

The surrounding stones started to dance as that imagined rumbling seemed to take on a truth.

Erik looked at Rugrat their eyes glowed in sync with Mana gathering formations, brightening as they drew upon the world's power, like desiccated roots finding new soil and water.

The pillar of elemental manas hit the first dungeon core. The water element split off, spreading over the floor. It reached into the Wood floor as trees underwent decades of growth in moments. The Fire floor erupted as magma boiled and swirled.

The Metal floor shone a brighter hue as pillars of metal grew and condensed across the floor.

On the Earth floor, crops grew to the size of trees.

Each stage, the mana had been stripped, leaving only pure mana.

Erik could *see* Alva as if for the first time, a complex web of formations and lines—a beautiful home that wrapped around them, protected them. Mana surged past the dungeon cores, into the mana storing formations, then remote dungeon cores.

Alva, then the Beast Mountain Range, then the newly renamed Alvan Empire... All of it shook as Erik saw the neon blue tracings spreading out in every direction.

Then it surged through the living floor, passing through Erik and Rugrat, making them cry out in pain and power. Their bodies *sung* with power. Fragments of the dungeon core fused with them, burned into their very being, attuning them to the dungeon in a way that only Egbert had been so before.

Formations flared to life, repairing and rebuilding. Mages felt a new vigor as their casting platforms glowed once more. Failed barriers surged and regrew against sect attacks.

Erik and Rugrat saw and sensed all.

They looked at one another, their faces passive and emotionless. They saw through every rock, through every person. This was a domain taken and stretched over dozens of kilometers. It burned in their minds as power tore them apart.

For Alva, Rugrat didn't move his lips, as much spoken as thought. His voice was a noble giant's, his eyes and veins aglow with power as mana vibrated with every syllable.

Erik reached up and grabbed his hand. Mana vapor and sparks from their dungeon core studded hands spread from their pores as Rugrat hauled him to his feet.

Erik nodded his thanks and looked to the entrance into Alva.

The defenders activated their Conqueror's armor. They held on, a militia of the wounded and willing.

The Adventurer's Guild crashed like a tide into the rear of the sects. The Tiger Corps rode with them.

Fighting had broken out in hand-to-hand combat along the bunker-line. The bunkers around the ravine had taken the worst of it. The Special teams and CPD fought along a fifty-meter-wide path nearly two hundred meters long.

Their backs were just tens of meters from one another, bodies laying stacked down the length.

Rugrat reached out and twisted his hand. Erik saw the formations within Alva as large as a child's hand activate, nudging another formation the size of a man, then another the size of a wagon, and another the size of a ship. *Time to wake up, Alva. We have power to burn.*

The formations stopped turning, falling into the correct alignment.

The clouds unnaturally rolled in, darkening and crackling with violent intensity.

Lightning struck the sect's lines, a few spikes at first, forking into the barriers below, growing rapidly in number and in size.

"We need to support them on the ground. Egbert, target the teleportation formations if you can." Erik's eyes searched through the city.

"Yes, Lord West."

Erik dumped out all his mana stones and threw the sky cornerstones up into the empty sockets in the ceiling. The mana storing formation grew and shrank as power was consumed, but more mana was being stored than they could consume.

Erik caught a movement of black and red, caught by the cold glow of the growing mana stone spider-web above the city.

"There you are." Erik pointed at Gregor's fleeing figure.

He jumped into the air, the mana density high enough for him to pull it together and step forward.

"Activate the Conqueror's armor now! Two hundred percent. Use everything you can control."

He saw the defenders surge, pushing the enemy at the tunnel entrance back. The Special teams and Close Protection Details in the ravine rallied and fought onward.

43

Alva Empire's Rage

"**J**ulilah, pull yourself together. Alva needs us," Taran said.

It snapped Julilah back.

"We need to feed the power into the formations right now. Activate the coffin formations. Ready the buffing formations and the lightning formations!"

Formation masters altered the surrounding formations, the changes spreading across the Beast Mountain Range as formations underground began shifting into position.

"Activate!"

The mana stones that had been poured out were drawn into the formations, directed across kilometers. The mana stones on the ceiling showered down in white powder.

Julilah didn't wipe away her tears, seeing outside the dungeon as the first formation activated.

The enemy's dead shifted and started to rise. Buffing formations reinforced the Alvan defenders, giving them a second wind as they activated their armor, pushing back the enemy, reclaiming their lines.

Lightning strikes dropped from the sky, spreading across the enemy formations, attacking groups of the sects.

"Here come the Tigers!"

In a rush, the Tigers and the Adventurer's Guild surged out from the forests, a spear in the back of the sects.

The sects started to fall into disarray as the forces of Alva converged on them.

Marco gathered up the sects, readying the next wave to head into the dungeon.

He paused, looking at the motion of a scrying spell. He felt it through his boots, the noise riding in the distance.

His eyes constricted as beasts charged out of the Beast Mountain Range forests. Banners and flags rose from the force, the banners of the Adventurer's Guild snapped in the dying light, standing firm beside the flags of a Tiger and Dragon. The marking the fiercest enemy soldiers wore branded into Marco's mind, a tower with a pillar of light that seemed to stab into the sky and into the depths of the earth at the same time.

He pulled out a map. His quick elation turned to a chill. The Alvans that they had always berated for hiding behind walls with their weapons surged into battle.

They were a tide, rushing across the bunker-line. Covered by their own weapons, they passed through barriers, using spell, blade, and gun to carve out a path. Fighters fell under their coordinated strike. It wasn't a battle. It was a slaughter.

He threw the back of his tent away, looking at the rear.

The banner of a Dragon fluttered in the distance, the force under it riding panthers as they emerged from the bunker-line. Their yells cut through the open ground.

They fired from their beasts' backs. Barriers covered them, defending against spell and scroll.

Their charge drove deep into the sects' forces, their blades and weapons cutting a path as they used spell scrolls to devastating effect.

Marino pulled Marco aside.

"We cannot win this," she hissed in his ear.

"But the totems, they control them," Marco shot back.

"We lie low, wait for an opening, and then head back to the higher realms. They cannot have the entire First Realm locked down. We will find a way. Come on." Marino hauled him into a jog. The guards moved with them, pushing people aside. Station and status mattered little in the face of survival.

A noise broke over the group. Marco looked up to see a bolt of fire like the one that had cut through the last corvette. Marco raised his personal barriers and yelled as everyone cast their strongest defenses.

The spell tore through their defenses, crashing into the ground, washing away the teleportation formations and command staff in a wave of heat and light.

Erik and Rugrat shot through the sky above Alva.

Gregor pulled out the corvette dungeon core, burrowing through the side of the city ahead of them.

"You deal with him. You have better control over Earth. I'll deal with the ones at the entrance!" Rugrat dropped from view, pulled out the Beast, and fired. The rounds were like artillery cannon shells, clearing sections of the tunnel.

Erik reached out to the ground. He shot into the stone and dirt. It rolled apart ahead of him and closed behind him naturally as he closed in on Gregor's best speed.

"Mana Chains. Mana Chains. Mana Chains," Erik muttered to himself.

He passed Gregor and stood in mid-air. Gregor's triumphant face darkened, seeing him in the sky.

Dozens of mana chains stabbed at Gregor. He defeated two of them and continued to run when he was struck with the first, then the second, and third.

Erik only dismissed the spell when his tombstone appeared. Collecting the body into his storage ring, he dismissed the chains.

He didn't need to turn to see the battle around him.

The sect forces had seen their opportunity and drawn their forces together at the breach to push into Alva. Now the bunker-line rolled inward like the sides of a trap.

Egbert cracked mana barriers with his attack formations while the Artillery rained down fire on the opened teleportation formations.

Erik dropped toward the new tunnel into Alva as Rugrat appeared with a Gatling gun on his hip. He cut down any that ran at him, his explosive shot-spell rounds tearing a swath through the enemy's advance, rolling them backward.

Erik could feel the power in his body moving chaotically. *Just a bit more there. Come on.*

He coughed, wiping away the blood as he looked at the pockets where sects were still gathering in force. They had lost nearly half of their numbers, including all their First Realm fighters, but still they were tens of thousands strong, enough to be a big problem and gathering themselves to create that trouble.

They seemed to have figured out the undead spell and made sure that the dead were stored in their storage rings. But there were thousands of dead in Alva Empire. Alva's skeletons rushed into the battle, detonating themselves if the fighting turned against them.

Erik surged across the sky, lowering his altitude. He arced over the bunker-line, over the contested ravine, and into the force readying their counterattack.

He hit the first line in a wave of mana that carved a cone through the force.

He stood on smoking ground. Hammers formed of the elements rose to his hands as beasts of flame appeared on his sides. A grand dragon formed of fire roared above him.

Golems of stone, earth, wood, and metal rose from the ground.

Erik roared with his conjurations as they ran into the enemy, putting them back on their heels and giving Alvans time to breathe and prepare.

Erik released his hammers. They rang against barriers and exploded. He called others to his hands and threw them, too.

His attacks crossed with the sect forces, turning into a wild uncontrolled melee, tearing through them.

Erik used explosive step to avoid a spell that cleaved through several golems and fire beasts.

He threw a hammer. It transformed into a spear, cracking against the mage's barrier and setting their steps back.

Erik could feel the power that sustained him was failing, weakening, burning up from the power he used.

He took out spell scrolls and tore them rapidly.

His steps slowed as his golems moved past him. He looked at the warships, broken upon the ground nearby, and found a section of the *Perseverance.* He pulled out his rifle and laid out magazines as the power from his body dimmed.

He stabbed himself with a revival needle, following it with a second. He fired, taking down the strongest sect fighters.

He ran dry, ducking down to reload. Breathing heavily, he felt the shards of dungeon core within his body, tearing him apart, the power too great for him to hold.

"Well, this wasn't the greatest idea." He stabbed himself with another needle and grunted, getting up to the top of the section he was using. He fired at a sect member fighting a fire bear. His barrier took the hit. Three more got his attention, and the bear finished him off.

The dead rose from the ground, attacking their allies as they fell under Alva's compunction.

Erik ducked his head as a mortar hit a nearby sect position, sprinkling him in dirt as he found a new target and fired.

Darkness leaked in at the edges of his vision, narrowing it as his reactions slowed.

"Roska!" Egbert's voice boomed around the Special Team.

"What is it?" she yelled, turning and firing on a sect fighter that rushed out from his position. She and the rest of her team fought beside the bunkers in the craters, supporting the complex that had been hammered with the airship's attacks.

"Erik needs your help. He's in a bad way."

"Marker, ping me." She switched channels. "Erik needs us. Get ready to boost. Storbon, you on my flank still?"

"Ready and waiting."

She got the marker ping, laying in the destruction of the airship.

"I am heading to support you. Air force is moving to support as well," Egbert said.

Roska moved to a channel for her and Storbon's Special Team. "We're going to move. Create a corridor to retrieve them and retreat behind the bunker line. Staggered line. Team Four, you have the right side. Team One, we have the left. We are not leaving him behind. Everyone, use a spell scroll and then we're moving!"

Everyone pulled out a spell scroll.

"Three, two, one!"

They tore them. Spells ripped down the hill, across the cratered and trenched landscape, into the distance toward the airships.

"Move!"

The teams moved out, spreading out as they ran.

Roska waited for three to pass her before she jumped out, moving to the left of the person ahead of her.

They ran across the spell littered landscape. A mana cannon's attack howled past her as they ran. The first team member dropped to the ground and fired up, watching the left side. The second person passed them, jumping over a trench, and hosing those inside.

The sects, already on their heels from the attack formations, artillery, and bunker-line push, were slow to react to their push.

The third person behind them cast dirt golems that charged toward the enemy.

The second person moved up to their position, firing mana blasts as powerful as the mana cannons, cratering the ground and striking a trench line.

They ran, people filing out and spreading down the line. The Fourth Team remained on their right as they pushed forward, opening a land of their own in this place of anarchy.

"Incoming," Egbert said.

She looked back to see him flying low.

He reached out his hand.

Roska jumped, gritting her teeth as he grabbed her carrier loop.

"Storbon!"

He ran and jumped from a rock. Egbert grabbed him and sped up, shooting forward.

They saw them. Erik was on a section of warship hull, defending against sect fighters encroaching on his position.

Egbert created swords of glittering sunlight. They hit the sect forces, exploding among their ranks and driving them off.

Egbert dropped to the ground, releasing Roska and Storbon.

Roska's scans of Erik's body made her shiver.

"Egbert." He was wounded, but his voice was clear. He pulled out a map, pointing to locations. "Hit these places. They're reforming, becoming cohesi—" Erik flopped.

Roska had out her aid bag, sticking him with revival needles.

She ignored how weak his vital signs were.

Egbert checked the storage rings and moved to Rugrat, pulling them

Michael Chatfield

off. "I can fly him to the teleport."

"They need care more than speed," Storbon said as he pulled out healing formation bands, dropping to his knee on the other side of Erik to Roska and slapping them to open skin.

Roska used an IO band, the formation powered drill digging into Erik's shoulder. She hooked him up to his own enhanced blood and stabbed him with revival potion filled needles.

His eyes were fluttering and twitching.

"Pull your shit together, Erik!" she yelled.

"Egbert, we're going to need cover to get back to the bunkers. He needs more than we can give him out here!" Roska yelled.

Lucinda from Storbon's team and Davos from Roska's slid to a stop near them, pulling out their trauma kits.

Egbert gritted his teeth. Holding the pouch and storage devices, his eyes dimmed.

The metal and stone of the warships creaked and groaned. Golems stepped out of their armored sides in the dozens. They turned and ran at the sects, reducing the pressure on the corridor the Special Teams were maintaining.

"All right, let's get him on a stretcher and we're moving. I don't want him out of my sight for a fucking second," Roska said. His life balanced on a needle's edge. In every direction was death.

Erik was barely conscious and unable to piece things together.

"This is Commander Glosil of the Alva Military. Members of the United Sect Alliance, put down your weapons and surrender. We control the totems in the First Realm, and we have destroyed your teleportation formations. We are at your front and your rear. There is nowhere for you to go. Save your lives. Do not force us to kill you!"

"They're breaking," Egbert said, his voice distant as Roska fought for Erik's life.

The United Sect Alliance collapsed. Without teleportation formations, and with the totems blocked off and their own dead attacking them, they surrendered in droves.

Mercy had been going from kingdom to kingdom to press their armies into the sects' use. She had been in a city that was under attack. She and her guards walked up to the totem, finding Adventurer's Guild members there. Seeing their armor, the Guild members opened fire, killing most of her guards. She had used the captain of her guard as a shield and fled.

Ever since, she had been hunted. All the totems were controlled by the Alvans. It had been several hours since she had last been able to contact someone. Niklaus, Cai Bo, her other cousins, no one in her clan, no one that had come with her down to the First Realm replied to any of her sound transmissions.

Mercy pulled the cloak tighter around herself. Her eyes darted around the streets. Gripping a dagger under her cloak in a shaking hand, she jumped at even the smallest noise.

There was a whistle of shifting cloth behind her.

She spun. Three men wearing cloaks stood in the middle of the street. The man in front pushed his hood back.

Mercy shivered under his gaze as he pulled down the scarf covering his nose and mouth.

"Domonos," she said, the word chilling her bones.

"You thought you could escape our realm?" Domonos shook his head. "We have lived here for years. We know every city, every town, every totem. We see all here."

His smile made her hold her dagger out. "You come closer, and I'll kill you!"

His smile grew wider. "Mercy, such an ironic name, don't you think?" Domonos said as he walked forward slowly.

"Look, just let me go. I'll give you anything you want," Mercy said, backing up.

Domonos shook his head, his smile fading as he straightened. "Your hands have so much blood on them it can never be washed away. You don't even possess the ability to regret your decisions."

Mercy's stomach pinched. Her breath came out in a hiss of pain as she reached down, finding a dagger in her stomach. Domonos' cloak settled as if floating on a breeze.

Burning pain radiated through the wound, through her stomach, spreading.

"Sometimes, there is no cure. You just have to cut out the infection, the evil." Domonos walked forward as Mercy staggered backward. Her legs failed her as she dropped to the ground, trying to get back up.

She dropped her dagger, her feet catching on the hem of her cloak as she fell backward, coughing as she looked up at the sky above.

"Good-bye, Mercy."

The burning sensation reached her neck; she raised her hand, seeing the black and green veins.

Poison.

Darkness took her.

44
Consolidate

Glosil wore bloody bandages, holding his left arm to his body and ringing his head. Another was tied to his leg. As soon as he could, he left the medical ward in a wheelchair this morning and was still catching up with the changes to Alva.

He put down the last of the reports. Pan Kun and Blaze had been focused on Alva. Some four hundred thousand sect members had surrendered in the fighting. Another one hundred and thirty thousand were wounded.

The scribes ran out of contract paper *twice* to print off all the contracts sealing the sect members from committing violence ever again, and bound them to Alva.

The police had taken over dealing with the prisoners. The Alva military worked on the wounded, ally or enemy. They worked as hard as they could, as they had been taught.

Citizens and those that had been in the Vermire Empire Cities and towns when the attack came were sent back to the surface, into the Alvan Empire.

Armor and weapons were melted down or cleaned and maintained. The smithies of the Empire worked around the clock.

Ammunition and armament factories worked through day and night. Ammunition and replacement armor were churned out. Loot was piled in the Alvan treasuries.

Everyone with medical training was sent to assist in the medical ward. Only a day had passed since the fighting, but it seemed the world had changed.

In taking the totems across the ten realms, the Adventurer's Guild had also removed the leadership of kingdoms that led the attacks on the Beast Mountain Range and placed the nations under Alva, nearly doubling the land under their empire's control.

Most of the nation and kingdom leaders were executed for their various crimes, including Alva's former Queen Ikku, while others became prisoners. A number had prisoners from Earth who were released and fled to King's Hill for protection.

The Tiger and Dragon Corps were mobilizing, preparing to launch their counterattack.

Three days and they will head to the higher realms supported by the Adventurer's Guild.

Glosil looked at the reports from Elan's people. They had continued to gather information. The members of the United Sect Alliance had sent their strongest, wary of the force they had fought in the Fourth Realm.

Now they just have their lower realm fighters. Glosil hoped to end the battles as bloodlessly as possible, parade the strongest figures in the sect as prisoners of Alva, and give them an offer to surrender and keep their lives.

With the totems closed off and the lack of magics in the Second Realm, none of the other realms had been able to access the First Realm, and none of the nations in the First Realm had been able to get any information on the state of affairs.

They would send a message to the other kingdoms. The last thing they needed was for one of them to attack their totem blockades. He made a note and passed it to an aide to be sent to Delilah and then Aditya.

Walking wounded were sent to their barracks to recover with stamina and mana potions, easing the stress on the medical facilities. The cultivation pods were being utilized to save lives. Alchemists and chemical factories worked around the clock to create concoctions to heal and save. Those who had just started their medical training were drafted in to help.

The bunker-line had been repaired and reinforced with the tower compounds pushed out to the outer city lines.

Pan Kun's reservists had taken over the defenses as the guild and full timers recovered their strength and readied themselves for their next action.

Glosil felt the iron tension dissipating as he dropped into a nearby seat, unnoticed in the command center's movements.

He looked at the map table of Alva and rubbed his face with his free hand.

We made it. We fucking made it. Now, we just have to keep it.

Delilah had appropriated a community hall used for weddings, parties and other gatherings as her command center. She needed to be seen by the people instead of hiding in a hole. The other council members had looked up at Alva's ceiling and mutually agreed not to mention it to their fearless leader.

She stood at the main table covered in reports and information. Secretaries and staff moved along the walls, passing information to one another or, rarely, handing it to the three heads in the middle of the room.

Delilah, Chonglu, and Aditya sat in middle at four large desks that had been thrown together to accommodate them all.

"Glosil handed me a reminder, and I sent out messages to the other leaders in the First Realm. They were quite agreeable once they realized we had locked down the First Realm," Aditya said. "Though the Associations weren't too pleased about it. They are demanding to talk with me and are ordering me to meet them at the headquarters of the Associations in the First Realm."

"Do any associations other than the Blue Lotus exist in the First Realm?" Delilah asked.

"Not really. There are a few branches here, mostly for people looking for a quieter time away from the chaos of the higher realms," Aditya said.

"Tell them that we will meet them tomorrow at Shida. Talk to the people at the totem in their city. Allow it to be free and then punch another guard."

"Yes, Council Leader," Aditya said with the glimmer of a smile on his lips.

Gilroy's eyes narrowed into beads as his mouth moved into tired wrinkles. He pursed his lips at the city beyond his carriage. *Impertinent fools, thinking that because they rebuff one attack from someone in the Second Realm they can look down on the Blue Lotus, no, the Associations.*

Groups of soldiers marched through the streets of Shida with a new emblem on their chests. The city was subdued, and people looked at the guards with new eyes.

The carriage arrived at Shida's castle. Passing under the portcullis, they rounded around the main fountain and reached the entrance into the castle proper.

Gilroy pressed his clothes, adjusting his emblem as the Head of the First Realm, aligning it perfectly with his attire. A step was placed in front of his carriage, and the door opened. His eyes watered against the bright light of day as he stepped out of the carriage.

He carried a cane for the finery of the worked metals and wood over any frailty.

His guards flanked him wearing their finest armor, rare sets of the High Apprentice grade.

They marched past the guards, who stood at the entrance to the castle. A woman walked out, greeting the captain of his guard.

"Please come this way."

She guided them inside and through halls. They reached a side room with guards in mis-matched gear, standing with odd weapons held with lazy comfort.

Gilroy felt his guards tense at the sight of these new fighters.

"Not befitting of my guard." His muttered words didn't cause them to relax.

The doors opened, showing an office on the other side.

Seems they know something of their position instead of trying to lord over me in some throne room. Still, if they think they are equal to me, they are mistaken.

Two men, one that looked like Emperor Aditya, and a woman stood around a fourth woman, younger than all three but clearly in charge. Their conversation cut off with the entrance of his guards.

"Ah, Head Gilroy." The woman smiled and indicated to the chair.

"I prefer to stand," he said. A guard moved the chair to the side and stood behind him as he faced the front of the desk.

"Very well. These are city Councilors Chonglu, Aditya, and the head of the trading guild, Elise. I am council leader of Alva, Delilah."

Delilah opened her inter-linked hands. "How can we help you?"

"We have come to discuss the current situation, the Association's stance, and the totems," Gilroy said, grinding his teeth at the impertinence of one so young.

"We will remove our forces from the totems in—" Delilah frowned and looked to Chonglu over her shoulder.

"Two days, Commander Glosil says."

"Right, so we thank you for your patience."

"You think that you can dictate to me when the totems will remain closed?" Gilroy snarled, hitting his cane against the floor.

The trio around the woman all straightened and looked at him, but made no motion to intervene.

The two guards in the corners of the room behind her lifted their eyes up to Gilroy. He now understood why his guards had tensed. These guards weren't decorations, they were killers. Reassured in his position, the thin sliver of fear turned into embarrassment, and he grabbed onto his anger instead.

"You have only defeated a Second Realm army and you think that you can dictate to the Associations what you desire? You think too highly of yourself, girl!"

The woman's face hardened, and he felt a lick of excitement in seeing the taunt register.

"Do not overthink your position." He leaned forward on his cane, the elderly lecturing the younger on the way of the world. "If you wish to survive, then you will need the support of the Associations to do so. Otherwise, as soon as you open those totems, you will be torn apart, which is the real reason you haven't. Defeating a group from one higher realm was impressive, but there are many higher realms!"

The door opened, and the guards looked over in alarm. A skeleton stood there, covered in glowing runes.

"Delilah, he is awake! I've come to take you there."

"What is this talking puppet!?" Gilroy demanded, smacking his cane into the ground.

"When we are connected to the realms again, talk to Elder Lu Ru. I'd rather deal with him," Delilah said over her shoulder. One of the men, who looked similar to Emperor Aditya, wrote down a note.

Delilah stood.

"Where do you think you are going, girl? Do you have no decency or decoru—" His words were washed away in a wave of power that surged from the woman as her eyes glowed with mana, pulling at her hair as the pressure threw his guards back and pinned him to the ground.

"They were not from the Second Realm, they were from the Sixth." Her voice was infused with mana. "This is the Alva Empire, not the Associations. When we were in Vuzgal, you stood on the sidelines. This is the contract for all Associations wishing to do business in the Mortal realms." A scroll shot out and landed on Gilroy's guard captain.

Gilroy's face blanched as he felt the waves of pressure coming off the men and women in the room, their eyes glowing with their advanced cultivation.

Delilah pulled out an Alchemist Association medallion that marked her as an Expert Alchemist. "My grand teacher is Master Alchemist Zen Hei. My teacher Erik West. I think he might be the first Four-Star hero in several decades. He just woke up. I have other things to deal with. Tell the Mission Hall to send down two emblems when they are ready. See, I serve *two* Four-Star Heroes."

"You!" Gilroy looked at the emblem in her hand. He knew it was real, but everything she said couldn't be real, could it?

"See yourself out. Egbert, with me." She turned and left. The skeleton's runes flashed in anger as he followed her.

"How goes the recovery?"

"We are looting Ubren's cave and Henghou. That, together with the loot from the battlefield, will fuel Alva for centuries."

"And if we add in the warship projects and the military re-armament?"

"It'll give us a much-needed boost to support our attack on the United Sect Alliance cities."

"Good."

45

Counterattack

Two months had passed and the streets of Alva, of Shida, and the route to King's Hill's new totem were filled with the sounds of marching.

The Tiger, Dragon Corps, and Adventurer's guild, healed, armed, and reloaded, marched on the higher realms. Men and women wearing their sect finery were linked by chains. Sect elders and leaders, with their heads bowed in shame, glanced at the armored men and women around them with respect and fear.

The procession was silent. Alvans stood in the roads, in their houses, their hands clenched in fists and held against their hearts.

Rubble had been cleared and walls repaired. Light shone over Alva even as she was cut off from the surface once again.

Delilah stood next to the totem, watching as the last soldier disappeared in a flash of light. She lowered her hand, looking at Alva.

Alvans had voted to keep the city underground. Those that wanted open skies were free to spread to King's Hill.

The main dungeon core had been shattered, but the shards could be refined by the other dungeon cores over time, and they had been added to them.

In the rush of mana unleashed from the center of the First Realm, three things had happened. Tectonic activity had created earthquakes and tsunamis as mana veins had been tapped and unlocked, releasing mana locked deep within the realm. It led to new hotspots of mana density and increased the overall mana density of the realm by a few degrees. Nothing like the Second Realm's, but enough that it would make it easier for people to cultivate mana and live longer.

The rush of mana had increased the mana density to the same passive density of the Seventh Realm. Most was collected in the mana gathering and storing formations, but enough was released so that the edges of the Alvan Empire held the same density as the Second Realm, the outposts equal to the Third Realm and King's hill the Fourth Realm.

The dungeon cores had expanded rapidly under the influx of mana, as had the grade of the resources in the different floors and volume.

Delilah smiled at people as she walked toward the temporary headquarters that had been set up in one of the military training bases. Her office was still being rebuilt. The dungeon cores had each had parts of the old dungeon core added to them, and had been separated out, each of the cores a little smaller than what they had been. They'd created another Earth grade dungeon core. Egbert volunteered most of his internal dungeon core, raising it to the Sky grade.

She looked at the jewel-like mana storing formation above, those lines of crystal, all of it mana stones of the Sky grade.

Aditya took a drink from a flask and passed it to her.

She accepted with a nod, enjoying the burn as she passed it to Chonglu.

"How are we looking?" she said.

"I have written up plans for expansion within the empire. Are we sure to not expand?" Aditya asked.

"What need do we have to expand to more than what we have? We can't hold the outer cities with our current forces. We must defend what we can hold. In the First Realm, we might stand a little taller, but there is no need to antagonize our enemies. Act fairly and be treated so. If there are others that conspire against us, Commander Glosil and his men are more than capable and Pan Kun still has all of his reservists."

"Yes, Council Leader."

"These plans, what do they look like?"

"Expansion of the outer cities, putting city at every strategic location into the empire. Changes to the citizenship to closely align with the same procedures of Alva. Expansion of the outposts into proper cities. King Hill Expansion—"

Delilah opened her mouth to speak.

"*And* plans for schools of education in every village, town, and city, with Academies in every city to mirror Kanesh Academy. The Consortium would take on the name Vermire Academy." He gave her a wry smile and accepted the flask again, storing it away.

Delilah smiled.

"Chonglu?"

"We have plans to take over the location of *Zahir*—" His voice caught. The city might have been renamed, but it was his city at one time. "Rebuilding it and making it part of Alva. That should be our only expansion. Alva's dungeon cores are growing faster than before. All factories are operating at maximum to supply the military with everything they need and print up supplies for the prisoners. They are currently clearing the battlefield of anything useful under the watch of the undead and the police officers. Judges are seeing to them on a case-by-case basis upon any other crimes to render judgements."

They stepped up to a waiting carriage. Guards flanked them as it pulled out into the street.

"The treasury is having one hell of a time going through all the storage rings that we collected. Broken weapons and sections of broken warships are shipped to the smithies and the factories. The healers' and medics' pace has slowed. All the medically trained members of the Dragon and Tigers have returned, and seventy percent of wounded have recovered. Another twenty percent in a week, ten percent in the month afterward."

"Any change with Erik?" Aditya asked.

"He's healing well, but it looks like the damage is permanent, as is Rugrat's." Chonglu cleared his throat.

"Repairs are underway on the living floor. Additional defenses have been added into the mountain above Alva and the totem guards are reporting no disturbances at their locations."

Gudriksson cleared his throat beside Stoorgard. They stood on the city's main tower, watching the Tiger Corps as they marched to the totem and teleported away.

"The newly formed council is looking to have your input on the breakup of the city's functions," he said.

"The *Alvans*?" She paused, tasting the new Empire's name that had torn through the lower realms over this last week.

"Same conditions as before."

Even in these summer heats, she felt a chill in her bones, deeper than the cutting northern winds of Reynir in the Third Realm.

The Alvan's tactics were relentless and repeated with terrifying efficiency.

They would have elders from the sect that occupied the city talk to the leaders. If they surrendered, then the Alvans would accept their surrender and take the prisoners, clearly mistrusting the other forces to treat any prisoners fairly. Another sect elder had grown angry, annoyed that they would take so many slaves, and took several prizes, young boys and girls from the sect, declaring them his property.

The Alvans had marched up to the manor they were using, killed the elder and the other sect members, and sent a message to the sect head that led the group.

No retribution had been taken. The sect had seen what the Alvans had done to any other city that had not surrendered. Massive weapons hidden under spying and detection spell sheets would rumble like a god's thunder. It took less than several barrages to destroy a city barrier and the Alvans would charge forward. The disciplined force didn't roar or yell as they moved up in units, firing and covering one another across the open ground, using their bare hands to smash through walls and enter the cities.

Ten thousand Alvans would quickly turn to one hundred thousand as they pulled out undead soldiers to support.

They didn't slaughter innocents, they accepted surrenders and marched row upon row in their faceless helmets.

In the first three days, they had attacked the headquarters of every sect that was part of the United Sect Alliance like a blade in the dark. The Dragon and Tiger Corps worked with the Adventurer's Guild, decapitating the sect's leadership, and worked their way down through the realms.

They had taken city after city, calling allies to their cause that they had contacted under the guise of Adventurer's Guild and Vuzgal.

The sects and clans, like the Grey Peak Sect, had reacted in support almost immediately. Few stepped out of line. The others followed their orders, and made quick ties with this new overwhelming force.

The Alvans didn't want any part of the cities. They didn't vie for controlling rights. They were sure to control any cities they desired. They established a non-aggression pact with every sect instead, and conditional alliance. It assured that Alva would not attack them, and they would not attack Alva, and that under the right conditions, they would support one another.

Stoorgard thought it odd until she read the contract. All the sects and clans that agreed to the contract were essentially safe from one another and could call on tremendous support.

The contracts will bring an age of peace not seen in the lower realms before.

Every force that could applied to join the newly formed alliance. the Alvans listed the criteria openly. Novice education was accessible by the people under the sect's control. Clean drinking water, food and basic general medical care, too.

It turned many away, but others joined, usually small groups coming under the protective umbrella of Alva.

With each city Alva took, they imposed that the same rules would be upheld in the city, that recruiters from Alva be allowed to set up a recruiting hall and their traders get good rates. They only asked for crafting materials.

Cleverly, they didn't state the amount of materials they should be given for each city, so the sects gave as many resources as they could to the Alvans. It seemed uneven as sects gained control over cities, forming councils, the Alvans got a few extras.

But their fame grew. They gained thousands of prisoners and their recruiting halls had a line outside as people vied for spots to join an empire from the First Realm.

They had turned the Ten Realms on their head.

"Storgaard?" Gudriksson said.

"Sorry, I guess that we need to figure out just how many materials we give the Alvans and where to set up their recruiting hall." She laughed and turned to the heavy-set man.

His lips quirked into a grin under his braided beard. "Just so."

She walked past him, her voice dipping low.

"I wonder if Alva would be willing to recruit an old Branch Head?"

He coughed on his breath as she walked into the castle.

Old Hei sat on his balcony, the back of his brush against his lip, his arms crossed as he twirled the brush in thought, a pill formula in front of him.

Captain Khasar cleared his throat as he walked out onto the balcony.

"Hmm?" Old Hei looked over, quirking an eyebrow as black ink fell from his brush onto the parchment.

"The First Realm has opened again. Master Alchemist Tenoch and Mission Hall Elder Hunt are on their way here. Delilah sent a message. She is the Council Leader of an empire called Alva, under Erik and Rugrat. They control a dungeon and defeated the United Sect Alliance. Now they are clearing up the rest of the sects to make sure that they will not be attacked in the future.

"From the reports I received, they are a strong force in the First Realm. In the lower realms, they attacked Henghou, capturing all the Willful Institute members. They have attacked locations in the Fifth Realm and are moving their way to the lower realms."

He coughed as the doors to Old Hei's office opened, admitting the two high powered leaders.

Old Hei put down his brush, his work forgotten as a wide smile spread across his face.

"Prepare a detail to head to the lower realms, if you could."

"Master Alchemist Hei." Tenoch tilted her head as he walked over to greet the duo.

"It is a pleasure to meet you both." Hei bowed lower, as was his position as a Mid-Master Alchemist. Tenoch was a High Alchemist, one of only a few in the Seventh Realm.

"Have you heard of the situation in the First Realm?"

"Ah yes, it seems that my student and grand student were keeping more than a little from me." He chuckled.

"Your student is to become a Four-Star Hero."

"A Four-Star?" Old Hei was excited by the fact that his students had survived, thrown off by the fact they controled a hidden dungeon and empire. This seemed to matter little.

"Are there any others?"

"There are some, but none in the First Realm," Hunt said.

"We have come to discuss your student. It is said that his forces are attacking cities in the lower realm. He could upset the balance of power in the lower realms."

"He could?"

"We want to know what you think that he will do."

"Erik and Delilah desire to get things done and to be left alone. I think that this will be their response. Do not worry. I shall head down there now to make an assessment of the situation," Old Hei said, slipping around them. Captain Khasar stood on the other side. "I will get you a most thorough assessment and make sure that they don't upset things too badly. They always were strong characters!" Old Hei talked rapidly and bowed as he backed away at the door. "Don't worry, it is a hard task, but I think that I will be up to it. Thank you for your support!"

With that, he turned out of his offices, picking up the hem of his robe as he half-jogged down the corridor with Khasar and his guards in tow.

"Quick, to the First Realm!"

Thank you for your support and taking the time to read **The Seventh Realm Part 2.**

The Ten Realms will continue in **The Eighth Realm.**

As a self-published author I live for reviews! If you've enjoyed The Seventh Realm, please leave a **review**!

Do you want to join a community of fans that love talking about Michael's books?

We've created this Facebook group for you to discuss the books, hear from Michael, participate in contests and enjoy the worlds that Michael has created. *Join now!*

Have you taken a look at the *Death Knight Series* yet? You don't want to miss it!

You can check out my other books, what I'm working on and upcoming releases through the following means:

Website: http://michaelchatfield.com/

Twitter: @chatfieldsbooks

Facebook: facebook.com/michaelchatfieldsbooks

Goodreads: Goodreads.com/michaelchatfield

Patreon (you can get sneak peeks about what I'm working on, signed books, swag and access to contests):

https://www.patreon.com/michaelchatfieldwrites

Thanks again for reading! ☺

Interested in more LitRPG? Check out
https://www.facebook.com/groups/LitRPGsociety/
And: https://www.facebook.com/groups/LitRPG.books/

Hope you have a great day!

Made in the USA
Columbia, SC
03 November 2021

48345401R00284